## Praise for *With Every Letter*

"Historical romance specialist [...] era series with a well-research[...] Army specialists whose pen-pa[...] line. Sundin has such a gift for c[...] details. WWII-era fans won't be able to put it down."

—*Publishers Weekly*

"Combining excellent research and attention to detail with a flair for romance, Sarah Sundin brings to life the perilous challenges of WWII aviation, nursing, and true love."

—*CBA Retailers + Resources*

"Sundin skillfully uses an alternating point of view between Mellie and Tom, and pulls readers into their lives. The themes of anonymity and growing love linking the two makes this story a romantic read."

—*RT Book Reviews*, 4½ stars

"I love the nostalgia and drama of the WWII era. No one takes me back there better than Sarah Sundin. *With Every Letter* is a beautiful love story and has everything you want in a novel: romance, suspense, and characters you care about from the very first page. A marvelous beginning for her new series. I can't wait to read the next book."

—**Dan Walsh**, award-winning and bestselling author of *The Discovery*

## Praise for *On Distant Shores*

"Sundin leaves no emotion unexamined in this mix of loss and hope. The author's experience as a hospital pharmacist gives her storyline credibility as it is matched by her extensive knowledge of WWII. With her nurse and pharmacist characters, Sundin has crafted an inspirational romance featuring a unique take on WWII that will pique the interests of readers who enjoy historical medical fiction."

—*Booklist*

"The second outstanding Wings of the Nightingale tale is about two people on the front lines of war overseas doing what they can to keep safe their loved ones back home. The characters are well defined within a fast-paced storyline, and the historical details of WWII are vividly described."

—*RT Book Reviews*, 4 stars

"Sarah Sundin is a master of World War II romance! *On Distant Shores* swept me back seventy years, into a whirlwind love story that took me to airfields, hospitals, and cities all over the Mediterranean. Kudos to Sarah for writing another exciting novel for those of us who love reading her historical fiction."

—**Melanie Dobson**, award-winning author
of *The Silent Order* and *Love Finds*

WINGS
OF THE
NIGHTINGALE

BOOK THREE

# IN *Perfect* TIME

*A Novel*

# SARAH SUNDIN

Revell

*a division of Baker Publishing Group*
Grand Rapids, Michigan

Published by Revell
a division of Baker Publishing Group
P.O. Box 6287, Grand Rapids, MI 49516-6287
www.revellbooks.com

Printed in the United States of America

Library of Congress Cataloging-in-Publication Data is on file at the Library of Congress, Washington, DC.

ISBN 978-0-8007-2083-4 (pbk.)

This book is a work of fiction. Names, characters, places, and incidents are the product of the author's imagination or are used fictitiously.

14   15   16   17   18   19   20          7   6   5   4   3   2   1

To my parents, Ronald and Nancy Stewart,
for believing in me and encouraging my dreams

# 1

## Over the Mediterranean
## March 25, 1944

For Lt. Kay Jobson, flight nursing meant more than physical care. It meant reconnecting a broken soldier with the shards of his humanity.

Kay assessed her planeload of patients en route from Italy to Tunisia. A restless lot, downhearted. That wouldn't do.

She headed to the front of the C-47 cargo plane, past six men confined to litters and eleven in seats along the sides of the fuselage. The soldiers had been wounded on the battered beachhead at Anzio or in one of the many bloody failed attempts to take Cassino. "Say, fellows, what do you think about the '44 baseball season? Starts soon, doesn't it?"

"Yeah, it does." Seated to her left, Sergeant Logan gave her a don't-worry-your-pretty-little-head look.

She knelt beside the patient and took his wrist to measure his pulse. What was more fun—showing off what lay inside her pretty little head or shocking people? "Do you think the Cardinals can come back from their World Series loss?"

"Um, sure." One bushy eyebrow sprang high. "But I'm a Tigers fan myself."

Kay rolled her eyes. "Hal Newhouser might be a great

pitcher, but the Cards have Stan Musial, and he batted .357 last season. Mark my words, they'll take the whole shebang this year."

Logan's mouth opened and closed around nonexistent words.

Kay tapped him under the chin. "I don't just follow the game, I play it. If I weren't a nurse, I'd be the star of one of those girls' teams."

"Well, I'll be."

Swishing her hair over her shoulder, Kay turned to the rest of the patients. "So, boys, who do you like this year?"

Over the roar of the twin engines, the men called out their favorite teams and players and stats.

After Kay noted Logan's vital signs, she scooted over to the next patient, a die-hard fan of the Philadelphia Athletics despite their dismal showing in '43. Friendly arguments arced through the stuffy air of the plane, and Kay smiled, her goal accomplished.

She loved everything about this job—the glamour of flight, the challenge of nursing, and the game of lifting spirits. Now she just needed to sweet-talk chief nurse Lt. Cora Lambert into recommending her for the Army Air Forces' chief nurse training program.

If only she could have an in-flight emergency to highlight her skills.

All the fun stuff happened to her friends. Mellie Blake put down a riot and dealt with medical trauma. And three days ago, Georgie Taylor evacuated an entire flight full of patients after her C-47 ditched in the Mediterranean. Kay could hardly be jealous of her friends' crises, but why couldn't a little adventure come her way?

"Improving morale again?" A deep voice rumbled behind her. Lt. Grant Klein, the pilot of the C-47 and one of her boyfriends.

"Always." She tilted a smile to him. "Shouldn't you be flying this bird?"

"Singleton's got it under control. I wanted to talk." His name and dark good looks used to remind her of Cary Grant, but a little flight time together had dimmed the resemblance in her eyes.

"I'd love to talk, but I'm busy."

"Come on. Let Dabrowski finish. Just give me a minute."

Rarely did she give in, but she handed the flight manifest to her surgical technician. "Sergeant Dabrowski, please take vitals while I slap some sense into our pilot."

"Sure thing."

Kay took her time leading Grant to the back of the plane. She straightened her gray-blue service jacket, tucked in loose blankets, and lit a patient's cigarette since no one required oxygen. Grant's purpose in this conversation was obvious—and futile.

Sure enough, at the back of the plane, Grant leaned one hand against the fuselage behind Kay. "Are you free tonight?"

"Sorry. I have a date."

"But I haven't seen you in forever."

Kay leveled her gaze at him. "It's Saturday. We went dancing on Wednesday."

"It feels like forever." He coiled a strand of her hair around his finger, strawberry blonde around tan, and he leaned in for a kiss.

Although his kisses were delicious, she planted her hand on his chest. "Not in front of the patients. You know that."

"I also know I need time with you."

"Not tonight. It's Harry's turn, and he hasn't seen me in two weeks."

Grant's eyes narrowed. "You'd rather go out with a dentist than with me?"

"He's a swell dancer and a lot of fun."

"And I'm not?"

Oh brother. She stepped to the side and opened the medical chest to get the meds for the litter patients. "Of course you are, but you know how—"

"Come on, baby. I miss you. I never get much time with you."

That was the idea. Kay pulled out the aspirin bottle. Maybe she should take a tablet herself. "When we started dating, right up front I told you how it would be. I date five or six fellows at a time. I'm not going to change."

"I don't want you to change. You're perfect. But I don't want to share you anymore. And I want . . ." He cleared his throat.

She faced him, dread slowing her movement and stealing her speech. This wasn't the kind of in-flight crisis she wanted.

He coughed into his fist, then gave her a silken gaze. "It's time we . . . it's time we got closer."

Kay's chest tightened. He'd never been pushy, always a gentleman, but now it was over. "I don't—"

He stepped nearer, his eyes smoky. "You told me when it was time . . ."

"It isn't time."

His forehead crumpled into accordion pleats. "But, baby, we've been seeing each other almost a year. How much longer? When *will* it be time?"

It never would. When you gave a man your body, you gave him control of your soul. Kay had never fallen into that trap, and she never would. "I need to get back to work."

He grasped her hand. "How much longer?"

She wiggled her fingers out of his grip. "I don't know."

"What about the other fellows? That dentist? Is that why you're so eager to see him?"

"That is none of your business."

"I'll say it's my business. You're my—"

"It isn't your business, and I'm not your anything." Kay planted her fists on her hips. "We're no longer dating."

"What?"

"We're no longer dating." She kept her voice calm and low. "I told you from the beginning—no commitment, no pressure. You just broke both rules. That's the end of it."

His mouth stretched wide, like a dog aiming to bite something.

She flipped up her hand. "Don't make a scene. It wouldn't make a difference anyhow."

His gaze darted over her head and down the aisle of the plane, where over a dozen patients would relish a scene. A snarl rose in his throat. "Who do you think you are, you little—"

"Don't. I've heard it all before anyway." She marched down the aisle to her tech. "How are we doing, Sergeant?"

Dabrowski handed her the flight manifest, and she listened to his report on the patients, asked the right questions, and made the proper notations. More importantly, she kept her hands and voice from shaking. Even when Grant stormed past.

Yes, she'd heard it all before. Floozy. Tart. Tease.

Her father's voice barked in her mind's ear. Irredeemable little sinner.

Kay sucked in air through her nostrils and knelt beside the patient in the lower litter on the right. "How are you doing, Private?"

Control. Only control silenced the voice.

---

**Sorrento, Italy**

"Wake up, Coop. You're dreaming."

Lt. Roger Cooper opened one eye, breath chuffing. Yes, he

could breathe. He wasn't trapped underwater in a sinking C-47, sinking because he never should have flown that day. A better pilot would have convinced his squadron commander to abort the mission.

Yes, he lay on his stomach on the beach at Sorrento. The scent of saltwater and sand filled his nostrils. His one open eye registered a sideways view of sheer white cliffs and tile-roofed homes, of the blue Bay of Naples and beyond that—Mount Vesuvius, still smoking from the eruption that brought down his plane. His cheek slipped on his crossed forearms, sweat moistening the leather sleeves of his flight jacket.

Roger kicked to the right and hit his copilot, Lt. Bill Shelby. "Come on, we take a dive in the drink, spend the night at sea, get interrogated for two days straight, finally get a day of rest, and you interrupt my beauty sleep."

"Hey!" Shell grabbed his skinny leg where Roger had kicked him. "You sounded like my dog, twitching and whimpering."

"What do you expect? I was chasing bunnies."

Technical Sergeant Gene Pettas let out a low whistle. "I know what I'd like to chase."

Roger rested his chin on his forearms and followed his radioman-navigator's gaze down the beach. A trio of Italian girls sauntered along, skirts ruffling around shapely legs, dark eyes surveying the four American flyboys, full lips curving in appreciation.

"One for each of us." Pettas pushed himself up to sitting. "Except old married man Shell here."

The tallest, prettiest girl targeted Roger. His dark red hair attracted too much attention in Italy. She paused and lifted an inviting smile. A dangerous smile.

Roger prayed for strength and turned away. "Leave me out of this. They're nothing but trouble."

Sergeant Fulton Whitaker, the flight engineer, flicked the

back of Roger's head. "Ah, you say that about everything in a skirt."

He rubbed his scalp. "'Cause it's true. Dames are trouble."

"C'mon, Whit." Pettas got to his feet. "Let's go get us some trouble. No fun with these two monks anyway."

One more flick to Roger's head, and Whit left too.

"Man alive." Roger winced and rubbed his head—again. "Everyone's beating me up today."

"Says the man who got nominated for the Distinguished Flying Cross." Shell sat cross-legged on the blanket, and a breeze lifted his wispy pale blond hair.

"Yeah." The word soured in his mouth. Only the US Army Air Forces gave a man a medal for getting out of a situation he never should have gotten into in the first place. He could have killed fifteen people that day. And he got a medal.

"At least I'm finally getting my own plane."

"About time." His best friend was an excellent pilot, better than Roger, but his small stature and quiet personality made him almost invisible in the 64th Troop Carrier Group. Getting trapped on Roger's crew hadn't helped either. "My new copilot will have big shoes to fill."

Shell stretched one leg in front of him and wiggled his foot—about a size seven. "Only if he's twelve years old."

"You kidding? I had bigger feet than that when I was born."

"Yep. They grow them large and stupid on the farm."

"Ain't that the truth?" Roger grinned, then pushed himself up to sitting, naptime over. He rolled his shoulders and gazed around. The midday sun gave off no heat, and Roger kept his flight jacket zipped.

"Say, Coop, you have any candy? Gum?" Shell nodded in the direction Pettas and Whitaker had gone in search of trouble.

Four Italian boys made their way up the beach, laughing and pushing each other and picking stuff up off the sand—

shells or rocks or whatever. Any minute now they'd spot the airmen and beg them for goodies.

A smile warmed Roger's face more than the sun did. "Can't spare any gum, but I've got a Mars bar. Here, give me your book."

"My book? No, you don't." Shell reached for it.

Roger grabbed it first and slipped out his drumsticks from inside his jacket. "It's for a good cause."

"You have no respect for the written word."

"What do you expect from a dumb farm boy?" He set the book on the blanket in front of him and rapped out a neat set of paradiddles.

Sure enough, the boys, about six to ten years old, looked his way. Brothers or cousins most likely.

Roger beckoned them with a grin, breaking the language barrier.

The kids ran over, sand shooting out behind their bare feet. They'd get candy, but first they'd get a show.

Roger twirled one drumstick around his fingers, then broke into a triple stroke roll, smooth and even, building up to a frenzy and ending with a tap to Shelby's head.

His friend cussed and scooted out of the way. "Should have known better."

"That's for waking me."

The boys giggled and gathered around. The littlest patted his own head, an irresistible invitation. Roger motioned for his four new cymbals to sit in a semicircle around him, with the tallest kid to his left, his "hi-hat."

Roger returned to his triple stroke roll, accented with light taps to hi-hat boy's head. The other kids squealed and patted their heads, and Roger obliged them. Then he returned to the book and switched things up to a ratamacue, nice and easy.

His eyes drifted shut, and the rhythm took over, flowing

through his arms and sticks and soul. Thank goodness the Lord had given him one thing to be good at.

That's why he practiced every single day, all forty rudiments, over and over. Not easy when he'd only managed to stuff a single tom-tom in his barracks bag. He hadn't played on a full drum set in ages, but he wouldn't let that stop him. If the Allies ever won this war, he'd go home and audition for the big bands. No more rinky-dink house bands for him.

His right foot worked an imaginary pedal for a bass drum, and he picked up the pace, swinging the rhythm.

The boys murmured in Italian, squirming in expectation.

Roger's eyes popped open. He shot them a mischievous grin, then tapped out a frenzied but gentle pattern on the four little heads. The boys ducked and shrieked with delight.

He laid the sticks in parallel on the book, lowered his chin to signal the end, then stuck out his hand to the oldest boy. "Gum, *per favore*? Gum?"

All four laughed at the role reversal.

"What do you have, Shell?" Roger dug the Mars bar from the pocket of his jacket, a bit squished from his nap, but boys didn't care about things like that.

"A Hershey bar." He handed it to the smallest boy and mimed breaking it in half.

"*Grazie, signore! Grazie!*" Eyes bright, the boys divided the candy and scampered away down the beach.

"The Pied Drummer strikes again."

Roger laughed and returned his drumsticks to his jacket, his fingers still tingling with the rhythm.

"Say, if this drumming thing doesn't work out, you should be a teacher. You're great with kids."

His hand clenched around the sticks, right over his heart. It skipped a beat. His laugh came out stiff. "Why would I want to be stuck in a school all day? Hated school."

Hated it because of dull teachers who made lessons as

tasty as chalk. He'd sit and watch and think how he'd make the lesson engaging with color and humor and flash.

Countless appointments with the principal's paddle showed him color and humor and flash did not belong in the classroom.

But the big bands welcomed it.

# 2

**Pomigliano Airfield, outside Naples, Italy**
**March 27, 1944**

"Need some help?" Mellie Blake leaned in the cargo door of the C-47. "My plane's already set up, and I have nothing to do."

"Sure." Kay motioned her fellow flight nurse inside. "Dabrowski isn't here yet."

Mellie climbed in and tucked her wavy black hair behind her ear. "Oh, you're almost done."

"You sound disappointed." Kay reached into a canvas bag affixed to the ceiling, drew out a coil of web strapping, and let the end flop to the floor. "Missing Georgie?"

"Of course, but I'm sure she misses us more." She released another coil of strapping a few feet away. "Can you imagine? They sent her to Capri as a reward for the ditching incident, but for Georgie, being alone is the worst form of punishment."

Kay laughed and knelt to secure the strapping to a pole running along the floor. "She's probably attracted a crowd of new friends. So how's Tom?"

"Wonderful." At the mention of her boyfriend, Mellie smiled, wide and bright. "His Engineer Aviation Battalion finished another airstrip in the Foggia area. He has a forty-eight-hour leave over Easter weekend to come to Naples. I can't wait. It'll be nice to worship with him." Her gaze slid to Kay, a question almost visible on her lips.

With a slight shake of her head, Kay scuttled that question. She tugged on the strap, nice and taut from floor to ceiling. That's what she liked about Mellie. Although her friend's faith was important to her, she never pushed.

Besides, if Kay walked into the air base church, the building would burst into flames and the chaplain would have a coronary.

Mellie tested her strap too. "I'm glad we're getting more planes with this new system. It's much better than the old aluminum brackets we had when we first came to North Africa."

"Sure is." Kay stood and slipped her hand in one of the loops that would hold a litter pole when the patients were loaded later that morning. "That's the last one."

A smile flickered on Mellie's face. "I'm glad I could be of such great help."

"Mellie? Ah, there you are." The chief nurse, Lt. Cora Lambert, poked her head inside the cargo door. "Your patients are ready to be loaded."

"Thank you, Lieutenant." Mellie left the plane. "Bye, Kay."

"Bye, Mellie-bird." Kay glanced around the cabin. All looked fine. "How about my patients?"

"Not yet. Maybe half an hour." Lambert pulled back, ready to leave.

"Wait." A moment alone with the chief couldn't be wasted. "Yes?"

Kay hopped to the ground and scanned the airfield. Yes, she had privacy. "A few weeks ago you said replacement nurses were coming at the end of the month. Do you still need volunteers to go home?"

"I need one more. Why? Did you change your mind? I thought you loved flight nursing." Her brown eyes widened, and she stared at Kay's abdomen.

Oh, for heaven's sake. She thought Kay was stupid enough to get pregnant. Kay tossed on a smile. "I do love flight nursing. So much that I'd like to go to the chief nurses' school."

"The . . . chief . . ."

Kay's heart twisted at the sight of her dream out in the open for the first time. She gazed away, toward the bulk of Vesuvius to the south. "I've been thinking about it since October when we were back at the School of Air Evacuation in Kentucky."

"You have?"

"Yes. It's perfect. I love nursing, but I'm also excellent at administration and organization. I'd be a good chief nurse. We all know this war will be over soon. Come spring, we'll go on the offensive again here in Italy, and all those troops gathering in England will invade France, and it'll be over before you know it."

"Most likely . . ." Lambert sounded wary.

Kay stroked the olive drab aluminum of the fuselage. "Ma'am, we both know flight nurses won't be needed after the war. I could go back to being a stewardess, but I'm twenty-eight, and they'll let me go when I turn thirty. That's just how it is. I could work as a ward nurse, but after the independence of flight nursing, how could I go back to kowtowing to physicians? But I could be a chief. I'm good with details—"

"Kay." Lambert raised her hand. Her expression oozed compassion but held the force of a red traffic light.

"Yes, ma'am?" Her smile twitched, and she hated it.

Lambert glanced away to the tents of the 58th Station Hospital by the flight line. "I don't know what to say. It never occurred to me that you'd be interested."

"I am. This is what I want."

She smoothed back her brown hair, and her mouth puckered. "If the decision were based on your skills alone, I'd send you. You're one of the best nurses in the squadron—levelheaded, clever, and warm but not sentimental."

"Thank you, ma'am." She winced at the word *however* hanging in the air.

"However . . . your reputation. Why, I can't keep track of all the men you date. I'm surprised you can."

Kay stiffened. "Nothing illegal or immor—"

"Maybe not, but it's the appearance." Her frown deepened. "I haven't said anything because you stay away from the married men, I haven't heard anything scandalous, and you keep curfew."

Kay fingered the side seam of her gray-blue trousers. "As I said, nothing illegal or immoral."

"But there are so many. The other girls don't take you seriously."

A slight shrug. "It's just for fun."

Lieutenant Lambert crossed her arms. "There's more to being a chief than nursing and administrative skills. The girls look up to you, and you have to present an image to strive for."

"But I'm a good leader."

"Are you?" She waved an elegant hand toward quarters. "Your flight of six nurses has given me the greatest headaches from the start. Things have improved, but still, after a year abroad, yours is the least unified of the four flights in the 802nd Medical Air Evacuation Transport Squadron."

She shifted her weight from one leg to the other. "They don't like each other much."

"I'm sorry, Kay." Lambert headed down to the next C-47.

All the wind whooshed out of Kay's lungs. Her father was right. The wicked didn't prosper.

---

### Comiso Airfield, Sicily

Roger walked over the stubbly grass toward Headquarters with Shelby. Patchy clouds hovered over the Sicilian plain, sloping down to the Mediterranean to the southwest. If his squadron kept getting grounded on good flying days, he'd never get the thousand hours of flying time needed to go home.

"Uh-oh," Shelby grumbled. "Here comes Klein."

Grant Klein marched in their direction, head down for once. The man usually strutted about like he owned the airfield.

"Say, Coop, the DFC," Shelby said in a loud voice. "Imagine that."

Klein raised dark eyes, snorted, and passed them by. "Didn't know they gave out medals for losing planes."

Roger turned and shoved down the smoldering, painful truth. "You see, it's called the Distinguished *Flying* Cross. You've got to fly to get it, not sit around schmoozing with Parrish."

Shell nudged Roger's arm, his eyes too wide. "Didn't you hear? Parrish is rotating stateside. We have a new squadron commander."

Roger rubbed his chin. "Come to think of it, I did hear. Good news for you, Klein. You won't be flying only milk runs anymore. Might get yourself a medal too."

Klein's look turned even darker. "You're a jerk, Cooper."

He grinned at Shelby. "More good news. I got promoted from lazy bum to jerk."

"With hard work and determination, anything is possible."

Klein stomped away. "Only promotion you'll ever get."

"True." Roger resumed his trek to HQ. Not like he wanted a promotion anyway. He just wanted to log his hours and survive the war.

"Heard anything about the new CO?" Shelby asked.

"Not even his name. About to find out. I'll fill you in later." Roger waved off his friend and ducked in the open flap of the Headquarters tent.

A tall officer in his forties leaned over a field desk, wearing a lightweight leather flight jacket, khaki trousers, and the crush cap favored by airmen. Same as Roger wore. Except this man had a major's gold oak leaves pinned to the collar of his khaki shirt.

Roger saluted. "Sir! Lieutenant Cooper reporting."

"At ease, Lieutenant." The officer raised light eyes. "I'm Major Bill Veerman, your new squadron commander."

Veerman? Like one of Roger's favorite bandleaders, a young up-and-comer. In fact, the major had the same kind of look about him, lean and blond and narrow faced. "No relation to Hank Veerman, I presume."

"My kid brother." He slid on reading glasses and picked up a paper for inspection. "He's done well for himself. I'm proud of him."

Roger's mouth went dry. Veerman's band sat at the top of his list, not too famous to be out of his league, and it fit his style—not too sweet, not too hot. He clasped his hands behind his back. "One of my favorite bands. The man can send it."

"Send it?" The major peered over the top of his glasses. "You're a musician?"

"A drummer, sir." Behind his back, his thumbs tapped out a new rhythm on each other.

"Drummers." Veerman groaned. "Hank can't keep a drummer for two weeks straight."

That was better news than the DFC. That meant openings. That meant God might have answered his prayers.

Veerman studied Roger. "Drummers are known for being . . . unreliable."

His thumbs stilled. Sounded familiar.

The major flipped through the papers. "That explains your record. Late all the time, sloppy reports, pulling pranks on the other pilots. Parrish said you questioned a direct order. And you've lost two planes." His expression dared Roger to defend himself.

He took the dare. "Sir, the first plane was destroyed in a ground collision. I'd parked her on the hardstand, shut her down, and left. Another plane lost its brakes, slammed into it." Grant Klein, the idiot. And two good people had died—navigator Clint Peters and his girlfriend, flight nurse Rose Danilovich.

"And the second? Just a few days ago. You flew in the middle of a volcanic eruption?"

Roger cleared the huskiness from his throat. "Sir, I knew it wasn't safe to fly. I was given a direct order, which I questioned. Then I got reprimanded for ques—"

"For questioning the order." Veerman nodded. "Then you successfully ditched, saved a planeload of patients, and earned a nomination for the DFC."

"Yes, sir."

The major came out from behind his desk and eyed Roger up and down, his expression vacillating between admiration and disapproval. "You have a good head on your shoulders and a mind of your own. That I like. Now show me hard work and reliability."

"Yes, sir," he said, but he'd only disappoint the man. Might as well scratch Hank Veerman's band right off that list.

# 3

**Naples, Italy**
**March 28, 1944**

Kay sashayed through the doors of the Orange Club with her friends, and a dozen heads turned. She never tired of the reaction she sparked when accompanied by blonde beauty Alice Olson and sultry brunette Vera Viviani.

Ever since they'd answered Pan American Airway's call for registered nurses to serve as stewardesses, the three women had worked together, roomed together, and played together.

Alice had a boyfriend in the Army stateside, but she didn't let that interfere with her nights out—her boyfriend certainly enjoyed his nights out. Vera had a man in her life but maintained mysterious silence. Probably an enlisted man. Georgie Taylor had dated an enlisted man earlier in the year, but she wasn't as secretive as Vera.

Kay, on the other hand, had a mission. She strolled around the tables in the darkened room, in time to the band's rendition of "Stardust," through billows of cigarette smoke, making chitchat with Vera and Alice to keep the men at bay while she sized them up. Her breakup with Grant left an unacceptable hole in her lineup.

Lambert wanted too much. Give up her boys? Unite Vera

and Alice with Mellie, Georgie, and their new friend Louise Cox? Why not ask her to hike up Vesuvius and put a giant cork in it?

Might as well enjoy life while she still had her looks. What then?

Kay gripped a chair back for support, laughed for her friends' sake, and pretended to slip her black pump back onto her heel.

What then? She had to set things up now to settle things later. Without the Army Air Force chief nurse program, she'd have to serve in a hospital ward and work her way up to chief. Might take years. Might mean moving from city to city, searching for an opening. And it might never happen.

Then she wouldn't have a home.

Pain squeezed her chest so tight she gasped.

Kay shook it off, swung back her hair, and scanned the tables. "What do you think, gals?"

"Plenty of partners tonight." Alice wiggled her fingers at a man across the room.

Sure, plenty of partners, but such young pups. This got more difficult each year as the mature men married off.

The band eased into another soft number, almost lifeless.

"Come on!" a man called, hands cupped around his mouth. "Enough with the sweet stuff. We want to jive."

The bandleader lowered his baton, glared at the heckler, and turned to the microphone. "As I mentioned at the start of the set, our drummer didn't show. We have to make do."

Vera rolled her eyes. "If this war's taught us anything, it's how to make do and do without."

"Coop!" a flyboy yelled. "Hey, Coop! Get up there and help."

Coop? Kay followed the man's gaze. There at the front corner table sat a bunch of boys from the 64th Troop Carrier Group, including Roger Cooper.

He shook his head and waved off his pal.

Kay returned Vera's eye roll. Roger Cooper, the fuddy-duddy? Whenever Kay said one word to him, he'd say something religious and scram.

As far as Kay could see, religious people came in three varieties. Some held a can of white paint and wanted to slather it all over her, people like Georgie Taylor, although Georgie had wisely lowered her paintbrush. Some, like Mellie Blake, offered the paint can but didn't get huffy when Kay turned it down. And some, like Roger Cooper, acted as if she held a can of black paint and wanted to slather it all over him.

Bert Marino, one of the pilots, stood and tugged on Roger's arm. "Yeah, Coop's our man. Used to play for a band in Chicago."

Kay nudged Vera. "His high school marching band maybe."

However, the clamor built, and Roger stood, raised one hand to quiet the crowd, and made his way to the bandstand.

Oh dear. He might be a fuddy-duddy, but she had no desire to see him humiliated. He was a good pilot, and all the nurses liked flying with him. Georgie had survived the ditching because of him.

Roger conferred with the bandleader, then drew drumsticks from inside his olive drab service jacket and shrugged off the jacket.

Kay lifted an eyebrow. Someone once told her Coop was an Iowa farm boy, and he was built like one, with thick arms and a solid chest.

Too bad he was so boring.

"Excuse me, miss? Would you like to dance?" A skinny blond kid blocked her view, half a foot taller than Kay, but she probably outweighed the poor thing.

"I'd love to." She smiled back and gave him her hand. "I'm Kay Jobson."

"Enchanted." He kissed her hand. "I'm Bob Sperling."

She would have found him charming. When she was eighteen. "Come on, Bob. Let's cut a rug." She led him to the dance floor.

On the bandstand, Roger stared at the drums and cymbals like a kid at the fair. The trumpet section stood and pumped out the opening chords of "Sing, Sing, Sing."

Bob broke into a jitterbug, but Kay winced for Roger's sake. No mistaking why the bandleader chose Benny Goodman's big hit. The complicated drumming had made Gene Krupa a star but would prove Roger Cooper an imposter. Then the band could return to their lazy love songs.

Kay ducked under Bob's arm, her hips swinging, legs kicking. Bob whirled her so she faced the band again.

Roger tapped out a lively beat, his chin, his whole body bouncing. He actually sounded good.

Kay lost herself in the dance and gave Bob her full attention, knowing she'd attract other partners who could shave and vote.

The band shifted into the solo section. The dancers stopped to watch, and Kay caught her breath and smoothed her hair.

On his feet, the clarinetist dove into his solo, nowhere near as complex as Benny Goodman played, but engaging.

And the drums . . .

They rumbled and pounded and drove the clarinet on, complementing, never overpowering. Roger's playing softened when the clarinet wailed and picked up when the clarinet quieted, a perfect seesaw. Someone in the audience whistled, then another.

Roger grinned, his sticks flashing in the air.

Kay stood, transfixed. She'd always thought him a good-looking man with his square face and auburn hair, but now he was flat-out handsome. The energy, the vigor, the power. His music pulsed inside her, quickening her heart and her senses.

When the song concluded, everyone cheered, and Kay joined them.

The bandleader held out his hand toward the drum set, and Roger bowed his head.

Kay switched partners, another youngster, but she already had a man in her sights.

Behind his fuddy-duddy exterior, Roger Cooper had hidden a fascinating man, a man she wanted to know. She'd never bothered pursuing him since he'd given her no encouragement, but that was going to change.

Sure, he talked about God too much, but so did Mellie and Georgie, and they'd turned out to be the best sort.

Besides, he was a fellow redhead. Imagining her father's fury, Kay laughed.

————————

Man alive, he hadn't felt that great in years. His set over, Roger swept his handkerchief over his forehead, wiped the back of his neck, and slung his jacket over his shoulder.

He headed back to his table and took the chair in the corner of the room next to Bert Marino, his friend from training days, and Mike Elroy, his new copilot.

Bert slapped him on the back. "Haven't heard you play since we were stateside. Sounded good."

"Sounded rusty, but thanks." Rusty or not, his instincts remained and his training and practice had imprinted in every move.

"That was really something, Lieutenant." Mike pulled on the bill of his service cap to adjust it over his brown hair. The kid was so new, he still hadn't removed the spring in the crown to convert it to a crush cap.

"I told you. Call me Coop or Roger. None of this lieutenant stuff."

"May we join you, gentlemen?"

Kay Jobson, Vera Viviani, and Alice Olson stood in front of the table, wearing their gray-blue skirts and white blouses, their jackets folded over their arms.

Kay sent Roger a flirty look that had felled many foolhardy men. But not him.

Bert and Mike jumped to their feet and pulled out chairs. Roger stood too, as was polite, but he wanted to groan. Why did dames have to ruin a perfect evening?

Kay took the chair to Roger's left, Bert hemmed him in on the right, and the walls formed a V behind him. When Bert twisted toward Alice, his back created another barrier.

Roger was trapped. He sipped his cold coffee to hide his grimace.

"Well, Roger Cooper. I didn't know you had it in you." Kay leaned her elbow on the table and turned the full force of her green eyes on him.

He sloshed the coffee to suspend the grounds. "Played in house bands before I enlisted."

She'd taken off her tie and undone the top two buttons of her blouse, completely modest, but enough to expose the sweet hollow at the base of her throat. "I thought you were a good little church boy."

Roger chuckled in spite of himself. "Don't know about that, but I love the Lord." And invoking the Lord's name always sent Kay running. Maybe he could whip up a sermon.

She rested her chin in her hand, a teasing glint in her eyes. "I thought the drums were the devil's instrument."

Another chuckle. If he wasn't careful, she'd think he was enjoying himself. "Heard that a lot growing up. That's one reason I play."

Kay's jaw flopped open. "You—"

"I wasn't always a—what you call a church boy."

"You weren't?"

Roger took another slug of coffee. He certainly didn't

want to tell his story to a woman like Kay Jobson. Best to switch gears and then state his case for a fresh cup of joe. "God and I weren't well acquainted, not until I left home, started playing in Chicago. Then I figured out drums were an instrument, nothing more."

Kay fiddled with a lock of her reddish-blonde hair, her expression unreadable—almost confused, almost intrigued.

Roger glanced to his right. Bert and Mike chatted with Vera and Alice, Bert's back as impenetrable as the side of a barn.

"How did you get started with the drums?"

His sticks lay on the table, and he rolled them under his fingers. "Wanted to play football. Tore my hamstring my sophomore year, and I hated the sidelines, sitting still. The band's drummer was a puny guy, always sick, so I took his place just for fun to see what it was like."

"And you liked it."

"Yeah. The drum is the heartbeat of the band." He picked up his sticks and tapped a heartbeat rhythm on the edge of the table. "When it's slow, it relaxes you." He increased the pace. "When it's fast, it's exciting. And when we mix it up, throw in a surprise—we like that, don't we? The unexpected. Like a skipped heartbeat." He demonstrated, mixed it up.

"I see." Kay cocked her head and studied his hands at work—intelligent interest rather than flirtation.

So he proceeded. "And drums send messages. Lots of cultures use drums to communicate. Even the Morse code is like a drumbeat. That's how I taught myself Morse. I drummed it out." He went into his alphabet, soft for the dots, loud for the dashes.

"That's clever." Her lips curved, but more girlish than womanly, something he'd never seen in her.

Dangerous, dangerous, dangerous. "I think the heartbeat itself is a drum message from God. With every beat, he sends his message. His life, his love. His life, his love." The sticks accented his words, and his words would send Kay packing, as he intended.

Indeed, her eyes darkened. She looked down to the table and pressed her fingers to her neck, right below her pretty jaw, as if taking her pulse.

Then she snapped up her usual bold gaze and rested her chin in her hand. "You play the drums extremely well. I'm impressed."

"Um, thanks. I plan to join a big band after the war." Her eyes weren't large, but they were striking, and she knew how to use them. She knew how to use everything God had given her—her hands, her hair, her shoulders. Everything choreographed to bring a man to his knees.

He had to escape.

"Everyone together now!" An officer stood and waved his arms in the air. "Let's sing 'Mairzy Doats.'" He belted out the nonsense tune that had swept the nation and now the troops overseas.

Roger joined in with the rest of his table. Good. After the song, he'd insert himself into Bert and Mike's conversation.

Kay didn't sing. She smiled as if enjoying herself, but not one word came out of that perfect mouth.

The song continued, but Roger couldn't resist teasing Kay. "What's the matter? Don't know the words?"

"I don't sing."

That meant she didn't sing well. "So, you're afraid you'll sing off-key and tarnish your glamour girl image." He grinned.

She didn't. Hurt flickered through her eyes. "I just don't sing."

"Sorry. Didn't mean to hit a sore spot." He wanted to discourage her romantic interest, but he didn't mean to cut her down.

Her eyes softened, and she lifted a wobbly smile.

With that flash of humanity and vulnerability, she was far

more attractive than when she flirted. And her flirting was mighty effective. How on earth could he get away?

The song had ended. His friends had resumed their conversation, excluding him.

Captain Craig, the bandleader, approached the table. "Lieutenant Cooper, if you're interested, we'd like to start another set in five minutes."

Was he interested? Boy, was he. "Absolutely, sir. I haven't had this much fun in years."

After the captain left, Kay leaned closer. "You need more fun in your life."

Back to the vixen, huh? Roger's jaw clenched. "I'm fine."

"You know, I've enjoyed this. I've worked with you for a year, and I don't think we've ever had this long of a conversation."

"True." He had to admit it hadn't been all bad.

"We should do it again sometime." She trailed one finger up his forearm.

Fire raced through his shirt, through his skin, through his veins, and he eased away and looked her firmly in the eyes. "You have enough men."

She flapped her hand in front of her face and laughed. "I broke up with Grant this week. It's too quiet now."

He almost smiled about her breakup. That explained why Grant had been snapping like a cheap drumstick.

Kay opened her mouth to speak.

"I'm flattered." Roger cleared his throat. "But I'm not the dating kind."

Her thin eyebrows twisted. "Not the dating—"

"Nope. Way I see it, there are only two reasons to date." He held up one drumstick. "First, to find a wife."

She gasped and leaned back. "I do *not* want to get married."

"Neither do I. After the war, I'm joining a big band. That means lots of time on the road. I'm not dragging a wife along. I've seen too many unhappy band wives, too many divorces."

Kay's cheeks reddened. Her lips drew in tight. "As I said, I'm not—"

"So you date for the second reason—just for fun."

"Exactly." She brushed her hair off her shoulder and sniffed. "That only leads to trouble."

"Not in my experience."

Roger chuckled. "No offense, doll, but I've seen giant waves of trouble in your wake."

Her chin rose, and her expression hardened. "So you choose no fun at all."

"And no trouble." He gave her half a grin. "Sorry, but you're better off. Trust me. Now if you'll excuse me, I've got to get back to the drums. *Arrivederci.*"

She swung her head to the side. Not even a good-bye.

Fine by him. He tapped Bert's shoulder. "Hey, pal. Can I get past you?"

"Sure thing." Bert stood.

Roger returned to the bandstand and sat on the stool.

Bert had followed him. "Say, Kay looks annoyed. What'd you do? Turn her down?"

"Yeah. The dame's dangerous."

"Dangerous?" Bert laughed and leaned closer, a glint in his dark eyes. "She's not dangerous enough."

Roger frowned. "What do you mean?"

Bert squatted next to the stool. "I heard Klein crying into his beer last night. Seems that if you want a fun night out, she's your gal. But if you want payback, forget it. Not the first time I've heard that about her. All promise, no pleasure."

Roger's mind spun. He looked out over the dance floor. Kay had already found herself a fellow, and she hung on his shoulder and smiled enticingly at the man.

Why did she act that way? If not for pleasure, then why?

The bandleader announced they'd play "Jersey Bounce."

Roger sent his energy through his drumsticks. What made that girl tick? Why did the name of the Lord make her run? Why did she . . . ?

The questions ran ahead of the rhythm, but the only way to answer them would be to talk to her again. His original conclusion stood fast. The dame was dangerous.

4

**Pomigliano Airfield**
**March 30, 1944**

Nothing Kay hated more than solitude.

Georgie was still on Capri, and Mellie and Louise had a Remain Overnight in Mateur, Tunisia, after an evac flight.

Kay paced in the chilly four-man pyramidal tent, past the cots and crates. Empty quarters bred self-pity, and this morning it overwhelmed her. Her dreams were being ripped away, and Roger Cooper's rejection smarted. But why did she care? Two days before, she'd written him off.

She dug to the bottom of the barracks bag until her fingers closed around Sissy's cloth form. Kay needed her, and she pulled out the rag doll Mother had made back when she loved her middle daughter.

She hadn't held Sissy for months, and her throat clamped at the sight of the green button eyes that had been replaced twice when her little sister, Keren, tore them off. She stroked the orange yarn hair, fresh strands sewn on after Kay's older sister, Jemima, ground Sissy into the mud. That was when Kay started hiding her doll.

Kay grunted in frustration and swiped away the moisture in her eyes. She stuffed Sissy back down to the bottom of her bag, stomped to the crate she used as a bedside table, and whipped open her compact. A few puffs of powder concealed her loss of control.

She put the compact back into her cosmetics bag and set it in front of the photo.

The photo, her only open concession to sentimentality. The black-and-white square showed Kay and Georgie and Mellie in front of Georgie's home in Virginia in October. She let everyone think she displayed the photo because of her friends, but it was really because of the house.

The Taylors didn't know what those weekends in their lovely white frame house meant to her. She'd never lived in a real house. A tent with her family as they zigzagged across the Midwest. A crowded apartment after she ran away from home. Cramped quarters in nursing school. Another crowded apartment with Vera and Alice when they flew with Pan Am. Military housing ever since.

In the picture, Kay and Mellie flanked Georgie as if holding her up after the death of her lifelong best friend, Rose Danilovich. In reality, they all propped each other up.

"It doesn't make sense." Rose was so good. Why did God take her? It should have been Kay.

She set down the photo and marched out of the tent and along the log-paved "corduroy road" that kept her feet out of the mud somewhat. She didn't need to report to the flight line for another hour, but she couldn't let the quicksand of self-pity claim her.

What good did ruminating do? No one could answer her questions. Georgie and Mellie tried but offered baloney about God not being done with Kay. Since when had God wanted anything to do with Kay?

*"God has rejected you,"* Father always said. *"Evil to the core."*

Kay stepped onto the pierced-steel planking that formed the airfield's hardstands and runways. A dozen C-47 cargo planes sat in the morning sunshine. In the distance, P-40 Warhawk fighter planes roared into the air, off to strafe German positions at Cassino and Anzio.

Beside the tail of a C-47, a man sat cross-legged, head bowed over a book.

Roger Cooper.

Kay's stomach jolted, and she turned on her heel. She'd been assigned to his flight today but didn't intend to say one word to him.

And yet . . .

She pivoted back. Since he hadn't noticed her, she studied him. Things he'd said at the Orange Club intrigued her. He hadn't always been a church boy. He chose the drums to shock people. He and God hadn't always been well acquainted. How did a rebel end up so good?

She edged forward, stopping about ten feet away from him. "Hi."

His head jerked up, and he gave her a wary expression. "Hi."

She glanced away to the plane, olive drab with minimal markings—just the Army Air Force's blue-and-white "star and bars" insignia and a narrow white stripe around the rear fuselage to identify the squadron. "I'm assigned to your flight today. Since you have a new plane, I should get oriented. Does it have aluminum litter brackets or web strapping?"

"Web." A page of his book crackled in the wind.

"Good. More efficient."

"And lighter. Can carry more cargo."

She walked beside the plane, behind him, and peeked down—the Bible, of course. When she reached the wing, she followed the edge to the wingtip. Six square windows ran the length of the cabin, and a round bubble of a window in the roof of the plane marked the radioman-navigator's room. "What's it like flying without a navigator?"

"Pardon?" Roger raised his head from his Bible again.

She'd never seen an unmarried man so blind to her charms. "What's it like flying without a navigator?"

"Not great." He stuck a finger in his place in the Bible. "The Twelfth Air Force decided the B-17 bombers need navigators more than the lowly cargo planes do. Pettas does fine, gets us where we need to go, but he's not Clint." His voice hitched.

Clint Peters had been Roger's best friend. "He was a good man," Kay said.

"Yeah, he was." A breeze ruffled his auburn hair.

"Rose was good too." Had it been six months since they'd died? Seemed like yesterday. "Doesn't make sense."

Roger shrugged. "Life doesn't make sense."

She cocked an eyebrow at him. "I expected more from a man with a Bible in his lap."

He grinned, reminding her of the energy she'd seen at the drum set. "God makes sense, even if we don't see it."

Kay crossed her arms. "I certainly don't see it. If God made sense, he wouldn't have taken Rose."

"Why not?" He gave her a matter-of-fact look.

She waved toward his Bible. "You know. 'Remember, I pray thee, who ever perished, being innocent? or where were the righteous cut off?' "

"Huh?"

"Job 4:7."

If he weren't careful, his jaw would get caught in the pierced-steel planking. "I—I don't know Job that well."

"I do. My father preached from it in every sermon. Every single sermon." As always, she gained devious pleasure from shocking people.

"He . . . preached?"

Kay shook back her hair. "He's a preacher. Are you shocked?"

He nodded slowly, his brown eyes wide.

"You can imagine how shocked he was to have a daughter like me. Irredeemable." Her voice quivered. Why on earth had she said that? But there it was, out in the open.

Roger closed his mouth, and compassion replaced shock. "Anyone can be redeemed. Even me."

Heat roiled in her chest. "What would you know? You're one of them. You're good."

"Good? Don't know about that. And believe me, no one called me good when I was a boy."

"No one?" Her hands grasped the tip of the wing, the aluminum cool to her fingers.

One side of his mouth twitched up. "I'm the seventh of eight kids. More energy than sense, my ma always said. Pestered my brothers and sisters, pulled pranks on my teachers, painted some of the pigs blue one winter to make my dad think they'd frozen solid. Got my backside tanned so much I'm surprised it's still there."

Kay fought a smile and lifted one shoulder. "Harmless childhood—"

"It got worse. Real bad. Did things I'm ashamed of." He smoothed a page in his Bible, and his voice lowered. "People got . . . hurt. Couldn't live with myself."

Kay strained to hear, and understanding drew her nearer.

Roger looked up with pain in his eyes that wrenched her heart. His mouth squirmed, and he patted his knee like a drum.

Did he understand what it was like to be bad? "What happened?" she said, just above a whisper.

He shook his head, and the rhythm changed. "That's not what matters. What matters is what happened next. After I graduated, I left home. Thought I could run away from myself, but I couldn't. Then I met Lou."

"Lou?" She gripped the trailing edge of the wing.

"Trombone player. He showed me the way out of my sin

39

and pain and shame. He showed me even I could be redeemed. Gave me this Bible."

Kay realized she'd moved closer. She took a step back. "Nothing in there for me."

"That's what I thought until I read it. Look." He beckoned, his face composed again. "See all the notes in the margins?"

She edged forward as if walking toward a cliff. Sure enough, scrawls filled the margins. "You write in the Bible? Isn't that illegal?"

He winked. "Told you I was a sinner."

A smile played on her lips.

Roger glanced down, flipped through the pages. "Anytime a verse speaks to me, I make notes, helps me remember. See? Proof that I've read Job once or twice."

The three black letters of the title glared condemnation. She flinched and stood up straight.

Roger's eyes widened. "Your name's Jobson. That's why he preached from Job, isn't it?"

The memory sliced, and she folded her arms over her stomach. "Sign from God."

"Did he—did he preach that suffering results from sin? That you have to be good to make it stop?"

For all the Bible reading he'd done, how could he be so ignorant? "Of course. That's what it says."

His forehead crinkled up, and he turned pages. "Those ideas are in here, all right."

"I know that."

"But they're not . . ." He tapped his finger on a page. "They're not God's words."

She shifted her feet and crossed her arms tight around her stomach. "They're in the Bible, aren't they?"

"Well, yeah. But they were spoken by men who claimed to be Job's friends but weren't. In fact, at the end of the book, God sets them straight and gives them a verbal whipping."

Kay's thoughts tumbled around and made her head shake from side to side. "But he said—my father said—are you saying he lied?"

Roger didn't speak, just gave her a steady gaze.

"Nonsense." Her voice wavered. "Complete nonsense."

"Have you ever read Job, the entire book?"

"Of course not. Father wouldn't let us read the Bible, said we weren't old enough to understand." Her eyes stung. Had he said that to conceal his lies? Fit better with everything else she knew about his character.

"You should read it. See what the Lord really says."

Steam expanded her chest. She stepped away. "Couldn't if I wanted to, which I don't. I don't own a Bible."

He chewed on his lips and rubbed his fingers over the black leather binding. "The chaplain—he has Bibles. Ask him."

Kay flung up both hands in front of her chest. "The chaplain? Last person I want to talk to."

Roger's face contracted, and he lowered his gaze to his Bible.

She'd never felt tinier, emptier, more confused, and she hated it, hated him, hated herself. *"Arrivederci."* She strode away.

"Kay! Wait!"

She waved her hand, wiping away his words.

His footsteps thumped up behind. "Wait. Take mine."

"What?" She spun around.

He almost bumped into her, then backed up as if she were the devil himself.

"What?" she barked.

"You don't have to go to the chaplain." He stared down at his Bible, his grip so tight, his knuckles popped up in little snow-capped peaks. "I want you to have my Bible."

"What?" Her voice sputtered out like a dying engine.

He thrust the book at her. "I'm giving it to you."

"But . . ." Wasn't it a gift from an old friend? Filled with his personal notes?

His brown eyes shone with determination. "It's a gift, and you can't say no."

The black leather had worn off in spots. The gold lettering had disappeared. The pages were warped and tousled from use. How could she take something so precious to him? "I don't want it."

He took her arm and pressed his thumb at the base of her wrist until her hand unfurled. Then he slipped the Bible into her hand. "Too bad. It's yours."

Her breath came hard and fast. He was so close, so incredibly attractive, his grip powerful but gentle, his message unbearable, his gift . . . unfathomable. "Why would you?"

Roger let go, but he didn't back away. "Because I remember."

# 5

**Pomigliano Airfield**
**April 1, 1944**

Roger's fingers itched for his drumsticks, but Veerman would think he was showing off. His energy had to go somewhere, so it flowed out his heels to the dirt floor of the tent.

On the camp stool beside him, Shelby glanced at Roger's bouncing knees and smirked. He got an elbow in return.

Veerman glanced from his watch to the tent entrance. "Anyone seen Marino?"

Grant Klein snickered. "For once, we're waiting for someone other than Cooper."

A quip danced on Roger's tongue, but the acidic look on Veerman's face stilled it. So Klein's little barbs didn't carry weight with the commander. Instead, Roger put on a bland smile and turned it to Klein. A startled reaction made a sweet reward.

Sunlight and a rush of cool air, and Bert Marino burst through the tent entrance. "Sorry I'm late, Major. I—"

"I don't want excuses. I want punctuality." He motioned to the empty camp stool.

Roger squirmed. That didn't bode well for him and his chronic tardiness.

"All right, men. We flew up here for medical air evacuation flights this morning, but plans have changed. Just got a telegram." Veerman tipped up his chin to look through his reading glasses at papers in his hand. "Seeing as how it's April Fools' Day, I didn't believe it at first. But it's officially confirmed. The 64th Troop Carrier Group received orders for an emergency deployment to the Tenth Air Force."

The Tenth? In India? Roger sat up straighter, and he chomped his chewing gum. He'd like a change in scenery and wouldn't mind steamy heat, primitive living conditions, or increased danger. But the China-Burma-India Theater demanded a lot from a pilot. What if the CBI demanded more than Roger could deliver?

Veerman flipped through the papers. "The situation in Burma isn't good. The Japanese launched a major drive early in March and are pushing the British back into India. Meanwhile, American and Chinese troops are fighting for their lives in northern Burma. The roads are abysmal. Air transport is the only way to supply our boys. The Tenth Air Force is overburdened, and since we have a stalemate in Italy, we've been loaned out."

Klein's eyebrows tented in mock concern. "Uh-oh, Cooper. We won't be flying over water. Next time you lose a plane, you'll have to do it in the jungle."

"I'm more worried about you. You might break a sweat."

"Gentlemen!"

Roger winced. That comeback wasn't worth it, and it wasn't even that good. "Just ribbing between friends." He grinned and punched Klein in the shoulder, a bit harder than necessary.

One narrowed eye told him he hadn't fooled his CO.

"As I started to say, we will not be taking any patients today. We'll head straight back to Comiso, pack up, and fly out tomorrow."

"Tomorrow?" Klein sat forward. "That—that doesn't give us much time to say good-bye. How long will we be gone?"

"A month. Maybe longer. And . . ." Veerman slapped the folder shut. "You men are officers. You know the routine. You can tell your sweethearts you're shipping out, but you can't say where. That goes for your crews too. They'll be briefed en route."

He dismissed them to their planes.

Roger headed outside with Shelby and Marino. He'd miss Italy but he wasn't sorry to leave. Not after the previous day's conversation with Kay Jobson. All his questions about her had been whipped into a frenzy.

Why had the Lord let him see her hurt and anger and shame? Why had the Lord moved him, of all people, to correct the lies she'd been told? Why on earth had the Lord prodded him to give her his Bible? God could have let him fetch a Bible from the chaplain for her, but no, the prompting was clear. It had to be Roger's Bible, filled with hundreds of personal notes. Very personal.

Why had he obeyed? Sure, the chaplain gave him a replacement, but the thing fit in the palm of his hand, only the New Testament, and no room to write. It could take two months to get a good Bible sent from the States.

Annoyance simmered, but he tamped it down. He'd done the right thing.

Bert elbowed Roger. "Your girlfriend wants a kiss good-bye."

"I don't have a . . ." His mouth dried out.

About a hundred feet away, Kay Jobson peered toward the men under a sun-shielding hand. She wasn't looking for him, was she?

Nope. Grant Klein strode up to her. "Hi, baby."

Relief and disgust mingled in Roger's gut. So much for the breakup.

However, Kay gave Grant a cool hello, stepped around him—and toward Roger.

"What's going on?" Shelby muttered.

"Nothing." Tomorrow he'd fly to another continent, away from swaying hips and swishing red hair and beckoning green eyes.

"Hi, Coop."

"Hi, Kay." He gave her a polite smile and walked past as if he didn't know she was looking for him.

"Rog—wait. I have a—can I talk to you for a second?"

He faced her, walked backward toward the flight line, and motioned with his thumb toward the planes. "Sorry. We're in a hurry."

Ouch. The force of that girl's glare. "Only a second."

Fine way to help the dame out. Might as well snatch back the Bible. He stopped and cocked a smile. "Yeah, sure."

"I'll tell your crew you'll be a bit late." Shelby gave him a mysterious look.

"Ah, they're used to it." He headed back to Kay and ignored Bert's chuckling. Shelby would get an earful about what happened at the Orange Club.

The temperature of her gaze rose from icy to chilly. "I have something for you."

Roger halted a safe ten feet from her. How often had he seen her give "good luck" kisses to men before missions? "Yeah?"

"An alarm clock." She opened her hand to reveal a small black case with a brass clasp.

Maybe the pressure of flying in a war zone was getting to her. "An alarm clock?"

She turned the case in her hand. "I heard your new CO is Hank Veerman's brother."

"True."

"That's good news for you."

He allowed a small smile. "If I don't make a fool of myself."

Her cheeks reddened, and she ground her foot into the dirt as if squashing an insect. "About an hour ago, I overheard Grant talking with Singleton."

That explained the insect-squishing, but not the clock. "Yeah?"

She chewed on her lips and didn't meet his eye. "Grant was being a jerk, said you'd never impress Veerman because you sleep too late. He said you don't even own an alarm clock."

The ends finally tied up. "They're forbidden at the Cooper homestead. No farmer worth his salt uses an alarm clock, my parents always say. They get up with the chickens."

Kay tipped a saucy smile. "You're not on the farm. No chickens here. You need a clock."

Roger shrugged. "I get by."

"That's not what Grant said." Her eyes gave off more sparks than Vesuvius's eruption last week. "You need to get up on time, impress your CO, get that big band spot, and prove Grant Klein wrong."

Volcanoes had nothing on scorned women. "Why? What did he do to you?"

"Nothing. Really, he didn't. But I don't like the way he talked about you. Not after what you did for me, giving me your Bible."

"Nah. I already got a new one."

She flipped the clock over and over in her hand. "I know it isn't just a book to you. I saw the inscription from your friend, all your notes."

His neck heated up. His Bible was as personal and private as a diary. How much had he revealed in those notes? What had he inadvertently confessed to this woman?

Kay thrust out the alarm clock. "It's a gift, and you can't say no."

Repeating his words, was she? Would she grab his wrist as

he'd grabbed hers? He could still feel the warmth, the tight-muscled stubbornness in her slim arm.

"Please?" Her green-eyed gaze reached out to him, just as warm and stubborn. And as fragile as a new blade of grass. "I want to do one little thing to help you achieve your dream."

His dream? His family saw his dream as foolishness. His friends saw it as wishful thinking. But she looked at him as if she believed he could do it.

"Thanks," he muttered through a too-thick throat. He took the clock, careful not to touch her fingers. But the black leather case carried the heat of her touch.

Kay gave him a shaky smile and gestured toward the flight line. "I kept you too long. You'd better get moving. I'll see you later."

Should he tell her? "Um, actually, you won't. We're shipping out tomorrow."

"Shipping out?"

"Group's deployed to a new theater. We're flying back to Comiso now, heading off tomorrow."

All the color left her face. She opened her mouth, closed it, blinked a few times. "Oh. I had a few questions for you. I tried to read, but it just—it isn't . . ."

The Bible. Oh, great. He'd given her the tool but not the instructions on how to use it. "I'm sure someone can—"

Kay shook her head hard. "Mellie and Georgie don't understand. Not like . . . well, never mind. It's fine." She raised her usual confident smile and walked away. "Good luck to you."

Ah, for crying out loud. Her friends didn't understand like *he* did. He understood how it felt to be a sinner, to be drowning, to grasp for a lifeline, any at all. The least he could do was throw her a line.

"Kay, wait."

"Yes?" Poise masked her turmoil again.

He pulled a notepad from the breast pocket of his shirt. "If you want, you can write me, ask your questions."

"I could?" The poise dissolved. He'd seen the same hunger in the faces of starving street urchins in Naples.

"Sure." With teeth gritted, he scrawled down his address and Army Post Office number. What on earth had the Lord gotten him into?

# 6

**Over the Mediterranean**
**April 4, 1944**

The rumble of the C-47's twin engines vibrated through Kay's backside as the words in the book of Job ricocheted in her head.

"Behold, God will not cast away a perfect man, neither will he help the evil doers." Kay squeezed her eyes shut. How many times had her father quoted Job 8:20 to her?

Willard Jobson's other favorite verse for her was Job 5:2: "For wrath killeth the foolish man, and envy slayeth the silly one," used to chastise her when she dared to argue with Jemima and Keren, the favored daughters, the songbirds with heavenly blonde hair.

Even as a child, it hadn't made sense to her. How could she be punished with red hair and tone deafness *before* she'd committed the sin of envying her sisters for their gifts?

Those verses—the verses he'd attributed to the Lord God Almighty—were spoken by Bildad and Eliphaz, not by Job and not by God. And if Roger Cooper was right, Bildad and Eliphaz didn't speak the truth.

Kay slammed the Bible shut and stuffed it in her small canvas musette bag. How on earth could she get through all forty-two chapters of the blasted book? She could barely handle one chapter at a time.

Kay pushed herself to her feet and snagged the clipboard with the flight manifest off its hook by the cargo door.

Tonight she'd add more questions to her list for Roger. After she filled a page, front and back, she'd mail it. Would he answer? He didn't seem terribly enthusiastic, but he also seemed like the kind of man who kept his word.

For now, she had work to do. Only a dozen patients today. Another lull had developed on the fronts at Cassino and Anzio, preparing for the big push, everyone hoped.

Kay opened the medical chest and filled a pouch on her belt with medications and supplies. Sergeant Dabrowski was busy distributing rations and water, lighting cigarettes, and reading letters, so Kay would take vital signs and administer meds.

She started at the bottom litter on the right, checked the patient's medical tag against the flight manifest, inquired how he was doing, looked for signs of bleeding or infection, and recorded his temperature, pulse, and respiration. After she gave him an aspirin, she repeated the process for the soldier in the middle litter.

Grant Klein talked about flying too much, but something he once said stuck in her brain. After the pilot got the aircraft in straight and level flight, he could use the automatic pilot system to keep it there.

Thank goodness Kay had her own automatic pilot, the skills she'd learned in almost a decade of nursing. Today she needed it.

Today she'd read Job 8:5–6, the words of Bildad: "If thou wouldest seek unto God betimes, and make thy supplication to the Almighty; If thou wert pure and upright; surely now he would awake for thee, and make the habitation of thy righteousness prosperous."

Father slapped the pulpit when he read that verse, and

he read it at every single tent meeting. The concept in those verses was the key to his success.

Just like Job, Father had lost everything. He'd lost four sons and his wife and his farm and his health. But he'd made himself pure and upright. The Lord rewarded him with a prosperous ministry, good health, a beautiful young wife, and three daughters, whom he'd named after Job's daughters—Jemima and Kezia and Kerenhappuch.

Kay stuck her foot in the stirrup under the bottom litter and hitched herself up to care for the man on top.

Her given name hissed in her ear. Kezia. Kuh-zzzzye-uh.

She drew up morphine into a syringe.

"What's that?"

"Morphine for your pain." She felt the inside of his elbow and found a good vein.

"I'm not in pain."

Kay looked into his pale blue eyes. Had she actually looked at him yet? "It's been four hours since your last dose. Better to give you another dose now than wait until the pain in your wound flares again."

Blond eyebrows tented. "I'm not wounded. I'm just sick is all. Can't shake this pneumonia."

Pneumonia? Bile chewed its way up her throat. She grabbed the medical tag—Pvt. Gerald Carson. The flight manifest—she was on Sgt. Joe Lazio.

Oh no.

Her cheeks tingled, and she glanced around the plane. When? Where had she gotten mixed up? When had she crossed to the left side of the plane? She didn't remember. The flight manifest showed data for seven patients, but she was taking care of the man in the sixth position.

She'd given morphine and sulfanilamide and aspirin. How many patients received the wrong drugs?

"I—I'm sorry, Private. You're right. You don't get morphine, but you need your sulfa." She opened the bottle and shook out tablets, far too many, and they sprinkled to the floor. With a shaky hand, she funneled the extras into the bottle and pressed one tablet into Carson's hand.

Kay lowered herself to the floor and picked up the wasted pills from among the dirt clods.

Her stomach turned over. She never made mistakes like this. Now she'd have to track down where she'd gone wrong, correct what errors she could, apologize for the errors she couldn't correct, and confess to both the physician and to Lieutenant Lambert.

What kind of chief nurse candidate made a grave mistake like this?

What kind of chief nurse candidate allowed herself to function on automatic pilot?

Grant had said the automatic pilot was no good in stormy weather or turbulence. How dare she rely on it in the middle of her own turbulence?

Bile bulged in her mouth and threatened to make an even bigger fool of her. She swallowed it back down, swallowed her shame.

But the truth couldn't be swallowed.

For the first time since she'd run away from home, she'd lost control.

---

**Lalmai, Lower Bengal, India**
**April 6, 1944**

Five thousand miles in five days.

Roger felt it in his back and arms and head. The stops in Libya and Egypt and Iran and India blurred together, and his chewing gum had turned stiff. One last landing, in far eastern India, close to the Burmese border. He gazed out the cockpit window to the steamy green jungle, the clearing for the airstrip, and the descending line of his squadron's C-47s. "Looking forward to a good night's sleep."

"Me too." Mike Elroy wiped his forehead. "And a day off, I hope."

"We'd better get one. Gotta adjust to heat and humidity." Roger wore his khaki shirt unbuttoned to the waist and his trousers rolled up to the knees, but sweat soaked his clothing.

On the downwind leg of the landing pattern, the C-47 drew opposite to the runway. Altitude and airspeed looked good. "Landing gear down."

Elroy moved the handle to the left of his seat. "Down."

After the green light flashed on the instrument panel, Roger secured the landing gear latch on the floor. He eased up the propeller controls to 2250 rpm, adjusted the throttles for descent, and scoped out the airstrip. A dirt surface. No more being spoiled with asphalt or even the temporary surfaces rigged by the engineers.

The 64th Troop Carrier Group was in for a rugged time.

Sweat slithered down his breastbone. Could he handle it? Or would he fail and endanger the lives of his crew, passengers, and bystanders on the ground? Would he let Veerman down and ruin his best chance at a big-time band?

His breath huffed out, loud enough to make Elroy look his way.

Roger put the bird into a ninety-degree turn toward the end of the runway. "Hotter than a blast furnace."

"Yep. Three-quarter flaps." The copilot readjusted the lever.

"Second power reduction." He pushed down the throttles, aiming for 120 miles per hour.

Elroy might be greener than the jungle below, but he probably cared more about crew and passenger safety than about impressing Veerman. Although Roger's body ached for sleep, his soul craved time with God.

He winced. His Bible.

Would Kay actually read it? If not, his sacrifice was in vain. And if she did read it? If she read the book of Job as he'd suggested?

He puffed out another breath. He'd only read the book once or twice and found it tough. Lou had started Roger off with the book of Romans and had been there to field questions. Roger had started Kay off with Job and bolted to another continent. What was he thinking?

"One twenty," Elroy said.

Roger turned for the approach. "Third power reduction."

"Full flaps."

The runway spread straight in front of him, and Roger kept up the play of ailerons, elevators, rudder, and throttles to make a good landing. Dozens of C-47s were parked around the airstrip, and trucks and people milled around.

"Fifty feet. Airspeed ninety."

Perfect. Roger tilted up the nose for the roundout, and the plane floated down onto two wheels.

The rough runway jiggled the plane and blurred the controls.

When the plane slowed down enough, she settled back onto her tail wheel. Not a bad landing. He and Elroy pulled the control columns toward their chests, and Roger tipped his toes forward on the pedals to apply brakes.

Outside, a ground crewman waved them to the side, and Roger followed his instructions and parked his plane. He and Elroy went through the shutdown and parking checklists, and silence rushed into the void left by the two engines.

Roger unfolded himself from his seat and found his clipboard with Forms 1 and F. He led Elroy through the radioman's compartment and the main cabin, filled with four giant auxiliary tanks that fueled the long voyage. He grabbed his barracks bag and hopped out the cargo door. Whitaker and Pettas waited outside.

The air smelled different—exotic. Instead of tents and tile-roofed buildings, Lalmai Airstrip had palm trees and thatch-roofed structures with lots of big open windows and doors.

Made sense. Even full sun and a breeze didn't dry him off. Had to be a hundred degrees, and humidity pressed on him like a wet wool blanket.

"Just like Florida." Elroy slung his bag over his thin shoulders. "Feel right at home."

"I think I'm gonna die." Whitaker flapped his unbuttoned shirt.

"Swell!" Pettas hefted up Whitaker's bag in addition to his own. "Dibs on your stuff."

In a flash, Whitaker flung his Oregon lumberjack frame at Pettas, knocking the smaller man to the dirt.

Pettas lay laughing on the ground. "Who'd want your ratty old stuff anyhow?"

With a grin, Whitaker gave his pal a light kick. "Yeah. Don't forget that."

Elroy nudged Roger. "If the heat doesn't kill them, they'll kill each other."

Roger managed a laugh, but more sweat trickled down his chest. He just prayed he wouldn't kill them all.

# 7

Naples
April 8, 1944

Kay escaped to the edge of the terrace at the Orange Club.

How much happiness could a gal take? Tom MacGilliver had just proposed to Mellie Blake, who gave her tearful, joyful consent. Kay did everything she was supposed to—smile, joke, loan her handkerchief, and prod her shy friend to action.

The full moon laid a trail of sparkles along Naples Bay. Sure, Kay could sparkle. She'd done it all evening, flirting with Lt. Hal Heathcock, the newest addition to her lineup of boyfriends, which had been depleted with the departure of the entire 64th Troop Carrier Group.

She'd met Hal here at the Orange Club. Two minutes after Roger Cooper's rejection.

A glance behind her confirmed Hal still chatted with Lt. Larry White, Georgie Taylor's blind date for the evening. Tall and blond, with lively blue eyes, Hal seemed like the perfect means to regain control in her life, but she'd been mistaken.

Tom and Mellie stood by their table, laughing with Louise Cox and Rudy Scaglione, Tom's friend from his Engineer Aviation Battalion.

Georgie Taylor approached Kay, brown curls bouncing.

"So, who's next, do you think? You and Hal?" Her Southern accent lilted even more than usual.

"Oh, please." Kay shuddered. "He won't get one more date out of me. All hands."

"Well, it won't be me and Larry." Georgie scrunched up her cute little nose. "The man's as interesting as an Army manual."

Kay frowned. Had she ever seen Georgie's previous boyfriend smile? Granted, she'd only met Hutch once, and apparently it had been a horrendous day for the man. "Sorry. Thought you liked them quiet and dry."

"Quiet isn't always dull." A wistful note lowered her voice.

Kay brushed her hair off her shoulder. Perhaps she'd misjudged Hutch, just as she'd misjudged Roger. She'd labeled Roger a fuddy-duddy, and he'd turned out to be energetic and compassionate. "I suppose not. Appearances can be deceiving."

Georgie looped her arm through Kay's. "Do you miss the flyboys?"

"India." Kay gazed east where the moon rose. "Can't believe he's gone."

"Grant?"

Kay's heart seized. What had she said? Why was she losing control like this? She made a face for Georgie's benefit. "Grant? I broke up with him weeks ago. Getting too serious."

"Then who—"

"No one. No one at all." She kept her voice as firm as the truth that Roger wasn't interested.

Georgie smiled, her eyes soft. "I won't pry. But I'll pray for him and for you."

"There is no him." Kay marched away from Georgie and from the other truth—Roger interested her far too much.

Guilt tightened the muscles between her shoulder blades. Georgie hadn't done anything wrong. In fact, she'd offered to pray. With all her questions about God, wasn't that what

Kay needed most? She turned back to her friend. "But thanks for the prayers."

Georgie looked more stunned than if Kay had broken out singing a hymn.

Kay crossed the terrace to congratulate Tom and Mellie. Louise and Rudy had departed, back to the dance floor, most likely.

Tom faced Mellie, the moon silhouetting the couple from behind. He cupped her chin in his hand, spoke to her, and gave her a gentle kiss.

Kay's steps halted. The moonlight must have addled her brain, because everything inside her felt as mushy as pudding. She didn't even like pudding.

What would it be like to have a love like that? Tender and sweet, tempered by the fire of a history together, forged to last a lifetime.

Kay huffed. For heaven's sake, she'd lost all control.

The more she read the Bible, the more she fell apart. Instead of gaining favor with Lieutenant Lambert, she was losing it. Although no one had been harmed the other day when Kay made her error and Lambert appreciated her honesty in confessing, the chief couldn't hide her disappointment.

"*Ciao, bella.*" Hal wrapped his arm around her upper back and nuzzled in her hair. "Off to greet the happy couple?"

"Yes." She stepped forward to do so and to dislodge Hal. The leech stayed with her, arm glued across her back.

"Congratulations, you two." Kay hugged Mellie. "I'm so happy for you."

"Thank you." Mellie pulled back, her dark eyes shining.

Kay shook Tom's hand. "When's the big day?"

"We were just talking about that." He gave Mellie an adoring gaze, his arm respectfully around her waist. "We'd like to get married this fall, maybe Christmastime, the Lord and Uncle Sam willing."

"Uncle Sam. Good luck convincing him." Hal chuckled and slid his hand further forward under Kay's arm.

She clamped her arm hard to her side. "An autumn wedding would be nice." She fought off a wave of sadness. How long before a baby came along and kicked Mellie out of the Army Nurse Corps? The war had better be over by then.

Hal pried his hand free and draped it over Kay's shoulder instead, dangling far too low. "You'll be lucky to stay on the same continent that long."

Mellie leaned her head on Tom's broad shoulder. "If the Lord wants us to get married this fall, he'll keep us together. If not, we'll just continue following his lead."

"God led us together, no doubt about it." Tom kissed the top of Mellie's head. "He kept dropping Mellie in my path, airfield to airfield. I couldn't get away, and then I didn't want to."

Kay squirmed, partly to urge Hal's drooping hand higher but mostly from discomfort. Mellie and Georgie talked about following the Lord as if he put up big signposts, and you turned and stopped and started when he ordered. He'd probably direct Kay off the nearest cliff.

Hal's hand slipped lower. "Why don't you hold off on the wedding until you go home and your families can attend?"

Kay winced. Mellie and Tom had each lost one parent, and Mellie's father was imprisoned by the Japanese. "Excuse me, Hal. I need to use the powder room. Mellie, would you like to join me?"

"Sure."

Kay led her friend across the terrace and into the dining room, dark and smoky. Why had she let Hal kiss her the night they met? She never did that. A man behaved better when he had to earn his way into her affections.

At the front of the room, a piano player plunked out "All or Nothing at All." Her chest squeezed. The night she met Hal, she'd been so enamored by a redheaded drummer, so humiliated when he spurned her, so desperate to put a man—any man—under her thumb.

She shoved open the door to the ladies' room. "I am sick and tired of fending off men's advances."

After Mellie set her handbag on the counter, she peered at Kay in the mirror, her dark eyes missing nothing. "I thought you enjoyed it."

Kay rummaged in her bag for her compact. Since ninth grade, she'd cultivated the image of the bad girl lining up boys in the dugout, convincing each he could hit a home run in time. No one knew she never let any man past first base. What man with any self-respect would tell his buddies he struck out every time he came to bat?

"Kay? Are you all right?"

"I'm fine." Where on earth was that stupid compact? She dumped her purse upside down, and cosmetics scattered over the counter. She grabbed her compact and flipped it open. "I'm just tired of men like All-Hands Hal."

"Mm-hmm." Mellie swept Kay's possessions toward her. "Maybe you're outgrowing your old ways."

Kay paused, her powder puff suspended before her well-powdered nose. Her eyes looked strange in the mirror, wide and unfamiliar and frightened.

Who would she be? If she gave up her old ways, who would she be?

Would she be the kind of woman who could be a chief nurse and attract one good man? Or would she fall to pieces?

Kay slammed her compact shut and snatched her lipstick from the counter. She painted her lips red, painted on a smile. "I wanted to talk to you about something."

"Oh?" Mellie reapplied her powder, worn off by tears and kisses and handkerchiefs.

"Yes. I'd like to train to become a chief nurse."

"You would?"

"I would." Kay's cheeks burned from the spectacle of her heart splattered on the counter among her possessions. She gathered the cosmetics and tossed them into her shoulder bag. "I love nursing, and I'm good with details, administration, and organization."

"I can see that." Mellie twisted up her lipstick but kept a puzzled gaze on Kay.

Kay sighed and threw down a bit more of her heart. "You look like Lambert when I told her."

"Oh?" Mellie outlined her full lips. Amazing how much she'd changed in a year and a half from the reclusive young woman who didn't wear lipstick and refused to smile. If anyone would believe people could change, it would be Mellie.

"She has two objections. She doesn't think the other nurses respect me because of all the men in my life."

"Mm-hmm." Somehow Mellie communicated agreement without condemnation.

Kay held up her chin and tugged down the hem of her waist-length uniform jacket. She usually liked how the bloused effect made her look bustier than she was, but not tonight. "I don't know how to change, and I certainly don't want to."

"All right. What's her other objection?" Mellie capped her lipstick.

"She says I haven't shown myself to be a leader. I'd like to unify our flight and prove her wrong."

One side of Mellie's mouth flicked up. "It'd be easier to break up with all your men."

Kay groaned and sat back against the counter. "I know. I wanted to ask for your help."

"Mine?" Mellie shook her head and pulled a brush from her purse. "I'm nice to Vera and Alice, but they don't want anything to do with me. And Georgie isn't good at getting over grudges. She isn't used to being rejected like I am."

Kay tapped her fingers on her purse. "I already talked to Vera and Alice. They think the problem's with you and Georgie, that you look down on them." Sometimes the truth needed to be stretched to be seen.

"Me? Look down on them? It's always been the other way around." Mellie looked at Kay with moist eyes. "I hope I've never given them that impression. Oh dear."

"Sorry." Kay patted her friend's arm. "I'm trying to unify, not hurt your feelings."

Mellie closed her eyes. "My feelings aren't hurt. It's just . . . oh dear. Vera will never trust me, not with what I know about . . ."

"What you know?"

If Mellie weren't careful, she'd chew off all her lipstick. "I can't say. I gave her my word and I'll keep it."

Kay puffed her cheeks full of air. Swell. A secret on top of everything else.

# 8

Dinjan, India
April 15, 1944

Roger tipped up his face. If only the warm rain could wash away his fatigue. Finally an afternoon off after flying two or three flights every day, with only one short break when they transferred to Dinjan Airfield in Upper Assam.

His squadron was in the process of transporting the 7th Indian Division from the Arakan in southern Burma up to reinforce Imphal in India, where the Japanese had besieged the vital British base.

Roger headed past Headquarters toward his *basha*, the thatch-roofed structure he shared with a dozen officers from his squadron.

"Lieutenant Cooper!" Veerman leaned out the door of the Headquarters building. "May I have a word with you?"

"Yes, sir." He tensed, changed course, and slipped on his shirt. Why was it when people wanted a word, it was always negative? And why did they say "*a* word" when they meant many?

Veerman led him inside to his office. Rain slanted through the open window and left a dark wet triangle on the raw wooden floor.

Roger stood at attention in front of the desk. How many times had he gotten chewed out standing in front of desks? At least Veerman didn't use a paddle like his grade school principal.

Veerman sat and spread out papers. "I've been going over last week's paperwork. Yours is sorely lacking."

"I know, sir. We only have fifteen minutes on the ground between flights to refuel and load."

"The other pilots manage."

Of course they did. The other pilots also wrote symphonies, climbed the Himalayas, and fed all the starving children in India in fifteen minutes. Roger barely managed to hit the latrines and do his basic load adjustment calculations. "I've got the essentials on the forms."

"It's all essential." Veerman held up a Form F. "You need to copy the weight and moment figures from Form C and the load weights from Form 1."

"I just keep C and 1 in front of me. Saves time."

"But we need those figures for record keeping. You know that."

Roger sighed. Back in Sicily, Bill Shelby used to fill out Roger's forms. He liked that kind of stuff. But Roger hated to dump it on Elroy with the crazy hours they pulled.

Veerman cleared his throat. "I see your final center of gravity figures but no intermediate numbers."

"I do it in my head."

The squadron commander's light eyes grew large. "You do it in your head?"

"I use the load calculator, of course. But everything else I do in my head. I like math." As a child, before he wised up, he wanted to teach math.

The corners of Veerman's mouth turned up a bit. "What's the first rule you learn in math? Show your work."

"I'm not fond of that rule."

"I bet you aren't. But this is the Army, and you have to do things the Army way. We need every form filled out completely—and neatly, by the way."

Taking a swipe at his handwriting now, was he? Roger didn't blame him.

"And I've had it up to here with this childish feud between you and Lieutenant Klein. The man comes in here every day complaining about something you did or said."

Roger gave him half a grin. "Aren't you thankful I don't come in here whining about everything he does and says?"

Was that a tic in Veerman's eyelid? "This morning he said you sewed a big pink bow on his service cap."

If Klein insisted on gossiping like a teenage girl, he might as well look like one. Roger kept a neutral face. "Where would I get a pink ribbon? I don't have a girlfriend." Good thing Shelby's wife sent him embarrassingly romantic gifts.

"This isn't high school. This is war." His voice deepened to a rumble. "At least you've been on time lately. I appreciate that."

"Thank you, sir." All thanks to Kay's alarm clock. His *basha*-mates hid the clock every night, so by the time Roger found the blaring thing, he was too awake and annoyed to go back to sleep.

"I need you to fill out your paperwork, knock off these pranks, and be more disciplined." He gestured toward Roger's shirt. "Don't think I didn't notice you walking around bare chested. I don't care how hot it is. Uniforms aren't optional."

"Yes, sir." He contained his sigh. As rigid as Dad was, at least he let Roger take off his shirt in the fields on hot days.

Veerman leaned his elbows on his desk. "I know you can do better, Cooper. You're a bright young fellow. Don't waste your talents."

The man could join the long line of family and teachers who lamented his wasted talents. "I'll try to do better, sir."

"Thank you. Dismissed."

Roger headed outside, over the damp airfield, and into his *basha*. He'd planned to hit the sack and take a nap, but now his hands yearned for his drumsticks. He pulled his tom-tom from his barracks bag and his drumsticks from the canvas aviator's kit bag he'd carried on today's flights.

He passed his snoring *basha*-mates, resisted the prime prank-pulling opportunity, and went out to the half-shelter he'd rigged under a palm tree for drumming.

Roger sat cross-legged with his tom-tom before him. He closed his eyes and concentrated on the sounds of the birds and insects, the breeze through the palms, the rhythm of the land. Then he joined in, softly at first, finding the tune in his head.

Frustration messed up the beat. How could he turn into a by-the-book pilot? Even now, right after promising Veerman he'd try harder, he was drumming instead of filling out today's forms more completely.

Yeah, he'd never amount to anything. He'd never earn a recommendation to Hank Veerman's band. He'd play with rinky-dink bands and wash out by the age of forty. Then he'd be back on the farm, begging for mercy, and he'd be sentenced to a lifetime of I-told-you-so.

He thumped the drum hard. *Lord, how can I bear it?*

"Hallo, Raji."

Roger opened his eyes. Two boys stood before him, Asad and Kavi. They'd turned his name into a good Indian name, and that meant the world to him. "Hi, guys. Join me?"

"Yes, please, Raji." Asad squatted beside him. The seven-year-old liked to watch Roger play. The boys spoke excellent English, thanks to the Brits, and seemed to be from a higher class in society.

"I am ready." Kavi had brought his child-sized *dhol*, a two-headed Indian drum. The nine-year-old wore it slung over his shoulder on a strap and played it with two sticks, one for each end. He had to stand to play it, but the palm tree would keep him dry.

"All right, Kavi. Give me a beat."

The boy grinned and pounded the bass end of the drum, nice and quick. Roger joined in, mixing it up, enjoying the interaction with the young drummer. The kid was good, had a natural sense of rhythm, and swayed to the beat.

Wouldn't it be swell to work with children for a living?

His childhood fantasy popped back into his head—standing in front of a class, bringing math to life, students leaning forward with eyes as bright as Asad's and Kavi's.

A stupid fantasy. Teaching required more than a love of children, a love of math, and an ability to make dull things interesting and difficult things comprehensible. Teaching required following rules and routines, doing paperwork. Being reliable.

He wouldn't even have become a pilot if it weren't for Lou Davis. Lou's ridiculously wealthy parents kept funneling money to their prodigal trombone-playing son. To keep busy when the band wasn't practicing, Lou took classes at the University of Chicago, dragging Roger along for company, paying his way. Somehow Roger built up more than two years of classes, the minimum required by the Army Air Forces for pilot training.

Roger hadn't even chosen a major.

At least he could drum. Drummers didn't have to be responsible.

Asad patted his head, and Roger rewarded him with a cymbal tap on the noggin.

How ironic that impressing Hank Veerman's brother required responsibility.

# 9

**Pomigliano Airfield**
**April 30, 1944**

"He lied to me!"

Kay stared at the open Bible, at the final chapters of Job. Rage shook the words into a blur as gray as the dress Father made her wear at the tent meetings.

She stood, shoved the Bible inside her bedroll on her cot, and ran her hands into her hair.

Sunday morning and all her roommates had gone to church services, because they were good enough to show their faces before the Lord.

Not Kay.

She pressed her palms hard against her forehead.

Father and Mother and Jemima and Keren, all in white, all pure blond, up on the stage singing with angelic voices. Dirty Kezia in gray with her red hair tied in a stark braid, collecting the offering. Father always told the audience his middle daughter was resting her voice, recovering from laryngitis.

"Liar." Why did it surprise her that he lied about God when he lied about everything else? He even lied when he said, "'My lips shall not speak wickedness, nor my tongue utter deceit.'"

Kay turned in circles, everything swirling around her—deception, betrayal, self-pity, fury, humiliation, grief.

Who was this God? If he wasn't who Father said he was, who was he?

She groaned and flung down her hands. Enough of this nonsense. She needed to take action.

A plan formed a solid rock in her chest. She wiggled out of her trousers and into her skirt. Since she couldn't scream at her father, she'd scream at the chaplain in his place. Oh, she'd be discreet. She'd sit in the back corner at the service, wait for everyone to leave, then unleash the barking hound inside her.

She marched out into the clear cool air. Dizzy and disoriented, she paused. Where did the church meet anyway? The theater building, wasn't it?

A good girl would know that. She headed down the road. If her father had told her the truth, she might have been good, might have been redeemed before it was too late.

A horn beeped behind her, and she jumped.

"Hiya, baby." Hal Heathcock waved to her from the driver's seat of a jeep. "I was looking for you."

Kay breathed hard and smoothed her hair. Did she look as bad as she felt? "Hi, Hal."

He tipped his cap. "How about a picnic on the beach?"

"I was . . ." She glanced toward the theater building. She was . . . what? Going to church to yell at the chaplain? They'd pack her off to the neuropsychiatric ward.

"Ah, what could be more important than a relaxing day at the beach?" He draped his arm over the dashboard and sent her his handsome smile.

What would be relaxing about fending him off all day? "I'd—"

"Please, baby?" He batted his blue eyes like an abandoned puppy. "Don't make me be the third wheel."

A couple sat in the jeep's backseat, another American officer with a beautiful Italian woman.

Kay never drove alone with a date and always met her boyfriends in public places. If another couple was present, men generally behaved themselves.

But it was Sunday. She never dated on Sundays, an old fear that God might deem that the final fatal sin.

"Come on." Hal patted the seat. "I know you're a fun-loving gal."

She had no use for silly superstitions. A defiant smile rose. "I am."

What would the chaplain tell her anyway? He'd tell her more lies. He'd condemn her evil ways. And he certainly wouldn't answer her questions.

What if someone did? What if Roger Cooper wrote her a letter that told her everything she wanted to know? Would she surrender control to this God?

Never.

Kay climbed into the jeep, sidled up to Hal, and kissed him on the cheek. "To the beach. I need some fun."

"Now we're talking, baby." He turned the jeep and headed down the road toward Naples.

Kay unpinned her cap, tore off her necktie, and flirted recklessly with Hal.

Controlling men was her revenge against her father, breaking his control over her, infuriating him, embracing the badness inside her. What did it matter? Her father rejected her, the Lord rejected her, but men accepted her.

Kay took off Hal's cap and played with his smooth blond hair. He talked about something or other, and she smiled and laughed and tossed her hair in the wind.

Hal thought he was in charge, but he wasn't. His interest grew, glinted in his eyes, and careened over the ledge into infatuation. Now she had complete and utter control. He'd do whatever she wanted, and he'd behave, trying to earn what she'd never give him.

"Here we are." The officer in the backseat leaned forward and patted Hal's shoulder. "Stop at the corner. Thanks for the lift."

"Any time, buddy." Hal stopped the jeep.

Kay spun around. Her hands lifted and opened, and everything she held slipped away. They were leaving? They were leaving her alone with Hal?

"Where are you . . . ?" The words creaked in her throat. "Aren't you coming with us?"

The officer—what was his name?—gave her half a grin and helped his girlfriend out of the jeep. "You're kidding me, right?"

Hal laughed and jerked the gearshift into first. "That wouldn't be fun for either of us. Bob's got a private hideaway in town."

The couple strolled up a cross street, glued to each other's sides. Bob looked over his shoulder. "See you at six."

"Six." Hal waved and drove down the street.

Kay struggled to gather her breath, her bearings. Where were they? Some village, creamy-plastered houses crowded together around a narrow road, like every other village she'd seen. How long had they been on the road? Half an hour? An hour? "Where are we?"

"Almost there, baby. You'll love it." One broad hand guided the steering wheel, and the other snaked around her shoulder.

The beach. She blew off her anxiety. What was she worried about? A nice big beach teeming with people. Romantic enough for Hal and public enough for Kay.

Not far past the village, Hal turned onto a road paralleling the rocky coast. He slowed down, scanning the roadside. "Yeah, here we are." He pulled over and parked.

A gray, slimy feeling oozed around Kay's stomach. She gazed over the jumble of rocks down to the sea. "I don't see a beach."

"You have to climb down the rocks to get there." Hal got out of the jeep and grabbed blankets and a basket from the backseat. "Should have warned you to wear better shoes."

The perfect excuse. "I can't get down there in these high heels."

"Take them off."

"I'll rip my stockings."

"Take them off." He set down the basket, covered his eyes, and turned around. "I promise I won't watch."

Hmm. A sign of chivalry. "Break that promise and you're taking me home."

"Absolutely."

With her eyes trained on the back of his head, Kay reached under her skirt and unsnapped her stockings from her garter belt.

"Mm." Hal's head sagged back. "Sweetest sound in the world."

"If you turn around, it'll be the last sound you ever hear." Kay rolled a stocking down her leg.

"I like girls with spirit."

And Kay liked fellows who knew better than to mess with girls with spirit. After she stuffed her stockings in her shoes and set them on the seat of the jeep, she stepped out onto the prickly, chilly asphalt. "Lead on."

He inched forward, hand still pressed over his eyes. "Sorry. You'll have to lead."

She laughed. "You can look now."

"May I? Thank you." He eyed her from head to bare toes. A smile crept up, and he shook his head. "Mm. Beautiful."

She waved him forward and grabbed the picnic basket. Hal headed down the rocks, assisting Kay in spots. Her gaze never strayed from the path. The last thing she needed was to fall and end up in the hospital for a few weeks.

Hal held out his hand and helped her leap down to the sand.

Kay drew a deep salty breath and gazed around. Her breath corroded her throat. They were alone in a grotto about a hundred feet square, hemmed in by rocky cliffs on three sides and the sea on the fourth.

"Isn't this swell?" Hal spread out the blankets on the sand close to the rocks. "Not a soul in sight. I like to come at high tide. At low tide it opens up, loses its appeal. Nice place to swim when it's warm."

The inside of her mouth felt sticky and grainy. Nonsense. Hal might have wandering hands but he wasn't dangerous. She could fend him off.

"Well?" He gave her a puzzled smile. "Bring the basket. I'm hungry."

A wave of relief relaxed her, and she joined him. She could stretch out the picnic for an hour or so, then coax him into a scenic walk down the coast road—in full sight of everyone.

Kay set the basket on the blanket. "What do we have here?"

Hal embraced her from behind and nuzzled kisses onto her neck. "One luscious woman, and one hungry man."

She pried off one arm. "Then we'd better eat lunch."

"That's not what I'm hungry for." He turned her to face him, his eyes glazed, and he covered her mouth with his.

All right, all right, she could handle this. She'd fended off advances for over a decade. She returned his kiss, circling her arms around his waist rather than his neck to block him better. Every time his hands worked too low or too far forward, she edged them back into place.

When he let out a soft moan, she pulled back and gave him a saucy smile. "That was a nice appetizer. Let's have lunch."

Hal drew her close again and burrowed in her neck. "Yeah, time for the main course."

Despite her hammering pulse, she forced a laugh. "That's not what I meant."

He kissed her—insistent, deep, dark with desire. One hand wormed between their bodies and fumbled with the buttons of her service jacket.

"Hal." She pushed on his chest, but he didn't budge. With effort, she yanked away his hand, but then his other hand worked on the button at the back of her skirt.

Panic quickened her breath. She planted both hands on his chest and pushed back, breaking his grip. "Stop it! You have the wrong idea about me."

His bleary eyes took a moment to focus on her. "Wrong idea?"

"Yes." She straightened her jacket and stood tall. "I don't know you well enough yet. A man has to be special, has to earn the right."

"Is that so?" He smiled and moved closer. "Aren't you cute, playing hard to get?"

"I'm not playing." She stepped back. Her bare foot banged against a rock, and she stumbled.

Hal caught her in his arms, kissed her even harder. "You don't have to play, baby. I saw the way you looked at me on the ride down here. I know you want this as much as I do."

"I don't." She struggled in his slithery grasp. How could he make his hands go in so many directions at once? "Take me home."

He chuckled. "Aren't you the little minx? Your words say no, but your body says yes."

"My body says no!" She slapped his cheek, not as hard as she wanted.

With one arm firm around her waist, he rubbed his cheek

and raised a sly smile. "There. Now you can tell your girl-friends you tried to stop me."

"Leave me alone!" She stomped hard, but her heel slid off the side of his shoe.

"So that's how you like it." He smiled, his grip tightened, and he backed her up, pressed her against the rocky cliff. "You know, it's more fun when you give up the pretense and admit you want it."

"I don't. I don't want it. I don't want anything to do with you." She tried to raise her knee to strike him in the crotch, but he had her pinned.

"All right, we'll do it your way." He ran his hand into her hair, almost tenderly. "I'll pretend to be the dastardly villain, you pretend to be the damsel in distress, and I'll ravish you. Sounds like fun."

No. No, it didn't. Her words swelled and blocked her throat.

*Lord, help me.* The prayer dribbled out, useless.

# 10

**Imphal Main Airfield, Imphal, India**

"Hurry. Come on." Roger beckoned the litter-bearers toward the plane. He didn't like the looks of the clouds to the northeast, the smell of the wind, or the sense of plummeting barometric pressure. A thunderstorm was coming, and he needed to get the C-47 airborne.

Imphal lay at the northern end of the Manipur Valley, surrounded by high mountains—and by the Japanese. For two weeks, C-47s and C-46s had been supplying 170,000 troops trapped at the British base.

"Welcome aboard." Pettas stood inside the cargo door and motioned a dozen healthy administrative personnel toward the folding seats in the front of the cabin. Ferrying out these "useless mouths" reduced the amount of supplies that needed to be ferried in.

A man lifted the foot of a litter to another worker crouched inside the plane. The litter tilted at a dangerous angle.

"Not like that!" Roger sprang forward and lowered the foot of the litter to the floor.

"Thank you, sir." The British soldier on the litter saluted with a bandaged hand. "This is more dangerous than the front lines."

"Sorry. We don't have an air evac team." Roger showed the native workers how to safely load the litter onto the plane, then how to anchor it in the web strapping.

He never had to do that in the Mediterranean Theater of Operations. In the MTO, teams of flight nurses and technicians could load a plane full of patients in ten minutes flat. The 803rd MAETS served in the CBI, but they didn't fly the Imphal run.

Kay's face flitted into his mind, and he couldn't shake it free. Again. The dame might be dangerous, but she was an efficient and competent flight nurse. He could see her doing the tasks he was doing right now—buckling straps and making sure patients were comfortable—only a lot better.

Roger knelt and tightened a strap attached to the securing pole that ran along the floor.

A cry rang out. Across the aisle, the top litter teetered and slipped. Roger lunged and grabbed it just in time. "It's not tight enough." He worked the pole into the loop of strapping and yanked as hard as he could.

For the first time ever, he missed Kay Jobson. And for the third time that day, he felt an overwhelming compulsion to pray for her.

He did so as he worked. All mail was being held in Sicily for their return next week, so he didn't know if she'd written or if she'd asked any questions. But he did know shame, remembered it with a knifing pain. That memory deepened his prayers.

Was that why God had chosen him? Why couldn't the Lord have chosen a Christian man eager to get involved with the gorgeous redhead, a stronger man who wouldn't be tempted like Roger was? Or a woman? Why didn't God choose a woman?

"Okay, Coop. That's the last of them." Whitaker wiped his brow. "Now we can do our own jobs."

"Yeah. Let's get this bird off the ground as soon as we can."

In the cockpit, Roger picked up his clipboard with Forms 1, C, and F. It would take him a good twenty minutes to fill them out the Army way, or he could do it in five his way.

Roger pulled out the load calculator and got to work. What was wrong with the military? They cared more about numbers than about the real men those numbers represented. Was it more important for the boxes to be filled in or for these soldiers to arrive safely at their destination, not struck down in enemy territory by a thunderstorm? Fifteen minutes could mean the difference between life and death.

"Ah, forget it." He skipped ahead and did it his way. He'd fill in the numbers later for Veerman's sake. Not now. Not with those black clouds forming over the mountains.

He leaned into the radio compartment, where Pettas sat at his desk with his radio sets and navigation charts. "You ready?"

"You bet. Let's get out of here. I get the jitters knowing we've got Japs on all sides."

Whitaker entered from the cabin. "Plane looks great, all passengers secured."

Roger thanked his aerial engineer, took his seat, put on his headset, and contacted the tower. "We're clear," he said to Elroy.

The copilot held the preflight checklist and called down the list. They checked the hydraulics and fuel and flight controls and everything else. Roger liked shortcuts, but not when it came to actual flying.

He gave the thumbs-up to the ground crewman, who rotated the propeller on the right engine three times.

"Clear!" Roger called.

After the ground crewman backed away, Roger positioned his finger over the ignition button on the electrical panel over the windshield. "Start engine."

He pushed the button while Elroy worked the wobble pump beside his seat to raise fuel pressure. The engine roared to life. They repeated the process with the left engine.

Roger scanned the gauges—all looked good. After the tower cleared him, he taxied onto the narrow runway. He and Elroy ran up the engines, finished the final checks, released the brakes, and throttled forward. The plane sped down the runway and lifted into the air.

"Landing gear up." Roger released the latch, and Elroy turned the lever.

He had to build altitude and fast. In less than twenty miles, he'd be over enemy territory, and the Japanese ground troops loved to take shots at the C-47s. Thank goodness they didn't send up too many fighter planes. The Tenth Air Force bombers and fighters did a great job keeping the Japanese occupied.

Sure enough, as soon as he passed south over the hills rimming the valley, pops rang out. The left wing jerked.

Roger gritted his teeth and guided the plane higher. Everything looked fine—flight controls operational, no loss of fuel or oil.

At his cruising altitude of five thousand feet, he made the final power reduction and trimmed the aircraft.

"Coop!" Whitaker's voice rang over the interphone. "Bad news."

"What is it?"

"Zero coming in at nine o'clock high."

Roger's heartbeat slowed to a stop. A Japanese Mitsubishi Zero. The same nimble little fighter plane that wreaked havoc at Pearl Harbor.

A C-47 was a workhorse, an airborne truck, stable and sturdy and dependable, but not built for dives and rolls and the acrobatics needed to evade attack.

"What are we going to do, Coop?" Elroy's brown eyebrows bunched together over his wide blue eyes.

The beat returned, but faint and defeated. "We're going to pray. Nothing else we can do."

---

## Italy

The more Kay struggled, the more Hal laughed. He honestly thought the whole thing was a game, thought every no meant yes.

"Oh, baby, this is going to be so much fun." He unzipped her skirt.

Kay tried to zip it again, but his hands moved to her chest. She couldn't win, couldn't gain control. Her throat clogged shut, and her eyes moistened.

Oh no. She wouldn't cry. She wouldn't give him the satisfaction.

If only she could break free, but the harder she fought, the tighter he held her.

What if . . . ?

The idea was so strange, so counterintuitive.

*Lord, help me.* The prayer felt stronger now, straighter, as if bound for heaven itself. A few deep breaths, and she decided. It was her only chance.

"Oh, Hal." She wrapped her arms around his neck, gave herself completely to his kiss, and let his hands go where they would.

He moaned and came up for a grin. "That's more like it."

"Mm-hmm." She kissed him, played with his hair, and unbuttoned his shirt. "Want to go for a swim?"

He startled and looked her in the eye. "A swim? It's only sixty degrees today."

Kay gave him her most flirtatious look and traced a squiggly line down his breastbone. "Don't tell me you're chicken."

"No, but it's—"

"We'll have to warm each other up afterward . . . somehow."

Light grew in his eyes. "All right then." He reached for her blouse.

"Oh, I'll do that." Kay fiddled with the waist buckle on her jacket. "Not a man in the world has been able to undo this thing." Because she'd never given any man the opportunity.

"Faster this way anyhow." Hal backed up, ripped off his shirt, and undid his belt buckle.

Kay dipped her head as if concentrating on her jacket but watched Hal's feet out of the corner of her eye.

Standing at bat, one perfect moment hung in the air right after the pitcher released the ball. Swing too early or too late and you missed. But when you swung at the perfect moment, the ball soared out of the park.

Kay's fingers tensed, her feet dug into the sand, and her breath came hard but steady.

Hal lowered his trousers, leaned over, raised one knee.

The perfect moment.

Kay bolted and scrambled up the rocks.

"Hey! Kay!" A thump on the sand, a curse. "Where are you going?"

"Away." Rocks scraped her feet and hands, her stupid skirt bound her knees, but she didn't stop until she reached the road. She grabbed a fist-sized rock and whirled around.

Hal lay on the sand in his skivvies, trousers tangled around his feet. "What on earth?"

She brandished the rock at him. "If you lay your sleazy hands on me one more time, I'll bash your skull in."

"Ah, come on, Kay. We were just having fun." He got up to his knees.

She didn't want to find out if he'd turn violent. She ran for the jeep, but the key wasn't in the ignition. Her shoes—little good they'd do her. She could run faster barefoot than in high heels.

Down the road she ran, legs pumping as hard as the skirt allowed, feet screaming from pain. Would he chase her down? First he'd have to put on his pants. That bought her a minute or two.

The village lay in sight. A strange sensation heaved in her chest, and a sob burst out.

She'd accepted Hal's invitation so she could regain control.

A sharp pain in her foot, and she collapsed to her knees. She had no control. None at all. It was all an illusion.

# 11

**Over India**

"Gotta hit the deck." Roger shoved the control column forward, and the plane went into a dive.

He had a plump plodding aircraft and no guns. His only chance was to reduce the Zero's maneuverability by skimming the treetops. An Allied fighter plane or two would also be nice.

"Hope the passengers are secured," Elroy said.

"Better they get banged up than shot up." Roger spoke into his interphone. "Whitaker, station yourself at the astrodome, call out what you see."

"Okay. Not sure how much good that'll do."

"Better than nothing." And nothing was what he had. Fighters had cockpits with full visibility, bombers had guns facing all six directions, but cargo planes had useless little passenger windows.

"I see him," Whitaker said. "He's following us."

"Position?"

"About seven o'clock high. Can't tell how far away he is."

Elroy fiddled with the mixture controls. "Airspeed two hundred mph, altitude two thousand."

Pressure built in Roger's eardrums, and he longed for chewing gum. Maximum airspeed was 255, and the plane was supposed to fall apart at 300. But Zeros could fly at 350, no problem.

He huffed out a breath. What else could he do? He had to push the plane to its limits. And himself too, for the sake of the other twenty-one men on board.

"Two hundred ten. Two twenty. One thousand feet."

The needle shimmered and worked its way from the yellow zone to the red zone. The jungle zoomed up below, sprawled over steep hills. Evasive maneuvers would be tricky.

"He's firing!"

Roger banked the plane to the left, pulled up a bit so he wouldn't go into a spin. The tail buffeted. He must have been hit. "Where is he, Whit?"

"He passed us up, turning around. Looks like he's coming in again from the front."

"There he is!" Elroy pointed up, to about two o'clock.

"Okay." Roger eyed the sharp ridge ahead. "Watch him. When he opens fire, I'm putting her in a dive."

"Oh boy. This isn't what I signed up for."

A laugh escaped Roger's pressed-tight lips. "Ain't that the truth."

His gaze hopped between the gauges, the landscape, the Zero closing in. Pain stabbed his taut eardrums.

"Now!" Elroy shoved his column forward.

So did Roger. Bright tracer fire streaked past the windshield, and he instinctively hunched low in his seat. A series of thuds shook the plane down its length. "Check the gauges."

"He passed us again. Making another turn," Whitaker said.

"All right." Sweat dribbled down his temples. He aimed the plane over the ridge, toward the valley. More like a canyon. Oh, swell. This could be his stupidest idea ever. Or his last. *Lord, stop me if you've got a better idea.*

"Manifold pressure, hydraulic fluid pressure, oil pressure—

all normal." Elroy wiped his hand on his trouser leg, then back to the controls. "Looks like we didn't take any damage."

Yet.

The canyon ahead, below. No more than half a mile across. His ears popped, sound rushed into the void, and he sighed in relief.

"He's coming! Eight o'clock high."

From the left. Roger plunged over the ridge, down another hundred feet, banked to the left.

Elroy cried out, and Roger bit his tongue, tasted blood. He leveled off, the wings wobbling. What on earth was he doing? Flying in a valley? Wooded hills whooshed by on both sides.

A bend—Roger slipped to the right. "Whitaker! Where is he?"

Choice cuss words singed the interphone. "Knocked me over, you numbskull."

"Where is he?"

Three pops along the top of the fuselage, muffled screams from the back. Roger zigged to one side, zagged to the other.

More cussing from Whitaker. "Passed over us. He's coming down behind us, into the canyon. We've got wounded in the back."

"That has to wait. First we have to get out of this alive." That would require fancy flying.

He followed the narrow river below.

"He's closing in, opening fire."

"All right. Hold on." Roger wiggled the control column back and forth, making the plane hop, worked the rudder pedals to make her slip side to side.

"Watch the right!" Elroy cried.

Roger skidded away, but a shimmy ran through the right wing.

"Lost the wingtip."

His breath jerked around more than the plane. He'd lose

a lot more than a wingtip if the Zero didn't break off the attack. How far were they from British territory?

Roger mixed up his pattern. Up, right, down, left, right, left, up, down. Had to throw off the pilot's aim, had to avoid the hills, had to follow the river.

A cliff rose before him. The canyon was narrowing. He couldn't make the turn.

"Everyone hold on tight. I'm pulling up." Roger's fingers kneaded the control wheel. If only he could wipe off the sweat. He focused hard on the cliff. Timing had to be just right.

"Cooper . . ." Elroy's voice came out in a low, warning growl.

"Ready?" It loomed closer, closer, rocks and vines and skinny waterfalls. "Now!"

Roger yanked the control wheel to his chest. The engines whined. Something screeched along the undercarriage. More screams in the back.

"One, two, three. Level off." He pushed the control column forward, found himself a good hundred feet above the tree-tops. The plane shuddered in protest at the rough treatment.

Where was the thunderous collision behind him? If he were in a movie, the Zero would have slammed into the cliff. "Where is—"

A kick to the rear. Metal scraped on metal. The C-47 tipped forward.

Roger cried out, pulled back on the controls. They shook in his hands, fought him hard. Trees reached up to him, branches whacked the wings, the undercarriage. "Lord, help me!"

The land sloped away beneath. He gained some altitude, edged over the next hill, and mowed off another treetop.

Roger gave the plane more throttle. "Whitaker? What happened?"

"Whitaker got knocked out," Pettas said, "when the Zero hit us."

"The Zero? He hit us? Where is he?"

"Can't see him. Turn a bit, let me see."

"Turn?" Toward the enemy?

"Yeah. I'm looking through the astrodome, don't see nothing. Wait. There's smoke. Go back, Coop. Go back."

Smoke? Roger exchanged a glance with Elroy. "Let's have a look."

Mom always said curiosity would kill him. Today she might be right. He turned the wheel to the right and applied right rudder pressure. The plane tipped in the correct direction but slipped to the inside of the turn. "Uh-oh. We lost rudder control."

"Or we lost the rudder."

Roger puffed out a ragged breath. The Zero must have sheared off part of the vertical stabilizer on the tail. At least he still had elevator control. If the horizontal stabilizers had been hit, he might not have been able to pull up after the collision.

"Holy smoke!" Elroy pointed, then let out a nervous laugh. "Sorry about the pun."

Roger peered past his copilot. It might not be holy but it was certainly smoke, a gray plume drifting up from the jungle behind them. "He must have crashed."

A slow smile cracked Elroy's round face. "I think we're the first cargo plane in history to down an enemy fighter."

Roger laughed, a strangled sound. "Might be right."

"Let's go home."

"I agree. Pettas, you got a heading for us?"

"Not yet. Got wounded back here."

Roger clamped his lips together. "Okay. Get us a heading, would you? Elroy, head southwest in the meantime. I'll check on the passengers."

He unfastened his seat belt and stood. His knees felt loose, and his hands shook. After he drew a deep breath, he headed to the radio room. Pettas leaned over charts on his desk, and

Whitaker sat on the floor, holding a bandage to his bloody head.

"You okay, Whit?"

He grimaced. "Hurts, but I'm alive."

Roger patted him on the shoulder and went through the doorway into the cabin. Some of the passengers were out of their seats, helping others. "How many are hurt?"

"Six." A blond officer pressed a dressing to a wound on another man's shoulder. "None seriously. We located the medical kit."

"Good."

A thin captain wrapped a dressing around his calf. "I say, that was quite a show, Lef-tenant." Why on earth did the Brits insert an *F* into *lieutenant*?

Roger knelt to assist him with the bandage. "You know us Yanks. Always showing off."

"We need to instruct you in geography. This is India, not the Wild West."

Mischief turned up the corners of Roger's mouth. "India. That's why we were playing cowboys and Indians."

One dark eyebrow rose. "I see your navigator studied with Columbus and confused the East and the West Indies."

Roger laughed, tucked in the tail of the bandage, and went to check on the next patient.

What he wouldn't give right now for an evac team's big medical chest, full of medications and supplies. And what he wouldn't give for a flight nurse, full of expertise and cheer. Maybe a green-eyed redhead.

Roger grimaced and returned to the cockpit, since the able-bodied passengers had the first aid under control.

Pettas looked up as Roger passed through the radio room. "Got our coordinates, our heading, relayed them to Mike."

"Good work." Roger clapped him on the back, then settled into his seat, replaced his headset, and took the controls.

Once again, Kay's face flashed through his mind. Why couldn't he stop thinking about her today? Even after the ordeal he'd gone through, the urge to pray for her swelled inside him.

He obeyed.

# 12

## Pomigliano Airfield

"Stop fussing over me." Kay pushed down the blanket Georgie was trying to tuck under her chin. She didn't want to go to bed, even after today's drama. Thank goodness a military policeman had been stationed in the village near the beach grotto. He'd arrested Hal, taken statements, and called in Major Guilford, the commanding officer of the 802nd MAETS.

Georgie spun away to her own cot and pulled a box from underneath. "Mama and Daddy sent a Hershey bar in my last package. They'd want you to have it."

"And the tea's almost ready." Mellie peered at the tin pot on the little cylindrical Coleman stove.

Kay threw off the blanket and sat up cross-legged in her pajamas. "Stop fussing and listen to me."

Georgie pressed the chocolate bar into her bandaged hand. "We're nurses. Fussing is what we do. After what you went through this morning, you deserve some fussing."

"I can't believe they won't press charges." Mellie swirled the pot. "Hal can get away with what he did because there weren't any witnesses, but a fine man like Hutch isn't allowed to fraternize with Georgie because he's a noncommissioned officer—and I'm so glad you two are back together, by the way."

"So am I." Georgie peeled open the Hershey bar in Kay's hand. "But that Hal. He should at least be charged with conduct unbecoming an officer."

Kay didn't care about the charges. Hal had been reprimanded, scared out of his sleazy skull, and thoroughly warned by Major Guilford. He'd never bother her again.

"Here you go, honey." Mellie held out a tin cup of tea.

Kay's sigh came all the way up from her bandaged feet. "No chocolate. No tea. All I want is the truth."

"The truth?" Mellie glanced at Georgie, then back to Kay. "Do you think we've been lying to—"

"No." This morning, recklessness flung her into Hal's groping hands, and now a burning, driving recklessness propelled her. "Tell me the truth about God. Right now."

Mellie sank onto Georgie's cot. "About . . ."

"God?" Georgie sat beside the brunette.

"Yes, and I want the truth. No more lies. I'm sick of lies."

"Lies?" Mellie turned the cup of tea in her hands.

Kay thrust her jaw forward. Receiving the truth meant divulging the truth. "I read Job."

"Job? In the Bible?" Georgie's blue eyes widened.

Her past wriggled inside her, desperate to stay in the dark, desperate to come to light. She fixed a hard stare on her friends. "I'm only telling you this so you'll understand. I don't want pity, only the truth."

"Okay." Mellie leaned a bit closer, and her eyebrows inched together.

Kay tossed aside the chocolate bar, pulled her musette bag from under her cot, and slid out Roger's Bible. "My father's a preacher. One of those charlatan traveling tent preachers who cons everyone out of money then skedaddles to the next town."

"Oh my. I—"

"He considers himself a modern-day Job, with a past full of suffering and a present full of blessings because he's so righteous." Kay used the ribbon to open the Bible. "Like Job, he has three daughters, Jemima, Kezia, and Kerenhappuch. I'm Kezia. Bet you didn't know that."

One corner of Mellie's mouth tilted up. "I'm the last person to comment on unusual names."

"Is that right, Philomela?" Kay allowed a quick smile.

"Go on." Georgie leaned forward on her knees.

She smoothed open the Bible with her good hand, her fingers brushing Roger's handwritten notes. "They sing for the tent meetings, the whole family. Beautiful voices all of them, except me. Father said I was cursed because I was evil."

"Heavens!"

Kay glared at Georgie. "I said no pity."

She held up both hands. "All right. No pity. None at all."

"That's better." Kay hated the thickness in her throat. If her friends dissolved, she'd dissolve too, and that wouldn't do. "Father said if I were good, God would redeem me and make me able to sing. But no matter how hard I tried to be good, I still couldn't sing. Father said I was irredeemable, evil, God hated me."

"Oh, honey, no." Georgie's eyes glistened. "God loves you."

Kay jabbed her finger on the page. "Father never let us read the Bible, said we couldn't understand it. Now I know why. Because he lied. All those verses he quoted—they're not from the Lord, they're from Job's friends and they're lies."

"Oh." Mellie covered her mouth. "No wonder you didn't want anything to do with God."

"I want the truth." She riffled the pages. "But it's too much. It's too thick. I don't know where to start."

Georgie scooted over to Kay's cot and flipped toward the New Testament. "Let's start with—"

"Wait." Mellie's dark eyes scrutinized. "What exactly do you want to know?"

The swelling in Kay's throat rose, froze her tongue, and stung her eyes. She swallowed it down. "Is it true?" Her voice came out disgustingly watery. "Is it true anyone can be redeemed? Even someone like me?"

Georgie rested her hand on Kay's arm. "It's true. Jesus died for you."

"That's impossible. Father—" She scrunched up her mouth. Father lied. He lied. "My father said Jesus only died for the good people, not people like me."

Georgie turned the pages.

"Romans 5:8," Mellie said.

"That's where I'm going." Georgie flicked a finger under her eye and wiped it on her skirt.

Oh, swell. Now her friends were crying? How on earth could Kay keep it together? "What's it say?"

"I can quote it," Mellie said. "But I want you to see it with your own eyes."

"Here." Georgie pointed. "Read this out loud."

Kay found the verse. It must have been one of Roger's favorites. Tons of notes in especially small handwriting filled the margin. " 'God commendeth his love toward us, in that, while we were yet sinners, Christ died for us.' "

"Do you see, honey?"

The words swam in her mind. While we were yet sinners? Christ died for—for the sinners as well as the good? Anger loosened her throat. "This was in here all along? Why didn't he tell me? Why'd he lie to me?"

"I don't know." Mellie's voice was soft. "But I do know it breaks God's heart. Did you read all of Job? Did you see God's anger toward Job's friends? That's how he feels about your father's lies."

Georgie put her arm around Kay's shoulders. "God loves you, honey. He wants you to come to him."

"But I'm not . . ." Her thoughts swirled into a mess. Roger said he'd been a sinner, really bad, and God redeemed him. Was it true? Could she be redeemed? "I'm not good enough."

"No one is." Mellie let out a wry chuckle. "That's the point. God doesn't call you to come to him *because* you're righteous. God *makes* you righteous."

Kay pressed her unbandaged hand to her neck, and her carotid artery pulsed beneath her fingers. Roger said the heartbeat was a message from God: *His life, his love.*

For her?

Part of her longed for it and wanted to believe, but another part dug in its heels. "Would it mean I'd have to give up control of my life? To him?"

"Yes." Mellie never minced words, did she?

"Kay—"

"No. Don't say anything. Let me think." She shrugged off Georgie's hand and slid further down the cot. All her life, her goal had been to gain control. And she'd done it by running away, becoming a nurse and a stewardess, and making boys fawn over her. Now she knew it was an illusion. She had no control over her career, over men, over her life.

That strange reckless impulse compelled her to throw herself into God's hands.

"Kay, are you all right?" Mellie said.

She stared at her friends. She'd always envisioned them with their cans of white paint, their eager paintbrushes.

A new image formed in her mind. Kay sat in God's hand like a tiny china doll. And the Lord smiled at her with a kind and loving look no man had ever given her—not for taking but only for giving. He held a paintbrush in front of her, waiting for permission.

Only he could paint her white. Not her friends. Not Kay herself. Only the Lord.

Kay closed her eyes as something warm and unfamiliar and irresistible stirred in her chest.

He waited.

She opened her eyes. "It's time."

# 13

Dinjan, India
May 8, 1944

Growing up on a farm, Roger had been raised to view rain with both gratitude and caution. Rain was a blessing, necessary for growth, but too much at the wrong time was a curse.

Roger stood by the tail of his plane alone in the downpour. The heavy rains that had fallen in India in April and the first week of May reduced the amount of cargo the Troop Carrier Groups could transport to the besieged troops in Imphal. But the thunderstorms allowed the ground crews to repair battle damage and the flight crews to rest.

Monsoon season didn't even start until June.

He poked his toe at a shimmering puddle. Plop. Plop. Splash. How could he resist?

"And I was worried Roger Cooper might grow up."

Roger smiled at Bill Shelby approaching from behind. "If my mom were here, she'd cluck her tongue and say, 'Twenty-nine going on ten.'"

Shelby nodded at the plane. "How's she coming along?"

"The mechanics are top-notch. They said she'd be ready tomorrow." He worked the new rudder side to side.

"I like the artwork."

"Yeah." Combat pilots painted little Rising Sun flags on their planes' noses for each victory, and Roger's ground crew had painted one under the pilot's window. Officially, he only had a "probable" credit for the downed fighter plane since there were no other witnesses, but most of the men in the 64th Troop Carrier Group treated him like he'd shot up the entire Japanese air force.

Veerman was less impressed. In all the excitement after they returned to base, Roger had forgotten to finish his preflight paperwork. And he'd been so much better about it lately.

Shelby smoothed his hand over one of the thirty-two patches on the fuselage. "Another month in India."

"At least. Unless they extend our deployment again." Roger's stomach squirmed. Most of the men's complaints about the order centered on the nasty British Emergency Rations, the danger, and the shortage of parts and supplies in the lowest-priority combat theater in the world. Roger didn't voice his concern about Kay Jobson's letters piling up unanswered in Sicily. If she'd written.

A month ago, he'd been thrilled to get away from her. Now he had the strongest urge to write her, apologize, and find out how she was doing, but he didn't have her Army Post Office number. He certainly wouldn't ask Grant Klein for the information.

Shelby patted the aluminum patch and wiped his wet hand on his trousers. "If we ever get back to the Mediterranean, I'll never whine again."

Roger blinked and focused on the conversation again. He hadn't let a woman have this effect on him in over a decade. Maybe he should request a permanent transfer to the CBI.

"Ready for lunch?"

"Yeah." Roger turned, tilted his hat so it took the full force of the rain, and headed toward the mess. "If it's inedible, I can fry up some of the eggs I bought off the local kids."

"I'm surprised they don't give them to you. When you're around, they act like teenage girls at a Frank Sinatra concert."

He loved the kids here—bright and funny and generous. "I make them take the money."

"Imagine that." Shell's voice rose. "Oak leaves for your Distinguished Flying Cross."

Roger frowned and followed Shell's gaze behind him. Klein and Singleton were heading for lunch too. He gave Shell a giant grin. "How about your DFC? Lost an engine from ground fire and made it back to base."

Shelby's pale blue eyes looked serious, except for a sparkle he couldn't hide. "Every man in the 64th Troop Carrier Group has earned a DFC. Well, almost every man."

Grant Klein, the only pilot in their squadron without the red, white, and blue striped bar to pin to his uniform, marched past them. "I know better than to fly in dangerous conditions. I don't take unnecessary risks."

Roger tapped his chin as if deep in thought. "Not flying in dangerous conditions. Not taking risks. In the CBI, that would mean not flying at all."

"That's what he's doing." Shelby elbowed Roger.

"True." Everyone knew Klein was as fussy as a hen about his loads. They had to be just so, not a pound over the limit, everything in its place. How many times had the man refused to fly until the locals unloaded his plane and reloaded it with half the weight? He usually flew only one flight a day while everyone else flew two or three.

Klein stopped and glared at Roger and Shelby. "It'll be hard for you to impress Veerman when your guts are splattered all over the jungle."

Roger put his hands on his waist and cocked his head. "You know, you're absolutely right. It would be hard to impress anyone that way."

"Not just a jerk, but an idiot." Klein stormed off to the mess.

"Not just a jerk, but a coward," Shell muttered. "Don't mind him. I'm sure Veerman's noticing. You're a lot more reliable now."

Reliable enough? Enough to be a teacher?

He shook his head, and droplets and dreams scattered around him. He grabbed hold of the only dream that mattered, the one he could make come true. A fine dream. With work, he could be reliable enough to be a drummer.

---

**Pomigliano Airfield**
**May 14, 1944**

Six feet from the door to the base church, Kay stopped. "I can't do this."

"Yes, you can, and you will," Mellie said.

On her other side, Georgie squeezed her arm. "We let you off the hook last week, but it's time."

Louise Cox adjusted her cap over her light brown hair. "What's all the fuss? So it's been a while since you've gone to church. No one will mind."

Kay clutched the Bible to her roiling stomach. Louise hadn't known her very long.

"Come on." Mellie gave her a warm smile. "How many times have you talked me into doing something I didn't want to do? It always turned out well. Now it's my turn."

Kay steeled herself as if going into battle. Because she was. "All right. But if you're wrong, you're doing my laundry for a month."

"Fair enough. And if you leave before it's over, you're doing my laundry."

Her feet inched forward. The doorway yawned before her,

and the stairs lolled down like a jagged tongue, ready to scoop her inside, where she'd be chewed up and spat out like a bone in the chicken à la king. She didn't belong.

No. No, it wasn't true. She did belong. She did.

With a deep breath, she mounted the stairs and slipped through the doorway. Her eyes adjusted to the darkness. Dozens of airmen, nurses, and ground personnel found seats on crates and camp stools.

"Goosie" Gerber was there, and Evelyn Kerr and Lieutenant Lambert and Alice Olson. Alice's finely plucked blonde eyebrows arched, then she lifted her little nose and turned away, apparently still miffed that Kay had refused to go dancing last night.

"Hiya, Kay." Vern Johnson stepped in front of her. "Don't think I've seen you in church before."

Kay had broken up with Vern and all the rest of her boyfriends in the past two weeks. She edged away. "No, you haven't."

"Say, if you're not doing anything—"

"I'm not going out with you—or anyone. I already told you."

"Ah, Kay—"

"No." She shouldered past him and sat on an empty crate between her friends.

"Goodness gracious." Georgie patted Kay's arm. "You don't have to spurn all the menfolk. Mellie and I have boyfriends."

"No, I need to. I dated for the wrong reasons and I need to stop."

Mellie chuckled. "First you date half the men in the MTO, then you break up with them all at once. You don't do anything in half measure, do you?"

"No, I don't." Kay gazed, light-headed, at the raw wooden walls and makeshift pulpit and rickety piano. She hadn't been in church since she was fifteen. The last time, she'd sat at the back of the tent counting the offering, her usual job since she wasn't good enough to be onstage with the rest of the family.

That night she'd pocketed the entire offering so she could escape. Every penny. On top of the cash she'd been skimming for months. Why not? She was irredeemably bad.

Kay bolted to her feet. "I have to go."

Mellie touched her arm. "Laundry, Kay."

She looked down at her friend's benign smile. For heaven's sake, why had she made a deal? "Fine." She plunked down on the crate.

"That's better. Good girl." Georgie spoke in the same cooing voice she used on her horse.

It was oddly comforting.

Kay worked her finger between the pages of the Bible and felt the fine paper dimpled by Roger Cooper's handwriting. What would he think to see her in church?

Mail took forever. Had he even received her letters? After she turned her life over to God, she'd told him about everything, including the incident with Hal. What would he think of her?

A warm wave swept through her. She'd read enough of his notes to know his heart. He wouldn't look down on her, and he'd be glad she'd made her decision.

Giggles erupted across the aisle from nurses in one of the other flights. Frannie Teague smirked at Kay and spoke to Mary Newlin. "Looks like she found someplace new to find men."

Kay slammed her eyes shut. Mellie said Kay was changed, a whole new person, but no one else believed it.

Shame slunk into her heart and bowed her head. She fought it the only way she knew how. *God, you said I'm a new person. You said it yourself. Mellie showed me the verse. Help me believe it. And if you wouldn't mind, make those girls believe it too.*

That new feeling oozed through her, slowed her respirations, and relaxed her muscles. Peace. It felt even better than watching a man fall in love.

Was it her imagination, or did it even still the voices around her?

Mellie nudged her.

Kay looked up. No, the voices stilled because the chaplain approached the pulpit. Would he recognize her? Use her as an example of how *not* to behave? Banish her from the building?

She leaned slightly to her right, centering her head behind the man in front of her.

The chaplain greeted everyone and announced a prayer. Kay even remembered to bow her head and close her eyes.

After he prayed for the troops of the US Fifth Army and British Eighth Army surging forward in their spring offensive in the Cassino area, the chaplain lifted his head. "Please open your hymnals to number 229, 'Amazing Love.' "

Kay gritted her teeth. She knew this moment was coming. Her friends promised her she didn't have to sing, but silence could draw as much attention as off-key singing.

Everyone stood, and Georgie held the hymnal so that Kay was supposed to take the other side. She did, but with as few fingers as possible.

Dizziness rolled in her head and brought out an overwhelming urge to run. When had she turned into such a coward? Danger didn't faze her, but a hymn did? No, she could handle this.

The chaplain sat at the piano and waved his hand to get them started. Kay drilled her gaze into the hymnal. She'd just focus on the words.

And can it be that I should gain
An interest in the Savior's blood?
Died He for me, who caused His pain—
For me, who Him to death pursued?
Amazing love! How can it be,
That Thou, my God, shouldst die for me?

Long my imprisoned spirit lay,
Fast bound in sin and nature's night;
Thine eye diffused a quickening ray—
I woke, the dungeon flamed with light;
My chains fell off, my heart was free,
I rose, went forth, and followed Thee.

No condemnation now I dread;
Jesus, and all in Him, is mine;
Alive in Him, my living Head,
And clothed in righteousness divine,
Bold I approach th'eternal throne,
And claim the crown, through Christ my own.

The words wrapped around her and drew her in. How did this fellow know how she felt? How did he know what she needed to hear? She wanted to rip out the page and take it with her, but defacing a hymnal would undo her salvation, wouldn't it?

The music soared, lifting her from the inside. Mellie's bird-like soprano and Georgie's buttery alto flanked her—just like Jemima and Keren, but without the cruel jests. Now Kay was white too, she was redeemed, she was good.

If she was a new creature, then maybe . . . just maybe.

The chaplain directed them to number 41, "This Is My Father's World."

Kay listened to the first verse and built up her courage, turning the crank over and over until she opened her mouth.

Her voice creaked.

She cleared her throat and tried another line. Ouch. So sour.

Mellie's head turned slightly toward her, turned back.

Kay hadn't changed, and her cheeks heated with the shameful truth.

She was only partly redeemed.

# 14

**Dinjan, India**
**May 16, 1944**

The mule didn't budge.

Two native workers tugged on the rope attached to the harness, to no effect.

Roger didn't blame the creature. They'd awakened the mule in the middle of the night and were coaxing it up a plank into the plane's dimly lit cabin. He wouldn't have co-operated either.

Regardless, the troops in besieged Imphal required mules for transportation over rugged jungle trails. He slapped the mule on the rump. "Git on there."

A whinny ended in a hee-haw, and the mule skittered up the ramp, shoving the workers aside.

"Tie him up nice and tight." Roger shone a flashlight at his Form F, every box filled in with military precision. He wanted to scribble on it, just to mar the perfection.

Grant Klein said Roger only did this to impress Veerman, and he was right. Roger had volunteered for the mule-hauling mission, and Grant hadn't, the nincompoop. More concerned with his reputation than with the men in Imphal.

"All loaded, boss." Pettas leaned out the cargo door.

"Great." Roger climbed the ramp. The C-47 already smelled like a barn. Never thought his mucking experience on the farm would be used as a pilot.

Four of the beasts were tied up to poles along the sides of the plane, and a canvas tarp covered the floor. Roger patted each animal on his way to the cockpit. "Thank you for flying with us this evening. Our stewardess will see to your needs during the flight. If you want anything, just bray."

"I ain't no stewardess."

Roger shone his flashlight just below Whitaker's big lumpy face. "But you're pretty enough to be one."

A fine compliment like that, and Whitaker only cussed in response.

Up in the cockpit, Roger and Elroy ran through the pre-flight checks. Roger didn't like night flights, but round-the-clock missions brought more supplies to Imphal, and at least the Japanese didn't fly at night. Maybe the mules would sleep.

When they had clearance, they started engines, performed their final checks, and dimmed the cockpit lights to reduce glare off the windshield.

Roger taxied into position, his landing lights illuminating the runway. He and Elroy ran up the engines, and the plane jiggled and swayed more than usual. The passengers must not have liked the noise. "Say, Whitaker," he called on the interphone. "Sing them a lullaby, would you?"

"Shut up, Coop."

He grinned. Grant Klein would write up the sergeant for insubordination, but not Roger.

Bert Marino and Bill Shelby took off first. Roger preferred flying in formation, especially at night. The extra navigational help came in handy, even though they all could fly to Imphal blindfolded by now.

When word came from the control tower, Roger released the brakes, raced down the runway, and lifted off.

As soon as they raised landing gear, the plane tilted to the right.

"What on earth?" Roger turned the wheel to the left to compensate. His pulse thumped against his earphones. Maneuvers were stupid at such a low altitude.

She flew heavy in the tail now, making his climb steeper than he liked. He eased the controls forward.

"What's going on?" Elroy said.

A sense of foreboding filled his stomach, as deep and dark and stinky as the manure would be when they landed. "The mules."

"Think they broke loose?"

The plane jerked left, and Roger pulled right. "Must have. Whitaker, go check the mules. Something's wrong."

Whitaker swore. "Got one up in the radio room. Thought you made sure they were tied up, Pettas."

"Me? That's your job."

Roger's eyes drifted shut, but he forced them open. No, it was *his* responsibility. Whitaker, as the aerial engineer, needed to secure all cargo, but Roger needed to make sure his crewmen performed their duties. "Tie 'em up, Whit."

The plane nosed lower, slipped to the right, and Roger struggled with the controls.

"Elroy," Pettas called from the radio room. "Whitaker wants the cabin lights on."

"Sure." He flipped a switch on the overhead panel.

Light glared off the windshield and blinded Roger.

"Sorry." Elroy flipped it off, flipped another. "Sorry about that, Coop."

"It's all right." He blinked away the stars in his eyes and focused outside.

The C-47 lurched. Old swear words formed in Roger's throat, but he swallowed them down and leveled the plane.

"Coop," Pettas said. "Command set. Shelby."

Elroy turned the dial on the overhead panel.

"Cooper to Shelby. Over."

"Shelby to Cooper. What's going on? Your plane's bucking like—"

"Like a mule?"

"Um, yeah."

"They got loose. Whitaker's taking care of it."

"Didn't he—didn't you—never mind."

Roger let out a deep sigh. "No, I didn't." He didn't check. All his little boxes might be filled in, but that didn't make him a good pilot.

---

**Nettuno, Italy**
**May 26, 1944**

So this was the infamous Anzio beachhead.

Kay twisted in her seat to see out the C-47's cabin window. Below her lay a turquoise harbor studded with ships and a wide toast-colored plain circled by jagged hills.

Three days before, the American and British troops had finally broken out of the beachhead. Yesterday, the Allies driving north from the Cassino front had linked with the forces at Anzio. Today, for the first time, four months after the landings, air evacuation planes were sent to Nettuno, just south of Anzio.

Kay had never been this close to a combat zone. Near the base of the Alban Hills, puffs of smoke arose and P-40 fighter planes zipped around.

Now she could do some actual nursing. She was tired of babysitting convalescing patients between Naples and North Africa.

The plane made its final turn for the landing, and Kay settled back in the folding seat along the side of the fuselage across from Sergeant Dabrowski. Stacks of crates filled the rest of the plane, rations mostly, from the labels she could read.

A rough landing rattled her bones. The airstrip at Nettuno had been declared secure, but no one said anything about declaring it smooth.

After the C-47 stopped and the engines died, Kay and Dabrowski stepped outside into a clear and warm day. A row of khaki hospital ward tents stood near the landing strip, and a medic pointed them to the second tent.

Four US field and evacuation hospitals had been stationed at Nettuno during the siege of the beachhead, enduring near-daily shelling and bombing. Georgie's boyfriend, Hutch, served as a pharmacist in one of the hospitals, which had recently rotated back to the Cassino front. Georgie said his tales were horrific. Dozens of patients and hospital personnel had been killed.

Now the Allies had the advantage. Kay could almost smell it in the sea breeze.

She ducked inside the tent and inhaled the peculiar odor of a mobile hospital—canvas and antiseptic and mustiness.

An officer approached and extended his hand. "You must be one of the flight nurses. I'm Capt. Jim Kirby, the physician in charge."

Jim Kirby was a fine-looking man, tall, midthirties, no wedding band, wavy dark hair, and appreciative gray-blue eyes. Very appreciative.

"Lieutenant Jobson." Kay gave his hand a cursory shake and surveyed the patients on their cots. "Who do we have today?"

"Um . . . well . . . let's start over here." He sounded confused, a bit wounded, and he led the way to the first cot on the left.

How could she be so rude? But how else could she avoid

such a handsome temptation? A month before she'd have added him to her lineup. For heaven's sake, she would have swept her lineup clean to make room for him.

Captain Kirby introduced the first patient, Pvt. Corwin Bailey, who had received multiple gunshot wounds in his abdomen and thighs on the first day of the assault. He'd barely survived surgery.

Kay asked questions and took notes on the flight manifest, reserving her warmth for the patient, which made her cool tone to the doctor stand out starkly.

They proceeded to the next patient, Cpl. Wayne Anderson, who had extensive burns to his hands and arms from an explosion in his tank. Captain Kirby relayed his condition in a clipped manner.

Kay's face heated as she made her notes. What was wrong with her? The other nurses managed to talk to men professionally without flirting.

She patted the corporal's shoulder. "We'll take good care of you. It's a short flight to Naples, and then you'll stay in a nice new hospital complex, where you'll receive top-notch care."

He looked at her through pain-watered eyes without a hint of romantic interest.

That was the key, wasn't it? A happy medium lay between flirtation and rudeness. She could relate to good-looking unattached males the same way she related to patients and married men—a dialed-down smile, no dazzle in the eyes, no leaning close, no touching.

As the physician reported on the remaining patients, Kay relaxed her voice and manner, but Jim Kirby didn't reciprocate. What a shame. When they first met, she could easily have made him swoon. A lingering gaze, a flip of her hair, and he'd have crawled into the palm of her hand.

Except now Kay sat in the Lord's hand and she liked it there.

"That's all." The doctor slipped the last patient's records into a large manila envelope.

"Thank you, sir. I appreciate all the information." She raised one of her professional smiles.

One of his eyebrows hiked up in a curious way, and he excused himself.

If she weren't careful, she'd just replace one bad reputation with an entirely new bad reputation—odd and mercurial.

Kay headed outside into fresh air. The ground personnel would have unloaded the cargo by now so she could set up the plane for her patients.

In front of the next hospital tent, Vera and Alice stood chatting.

Kay waved and strolled over. "Hiya, ladies. Have a good flight?"

Alice shielded her eyes from the sun and frowned at the hills in the background. "I don't like the sounds of that artillery. Don't you think it's too early for us to be flying in here?"

"Not for these patients." Vera turned to Kay, and her dark eyes gleamed. "Have you come to your senses? Are you going dancing with us tonight?"

Kay's feet did itch to dance, and she couldn't unify the nurses in the flight if she became a hermit. But if she went dancing, she'd come home with three new boyfriends. "Sorry. Not tonight."

"Are you all right, sweetie?" Alice's blue eyes brimmed with concern. "You've been so quiet lately. You've lost your zest for life."

Actually, she'd never felt more zestful, as if she'd been faking it for the past twenty-eight years. She shrugged. "I'm still new to this—to God—and I'm trying to figure things out."

Vera eased back.

Alice sent a patronizing smile. "Going to church is good, but you don't have to go overboard and let it ruin your life."

A snort from Vera. "Too late for that. She's turning into a redheaded Georgie. Are you going to start preaching at us too?"

"Of course not." Kay sighed and gazed away, where hospital tents spread inland like sand dunes.

"Good." Alice shook back her blonde hair. "My mother says one should never discuss religion or politics in polite company."

Vera thrust both hands in front of her chest. "Then I am extremely polite company because I don't want to hear one word about it."

Sadness tugged down on Kay's heart. Vera's father went to church every Sunday, worked hard Monday through Friday, drank hard on Saturday, and beat hard on his family Saturday nights. Then on Sunday, he'd go back to church.

Until recently, Kay had been Vera's biggest ally in this matter. "Listen, I still want to be friends. But I have to make changes, and that means not dating six fellows at a time. For now I have to pull back and figure things out."

Alice cocked her head. "How are we supposed to be friends if you won't do anything with us?"

In the cloudless sky, three P-40 fighter planes zipped by in a V formation. Kay chewed on one side of her lip. "Why don't we play bridge? Like we used to do in North Africa?"

"We were in the middle of nowhere." Alice wrinkled her nose. "We didn't have anything else to do. Here we have nightclubs, and I want to dance."

"So do I." Vera gave Kay a scornful glance, grabbed Alice's elbow, and sauntered away. "Kay's turned into a fussy old lady. We'll go without her. She wouldn't be fun anyway."

Kay groaned, and her shoulders sagged.

"What was that about?"

With a sharp intake of air, she whirled to face Lt. Cora Lambert.

"Well?" Lambert's gaze wandered over Kay's shoulder to her retreating friends.

Kay smiled and fluttered a hand in their direction. "Oh, them. They're just annoyed because I don't feel like going out tonight."

A long silence painted two creases up the chief's forehead. "I'm worried about you. Ever since the incident with that Lieutenant Heathcock, you haven't been yourself."

"I hope not. I'm trying to change. I broke up with all my boyfriends."

"So you can become a chief nurse?"

Kay's breath formed a solid block in her chest. Was that how it looked? Like she was only trying to gain Lambert's favor? "No. I just—I had to make changes in my life."

"Hmm." She crossed her arms over her gray-blue jacket. "Apparently, Vera and Alice aren't fond of these changes. And I'm tired of the division. You ladies need to learn how to get along."

A deep sigh fluttered over Kay's lips. How could she gain ground on one front without losing it on the other?

# 15

Dinjan, India
June 8, 1944

Kavi and Asad ran to Roger with four other boys and girls. "Drum? Drum?"

He grinned. In Italy the kids asked, "Gum? Gum?"

Asad tugged on Roger's arm—and his heart. "Raji, play?"

"Sorry, kids." He sat on the steps of the *basha*. "I'm afraid we won't be drumming together anymore. I'm leaving India."

Kavi fingered the strap of his *dhol* and gazed down at the drum. "You are going back to America?"

Roger's gaze passed from one set of sad dark eyes to the next. Military secrecy decreed he couldn't say he was returning to Italy and escaping the dangers of the CBI right at the start of the monsoon season.

Back to Europe where the Allies had leaped out of stalemate. The US Fifth Army had taken Rome on June 4, and two days later the Allies landed in force in Normandy. The Nazis would be brought to their grimy knees in a few short months.

He offered the kids a smile since he couldn't offer time. "A soldier can't say where he's going. But we're leaving India."

Asad hugged Roger's arm. "I want you here."

He patted the boy's head. "I know, buddy. I don't want to leave you guys."

Kavi raised fiery eyes. "We need you here. The British Army needs you to fly food and guns to them."

"Not anymore. A new group of pilots arrived in India a few days ago. We were just borrowed."

Asad's dark brown fingers played with Roger's sleeve. "One more time on the drums?"

"Sorry." He sighed and beckoned for the kids to follow him into the *basha*. He needed to pack and maybe he could find some candy for the children. He'd used up his gum weeks ago.

Roger snatched his drying laundry from the line strung across the room and shoved it—still a bit damp—into his barracks bag. He knelt beside his cot and pulled out his last package from Mom, which arrived just before they left Sicily. Two months in the boonies had decimated the contents. All he had left was a box of lemon drops. Mom could never remember Roger didn't like lemon drops. But with eight kids, who could blame her?

"You guys like lemon drops?"

Kavi held the *dhol* in front of him, right in Roger's face.

"I wish I had time to play, but I don't." Roger got to his feet.

Two shimmering lines ran down the boy's face. He shook his head. "No, it is a gift. I give to you."

Roger's chest constricted. The *dhol* was Kavi's prized possession, and although his family seemed well off, they had so little by American standards. He laid his hand on the boy's shoulder. "I couldn't take . . ."

Kavi's big black eyes went from sad to devastated before Roger could finish his sentence. Accepting the gift would deprive the boy of his favorite possession, but refusing the gift would insult him.

Roger leaned down to look Kavi in the eye. "Do you really want me to have your *dhol*?"

"Yes." He thrust it into Roger's hands then swatted away a tear and gave a dismissive shrug. "It is a child's *dhol*. My father said he will give me a man's *dhol* for my tenth birthday this winter."

Roger stroked the smooth drumhead, and his throat felt tight. How could he make things even?

Of course! He spun around and grabbed his tom-tom and spare pair of drumsticks beside his cot. "This is for you, Kavi. I want you to have this."

The younger kids squealed, and Kavi's eyes grew wide—but not as wide as his grin. "For me?"

"For you."

Kavi hugged the drum with one arm and rapped on it with both drumsticks in his other hand. "See me. I am big famous American drummer."

Roger laughed, but regret nibbled at his stomach lining. How could *he* become a big famous American drummer without an American drum to practice on? He'd order a new one from the Chicago music store that supplied his drumsticks, but how long would he go without?

The kids danced to Kavi's beat, and Roger shoved away the regret. What did a drum matter compared to the kids' joy? The gift would be used and treasured.

What about the other gift? Was his Bible being used and treasured? He pictured Kay's pretty face bent over the pages, inhaling the words, but that wasn't the Kay he knew. Even so. Even if she'd burned it and flung the ashes into the sea, it didn't matter, because he'd done the right thing.

Yet in the space of two months, Roger had given away the two things in the world that meant the most to him.

Once Dad said Roger wasted every good gift in his life—his mind, his legacy in farming, and his good solid Cooper reputation.

Kavi threw his free arm around Roger's waist and hugged him. "Thank you, Raji."

Roger smiled and ruffled the kid's silky black hair. What he didn't waste, he gave away.

---

**Rome, Italy**
**June 14, 1944**

"*Benvenuto a Roma!*" Georgie Taylor twirled in front of the gigantic Arch of Constantine. "I can't believe we're here."

"It's true, *la mia bella Giorgianna*." Her boyfriend, Technical Sergeant John Hutchinson, stood an unromantic distance away and grinned at her.

Kay smiled at the pair. Since Hutch was a noncommissioned officer and Georgie was commissioned, they weren't allowed to fraternize. Hutch played the role of tour guide to justify his presence. Could the Military Police arrest him for the adoring glances he lavished on his girl?

"I can't believe we're here either." Mellie gazed up at the hulk of the Colosseum to their left. "The first Axis capital to fall into Allied hands."

Lt. Tom MacGilliver clasped his fiancée's hand. "I'm thankful the Germans didn't sack Rome on their way out like they sacked Naples."

"For once they showed some heart and some sense." Kay shielded her eyes from a shaft of morning sun piercing one of the Colosseum's arches. "Can you imagine destroying something that's stood for almost 1,900 years, just out of spite?"

"With the Nazis, I can." Hutch beckoned the group onward. "Come on. Let's go inside."

Georgie walked beside him, taking three steps for every two of Hutch's. He stood at least a foot taller than she.

Kay fell in behind the two couples. With one hand, she

clamped her shoulder bag over her stomach, although she couldn't imagine what the locals would want with face powder and lipstick. Her other hand swung free and awkward. On sightseeing trips, this hand was usually wrapped around a muscular manly waist.

Had she ever been in a group like this without a date? Felt odd and unnatural.

The group wandered down the broad avenue leading from the Arch and running alongside the Colosseum. GIs on leave gawked at the sites, and Italian women and children offered items for sale.

Kay kept a firm watch on soldiers and locals and the cobblestone roads.

Hutch led them past a pair of MPs standing guard at the entrance to the Colosseum. Kay paid a dime of occupation money and entered.

Dozens of voices bounced off the stone walls and ceiling. Kay and her friends headed through a tunnel and up uneven ancient stairs to the first level, where the stadium opened before them in the warm sunshine. They circled to the right around the thickest part of the crowd until they found an open spot.

"Oh my." Kay leaned her elbows on a waist-high stone wall. Remains of stadium seating slanted up around her, pierced by arched tunnels and windows. Pilings sprang from the ground. Once they'd supported the floor—now they supported sun-browned vegetation.

"Imagine all the gladiators in battle." Tom waved his arm over the wall as if he held a Roman broadsword.

"You're such a little boy," Mellie said.

Georgie rested her chin in her hand. "The place makes me sad. Think of all the Christians martyred here, all the innocent animals slaughtered."

"Well, hello there, doll face."

Kay turned to her left. An officer draped his elbow on the wall beside her. Handsome and dark-haired, he wore a khaki shirt with lieutenant's bars on the collar, pilot's wings over his pocket, and a leather flight jacket with the patch for the US Fifteenth Air Force on the sleeve.

A bomber pilot showing off. Why else would he wear the jacket when the temperature promised to hit the high eighties?

His buddy stood beside him, dressed the same, taller, lankier, with a goofy grin as if he hadn't seen a woman for a year.

"Hello." Kay gave them a noncommittal smile and faced the stadium.

Officer A leaned closer. "A beautiful woman like you doesn't deserve to be alone."

How many times had she heard that line? She usually ignored the lack of originality and credited the man for the compliment, but today she heard the line in a new way.

"Is that so?" She cocked her head, letting her hair swing out to the side. "So if I weren't beautiful, I *would* deserve to be alone?"

He jerked back his head. "That—that wasn't what I said."

"Yes, it was." Kay gave the officer a sweet smile. "And you only sought my company because I'm beautiful. Shortsighted, don't you think? What do you know about my personality, my intellect, my character? Nothing."

"Say, Leo . . ." Officer B tapped his friend on the arm with the back of his hand, his smile as rigid as Kay's. "I think I see Jones and Davison over there."

Leo edged away from Kay. "Yeah, let's go. Later, ma'am."

"Good-bye." She fluttered her fingers and her eyelashes at them, and they scrammed.

Silence to her right. Her four companions gaped at her.

"Goodness gracious," Georgie said. "That was quite a show."

"Rubbed me the wrong way. Think about it. You two were friends first." Kay gestured toward Georgie and Hutch, then to Tom and Mellie. "And you two fell in love through letters, for heaven's sake. Those two—they just saw a pretty face."

Mellie's exotic dark eyes took on a gentle, playful gleam as if saying, "Now you want something more, something better." But she didn't open her mouth.

Neither did Kay, though her heart screamed yes.

Hutch pointed Georgie to a pair of Italian boys in a mock swordfight, and the couple laughed at the little ones.

"Let's go up to the next level." Tom led the group through the nearest tunnel.

Did Kay stand a chance? Every relationship she'd ever had started with her looks and charm. Could she attract a good man based on her character?

And what kind of man did she want? A strong man of faith, but still fun and energetic. She couldn't give that up.

Maybe someone with auburn hair and cocoa eyes and big thick shoulders.

"Oh brother." Her words absorbed into the brick walls of the staircase. Roger Cooper was in India, and he didn't like Kay one whit.

Maybe that was one of the reasons he appealed to her, because he didn't like the old Kay. But what about the new Kay?

Nonsense. She didn't even know who the new Kay was.

"Would you look at that view?" Georgie gazed through an arched window in the outer wall.

"The Forum to the right, Palatine Hill to the left." Hutch pointed over Georgie's curly head. "Amazing, isn't it?"

Columns, temples, arches, and remnants of buildings covered the hill before them. What once had been a thriving center of a decadent civilization now lay in ruins. But off in the distance, new structures poked up, shiny and clean.

A sense of warmth stirred in her chest. Perhaps the new Kay could be shiny and clean too.

Georgie clucked her tongue. "I should have asked Louise if we could borrow her camera. Poor thing."

Kay murmured her agreement. Louise Cox was in the hospital suffering from a bout of malaria.

"I forgot to ask," Mellie said. "Did you invite Vera and Alice to join us?"

"Yes." Kay grumbled so loud she thought the Colosseum would crumble beneath her. "They wanted to go shopping, find some nightclubs later on. Captain Maxwell agreed to take them and some of the other girls."

"Sorry. I hoped they'd join us."

Kay squeezed her friend's arm, grateful for her subtle help in building unity. Since Mellie had been most injured by Vera and Alice's cattiness, it meant a lot.

Georgie huffed. "Why would we want them along? They'd smirk at everything we said, as they always do."

"Please." Mellie's voice lowered. "You know I don't like gossip."

Georgie set her hand on her hip. "And I don't like how they look down on us because they think we aren't sophisticated. We're all nurses. We're supposed to work together."

"I know, but holding grudges makes things worse."

"Doesn't mean we have to socialize with them and take their snippiness either." Georgie flounced down the aisle into the stadium.

Kay grimaced. She was doing a swell job unifying the flight, wasn't she?

# 16

Capodichino Airfield, Naples
June 16, 1944

The new Form F annoyed Roger. Not only did he have to enter data he knew by heart, but now there were little boxes for each individual digit, as if he were a second-grader who'd get his columns mixed up when adding.

Sergeant Whitaker jumped down out of the cargo door. "Okay, Coop. All loaded and lashed in place."

"Thanks, Whit." He'd check everything again after he finished the stupid form. Crates of ammunition filled his C-47, bound for Grosseto Airfield, which the Allies had captured the day before. On the return trip, he'd evacuate wounded soldiers from the new US Fourth Corps.

A warm breeze fluttered the form on his clipboard, and he glanced around Capodichino Airfield for the hundredth time since he landed. Too bad he'd have nurse Alice Olson on his flight instead of Kay.

The day before, he'd arrived back at Comiso to find a dozen letters from Kay with lists of questions. She'd even numbered them. At first, she questioned God in a bitter tone, but as she neared the end of Job, her anger shifted from the Lord to her father, and her tone became desperate and longing.

Then on May 1, an abrupt change.

Roger scanned the airfield again. Kay Jobson had been saved? Of all people.

He chuckled. When he'd been saved, everyone said the same thing. Roger Cooper? Of all people.

Despite the warm day, goose bumps poked up against his khaki shirtsleeves. He'd argued with God about giving Kay his Bible, and look what happened. "Well, Lord," he muttered. "Guess you knew what you were doing."

"Hi, Roger."

Kay. He spun around. There she stood in her blue trousers and white blouse, smiling, her hair gleaming in the sun.

"Hi." That's all he could say?

"I heard you fellows were back. I—"

"Listen." He held up one hand. "I only have a few minutes before takeoff, so let me talk. I need to apologize."

"Apologize?"

He motioned with his thumb over his shoulder in the general direction of Sicily. "Just got back from India yesterday. They didn't forward our mail. You must think I'm—"

"I must think it takes a horribly long time for mail to get to India and back. I thought nothing of it."

His shoulders relaxed. "I read your letters last night."

"You did?" Her gaze wavered and flitted away.

"I'm real sorry for everything. Your dad, that jerk in Quartermasters—I want to beat up both of them."

She wouldn't look at him, but one corner of her mouth flicked up.

"You did the right thing. I'm happy for you."

She turned back to him, green eyes bright. "Now I can give you back your Bible."

"No, no, no." He waved his hand back and forth like a windshield wiper, sweeping away her concerns. "It's yours. I got a new one shipped from stateside."

Mischief sparkled in her eyes. "I hope it has big margins."

He laughed. "It does."

"Lieutenant Cooper?" The sergeant in charge of loading saluted Roger and handed him the invoice.

"Thanks." Roger scrawled his signature, returned the bottom copy to the sergeant, and added the top copy to his clipboard. He gave Kay a sheepish smile. "I don't want to be rude, but I have to get this bird in the air."

"I'm on your flight."

"You are?" He flipped to the flight manifest. "I thought—"

"Alice and I switched places. I hope you don't mind. I figure you owe me some answers." That mischief again—but not a hint of flirtation.

Roger's heart thudded into his rib cage with strange anticipation. "About ten pages' worth of answers."

Her cheeks turned pink. "I overdid it, didn't I?"

"Hardly. You should have heard me batter poor old Lou with questions back in the day." Tonight he'd write to Lou. Who would have thought the same Bible Lou used to lead Roger to Christ had now led Kay to Christ?

Kay hoisted herself through the cargo door without waiting for assistance.

Roger followed her inside and down the aisle past crates of bullets and artillery shells. He made sure each crate was secured, then headed for the cockpit. Kay sat in a folding seat on the right side of the fuselage.

He almost passed her by, but his conscience dogged his steps. He braced his hand against the bulkhead leading into the radio compartment and drummed his fingers on the metal. "Say, listen, Kay. We've got almost a two-hour flight to Grosseto. If you want, you can come up front. We can talk."

She studied him for a long, nerve-wracking moment.

His finger drumming accelerated.

Kay nodded.

"Swell." He escaped to the cockpit. What on earth was he doing? Why was he inviting conversation with the most attractive woman he knew?

He settled into his seat and put on his headphones. Why was he fussing? If God knew what he was doing when he told Roger to give away his Bible, then he certainly knew what he was doing today.

Mike Elroy joined him in the cockpit and ran through the preflight checklist. Roger trained his mind on his actions. With all that ammunition on board, he couldn't afford any mistakes.

He and Elroy started engines, taxied into position, and took off into a clear blue sky. Should be a good flight. If Pettas lost his way, Roger could just follow the coast. And they'd pass Rome. Maybe the brass would give the boys from the 64th TCG a pass. After two months in the jungle, they deserved it.

He felt Kay's presence behind him.

She stood with arms crossed and an uncertain look on her face. Had the woman ever been uncertain of anything in her life?

Roger slid his headphones off his right ear so he could hear both her and the radio. The first months after he'd given his life to the Lord had been an uncertain time too, as if he floated between two worlds, not belonging in either. "Have a seat."

"Thanks." She sat with her knees hugged to her chest and leaned against crates in the small cargo space between the cockpit and the radio room.

He returned his attention to the instrument panel. "Got a question?"

"Sure. How was India?"

"India?" A quick scan of the gauges, then he sent her a questioning look.

She cast a glance at the back of Elroy's head.

Understood. Personal spiritual questions wouldn't be appropriate. "Yeah, India."

While he flew over Italy's rugged hills sprinkled with olive trees and vineyards and tile-roofed homes, he told stories about *bashas* and jungles, about downing Zeros and drumming with little boys.

When was the last time he'd had a normal conversation with a young woman who wasn't his sister or cousin? Years and years, and it felt good.

Kay laughed at his stories and told about her trip to Rome. Thank goodness he had instruments to watch and headings to mind, giving him an excuse not to look at her too often.

"So what do you think?" she asked.

What was the question? He faced her. The brassy glint in her eyes had been replaced by a golden glow.

What did he think? He thought she was beautiful. He thought she was fascinating. And now they had an unbreakable bond because of his gift.

"Well?" She gave him one of those "you weren't paying attention, were you?" looks.

He cocked half a grin. "I think it sounds great."

A smile revealed neat white teeth, and she chattered about an orphanage and her friends and a plan. He'd actually chosen the right answer.

He veered his attention back to his job. Good thing he hadn't told her what he really thought—that he hadn't been in such a dangerous situation since high school.

———

Kay strolled across Grosseto Airfield in the sunshine toward the tent hospital by the flight line. Artillery boomed in the distance, competing with the noise of the engineers' bulldozers and graders. Maybe Mellie's Tom was here.

"Glad we're on the move again." Sergeant Dabrowski

walked alongside, gazing north as if he could see the US Fifth Army chasing the Germans up Italy's boot.

"Me too. It's—"

"Kay! Wait up!" That was Roger.

Her heart lurched in a way it had never done in all her dating years. "Did I forget something?"

He thumped to a stop a good ten feet from her. "I want to apologize."

"Apologize? Again?"

Dabrowski tapped her on the arm. "I'll go on ahead."

"Thanks, Sergeant." After he left, she returned her attention to the pilot. "Why do you want to apologize?"

His square jaw worked from side to side. "You see, I promised. I said I'd answer your questions, but I didn't think about Elroy being there. I still haven't given you a single answer."

"It's all right."

"No, it isn't. Maybe . . ." The expression in his eyes froze. His Adam's apple slid down to his open collar and back up to that strong jaw.

Maybe later. Only two months ago, she would have given him a coy look and said, "Maybe over dinner tonight."

But that was the old Kay. Not the new Kay. "I'll see you around."

His eyebrows arched in appreciation, then a smile spread. "Yeah. I'll see you around." He waved and trotted back to his plane.

She chuckled. Yeah, she'd see him on the return flight.

Kay headed for the hospital. What a strange day.

Roger had always fled her presence. At best, he was guarded. But today, he seemed genuinely glad to see her, and their conversation in flight was comfortable and easy. She'd never seen him so relaxed and animated, one square hand leaving the control wheel to emphasize his stories, one leg jiggling as if playing the pedal for a bass drum.

The man never stopped moving, and she liked that, liked the colorful way he told a story, his down-to-earth wisdom, even liked his lack of attraction to her.

He kept his eyes on hers, his hands to himself. Once that would have bugged her, but now it made her feel safe, special, as if she were good enough *not* to make a pass at.

And it completely unraveled her inside.

Kay drew a deep breath to clear her head.

A dozen patients lay on cots outside the tent, and Dabrowski waved her over. "Lieutenant Jobson, this is Captain Arnold."

Kay shook hands with a balding man in his fifties with the sweetest grandfatherly smile. "Good afternoon, Captain."

"I'll warn you, young lady." The physician leaned closer. "That fellow on the far right is a screamer. I gave him half a grain of phenobarbital about thirty minutes ago, but it didn't sedate him much."

The patient moaned and writhed on his cot.

"What happened to him?"

"Nothing worse than the other fellows. Bullet to his upper thigh, avoided the major vessels, no bone damage. He had minor surgery, needs a few weeks to recuperate."

Kay made a note on the flight manifest. "Anything in your records about an indulgent mama who honored his every boyish whim when he was sick?"

Captain Arnold laughed. "The X-ray failed to detect that."

"A little fussing over, and he'll be fine. Why don't you introduce me?"

"Kay! There you are." Grant Klein approached from the airfield.

"Hi, Grant." She squelched a grimace, gave him a polite wave, and followed the doctor to the patient.

Grant jogged up behind her, settled his arm around her shoulders, and kissed her cheek. "Hi, baby. I sure missed you."

Kay shrugged him off. "I'm working. And I'm not—"

"Excuse me, Captain." He tipped his cap to the physician. "I haven't seen my girl for three months."

"Well then, I'll give you a few minutes to catch up." The doctor's eyes hardened and erased the grandfatherly image.

"I'm sorry, Captain. This will only take a minute." She marched about twenty feet away and faced Grant.

"I heard your good news." He reached for her hand, his smile gentle.

She crossed her arms over her clipboard. Good news? Since when would he care about her relationship with God? He reserved the Almighty for Christmas, Easter, and flight emergencies. "My good news?"

"I heard you broke up with all your other boyfriends." His eyes turned smoky. "I'm honored."

Kay could only stare. When she met Grant Klein, she'd been attracted to his self-assurance. Now she saw it as pure arrogance. "You think I did that for you? Did you forget I broke up with you first?"

His dark eyebrows met in the middle. "If not for me, for whom?"

"No one."

"I saw you talking all cozy with Cooper."

She huffed. "It's not like that. We're just friends. I'm not dating anyone."

He stepped closer, suspicion and curiosity mingling in his eyes. "Why'd you do it?"

Kay pressed her lips together. He deserved an honest answer. "All right. I started reading the Bible, going to church, getting to know God. I realized I was dating for the wrong reasons—to get back at my father by controlling other men. I had to start over."

Grant peered at her, one eyebrow high. He probably thought she was crazy.

She lifted her chin. "I owe you an apology. I used you, led you to believe there could be more between us when I had no such intention. I'm sorry. You don't deserve to be treated like that. No one does."

He gave his head a quick shake. "You're not making sense."

Kay's shoulders slumped. "No, I suppose not. But let me make one thing clear. I'm not going out with you again."

Grant's gaze darkened and shifted over her shoulder toward Roger's C-47. "What's Cooper have to do with this?"

"Grant, jealousy is never attractive."

He glared at her. "Neither is deception."

"For heaven's sake, we're just friends. He gave me his Bible, answered some of my questions about God, that's all."

Grant chuckled. "So he's responsible for you getting religious?"

"Hardly. Now, excuse me. I have patients to see." She strode past him.

"That man's smarter—and more devious—than I gave him credit for," Grant said.

"What?"

"Don't you see?" He spread his hands before him. "You're his pawn. He can't stand me. He can't beat me as a pilot, so he plays stupid pranks on me. Now he's turned my girl against me."

Why on earth had she ever found this man attractive? "Turned me against you? Oh no, Grant. You did that all by yourself."

# 17

**Ciampino, Italy**
**July 13, 1944**

Roger flailed his arm in the darkness. What was that racket? The alarm clock. He shoved aside the mosquito netting, swung his bare legs over the side of the cot, and stood.

Swaying, he pried his eyes open. Where had he hidden the clock last night? Oh yeah, under the cot. Down to his knees, he fumbled on the tile floor. There it was. He slapped the fool thing off.

What time was it anyway? He held the clock to the open window in the house serving as officers' quarters.

Pale moonlight illuminated the dial. One o'clock? That couldn't be right.

His head sagged back. Yeah, it was right. He and Bill Shelby and Bert Marino had volunteered for a night mission dropping supplies to Italian partisans behind German lines. Veerman lifted a proud, satisfied smile when Roger volunteered.

But why did Roger decide to catch a few hours of shut-eye rather than stay up late like the other fellows?

He scratched his bare chest. Too hot to sleep in anything but skivvies. He grabbed his flashlight from the desk and found his trousers and khaki shirt draped over a chair. Felt nice and civilized to live in a house again after so many months in tents. A few days ago, the 64th had transferred up to Ciampino Airfield outside of Rome.

Someone rapped on the door. "Coop? Coop? You awake?"

"Barely." He opened the door.

Lt. Gerald Singleton stood in the hall. "Veerman sent me over from Operations. Seems the weather up north hasn't cleared. They canceled the mission."

Roger leaned against the doorjamb, and a tired smile crept up. Not bad. He'd get to sleep all night, but he'd still impressed Veerman by volunteering. "Thanks, Singleton. Appreciate it." Decent of the fellow, considering Singleton and Klein were pals.

"See you in the morning."

"Yeah. Morning." Roger shut the door and slipped under the mosquito netting over the cot. His bedroll had never felt so good.

"Coop! Coop!"

A light blazed in Roger's face, and he covered his eyes with his forearm. "What . . . ?"

"Coop, what're you doing in bed? We got a mission." That was Whitaker's voice. "Get your lazy tail moving."

"What?" He sat up and batted the flashlight out of his face. "What time is it?"

"It's 0145. Briefing started fifteen minutes ago. Veerman's fit to be tied that you're not there."

"Briefing? But the . . ." He shook the fog out of his head. "The partisan supply drop mission?"

"Yeah. Did you forget?"

"No." He tried to rub consciousness into his eyes. "Singleton. He came by. Said the mission's canceled."

"You must have been dreaming." Whitaker thrust Roger's trousers at him.

Sitting on the edge of the cot, he poked his feet into the trouser legs, then stood to yank up his pants. Singleton. Should have known better than to trust Klein's copilot.

Roger shoved his feet into his shoes without bothering to put on socks. The feud had quieted down lately. Sure, a few weeks ago, Klein had interrogated him about his relationship with Kay. Ridiculous. Roger told him he knew better than to get involved with a dame like her.

That was only partly true. Roger was involved, just not in the way Klein thought.

"Let's go." He snugged his cap onto his head, grabbed his shirt, and headed out the door.

His feet pounded down the stairs, and he dashed outside into the warm darkness. He and Whitaker jogged down the pathway, past spindly little trees toward the house they used for Operations, all lit up inside. For a briefing.

Old swear words knifed through Roger's head, but he shoved them aside.

Was Klein that big of a jerk? Or was he jealous?

Sure, he and Kay talked. He tried to keep his distance, but the connection of his old Bible and her new faith acted like a rubber band. Every time he tried to get away—boing!—there she was again.

He still didn't quite trust her. What if she reverted to her old ways? What if she bent with the first wind? People did that.

Roger tripped on the rough path, and his shoe almost came off. He hadn't bent. He hadn't reverted. But he remembered everyone eyeing him, suspicious, certain he'd slip.

Lou had been there for him, guiding him, encouraging him. Trusting him.

Today, after the mission and a nap, he'd write Lou for advice. He'd written Lou more in the past month than he had all of 1943.

Roger turned onto the pathway to the Ops building. At

least Kay didn't flirt with him anymore. Or was this good-little-church-girl routine just an act, a strange new way to flirt with the good little church boy, as she'd once called him?

He groaned and pushed open the door. Man alive. He sounded as arrogant as Grant Klein.

Speak of the devil. Klein and Singleton sat in the large front room they used for briefings, along with Bill Shelby, Bert Marino, and their crews, gathered around a large wooden table. Cigarette smoke wafted around the room.

Alarm flashed on Mike Elroy's round face. "Where have you been?" he mouthed.

Veerman stood. "Lieutenant Cooper. How kind of you to grace us with your presence. Although I see, once again, you forgot to wear clothes."

Swell, his shirt. He planned to put it on while he ran. He punched his hands through the sleeves. "Sorry, sir, I—"

"You're twenty minutes late. Don't you know how important this mission is? Those partisans put their lives at risk every single day fighting the Nazis, never knowing when the Gestapo will hunt them down or their neighbors will turn them in. And you can't be bothered to be punctual."

Roger stiffened. He would have been on time except for Klein and Singleton.

He fixed a hard gaze on the two men. Singleton glanced away, and his cheeks reddened. But Klein smirked.

The truth parted Roger's lips, but he pressed them shut again. That's what Klein wanted. He wanted Roger to rat on him. Sure, Klein and Singleton would get in trouble, but Roger would look like a sniveling tattletale. The feud would escalate again, and Veerman would lose what little respect he had for Roger.

No, he'd take his licks like a man. Roger faced Veerman, pulled himself tall, and set his jaw. "I apologize, sir. It won't happen again."

"I should hope not." He clasped his hands behind his back. "I thought you were getting better."

Roger's face warmed. He *was* getting better. This was the first time he'd been late since Kay had given him the alarm clock. "I'm sorry, sir."

Veerman waved his hand toward the conspirators. "Lieutenant Klein offered to take your place. I'm glad someone around here can be relied on."

Yeah, Klein could be relied on, all right. Relied on to stab Roger in the back.

"Thank you, sir." Klein wore the smarmiest smile. "I'm glad I can help you tonight."

"That won't be necessary, Lieutenant." Veerman leaned over the large map of Italy on the table. "I might value dependability, but this mission needs Cooper's brashness and courage."

Small victory. Very small.

# 18

Ciampino Airfield, Italy
July 23, 1944

Kay knelt by the C-47's open cargo door and ushered in the last patient for the morning's flight. She checked his emergency medical tag against her flight manifest—Sgt. James Yamaguchi of the 442nd Regimental Combat Team, gunshot wound to upper left abdomen, two weeks postsurgery.

Serving as a stewardess for four years had introduced her to all areas of the country and many ethnicities. Excellent training for flight nursing. "Good morning, Sergeant Yamaguchi. I'm glad you can fly with us today."

A wan smile rose on his angular face. "Thanks, ma'am. Is it true they have a swimming pool at that hospital in Naples?"

"It's true. Quite a facility. Used to be Mussolini's fairgrounds." She addressed the medic carrying the head of the litter. "He'll go in the top position on the left."

After they carried the patient inside, Kay stood in the doorway and inhaled the fresh balmy air. A brilliant blue sky arced overhead. What could be better than to be quartered in a seaside villa in Lido di Roma outside of Rome?

Her next day off, she'd bask on the beach with her friends and splash in the warm turquoise sea.

Irony tugged up a smile. "The sacrifices I make for my country."

Could her life possibly get any better? Plenty of friends, a stimulating job, a glorious setting, and this bubbly joy and relaxing peace.

Kay bounced on her toes and laughed at her giddiness. She'd never been the giddy sort.

The last medics hopped out of the plane, and Kay backed up to let the aerial engineer close the door. "Thanks, Sergeant Whitaker. Lovely day, isn't it?"

Big and burly, the man hunched his shoulders, ducked his head, and lumbered toward the cockpit. "Yes, ma'am."

Kay checked the web strapping that secured the six litters and checked the seat belts for the ambulatory patients. Roger's crew was her favorite—the shy and polite copilot, the engineer uncomfortable with women, the radioman who looked quite comfortable with women but knew better than to flirt with officers, and Roger. Competent, energetic, inspiring Roger.

The first engine roared to life, as if the pilot were trying to silence her thoughts.

She'd have to add "humble" to his list of attributes.

Kay strolled to the front of the cabin and faced the patients. "Good morning, gentlemen. Welcome aboard. We have a short flight to Capodichino Airfield in Naples, under an hour. I'm Lieutenant Jobson, and this is Sergeant Dabrowski. We'll take care of you in flight. If you need anything, give us a holler."

"I'm hollering, baby." One of the ambulatory patients, Lieutenant Schaeffer, a dark-haired man with one foot in a cast, beckoned her with a finger.

One of those. She could deal with him. "It's Lieutenant Jobson, not 'baby.' What do you need?"

Wide-set eyes swept up and down, checking out her figure. "You tell me. What services do you provide?"

Kay knew her way around a double entendre. "Medical care, water, and sedatives for men who can't behave."

Some of the men laughed, but not Schaeffer. The plane rolled forward, taxiing toward the runway.

"All right, gentlemen." She smiled at the patients and strode down the aisle. "Everyone's secured. The sergeant and I are getting seated for takeoff, and then—"

Schaeffer grabbed her arm and pulled her onto his lap. "I've got a seat for you, baby."

"Let go of me." Kay struggled in his tight embrace.

Sergeant Dabrowski glared down at Schaeffer. "Let her go immediately."

The private sitting next to Schaeffer stared, eyes huge. "Sir, you shouldn't do that."

Kay jabbed him with her elbow. When he loosened his grip, she scooted off his lap and stumbled away. "You ought to be ashamed of yourself."

Dabrowski leaned over him, fists coiled. "Control yourself, sir. That's no way to treat a lady."

"Lady? She's no lady." He flicked his chin in her direction. "See the way she walks, the way she moves? She knows how to please a man."

"Sir!" Heat inflamed her face. "I am a nurse, not a prostitute."

Schaeffer shrugged. "You like to touch men's bodies, don't—"

Sergeant Dabrowski slugged him, right in the jaw.

Men yelled and gasped. Kay cried out.

Schaeffer held one hand to his jaw and cussed. "Assaulting an officer? I'll have you locked up—"

"No, you won't." A lieutenant across the aisle leaned forward, eyes burning. "Not a man on this plane would testify in your favor. You deserved that punch. Now, shut up and keep your lousy hands to yourself, or I'll have *you* charged with assaulting Lieutenant Jobson."

"Thank you, sir." Kay tried to smile at him, but her facial muscles twitched.

"I'll testify for you, ma'am." From a litter in the back, Sergeant Yamaguchi raised a hand. "You're just doing your job, and we all appreciate it."

"Thank you." Her voice wavered in a way she hated.

The engines built to a roar, and Kay made her way to the back of the plane to sit down.

Everything inside her quivered. Not from danger—even if the rest of the men hadn't protected her, she could have handled him.

Schaeffer thought she was easy, an image she used to cultivate—that's what made her quiver.

Kay sat on the floor behind the litters and hugged her knees to her chest. Three months of trying to act like a good girl, but she still came across as a good-time gal.

────────

## Capodichino Airfield

"That's the last of it." Kay forced her trembling fingers to roll up a length of web strapping.

"Everything's clear and ready for cargo." Dabrowski took the coiled strapping from Kay and tucked it into a canvas bag on the ceiling.

Roger Cooper and Mike Elroy came out of the cockpit, laughing at something.

She didn't want to talk to anyone, much less Roger. Kay picked her musette bag off the floor.

"Hey, folks. How was the flight?" Roger asked.

Kay slung her bag over her shoulder, not trusting herself to meet his eye. "Fine."

He stopped, right beside her. "You all right, kid?"

"She's a little shaken up," Dabrowski said. "Some jerk made a pass at her."

"On my plane?" Roger's voice rose. "I won't have any of that. Any man gives you problems, you let us know up front."

Kay unbuckled and rebuckled her musette bag. "Nothing I couldn't handle. I've done it a hundred times before."

"Yeah? So why'd this fellow get you out of joint?"

She raised her chin in defiance. "I'm not . . ."

Roger's mouth drifted open.

Oh no. How red were her eyes? She moved toward the doorway. "I'm fine."

He blocked her way. "Sure you are. And I'm a ballerina."

At the mental image of his stocky build in a pink tutu, a giggle escaped. And a tear. Stupid faulty tear ducts. She swiped away the evidence and tried to get around the pilot.

He didn't budge. "Dabrowski, you about done?"

"Yes, sir. Anything else you need, Lieutenant?"

Kay shook her head. "I'm fine. Thanks for—for everything."

"All right." The sergeant didn't sound convinced, but he hopped out of the plane.

More than anything, Kay wanted to leave too, away from the heat and stuffiness and Roger's discerning eyes. "Excuse—"

"You want to keep pretending you're fine, or you want to tell me what's wrong? Maybe I should get Mellie or Georgie. Want me to do that?"

Grief swelled in her chest, her throat, her mouth. "I thought I'd changed. I thought I was good now." Her voice came out high and constricted.

"What'd you do wrong?"

"Nothing." She hadn't encouraged Schaeffer, had she? "He—he thought I was loose. But I haven't been on a date in almost three months. And I never once flirted with a patient.

Never. But he said he could tell—tell by the way I moved." Her throat closed off, and she scrunched up her eyes to slam the tear ducts shut.

Roger stood there, silent, unmoving. He probably thought she was loose too. At the Orange Club not so long ago, hadn't she purred over him, trailed her finger down his arm, and asked him out?

A sob ballooned in her mouth. "Maybe I can't be redeemed after all."

"Hey, now." He patted her shoulder, then stuffed his hand in his trouser pocket. "If I can be redeemed, you can too."

"You don't know what I did."

Roger sighed and gazed out the cargo door behind him. "Say, they've got to load the cargo, and I need to do my pre-flight inspection."

Kay's mouth tightened. "I'll get out of your way then." She darted for the exit.

"Hey." He flung his arm across the doorway. "Let me finish. Why don't you come along while I do the inspection? It'll give me something to do while we talk, since you don't want to look at me anyway."

True. She ventured a glance. He stood only a foot away, and his brown eyes overflowed with firmness and compassion. But did he have the truth? That's all she wanted. "All right."

"Great." He jumped out of the plane and held out a hand to assist her.

She ignored it and got out all by herself, as she'd always done.

Roger went around the wing toward the nose of the plane, stood in front of an engine, and made a note on a clipboard. "Tell me why you think you can't be redeemed."

Kay crossed her arms, making the musette bag stick out by her belly. "You want to know what I did? I'll tell you. I lied. I lied to all the men I dated, promised something I never planned to give. And I stole. You didn't know that, did you? I skimmed off my father's offering for months so I could escape. Then the last night, I pocketed the whole amount. And I conned some lovesick boy into driving me into Tulsa, promised him a night in a ritzy hotel. But I ditched him while he was checking in. I used him."

"Mm-hmm." Roger ran his hand over the edges of each propeller blade. "Did you ask God to forgive you?"

Kay nodded. "Guess it didn't take."

He shot her a glance, then peered at the underside of the engine. "So you think God lied."

"That's not what I—"

"First John 1:9 says, 'If we confess our sins, he is faithful and just to forgive us our sins, and to cleanse us from all unrighteousness.' That's what the Lord said. If there are any sins he won't forgive, he's a liar." He made checkmarks on his clipboard.

"But what I did was so bad."

Roger squatted by the wheel and inspected the length of the landing gear. "Kid, you aren't the only one with a past."

Kay glanced away to Vesuvius in the distance. "What'd you do? Sneak a smoke behind the barn?"

He was silent so long, she turned back. His hand lay motionless on the tire, his auburn head bent. "I never told anyone but Lou. And—and Clint. Even Shell only knows part of it."

Clint Peters. Kay hadn't heard his name spoken in far too long. It seemed to cost Roger a great deal. His shoulders rounded, and his jaw worked back and forth.

A better friend would know the right words to encourage him. Kay chewed on her lips. "You don't have to tell me."

A dry laugh. "Yeah, I do. But it isn't easy."

Her stomach squirmed. What exactly had he done?

Roger got to his feet and headed around the wing, touching the light on the leading edge of the wing and curving his hand around the wingtip, scrutinizing it. "I had a lot of girlfriends in high school, had my way with most of them."

"Oh." She squeezed her lips together to cut off her shock.

"My senior year, I got a girl pregnant."

"Oh no."

"Yeah, that's what I said." On the trailing edge of the wing, he wiggled the aileron up and down. "I didn't love her, but I wanted to do the honorable thing and marry her." He strode toward the tail of the plane.

Kay struggled to keep up, to hear his low voice. Was he divorced? Widowed? What about the baby? "You married her?"

"She wouldn't have me." Behind the tail, he moved the elevator flaps up and down. "Said everyone knew I'd never amount to anything. She didn't want to be stuck with a no-account for life."

Kay clapped a hand over her mouth. Her "oh my goodness" came out muffled.

"Yeah. Well, she had a point." Roger's face reddened, and his jaw jutted forward as he made more notations on his clipboard.

What a horrible thing for the girl to say—for him to say. Of course, he wasn't a no-account anymore. Kay lowered her hand from her mouth. "She raised the baby alone?"

Roger's shoulders curled in, and his muscles pressed out in lumps under his khaki shirt. "If only she had."

"What—"

"She . . ." His voice stiffened, lowered.

Kay stepped closer, drawn by his distress, her breath captured, waiting.

The muscles under his jaw stood out in ropes. "She—one of her friends knew someone in Chicago who could—who could get rid of the baby."

Kay had been around enough to hear of such things, but this time it socked her in the gut. "Oh no."

"That's what she did." Roger shoved the plane's rudder side to side. "Couldn't talk her out of it. Promised to drop out of school, get a job, give up my big band dreams, but she wouldn't listen. Said she knew—knew I'd be a lousy husband."

"Oh, Roger. I'm so sorry." An urge grew within her to hug him or at least stroke his shoulders, but he might misinterpret her actions.

He tested the other elevator flap. "I'm responsible for my baby's death, you know that?"

"Nonsense. She's the one—"

"No!" He faced her and jammed his thumb into his chest. "If I were a better man, she would've married me, and we'd have a son or daughter who'd be eleven years old now. Eleven." His voice cracked.

Her chest caved in from the weight of his grief. "I'm so sorry."

He marched toward the other wing.

Kay dashed to catch up. "Wait, Roger."

He spun to face her, and she almost ran into him.

He thrust a finger in her face, pain and fire mingling in his eyes. "Stop feeling sorry for yourself. Stop thinking your sins are so big, so much worse than anyone else's that even the almighty God who created the universe is incapable of taking them away. Understand?"

She stared at that fingertip, only an inch from her nose, while the words wedged into her heart. She nodded.

He opened his hand before her, palm to the sky. "His mercy is a gift. Not something you earn, not something you deserve. But like any gift, it isn't yours until you take it."

Kay's gaze flowed over his open palm to his eyes of unyielding bronze. "A gift."

His fingers coiled into a fist. "You've got to grab hold of it. Claim it."

She cupped her hands before her stomach and stared into their emptiness . . . no, their fullness. If God could forgive Roger, he could forgive her.

He already had.

Kay took a deep breath of sea air and aviation fuel and certainty, and she curled her fingers tight.

# 19

Over Italy
August 4, 1944

"Magnetic heading 336," Mike Elroy said.

Roger nodded and kept his hands steady on the C-47's control wheel. As the head aircraft in his nine-plane "V of Vs" formation, he had to keep a constant watch on his heading, altitude, and speed. Ahead of him, Veerman led the flight of thirty-six planes. An hour later, the remaining twenty-seven planes of the 64th Troop Carrier Group would follow.

Morning sunlight spilled through the cockpit and illuminated the instruments. The altimeter read three thousand feet, airspeed one hundred forty.

Good. Roger chomped on his gum, thankful that Wrigley's had requisitioned enough sugar to provide chewing gum for the troops. Helped with his nerves.

Especially today. Two paratroopers from the British 2nd Parachute Brigade rode in the back of the plane, ready to jump over a practice drop zone north of Rome.

Some big operation was coming. A betting pool kept the boys busy at Ciampino Airfield. Where would the US Seventh Army land? At Genoa at the top of Italy's boot? Or at any of a dozen potential sites in Southern France? Roger wasn't a betting man anymore, but he would have put his money on someplace near the mouth of the Rhône River, near the huge port of Marseille. He'd ferried enough cargo to know how vital supply routes were to an army.

The sun finished poking its head over the rugged hills to Roger's right and brought out the blue-green of the Mediterranean spreading to his left. The coastline ran in a jagged line to the northwest, pointing to France.

Roger rolled the ball of gum around in his mouth. He had to do his best today so he could do his best when it mattered, when he was dropping more of these men into enemy territory.

How had Dad worded it in his last letter? "Your mother and I are pleased and surprised that you haven't gotten yourself killed—or worse, gotten someone else killed."

No one knew how to raise his morale better than Harold "Copper" Cooper.

Then Dad went on for another two pages about the farm, and his brothers' farms, and his sisters' husbands' farms. All of them good Coopers, patriotically growing food for the Allies.

And here was Roger, three thousand feet above the earth, playing in his aeroplane, as his oldest brother Joe had put it when Roger joined the Army Air Forces.

Yeah. Playing. Roger shook his head. The men in the back of his aeroplane weren't playing, and neither was he.

"Coop, I've got the homing station at Lido loud and clear." Pettas's voice crackled on the interphone. "Time to start our descent."

"Thanks." With radio silence required, Roger waggled his wings to signal the eight planes behind him. Then he edged the control wheel forward to descend to eighteen hundred feet.

The radioman was doing much better as a navigator, really applying himself.

Just like Roger was trying to better himself as a pilot. His reports were neat and complete. He was on time or early for briefings. He'd even read Elroy's meteorology book after he finished teasing his copilot for bringing a big fat textbook.

Most difficult of all, he'd resisted the temptation to get Grant Klein back for lying to him about the partisan supply mission.

Roger tapped out a rhythm on the control wheel. Man alive, what an opportunity. A local woman had delivered a package to the house at Ciampino—Klein's laundry, spanking-clean white underwear.

And Roger had received a red scarf from his mother. Making sure he got it in time for Christmas, she said. Couldn't trust the Army Post Office, she said. But red? Had Mom forgotten he was in the Army? Drab colors only.

He'd pictured the tiled kitchen in the house, the big kettle, the red scarf and white undies swirling together on the stove.

Instead, Roger had scrawled a message on the paper wrapper: "Decided not to dye your lingerie pink. One of us has to grow up. Coop."

Although Klein liked to report Roger's every doing to Veerman, apparently he hadn't reported that.

Below, a spit of land stuck out into the Mediterranean. Looked like Lido di Roma. The altimeter read eighteen hundred feet. Perfect. Ahead of him, the other planes turned right.

"Coop, we're at the IP," Pettas said.

"Thought so. Thanks." Roger waggled his wings again to signal the initial point, the start of the run to the drop zone. He put the plane into a dog-leg turn until the heading read thirteen.

"Ten minutes to the DZ," Elroy said.

"Check." On the overhead electrical panel, Roger rang the bailout bell to signal the men in the back that the drop zone was approaching.

The beachside town of Lido di Roma slipped underneath

his plane. That's where Kay was stationed. Was she down there right now, shielding her green eyes from the sun, watching the C-47s trail overhead?

Oh brother. When had he turned into a sentimental fool? He was a fool, all right. Never should have told her his secret. Never.

Once again, the Lord hadn't given him a choice.

Roger throttled down from 140 to 110 mph.

He wouldn't have minded sharing if his sin involved espionage or murder or armed train robbery. But his sin was sexual, and she was a beautiful woman who used to flirt with him.

He preferred it when she thought he was a prudish monk.

"Coop, the Rebecca picked up the Eureka beacon at the DZ," Pettas called on the interphone. "It's working."

"Good." They hadn't used the new Rebecca radar system yet. "How long until the drop, Elroy?"

"Two minutes."

"All right." On the overhead panel he switched on the red light to signal the paratroopers to stand to the door.

He had to keep the plane steady and level. He reached to the side of the copilot's seat and flipped the lever to raise the flaps.

"Ninety seconds."

Roger throttled back the left engine to lessen the impact of propwash on the paratroopers when they jumped from the cargo door on the left side of the plane, while he throttled the right engine up to compensate.

"Thirty seconds," Elroy said. "Heading thirteen, altitude eighteen hundred, airspeed one ten."

"Right on target," Pettas said.

Roger's hand hovered over the light switch, and his jaw set hard. *Lord, keep those men safe.*

Memories of failure galloped through his head. Most of the Allied airborne missions at Sicily and Salerno hadn't gone well. Men had been scattered far from their drop zones, far from each other. Too many men had been lost.

"Coming up," Pettas said. "Three, two, one."

Roger gritted his teeth and flipped the light to green.

While he kept the plane level and true, he ventured a glance out the window behind him. The two paratroopers flung themselves out the door, hurtling toward the ground below, trusting in a flimsy piece of silk to save their lives.

They had no choice but to obey.

After a minute or two, Roger made a climbing 180-degree turn to the right.

He had no choice but to obey either. God had a reason to make Roger yank his secret from hiding. The peaceful look had returned to Kay's face.

There'd better be some reward for all this painful obedience—like never seeing Kay Jobson again. The dame was dangerous.

Roger headed south toward Ciampino and huffed out a sigh. More accurately, Kay had the power to bring out the dangerous in him. And he never wanted to see that part of himself again.

# 20

Rome
August 5, 1944

"Watch out!" Mellie called.

Kay ducked, and the soccer ball soared over her head.

"Ha!" Roger caught it and bounced it like a basketball, up and down, one hand to another, eyes alight. "Guess you're one of those fraidy girls."

"No hands in soccer." Kay kicked the ball away from him and toward the children. "Guess you're one of those milksop boys."

"Funny girl, are you?" He jogged past her to where the children jostled the ball back and forth in the orphanage's dining room, tables and benches shoved against the walls for the game.

"Sure am." She smiled at the back of his mussed-up head. This was such a great idea.

Georgie had organized visits to an orphanage in Naples earlier in the year, and now she'd found a place in Rome. Mellie had expressed concern that the children only had females in their lives—the nuns, Red Cross workers, and flight nurses. With only occasional visits from a priest, they were starved for adult male influence, so Kay had suggested recruiting the flight crews. Today some of the men had joined them, since they were grounded in bad weather.

The children did fancy footwork, bypassed Roger, and kicked the ball between the chair goalposts.

"You guys are killing me." Roger scooped up two of the smallest boys and tucked them under his arms like sacks of corn. "I need a break."

Two little girls clung to his legs, laughing and calling to him in Italian.

Kay smiled. These children might not have families, but at least they had a home. The old longing for a house swelled inside her—four walls, a floor, a ceiling, doors, and separate rooms.

Perhaps today's outing would put her another step closer to her goal. If she could bring Lambert an offering of a unified flight, maybe she could persuade the chief to write a recommendation. Today all the nurses worked for the same purpose. In the classroom across the hall, Vera, Alice, and Georgie did art projects with some of the children, after distributing clothing sewn and knit by the nurses.

Kay "knit her bit" because she had to, but knitting reminded her of evenings in the family tent. Mother and Jemima and Keren sewing industriously, her sisters scoffing at Kay's uneven stitches, her younger sister Keren smugly proclaiming that even *she* sewed better than Kay.

They did everything better than Kay.

Until Kay realized she earned better grades, played sports better, and made friends more easily—all worldly, sinful things in her father's eyes. So Kay embraced them all the harder.

"Some teammate you are." Mellie tapped Kay on the arm, her golden cheeks glowing from the exercise. "Mike and I need your help. Roger, Louise, and Bert are plotting something."

Kay hauled up a grin. Self-pity only wasted time and energy.

Mellie pulled Kay to her team's side of the room. On the far side, Roger gathered his kids in a huddle as if they were playing American football. His rich voice carried even though he spoke low. He used lots of hand motions, patting kids on the head, and they looked up to him with rapt attention.

His care for the children shone in every gesture and word, and they soaked it up like dry little sponges.

But she had to defeat him. She turned to Mellie and Mike. "He thinks he's playing football. How can we use this to our advantage?"

Mike Elroy squinted at his pilot. "I bet he'll go long. He's thinking like a quarterback. He'll send one kid down deep on each side, go for a long pass."

"That's not how you play soccer." Mellie raised a mischievous smile. "Long passes are easy to intercept."

"All right then." Mike crouched down, pulled a handful of pebbles from the breast pocket of his khaki shirt, and used them to show the children what was going on.

The older boys pointed to the pebbles, laughed, and elbowed each other.

Kay smirked at the auburn-haired jock. "He doesn't stand a chance."

Roger clapped his hands, and the kids spread out in a line, just like in football.

Sure enough, the girl in the center kicked the ball backward to Roger, who booted it long and low down the left side of the room. Before it could reach the boy who was loping for it, two of Kay's teammates rushed in. The children dashed down the room, and the ball zigzagged between them in a series of short passes until—boom!—"*Gol!*"

Roger tossed up his hands. "I do *not* understand this game."

"Obviously." Kay burst out laughing. "Stick to badminton."

"Badminton? Badminton?" Roger dribbled the ball toward her like a basketball, eyes flashing. "I'll show you badminton."

Kay grinned. He had no idea how good she was at basketball. She snatched away the ball and twirled to get around him. For a big man, he moved surprisingly fast. He blocked her.

She spun the other way, shouldered up against him, spun again, bumped again.

He was so solid, and he didn't stop laughing. "Say, you're not half bad, kid."

"I'm not a fraidy girl."

"I'm not a milksop." His big hand swatted at the ball.

She whirled around and thrust the ball in his face. "And this is not a basketball or a football. It's a soccer ball. You kick it with your feet." She tossed it over her shoulder.

The children pounced on it, falling naturally into the game, free of the American pilot's game plans.

Roger didn't follow the ball. He didn't follow the children. His brown eyes focused hard on her, and one side of his mouth twitched up. Sweat darkened his hair to a deep russet brown around the hairline.

Her heart did some fancy footwork of its own. He was too close and too handsome.

His smile grew. "Guess you're not a fussy kind of dame after all, kid."

"Never was."

Roger nodded, broke his gaze, and ran back into the fray of the game.

Kay blew out a hard, hot breath. Goodness, what he did to her!

That was the closest she'd seen to admiration from him— but nowhere near attraction. His "kid" nickname for her rang of brotherly platonic affection.

What kind of woman did he like? Since he'd confessed his past to her, she kept tripping over that thought. Her image of him continued to shift—from fuddy-duddy, to a vigorous man immune to feminine charms, to a man with a healthy appetite for women. A man of passion.

She'd been better off not knowing that.

Why had he never shown any interest in her? Had the Lord taken away his appetite? Had he sworn off women for good? Did he find her unattractive? Maybe he liked his girls voluptuous, or blonde, or giggly.

Or maybe Kay wasn't good enough.

"Stop it," she murmured to herself. "No self-pity."

The game had wound down, and a nun gestured for the children to line up.

Roger worked his way down the line, shook hands with each child, and addressed them all by name.

Kay's throat closed off. To the rest of the world, these orphans were a burden, a waste, a hassle. But Roger Cooper saw the value in each and viewed them with interest, understanding, and respect.

He turned to the American visitors and clapped his hands. "All right, crew. Let's put this place back to rights."

Along the wall, Roger and Mike rocked one of the tables onto its feet and wrestled it into position.

Kay and Mellie grabbed a bench, while Louise Cox and Bert Marino carried another.

Mellie puffed a strand of hair out of her eyes. "So, Roger, what did you do in the real world before the war? Were you a teacher?"

"What?" He stared as if she'd said he were a bank robber.

"You're so good with children." Mellie set down her end of the bench.

"You are." Kay straightened the bench.

"Nah, I'm a drummer."

Mellie laughed. "Of course. I forgot. Well, if drumming doesn't work out, you'd be an excellent teacher."

"Hardly." His voice came out low, and he headed for the next table.

Kay fetched another bench. An image of Mr. Warburton flashed in her mind. She'd never stayed at any school more than three months in a row, but she'd never forgotten the tenth-grade history teacher.

Big and loud, Mr. Warburton used to perch on the front of his desk and tell stories. In his classroom, history was more than terms and dates—it was real people in the sweeping arc of life, caught up in grand events. And he cared. The students responded.

"Little more this way." Roger tugged a table to the side, face red.

Kay pictured Roger as that sort of teacher, the once-in-a-lifetime sort who could engage children and change lives. "I can see you as a teacher too. I really can."

Roger scrunched up his face. "Hardly. Kids only like me because I'm an overgrown kid myself. I'm not a teacher."

She frowned and helped Mellie carry a bench over to his table. "It's more than that. You have a gift."

He shot a glare at her. "I'm not good enough, all right?"

She almost dropped the bench on his toes. "Not—not good enough? I thought—I thought you were redeemed."

He stared down at her with a look in his eyes she'd never seen before—a strange mix of shock and . . . insecurity?

Kay's heart shriveled up. Deep down inside, he didn't really believe he'd been redeemed, did he? And if he hadn't been . . .

Roger blinked, and the insecurity vanished. "Not *that* kind of good. Just meant I wouldn't be good at teaching. All those routines and regulations and stuff. I can barely fill out my forms right. Ask Elroy."

"He does fine," Mike said with his shy smile.

"Fine. Yeah. Those forms about kill me. Couldn't do that for the rest of my life. Okay, the room's back to normal.

Somehow we managed not to break anything." He strode out of the room.

The shriveled-up feeling didn't go away.

"Come on." Mellie touched her arm. "Georgie and the other girls are waiting for us."

"Yeah." She walked with Mellie and Louise into the foyer.

"The children had so much fun with the art projects." Georgie stepped forward, blue eyes dancing. "How was the soccer game?"

Mellie smoothed her hair and smiled. "The nuns will have a hard time settling our little soccer players down again."

The ladies headed outside, and Kay hung back to walk with Vera and Alice. "Did you have fun?"

"How could we not with Shirley Temple herself in charge?" Vera rolled her eyes and trotted down the outside steps.

Alice hummed "On the Good Ship Lollipop" and did a little tap-dance move.

A sour taste filled Kay's mouth. True, Georgie was cute and perky and curly-haired, but what had she ever done to hurt Vera and Alice? "She's just trying to do something nice for the orphans. Don't act so superior."

Vera's upper lip curled. "Aren't you the one acting superior right now?"

"Because she *is* superior." Alice batted her blonde eyelashes and pressed her hands together as if praying. "Forgive us, Sister Kay, for we have sinned."

The sour feeling dribbled into Kay's stomach.

Vera and Alice strolled on ahead of her, shaking their heads and laughing. They hadn't invited Kay to go dancing for over a month.

Because of her faith, Kay no longer bridged the two factions. She'd joined one.

Vera and Alice had it wrong. The last thing she felt was superior.

# 21

**Over the Mediterranean**
**August 15, 1944**

Despite the cool night air in the cockpit, sweat tickled Roger's upper lip. "You got it, Pettas?"

"Position Hoboken coming right up."

"Good." Hoboken was the last naval checkpoint before the French coast. Two thousand feet below, a ship guided the planes with Eureka radar beacons and Holophane infrared lights. Although Roger flew toward the end of the hundred-mile-long string of 396 C-47s, he was responsible for his flight of nine planes and for the twenty-eight British paratroopers in the cabin. He couldn't afford to stray off course.

"Thirty-nine miles to the IP." Mike Elroy swiped a hand over his forehead, then adjusted the throttles.

Thirty-nine miles to the French coast. Roger ran the numbers in his head—less than seventeen minutes until he crossed into enemy territory.

Today the Allies would open a fourth front against Nazi Germany. The forces from Normandy streamed east toward Paris, the Soviets marched west through Poland, the Allies in Italy pushed up through Pisa and Florence, and today the US

Seventh Army would land in Southern France near St. Tropez, not far east of the major ports of Toulon and Marseille.

Operation Dragoon.

"Passing over Hoboken," Pettas said on the interphone.

"Thanks." Roger flipped off the amber downward recognition lights meant to protect them from Allied naval fire, but now likely to draw enemy fire.

The amphibious landings were scheduled for 0800, with the first paratroopers jumping at 0330. The clock read 0441, and Roger was scheduled to make his drop at 0505.

He scanned the instruments and checked his grip on the control wheel.

*Lord, don't let me mess up.* The lead position was a great responsibility with dozens of lives at stake—and it was an honor. Just this week, Major Veerman had praised his improved reliability and said he might be able to put in a good word with his brother.

Roger's heels tapped a pattern on the floor. Finish his thousand-hour combat tour, fly stateside for the duration of the war, then audition for the Veerman band. A gift.

*"You have a gift."* Kay's words speared through his head, but she was wrong. He might have a way with kids, but teaching was entirely different.

He could still see her as she said it, lowering one end of a bench, hair falling into her face, a soft smile pushing up her pink cheeks.

Man alive! He never should have gone to the orphanage.

Roger tumbled his gum around in his mouth and fixed his mind on his instruments. Looked good. A crescent moon barely illuminated the scattered clouds above and the land ahead.

The land looked—he squinted—pale and puffy? Oh swell. The meteorologists had been concerned about fog over the drop zone. They got it right. "Fog," he said.

Elroy leaned forward as if six extra inches would improve visibility. "Oh great."

"Pettas, here's hoping your toys work. We've got fog over the shore."

"The Rebecca radar hasn't picked up a Eureka beam from the drop zone yet."

"It's early, isn't it?"

"Yeah." The radioman's voice crackled. "Hope Veerman's radar works."

Roger peered ahead at the dark planes in their V formations silhouetted against the pale gray fog ahead. In the lead of the serial of thirty-six planes, Veerman's navigator had an SCR-717 set which distinguished land from sea, so they'd know when they crossed the coast at the harbor at Agay.

Elroy fiddled with the oil mixture. "Sure hope the Pathfinder teams landed all right."

"Yeah." The first men to jump carried Eureka beacons, lighted panels, and other navigational aids to guide the rest of the planes to the drop zone.

Was it his imagination, or did the stream of planes bend slightly to the west? "Pettas, are we close to the IP?"

"Yeah. Dead reckoning says we should be there in two minutes."

Elroy nodded. "I'll count it down."

While Elroy ticked off the seconds that would determine whether twenty-eight men lived or died, Roger made sure everything was ready. Oil and fuel mixture, manifold pressure, heading, altitude, airspeed.

His gum turned stiff and flavorless, and he clamped it between his molars.

"I've got it!" Pettas shouted in the interphone. "I'm picking up the Eureka."

Roger lifted his earphone away from his head. "And we're picking you up—loud and clear."

"Sorry, Coop."

He grinned. "That means the Pathfinder team landed safely. Hallelujah."

Elroy tapped Roger's upper arm. "We should be at the IP."

"The boys ahead of us agree." Roger waggled his wings and then put his plane into a descending four-degree turn to the left, following the stream of troop carriers. Since the IP was only ten minutes from the drop zone, he rang the bailout bell.

He and Elroy worked together to ease back the throttles, their hands coordinating from months of practice. Had to get down to fifteen hundred feet and 110 mph.

Spots of light flashed in the fog below. The Nazis had discovered them.

Roger drew in a deep breath, reassured by the weight of the flak vest. First time the Twelfth Air Force had ever issued them to troop carrier crews.

A crack rocked the plane.

"Elroy, do a check. Pettas, how's our heading?" He had to keep them on target.

"Half a tick to the right," Pettas said.

Roger adjusted his course and eyed the fog below. The drop altitude of fifteen hundred feet was much higher than usual due to high terrain features, and he didn't want to meet one of those terrain features face to face.

Elroy shifted in his seat. "Everything's fine. Don't think we took any damage."

"Good." He definitely didn't want to meet the Nazis face to face. In the pocket of his trousers, he carried a clicker, issued to all the crewmen today to differentiate friend from foe if they crash-landed. The brass expected minimal losses since the Germans focused on the Allied threat in northern France. "Minimal" might make the generals happy, but not the man testing his clicker behind enemy lines.

"Two minutes," Pettas said.

Roger flipped on the red light and raised the flaps. Back in the cabin, the Brits would queue up, do a final check, and prepare themselves.

Those men would be using their clickers today. And their guns.

"Altitude fifteen hundred, airspeed one eleven." Elroy wiped one hand on his trousers.

Roger eased the left throttle back and the right throttle forward.

"Signal's nice and clear," Pettas said. "We're on course. Thirty seconds."

Ahead and below, parachutes blossomed and sank into the fog.

Roger stuffed his gum into his cheek and willed his muscles still and steady. He had to amount to something today. For the sake of the men in the back, he had to.

Pettas ticked off the seconds, and Roger's hand rose to the light switch on the overhead panel.

"And . . . now!"

His thumb froze in position. *Lord, please. Please let them live, let them do their job.*

He flipped the switch from red to green, flung the men from friendly to enemy territory, from safety to danger.

Slowly the plane lightened and lifted, emptied of twenty-eight men laden with gear.

"All right, Coop." Whitaker spoke on the interphone back by the cargo door. "They're out, every one of them. All clear."

"You know, I've never been to France." Roger chomped on his gum. "Who wants to do some sightseeing?"

Pettas cussed. "Are you joking? Get us home."

Elroy laughed. "Would Coop ever joke? Never."

Roger turned the wheel to the right and drew it closer to his chest. "We'll come back another day."

No joke this time. Once the Americans had secured the beachhead and built an airstrip, they'd fly in supplies.

Roger finished the 180-degree turn and adjusted his rate of climb so he'd reach the return altitude of five thousand feet.

What next? Running cargo from Rome to Toulon? How about medical air evacuation? Would the ladies of the 802nd stick to the Rome to Naples route, or would they join the men of the 64th TCG? Maybe he'd get his wish and he wouldn't fly with Kay anymore.

The flak vest pressed hard on his chest. Yeah, that had to be what he felt. He couldn't be disappointed, could he?

He checked his heading, airspeed, altitude—state of mind. Yeah, he was disappointed at the thought of not working with her, not seeing her.

More than anything, he wanted to spit out his stale gum. Shelby was right—he shouldn't have gone to the orphanage. Shell had declined. As a married man, he kept his distance from women to avoid temptation. A wise policy Roger had followed until lately.

But Kay and her friends had pleaded on behalf of the children. Did she know kids were his weak spot?

Worse, the kids softened him and stole away his defenses. And there was Kay, playful and sassy, bumping against him, making him want to grab her around the waist and stop the game with a good long kiss.

Roger rapped his hand against the control wheel.

The plane dipped, and Elroy shot him an alarmed look.

"Sorry. Forgot something." Yeah, forgot his brain, forgot his common sense, forgot all the lessons he'd learned the past decade.

He was tumbling into territory almost as dangerous as the land below. Not just for him, but for her. She already had to fight off one lecher recently. She shouldn't have to fight Roger off too. Or worse—what if she didn't fight?

Roger grimaced. Somehow he had to get some distance again. *Lord, please let us go our separate ways. I've done my bit. Now pull me off the assignment.*

The flak vest pressed hard.

# 22

*"Vive la France!"* Mellie Blake crossed the sod runway, arms outstretched as if to hug the country.

Louise Cox giggled and nudged Mellie. "You're just happy because Tom's here."

"Right here at Sisteron. Rudy's here too." Mellie's tone took on a teasing lilt for Louise's sake, then she turned to Georgie. "And I do believe a dark-haired pharmacist is in the area."

"He is." Georgie sighed. "France is already living up to its romantic reputation."

Too much romance for Kay, especially since Roger remained in Italy. And especially since Roger had no romantic interest in her. She fell back to walk with Vera, Alice, Lieutenant Lambert, and Capt. Frank Maxwell.

"Isn't the light exquisite?" Alice shielded her eyes and gazed around. "The Impressionists said Provence has the best light in the world, and I have to agree. I can't wait to get out my paints."

Kay didn't know anything about light or paint, but the scenery was gorgeous—the rolling Durance Valley, the mix of golden grasses and deep green trees, and the sudden white of limestone cliffs, one topped by an ancient citadel.

Vera shook back her shiny sable hair. "I'm looking forward to Paris. The way we're charging up the Rhône Valley, we might beat the Normandy forces there."

"They have too much of a head start on us." Captain Maxwell chuckled. "But never fear. You'll be shopping on the Champs-Élysées before long."

Kay rolled her eyes. The flight surgeon thought women only cared about shopping.

Lieutenant Lambert wore a satisfied smile. "That's why I chose these two flights for this assignment. The twelve of you ladies have been overseas the longest, and you deserve to be the first to fly from France."

"Thank you, Lieutenant. We appreciate it." Kay's smile felt as fake as her words. France didn't feel like a reward when Roger was in Italy, and when Lieutenant Lambert would return to 802nd headquarters in Lido once she got the French detachment settled in. How could Kay convince Lambert she was chief nurse material if Lambert never saw her?

Kay fanned the open neckline of her blouse for relief from the heat. Since April, her spiritual tumult had thrown her off her goal and driven a wedge among the nurses. But soon the war would end and she'd lose her opportunity. Somehow she had to bring the group together. Unity would be more important with the women isolated, away from the other two flights in the squadron.

Unity. That was the key. Kay hefted her barracks bag higher on her shoulder and smiled at her friends. "We'll have to work together like never before, like sisters. And here we are at Sisteron."

She almost gagged on the corn in her mouth. Corn? She'd never been corny in her life. Where on earth had that come from?

Alice glanced to the side as if embarrassed for Kay, and Vera's upper lip twitched, a look Kay had only seen directed at Mellie and Georgie before. And Lieutenant Lambert gave her a quizzical look.

Kay laughed it off. "On the other hand, maybe not. I don't even like my sisters."

Vera's lip stopped its twitch, and Lambert raised a slight smile.

"Where are we staying?" Changing the subject seemed wise. Kay waved her hand around at the scenery. "Where's our grand château?"

"I'm afraid it'll be the Château de Canvas de l'Armée." Lambert's brown eyes crinkled.

"Tents." Alice scrunched up her nose.

"Not just any tent," Kay said. "A tent in Provence with Impressionistic light filtering in."

"Romantic." Sarcasm colored Vera's voice, but she smiled. "So many happy memories under canvas."

"Many more to come." Captain Maxwell gave her a warm smile.

Kay fought a frown. For a married man, he was far too familiar with the nurses.

Then there was Roger, who acted more like a married man than Maxwell did. And people said women were hard to figure out.

---

**Istres/Le Tubé Airfield, France
September 8, 1944**

Two asphalt runways and one earthen runway. Nice. No wonder the Luftwaffe had liked the airfield. But now the Americans ran Istres/Le Tubé.

Roger carried his bag across the runway with the Indian

*dhol* drum strapped across his chest. He hadn't received a replacement drum from Chicago. The music store apologized—shortages of metal, you know, but if they received anything in stock, they'd send it. He was getting good on the *dhol* though. If only that impressed the big band leaders.

Major Veerman beckoned Roger and Elroy to the Army truck that would take them to officers' quarters.

Warm sea air filled Roger's lungs. The airfield lay close to the Mediterranean, not far west of Marseille. To the surprise of the Allied commanders, the French had taken both Marseille and Toulon before the end of August, and the US Seventh Army had already linked up with the Normandy forces over a hundred miles to the north. The Allies held a line from the English Channel to Switzerland and down to the Franco-Italian border. Maybe this war would be over by Christmas.

Roger would do his best to speed the process. In France he'd fly new routes and face new dangers and challenges. For the first time in his life, he felt prepared.

"Hey, Coop. Elroy." Bill Shelby waved and approached with his copilot, Irvin Bernstein. "Can't believe we're stationed in France."

"Swell, isn't it?" Roger tossed his bag into the back of the truck and climbed in.

"Do you know . . . has anyone heard if the gals are here?" Mike Elroy hoisted himself up over the tailgate, but his voice sounded stiff.

Roger plunked down onto the bench seat, and a brotherly urge rose in his chest. The poor man needed help talking to women and asking them out. However, Roger's bad experience would only lead to bad advice.

"Sure thing." Bernstein shoved his barracks bag under his seat. "Heard some of the gals of the 807th are up at Le Luc, and the gals of the 802nd arrived here at Istres a few days ago. Good news for you, Playboy Elroy."

Mike's cheeks flamed. "I've never . . . no one's ever . . ."

When the men broke down in good-natured laughter, Mike laughed too and exchanged shoulder slugs with Bernie.

Roger patted out a quiet rhythm on both drumheads of the *dhol*. The gals of the 802nd were here at Istres. He was afraid of that. No matter where in France Kay was stationed, he'd fly with her. But to be quartered at the same base, sharing a mess, church services, all that?

"Oh boy," he muttered and shifted his tempo.

The truck rumbled across the field and down a road running east. The wind cooled Roger's face, ruffled his hair, and mellowed his beat. Kay or no Kay, this was a first-rate location. The airfield lay on a large coastal plain. Far inland, limestone ridges jutted up.

They turned into town. The streets were lined with two-storied homes, plastered in shades of tan or yellow, with colorful shutters and red tile roofs.

The truck eased onto a side street and filled it from curb to curb. A staircase ran up the exterior of one of the houses, and four ladies sat on the stairs, top to bottom.

Roger's heart lurched in his chest, throwing off his rhythm.

Kay Jobson sat on the bottom step, hair glowing in the sunshine. She raised one hand to shield her eyes, then grinned and waved.

His heartbeat gave a whole new meaning to syncopation.

He returned the smile and the wave. At least the rest of the boys were whooping and waving, so he didn't stand out.

The truck stopped. Veerman pointed to the house across the road. "That's your home, gentlemen."

Right across the road from Kay.

Not good.

He grabbed his barracks bag and hopped out of the truck.

Now Kay stood at the cyclone fence at the curb, not even

four feet away, leaning her elbows on a cement post. "Hi, Roger. Boy, it's good to see you fellows."

"Good to see you too." Her eyes sparkled, her mouth . . . oh, her mouth.

He yanked his gaze back to her eyes.

Thank goodness she was studying his drum and missed that slip. "Is this the drum the little boy gave you in India?"

"Yeah. It's called a *dhol*."

"I'd love to hear you play it. Now we're stationed at the same base. Maybe someday . . ." She tucked her lower lip between her teeth, and her eyebrows clumped together.

He had to reassure her. "Yeah. Maybe someday. Maybe even now." He slapped out a lively beat.

His reward was the prettiest smile he'd ever seen. "That's swell."

So was she. Roger backed up and motioned over his shoulder with his thumb. "Better get settled in. See you around."

"See you." As she walked away, the motion of her hips inspired an even livelier beat.

With a huff of breath, Roger spun away and headed to his new home. The Bible promised the Lord would never tempt a man, so what was going on here?

Major Veerman opened the blue door of the house. "Kitchen and living room downstairs. The French couple who own this place will reside down here. Three rooms upstairs, four of you to a room. You numbskulls know the drill. No late hours, give them their privacy, ask for nothing, accept anything offered with grace. Be kind, respectful, and quiet." He glanced at Roger's drum.

"Only for outside use, sir. Far from the house." He gave his CO his most serious look and sharpest salute.

Veerman headed up a steep, narrow staircase. "Never had a complaint yet."

"Except from Klein," Shell murmured.

Thank goodness Grant Klein came to Istres earlier today. He'd be quartered in another house.

Roger tried not to bump against the wall along the staircase. Uneven steps, chipped tiles, and no banister. He wouldn't want to navigate the stairwell until he was fully awake each morning.

At the top of the stairs, Roger followed Elroy, Bernie, and Shelby into one of the rooms. He shoved open blue shutters, and sunshine and a breeze filled the room. The men's four cots didn't leave much standing room, but they didn't need much anyway. Sure beat a tent with a mud floor.

But why did they pick the room that faced the road? That faced Kay's house? That looked down on the gorgeous nurse lounging on the steps, long legs stretched in front of her, laughing at something Mellie said?

Roger marched across the room and tossed his bag onto the cot farthest from the window.

Elroy set down his bag too and backed out of the room. "Say, fellows, I think I'll check out the neighborhood."

"Me too." Bernie slugged Elroy in the shoulder again. "Let's see if the French mademoiselles are everything they're cracked up to be."

The two men thumped down the stairs.

Roger chuckled and set down the *dhol*. "Elroy's going to end up with a girlfriend whether he wants one or not."

"What about you?" Shell laid his bedroll on the cot. "Changed your mind?"

The contents of Roger's barracks bag became fascinating. "Changed my mind?"

"About dating? Women? Kay Jobson?"

He grimaced at his shaving kit and set it next to his cot. "Nah. You know where I stand."

"Sure. Only two reasons to date—for fun or for marriage, and you're not looking for either."

"No change there." Fun led to steamy temptation. And marriage? Well, no woman should have to put up with a husband who lived on the road.

"Then what's going on with Kay?"

"Nothing. Just friends."

"You know my opinion. If you want to avoid romance, avoid friendship."

"No choice this time. Kind of fell into the friendship." More like God shoved him. "But I won't fall into temptation."

"Why not? You find her unattractive?"

Unattractive? Lt. Kay Jobson was about the best package of womanhood ever—mind, soul, body, and spirit. Roger kicked his barracks bag under his bed. He'd set out his stuff later.

"Yeah. I thought so." The cot squeaked under Shell's slight weight.

"I'll be fine."

"Sure. But what about her?"

"Her?"

Against his summer sunburn, Shell's eyes seemed lighter, more probing. "So you have masterful control of your emotions. Great. But what about her?"

Kay's laughter floated up through the open window, tingling in his ears.

Roger swallowed hard. "She's changed. She's not the same woman. She won't throw herself at me."

"Of course not. Who would?"

"See? What'd I tell you? Nothing to worry about."

"That wasn't what I meant. I meant, what about her heart?"

"Her heart?"

"Yeah. She has one, you oaf." Shell lay back on the cot, hands laced behind his head.

"I know that." Roger poked his barracks bag with his toe, poked harder.

"What if she falls for you? Does she know you've chosen the life of a monk?"

"Sure. Sure, she knows. I told her." His stomach folded in on itself.

Once. He'd told her once. At the Orange Club a good six months earlier, he'd told her he didn't date and his reasons why.

Everything had changed since then. Kay had changed. Even Roger had changed. But his reasons not to fall in love, not to let a woman fall in love with him—those hadn't changed and never would.

His pulse thumped out the truth. It might be too late.

# 23

With six litter patients on board the C-47, Kay knelt in the cargo doorway to admit the ambulatory patients. Some walked on their own, some hobbled on crutches, and some were assisted by medics.

The first man climbed the ladder with a crooked grin on his freckled face. "Morning, ma'am."

"Good morning." Kay checked his emergency medical tag against her flight manifest. Pvt. Elwood Scott lost most of his right hand to a German bullet in the fighting for Meximeux.

"Shame to go home when we're knocking on Hitler's front door. I wanted to be the man to carry Old Glory into Berlin."

Kay smiled into his eager blue eyes. "But look how far you came. All the way up to the Swiss border." The American and French armies had driven so far, so fast, the US mobile hospitals had to leapfrog each other to keep up.

The 802nd and 807th flew the sick and wounded to Istres, and then to Rome or Naples, sometimes directly from the front to Italy.

"Look." Private Scott held up the bandaged stump of his

hand. "Got me a swell war wound to show off. I'm left-handed, so it don't matter."

If only all patients had Scott's cheerful attitude. Kay ushered him inside and addressed her next patient, whose dark eyes peered from a mask of gauze bandages. "How are you this morning?"

"Read the tag." He flicked the piece of pasteboard pinned to his bathrobe.

The chill of his voice felt like a slap, but she smiled and read the tag. Oh bother, how could she forget? Pvt. Leonard Hayes, multiple facial injuries from a grenade burst—and he'd lost his hearing. The physician said he was touchy about it, not that he could be blamed.

Kay wrestled a notepad from her trouser pocket and scribbled a note on it: "I'm nurse Lt. Jobson. Just ask if you need food, water, medicine—anything."

He read the note and thrust it back at her. "I don't need this. I can talk fine."

All right then. So if she talked to him, he was annoyed. If she wrote a note, he was annoyed. What about pantomime? The poor man might explode. Nevertheless, she smiled and beckoned him up the ladder.

Kay checked in the remaining ten patients. Their attitudes varied as widely as their injuries. Some were relieved to be done with the war, some depressed, some drained, some stoic, and some bore up with grace.

On the 150-mile flight to Istres, Kay's goal was to make each man a bit happier than when he boarded. Except Private Scott, perhaps. The man was plenty happy already.

Kay straightened to standing, rolled her shoulders, and kicked out kinks in her legs.

Five other C-47s were loading patients at Ambérieu today, the first evac flights out of the brand-new airfield. About a hundred feet away, Roger inspected his plane with a clipboard in hand.

Kay's heart did an odd lurch. Something about his relaxed but powerful gait, the tilt of his head, the way he held his pen.

She'd never fallen for a man like this. Why, she'd never let herself fall for a man at all. Men had come in handy for fun and amusement and the sheer physical pleasure of a good kiss. Other than that, they were objects to control. By dating half a dozen men at a time and cutting them off when they got too serious, she'd avoided entanglement.

Now she was entangled. In a one-sided way.

Kay sighed and turned back into the stuffy plane before Roger could catch her mooning over him. If only she were on his plane, but Georgie had the privilege today.

Perhaps now things would change. Georgie and Mellie talked about God orchestrating events, and being stationed with Roger Cooper sure felt like heavenly orchestration.

They'd be together not just on flights but in day-to-day life. Last night while Kay lay falling asleep, the sound of his deep voice drifted across the road to her, muffled by distance but undeniably his. Oh, the intimacy of it.

Kay smiled and made sure her patients were secured for the flight. Surely the Lord wouldn't mind a little help with his orchestration.

---

### Istres/Le Tubé Airfield

"Everything looks good." Roger gave the wheel chock an extra kick. After two round-trip flights between Ambérieu and Istres, he was finished, with plenty of day remaining, and he planned to spend it drumming. He'd find a spot down by the lagoon, the one called Étang de l'Olivier, and drum to the beat of the *cigales*, the French cicadas.

"Hi, Kay!" Mike Elroy said. "Hi, Georgie."

Roger's head jerked up. The two nurses strolled down the runway, straight to him.

"Hi, fellas!" Kay waved. "Do you have the rest of the day off too?"

"Yeah. Swell, isn't it?" Roger's plans evaporated in the warmth of her smile.

"It is." Georgie tipped her head to the side. "You gentlemen are cordially invited to a musical evening."

Roger crossed his arms. "Why do I have a feeling I'm meant to be entertainment rather than a guest?"

"Because you are." Kay winked at him. "Bernie has his clarinet, Marino has a harmonica, and Mellie and Georgie have voices to die for."

"I'm not a bad singer either." Elroy's round face reddened.

"Good," Kay said. "We can use a strong manly voice, and Coop sings like a little girl."

He barked out a laugh. "Says who?"

"Just bring the drum, flyboy."

Elroy stepped forward. "Where? When?"

Georgie pointed to the east. "We thought we'd go down by the lake so we don't bother the locals, right after dinner."

"Sounds great." Roger's original plan, but better, with more instruments, with singing . . . with Kay Jobson watching him, admiring him, snuggling close in the moonlight.

Oh boy, he was in big fat trouble.

"See you then." The girls walked away.

"Wait up, ladies. I'm going that way." Mike jogged to catch up. "Coming, Coop?"

"Nah, I've got to turn in my forms." Roger darkened one of the numbers on his clipboard to look busy. He headed down the runway toward the tent used for HQ, and he pulled his latest letter from Lou out of the inside pocket of his flight jacket.

Lou had married a British girl from a village near his fighter base. He'd finished his combat tour and married her once he got assigned to a desk job and knew he wouldn't be shot down in flames by the Luftwaffe.

Roger read over the part in the middle, the part he couldn't grasp.

> I'm glad you decided to trust this gal, Kay. She went through the same transformation you did. You both grabbed onto Jesus and let him thoroughly change you.
>
> I'd like to see you trust yourself too. You were smart to avoid women in the past, but you've grown. You're stronger and wiser, and the Lord will help you handle temptation.
>
> Maybe I'm wrong—I've never met Kay or seen the two of you together—but it sounds like the Lord's given you a gift.

Roger folded the letter and stuffed it back inside his jacket. Marriage must have addled Lou's mind.

A gift? A gift of love, of a good woman in his life, of marriage and family?

The Lord knew better than to waste a gift like that on him. God had already given him a girl, and Roger had ruined her. God had already given him a baby, and the baby was dead.

Roger's throat thickened, and he picked up his pace, his shoes slapping the asphalt. The Lord loved Kay too much to let Roger ruin her, and Roger . . . he cared too much too.

"Hey! Cooper!" Grant Klein's voice pummeled him from behind.

What now? Roger's shoulders sagged, and he turned around. "Yeah?"

The pilot marched up to Roger, his tie knotted perfectly. "You told me nothing was going on with you and Kay."

"That's right." He'd make sure of it.

"Liar."

His eyes flopped shut. "I'm a lot of things, but a liar isn't one of them."

"More lies." Klein poked Roger in the chest. "Every time I turn around, I see you two together. I see the way you look at each other. Everyone knows you're sleeping together."

A dozen arguments and wisecracks pinged through his head, and he snatched the closest one. "What's the matter, Klein? Jealous 'cause she wouldn't sleep with you?"

Klein's face darkened to a shade the locals would be proud to see in one of their wines. His hand rolled into a fist. "Why you—I ought to—"

"Just a joke." Roger stepped back and flung up both hands, clipboard in his grip. Smashing that pretty-boy face might feel good for a moment, but a fight on his record would destroy his big band dreams. "I haven't laid a hand on the dame."

"What's going on here?"

Roger spun to his left and lowered his hands.

Major Veerman strode to them. "Lieutenant Klein, do you have a reason to pick a fight with Lieutenant Cooper?"

Klein's black eyebrows shot up, and he tugged his flight jacket straight. "I wasn't picking a fight, sir. Unlike some people, I follow regulations."

Since when was it against regulations to talk to a girl? Roger mashed his tongue between his molars to keep the words inside.

Veerman's gaze darted back and forth between the men and then settled on Klein. "No woman is worth it."

"Sir! That wasn't—"

"Enough. You're dismissed, Klein. Go cool off."

Klein fiddled with the hem of his jacket, and his face twitched. "Yes, sir."

Every bit of control Roger possessed went into freezing his facial muscles. For once, Klein had been caught acting like a ninny, and for once, Roger hadn't given in to his baser instincts.

Except the one comment. But boy, did it feel good.

Roger slipped his paperwork off the clipboard. "My forms, sir."

"Thank you." He studied Roger. "I appreciate how you kept your temper there."

He shrugged. "Yeah. Well . . ."

"Well, I know Klein can be a jerk. Remember, he used to dismiss you as a lazy goof-off, but you've changed. Now you're one of my best pilots, and he's jealous. And jealous men don't always act rationally."

"Yeah." Roger chuckled and rubbed the back of his neck.

"Now he has more to be jealous about. A girl?"

Roger grimaced. "Only in his imagination. I'm just friends with her."

Veerman leaned closer as if ferreting out the truth. "Let me repeat what I said to Klein. No woman is worth it."

"Yes, sir." But Veerman was wrong. Kay Jobson was worth it.

# 24

**Marseille, France**
**October 5, 1944**

The woman waved a fish in Kay's face, then slapped it down in the water-filled tray, sending up briny droplets.

Kay yelped and sprang back. So did the other five nurses, and then they broke down laughing. "Awful squeamish for nurses, aren't we?" Kay said.

"If it were blood, you wouldn't even have blinked." From behind, Roger handed her a handkerchief.

"Thanks." She wiped a drop from her cheek.

On Marseille's waterfront, at the foot of the Vieux Port, fishmongers sold their wares from table-height wooden trays. All the fishmongers were women, their hair tied back under dark scarves.

Mellie bartered in French, and Kay's mouth watered at the thought of fresh fish for dinner. Knowing Mellie, she'd buy a bushel for their French host family as well.

Louise Cox tapped Mellie on the shoulder. "Maybe we should buy the fish at the end of the day so we don't have to carry it around with us."

"That's what I'm trying to tell her." Mellie returned to her French, pointing at her wristwatch.

Meanwhile, Vera, Alice, and Captain Maxwell drifted away from the group and headed along the waterfront.

Bother. Kay wanted to keep the group together. She should catch up, but she disliked being alone with the three of them. Captain Maxwell was a married man, and although Vera and Alice insisted friendliness was perfectly acceptable, Kay didn't want people to get the wrong idea about her. She might have been a flirt, but she'd never been a home wrecker.

"Come on, Kay." Roger tipped his head toward the drifters. "We shouldn't let them get too far ahead. The others will catch up."

"I'm almost done." Mellie shot them an apologetic look.

"Say, Elroy . . ." Roger pointed with his thumb to Mellie.

"Sure. I'll chaperone."

Kay's heart went into happy palpitations. Time alone with Roger. "Thanks, Mike."

He blushed and smiled. Poor Mike had a bad crush on Kay, but he seemed to know her heart swayed toward Roger alone.

The past few weeks in France had been wonderful—seeing Roger at meals, in flight, in church, and best of all, the musical evenings by the lagoon. She loved to sit by him as he drummed, marveling at his intensity, joy, and energy.

"How are things going, fish-face?"

"Fish-face!" She backhanded Roger in the arm and marched down the walkway along the docks and toward the ocean.

His laughter caught up to her, and then his footsteps, and then his glorious, mischievous grin. "What's the matter? Got your pretty new uniform all dirty?"

She resisted the impulse to glance down at her new olive drab uniform with its smart waist-length jacket, knee-length skirt, and khaki shirt and tie. She'd only prove him right. "I'm not a fussy kind of dame, remember?"

"True." He stuffed his hands in the pockets of his leather

flight jacket. "How are things going? You got the whole gang here today, thanks to lousy flying weather."

Kay glanced up to the thick overcast, glad she had her umbrella and coat. "The worst thing about being a flight nurse is we only get days off when the weather's bad."

"Lots of that lately. At this rate, I'll never get my thousand hours."

"You're close, aren't you?" The words felt heavier than the clouds.

"Depending on the weather, one or two months. But you know how it is. Bert Marino's already logged his hours, and they still haven't sent him home. I'm here as long as the brass wants."

Kay bit back the word *good* on her tongue. "Then you'll go stateside, fly there?"

"Yeah, and I think Veerman will give me a recommendation for his brother's band. Who'd have guessed it?"

"I would. You're a first-rate pilot."

His brown eyes turned to her, grateful but hesitant. "Thanks."

With most men, she'd wrap her arms around his waist and burrow a kiss onto that square jaw. But with Roger, she resigned herself to hugging the overcoat draped over her arm.

He stepped around a stack of crates by the dock. "'Course, even if I get an audition, even if I pass the audition, I wouldn't be able to join the band till after the war. At least when I'm based stateside, I'll be able to practice, get back up to speed."

"That'll be good." Where would he be stationed? Unlikely he'd be anywhere near the School of Air Evacuation.

"And you." He tapped the umbrella hanging over her arm. He always had to touch something, although he never touched her. "Bet you'll be back in Italy soon."

"I've heard the rumors." With the Seventh Army so far north, flying the wounded to Italy wasted time and fuel. It made more sense for the Medical Air Evacuation Squadrons based in England to take over. "I wish I had more time here. I'd hoped to impress Lambert with a unified flight when I returned to Rome, but I'm no closer now than before."

"I can see." He gazed behind him, where the rest of the nurses lagged. "What's the big deal? You work together, don't you? Why does Lambert care if you're not all best friends?"

"We don't always work together. That's the problem." She sighed and gazed over the Liberty cargo ships to Notre-Dame de la Garde on the hill across the port. "They don't like each other, and nothing I do or say makes a difference."

"You need a real good crisis to bring you together."

Kay nudged him with her shoulder. "Wish bad things on us, why don't you?"

"All right." He stopped and raised his hands over her head like an old-time prophet. "May you be cursed with a shortage of lipstick and face powder."

"Oh, you're funny. How about I call down a breaking of the drumsticks?"

Roger clutched his chest. Sure enough, two drumsticks clicked together inside his jacket. "Hey, I'm not the one who needs a crisis. You are."

She gave him a saucy tilt of her head and strolled away. "No, I need a pilot who isn't a smart aleck."

"Boring." He fell in beside her. "Why would you want that?"

She didn't. She wanted him. She wanted him as more than a friend, wanted his thick arms around her, wanted his lips on hers, wanted to know if his hair was silky or coarse. For the first time in her life, she didn't want just *any* man, but *this* man.

But this man didn't date, a cruel situation. With his past she understood why he didn't want to date only for fun, but what did he have against marriage? And here he was making her think of marriage.

Kay stepped in front of him, so he had to stop and look down at her. She gave him her best mock glare. "You are a pest."

"Why, thank you, ma'am," he said in a Western accent, tipping the bill of his service cap. "Makes me right proud."

Made her want to pull him down into a kiss so long and luscious he'd propose on the spot.

"Kay! Kay! Look what we found," Georgie called.

She tore her gaze from Roger and peeked around his solid form. "What?"

The three nurses dashed up. Georgie flourished a piece of lace. "Isn't this perfect for Mellie's wedding? We were wondering what to use for a veil. Didn't you see the stall? Right down there. We didn't have to look twice, didn't even barter, just bought it on the spot."

"It's beautiful." Kay fingered the creamy lace, which would be gorgeous with Mellie's darker complexion.

The four ladies huddled together, but Roger and Mike dropped back and faced the docks, pointing at the cargo ships and cranes and such. Inside, Kay winced, but on the outside, she gushed over the fabric.

Georgie draped the lace over Mellie's black hair. "I'm almost done with the dress. It isn't easy working with odds and ends, but it'll be done in time."

Mellie sighed, her eyes dreamy, and she patted the impromptu veil. "Next time Tom can get a forty-eight-hour leave, but he's so busy building and repairing airfields. And who knows if I'll still be in France when he gets his leave?"

"No worrying allowed." Louise fluffed out the lace around Mellie's shoulders. "You'll be a bride by the end of 1944."

"Thank you." Mellie pulled off the veil, folded it, and wrapped it up with brown paper.

Kay glanced ahead, where Vera's group stood by one of the two forts flanking the harbor entrance. "We should catch up."

The ladies continued on their way, with Roger and Mike trailing behind. Too far behind.

Louise sidled up to Georgie. "How was your Remain Overnight in Luxeuil? Awfully close to the 93rd Evacuation Hospital in Plombières, isn't it?"

"You know it is." Georgie colored prettily. "Hutch and I had a real nice visit. He took me stargazing."

Kay propped her umbrella on her shoulder. "Why do I have a feeling you weren't gazing at stars?"

Georgie clucked her tongue. "Were too! I have proof."

"Proof?" the ladies asked in unison.

She pressed her fingers to her breastbone. "Well . . . he showed me the constellation Lyra and pointed out something in his telescope. He asked, 'What do you see?' I had to peer hard because it was fuzzy, then I said, 'It looks like a ring.' 'It's the Ring Nebula,' he said. Then he asked . . . he asked if I was seeing rings. And he gave me this." She reached under her collar and pulled on a gold chain.

A ring with a cluster of little diamonds dangled from the chain.

Kay gasped, and Mellie and Louise squealed.

"You're engaged?" Louise cried.

"Shh!" Georgie pressed a finger to her lips. "You know we have to keep it a secret, and we can't get married until after the war unless God miraculously bestows an officer's commission on him, but he wanted to ask and make it official."

Mellie squeezed Georgie's shoulders. "You're officially happy, that's for sure."

"I'm officially ecstatic." Georgie rolled her eyes heavenward. "Now we just have to work on Kay."

"Me?" Her chest contracted, and she stopped in her tracks.

"Yes, you." Louise grabbed Kay's arm and pulled her forward. "How are things with Roger?"

Her face tingled as all the blood drained. She had never

told anyone about her crush. "I don't know what you're talk-ing about."

The three nurses laughed harder than they had at the Ab-bott and Costello movie at the airfield the week before. Kay did a quick check over her shoulder. Thank goodness Roger and Mike walked almost a hundred feet behind them, and the mistral wind from the north would blow the ladies' con-versation away from the men.

"Come on, Kay." Georgie's face shone with laughter. "Everyone knows you two are crazy about each other. When we're down at the lagoon, it's like he's playing just for you, and you're gaga over him."

Kay swung back her hair and picked up her pace. Fort Saint-Jean loomed before her, guarding the harbor with mas-sive stone walls. "You don't know what you're talking about."

"Has he asked you out yet?" Louise asked.

"He won't. He isn't interested."

"Does, he know you're interested?" Mellie's voice came out gentle and compassionate.

Kay wrinkled her nose. A crack rumbled through her stone wall. "I'm not—"

"Don't lie." Georgie scooted up and looped her arm around Kay's. "You glow when he's around. I've never seen you like this before."

Way too many emotions churned in Kay's chest. The im-pulse to lie and save face swam to the top, but what good would it do? They already knew the truth. She breathed out all the emotions until only honesty remained. "I've never felt like this before."

"All right, ladies. Time to do some thinking." Georgie led the way up the hill to the north. The Germans had razed this section of Marseille almost two years earlier to flush out French partisans, leaving only a few churches and historic buildings.

In the past Kay had a wide repertoire of flirtatious ways, but now her options had been razed too. "How can I let him know I'm interested? He didn't like me at all when I was a flirt. If I so much as bat my eyelashes at him, he'll run for the Alps."

"Hmm." Georgie scrunched up her mouth, then nodded. "You need to titrate to effect."

Kay laughed at the nursing reference. "Titrate?"

"Think about it. You have a patient in pain, but he has a head injury so you're worried about sedation. You give him a tiny dose of morphine, monitor him. How's the pain? Is he feeling woozy? You give him a little more, monitor again. Then you stop when he's feeling fine but before he falls unconscious."

Kay leveled her gaze at her friend. "So you want me to flirt with Roger until I knock him out."

"Yes!" Georgie thrust a finger high. "Knock him out."

Kay had to smile even as she shook her head. Flirtation titration. It might work.

At the top of the rise stood an ancient little church of pink limestone. Mellie looked at a map. "Eglise Saint Laurent, from the twelfth century. My goodness. Isn't it darling?"

"It is." Kay pressed her hand to the cool, rough stone that had stood for eight hundred years. How many people had come here through the centuries, praying for guidance? How many couples had been wed?

Kay added a prayer for guidance with the man she loved. *Lord, you knew I loved him before I knew it myself. Show me what to do. I don't know how much longer we have together here in France, if we'll see each other when we return to Italy, and what about when we both go stateside?*

Kay shuddered, and her fingers pressed into the stone. *I should ask if you even want us together, shouldn't I? If you do, please help me.*

"Those are called raindrops, kid." His voice, right behind her.

She opened her eyes. Yes, raindrops glistened on her hand and made dark spots on the olive drab of her new uniform sleeve. She faced him, looking up into his sparkling brown eyes.

"And this is an umbrella." He lifted it off her arm and opened it over her head. "Unlike the stupid menfolk who didn't bring umbrellas, you don't have to get wet."

Titrate to effect. Kay smiled, not coy, just sweet. "We could share."

His forehead rippled, then relaxed. "Sure."

She stepped close to his side so the umbrella arched over both their heads, and they strolled up the road. Rain tapped out a sweet melody.

# 25

**Istres/Le Tubé Airfield**
**October 18, 1944**

Major Veerman leaned over the briefing map spread on the table. "Weather's dicey. I won't make any man fly who doesn't want to."

Roger crossed his arms. The route was treacherous, flying low under the clouds over mountainous terrain. Although they didn't have radio navigational aids, Roger could fly to Luxeuil and back blindfolded. He knew every landmark—each hilltop castle, each bend in the river, each crossroads town. "I'll go, sir."

Grant Klein snorted. "You just want to run up your hours and get out of here."

"Who doesn't?" Shell asked.

Roger turned to Klein. "I want to go because our boys are up there in the Vosges Mountains in the rain and mud, getting shot up by the Germans, and they're low on ammo and gasoline and food and medical supplies."

Veerman clapped Roger on the back. "Thanks, Cooper. Knew I could count on you."

Probably the first time in his life Roger had heard that, and it felt good.

He collected the forms he'd need for the flight, stashed them in his kit bag, and headed out of the house.

Half a dozen children waited outside, climbing the cyclone fencing, their thin little shoes stuck in the holes. "Monsieur Ro-zhay!" they called.

"Hiya, kids." He grinned and joined them on the street.

The fence jangled as a dozen feet pulled free and jumped to the ground. The children hung on his arms and legs and chattered in French embellished with American slang words. He made exaggerated grunting noises and lumbered down the street, shedding giggling children with each step.

The languages changed, the clothing and customs, but all around the world, kids were kids.

The ringleader, a ten-year-old boy named Philippe, tugged on Roger's sleeve. "Drum, *sil vous plait?*"

"*Non. Désolé.* Today I fly." He stuck his arms out like an airplane and made a puttering sound.

Half a dozen frowns, half a dozen droopy heads.

Roger squatted down and ripped six pages from the back of his logbook. With his hours almost up, he wouldn't need those pages anyway. "I'm a pilot." He pulled aside his jacket collar and pointed to the silver wings over his breast pocket. "Pilot."

"*Oui, pilote.*" Angelique, Philippe's little sister, moved her hands like on a steering wheel.

Roger handed each child a piece of paper. "Angelique is *pilote* too. Philippe is *pilote.* Paper airplane." He folded the last piece of paper.

"*Oui, oui.*" Philippe folded his paper without watching Roger and called out instructions to his friends.

Roger handed his paper airplane to the tiniest child. "For you, Jean-Paul."

"*Merci*, Monsieur Ro-zhay."

"*Merci! Bon voyage!*" The children smiled and waved.

Roger waved back and jogged to the end of the side street, where the men from his squadron waited in the open back of an Army truck. As soon as he climbed in and sat, the truck rumbled down the street.

Roger unwrapped a stick of gum and stuck it in his mouth. "Guess we're all braving the weather today." Since two squadrons of the 64th Troop Carrier Group had been sent back to Italy, the two remaining squadrons shouldered more work. In lousy weather.

"Not Klein." Bert Marino slouched back on the bench. "Man's a big fat chicken."

Murmurs of agreement circled the truck, but Roger refused to join in. Klein had been a strutting rooster back when they flew in North Africa and Sicily. But when he crashed into Roger's parked plane and killed Clint Peters and Rose Danilovich, the rooster turned chicken.

Roger propped his elbows behind him on the side of the truck. Before the crash, Klein had been the top pilot and walked around with Kay Jobson on his arm. Now Roger had passed him as a pilot. He had Kay's heart as well.

His hands balled up. Despite his intentions, it had happened. Kay had fallen for him. He saw it in her eyes and heard it in her voice. He'd fallen hard for her too.

The truck turned onto the road to the airfield, away from the lagoon. How could he turn down her invitations? Music, fun, friends. Their conversations ranged from playful joking to serious discussions. The more time he spent with her, the more time he wanted to spend with her.

Their friendship had sliced deep through his defenses, and now the breach had widened into love. How long until she realized she'd broken through and came storming in?

The truck lurched to a stop on the airfield, and Roger climbed out with the other men. He walked to his plane at a fast clip, leaving Elroy behind so he could think things through.

What would happen if Kay stormed his heart? Disaster.

He could ruin her like he'd ruined his girlfriend in high school. He couldn't even resist Kay's invitations for sightseeing excursions and evenings by the lagoon. How could he resist if he held her in his arms? He'd never had any self-control.

He'd have to marry her right away, but that would turn a short-term disaster into a lifelong disaster. Veerman was sure to give him the recommendation, and with practice, he stood a chance of passing an audition—if not with the Veerman band, then some other. He'd be on the road, city to city, hotel to hotel. Sure, it'd be fun for a year or two. Until kids came along. He couldn't haul a family around. What about school? Church? Kids needed stability. Wives needed stability. So husbands needed to have a stable job, like a farmer.

Or a teacher?

Roger stopped by his plane and examined its familiar lines and the unfamiliar idea. He'd never allowed himself to examine it for long, always shoved it aside.

What if he could become a teacher? If he was reliable enough for Veerman, maybe he was reliable enough to teach. Sure, he chafed at routines and regulations, but he followed them now. And it didn't kill him. He had a purpose—at first to impress Veerman, but now because he saw the importance of documenting his work so others could do their work.

Perhaps he could follow the rules and regulations the teaching profession required. He'd have a good purpose—for the children. For Kay.

Vertigo struck. He planted his hand on the fuselage to regain equilibrium. Kay would make anything worthwhile. When he was with her, he didn't feel like a no-account. He felt like the kind of man who could support a wife.

But could he? Above him, scattered clouds tumbled with the wind. "Lord, what do you want me to do? You got me into this mess. Help me out of it."

Footsteps approached, the sound of gravel skittering on asphalt.

Roger turned around.

Mike Elroy patted the tail of the plane like a dad patting a baby's bottom. "You took off, Coop. In a hurry?"

"Yeah." Roger pulled his clipboard from his bag. "As Veerman said, weather's dicey."

"Good thing we're not flying air evac today. Still . . ."

Roger recognized the wistful tone of a man enamored. "Why? Got your eye on one of the flight nurses?"

He flushed. "Ah, she's out of my league. Doesn't even know I exist."

Kay was nice to Mike. Thank goodness it wasn't her. The flood of relief came as a shock.

But who was it? Mike was too good a man to fall for a woman with a boyfriend. Who was left? Vera Viviani sure was a looker and she was single, but she was haughty.

Roger poked his clipboard at his copilot's chest. "A man like you deserves better than a dame who won't acknowledge you. Look around. Plenty of nice girls."

A twitch of a smile, but a strained one. "Yeah, thanks."

They started the preflight inspection, and a truck pulled up, loaded with five-gallon jerricans of gasoline for the Seventh Army front.

Roger studied Mike as they did their inspection. A good-looking fellow in a boyish way, seemed younger than his thirty-one years. Smart, steady, kind. A banker. The sort of man who'd make something of his life and never doubt he could be a good husband, a good provider.

The sort of man Kay Jobson should fall for.

# 26

Another memorial service.

Kay sat with her friends in a church in Istres, waiting for the service to start, the walls cold and gray and stony, the organ blasting somber tones. The day before, a C-47 from Roger's squadron had crashed in a storm on a flight from Luxeuil, killing the entire crew, flight nurse Lt. Aleda Lutz, a medical technician, and over a dozen patients.

The church was packed with personnel from the 802nd Medical Air Evacuation Squadron and the 64th Troop Carrier Group, as well as locals who considered the Americans "their" boys and girls.

Kay patted her shoulder bag, over and over. Why did her lap feel empty?

Her Bible. She didn't have her Bible.

She sprang from her seat.

Georgie looked up to her with red-rimmed eyes. "Are you all right?" she whispered.

Kay leaned down to whisper back. "I forgot my Bible."

"We can share."

"No." On a day like this, nothing but her own Bible would

do. She lowered her head on her way down the aisle, as if that would make her less obtrusive.

A flicker of motion to her left.

Roger sat on the aisle and waved low. "You okay?"

She nodded, a lie. He didn't look okay either, pale and drawn. Had he been close to the flight crew, or was he reliving Clint Peters's death, just over a year earlier? "Forgot my Bible."

He lifted a wan smile. "I can give you another one."

What would she do without him and his sweet friendship? "That's all right." She gave his shoulder a squeeze on her way out.

The organ quieted, and the chaplain approached the pulpit. Oh dear. She'd miss some of the service and make a disturbance when she returned, but it didn't matter. She needed her Bible.

Everyone mourned. Some had gotten drunk last night. Many cried. Some shared stories. All came to the memorial service to pay their respects. All but Vera. For her, setting foot in a church would be more painful than the loss itself. Poor thing.

A horrid drizzle moistened her cheeks. She'd left her coat in the church, so she'd just have to put up with limp hair. Who would notice anyway?

She turned onto her side street and approached the house she shared with eleven other girls. No, only ten now. The drizzle on her lips tasted salty, and she wiped her eyes. Somehow crying seemed right.

Another hole in their squadron. The hole left by Rose's death the year before had never been patched. Everyone loved Louise Cox, but no one could replace Rose, and no one could replace Aleda either.

Kay climbed the outside steps to reach her room on the second floor. The dampness had darkened the walls to a mustard color. Even the house wept.

Her room sat to the left, but faint sobs rose from behind the closed door to the right.

Vera.

Kay's heart wrenched for her friend. Vera's aversion to church didn't erase her need to grieve, and why should she have to grieve alone? Maybe this was why Kay came back.

She opened the door.

Vera didn't grieve alone. She sat on her cot, cuddled up beside Capt. Frank Maxwell. He held her in a familiar manner, caressing her arm, kissing her forehead.

Kay sucked in a breath, icy cold, freezing every muscle, every thought but one.

Vera scrambled to her feet. "Kay! What are you doing here?"

"I—I forgot . . . What are *you* doing here? In women's quarters?" She turned a pointed glance to the flight surgeon.

He put on a flat smile, stood, and fumbled with his shirt buttons, as if checking to see that he was dressed. He was. A wormy feeling in Kay's gut told her that wasn't always the case when he was with Vera.

Captain Maxwell smoothed his tie. "I was comforting Lieutenant Viviani."

Kay's upper lip curled. "Your wife must be very proud of you."

"Kay!" Vera swiped tears off her cheeks. "What's wrong with you? The old Kay wouldn't have batted an eye."

"Baloney. Even I never stooped so low as to date a married man."

Maxwell's dark eyebrows bunched up. "Don't jump to conclusions. Nothing unseemly is going on here."

"More baloney. How long has this been going on?" Her head swam, and she pressed her hand to her forehead. "Oh my goodness. This is why you're always so mysterious about your boyfriend, your dates. You're embroiled in a tawdry affair."

"It's not like that." Vera fiddled with the ends of her hair. "It isn't tawdry. We're in love. After the war is over, Frank will divorce his wife and marry me."

Kay's mouth dangled open. "I can't believe you fell for that. That's what every married man promises his mistress."

She wrinkled her pert little nose. "It's different with us."

"Is it? And what then? What if he actually divorces her and marries you? Don't you think he'll tell his next mistress the same exact thing?"

"Enough, Lieutenant." Maxwell stepped between Vera and Kay. His green eyes burned. "How dare you talk about me like that? I outrank you."

Her green eyes could burn too. "How can I speak respectfully to someone I no longer respect?"

His expression darkened, stiffened. If he hit her, she'd hit him back.

"Now, Kay." Vera darted around her lover, took Kay's arm, and turned her aside, her voice sugar-sweet. "There's no need to get worked up. We've been friends for ages. You mustn't be cross with me."

Heaven's sake, the woman talked as if she'd done nothing worse than borrowing one of Kay's dresses without permission. "You've got to be kidding. You're having an affair with a married man. It's wrong and you know it. Not to mention it's against regulations."

Vera grasped Kay's hand, tilted her head, and dimpled one corner of her mouth. "Oh, you wouldn't say anything. I know you wouldn't. After all, how many times did I cover for you when you broke curfew?"

Kay pried her hand free. "It's not the same, and you know it. You expect me to ignore this?"

"Well, of course. Mellie knows and she's never blabbed."

Kay blinked her eyes as if that would clear her ears. "Mellie knows?"

"She's known for ages and not one word. And you know what a stickler for rules she is." Vera chuckled in a conspiratorial way.

Kay didn't chuckle back. Mellie knew? Good, sweet, honest-to-a-fault Mellie Blake blithely ignored adultery? How could she?

"You're my friend." Affection shone in Vera's dark eyes. "I'm not asking you to lie. I'm just asking you—begging you—not to say anything."

Kay's stomach and mind and heart churned. She backed out of the room. "No promises."

Roger's leg jostled. He glanced down the aisle of the church and at his watch. Again. Kay had been gone twenty-two minutes. She should have been back by now.

Had something happened to her?

He couldn't just sit there. He leaned closer to Mike Elroy. "Be right back."

After Mike nodded, Roger slinked down the aisle and out of the church. Let them think he was rude, overcome by grief, had to go to the latrine. What did it matter? Kay needed him.

Out in the drizzle, he jammed his cap on his head and stuffed his Bible inside his service jacket to keep it dry. He strode down the street, around the corner, past the *boulangerie*, onto the side street.

There was Kay.

A sigh rushed from his lungs. Thank goodness, she was okay.

Or was she? She marched down the street, head down, arms swinging. With each step, her skirt snapped into a thin line between her knees.

"Kay?"

She looked up, pushed her hair off her face, and swayed a bit.

What happened? He ran up to her. "You all right?"

She shook her head and pressed her hand over her garrison cap.

He wanted to fold her in his arms, but instead he laid one hand on her shoulder. "What's the matter? Where's your Bible?"

"My . . ." She looked over her shoulder to her house. "I forgot all about it after—" She clamped her mouth shut.

"After what? What happened? Someone hurt you?"

"No. Nothing like that."

"So, what—"

In one second flat, her expression switched from dazed to determined. "You always give me good advice."

"I do?"

"Yes, and I need advice." She headed down the street. "Come on. We need to go somewhere private to talk."

What could be more dangerous than privacy with a gorgeous redhead?

Kay stopped and motioned to him. "Come on."

"We should—we should go back to the church."

"They don't need us, and I need to talk to you right now."

Roger shifted from one foot to the other. "Your friends will worry."

She continued on her way, ordering him forward with a flap of her hand over her shoulder. "I hope they don't look for me at quarters. They'll be in for a rude shock. Except Mellie apparently." She huffed.

Roger sent a groan heavenward and followed the nurse. *Your idea, Lord. Not mine.*

Catching up wasn't easy at her skirt-snapping pace. In a few minutes they reached the Étang de l'Olivier. Alone.

Roger sat on a rock and pulled out his drumsticks to look casual. "What's up?"

Kay paced in front of him, one hand wrapped around her slender waist, the other bracing her pretty chin. "Your friend Shell's married, right?"

"Right."

"What would you do if you caught him with another woman?"

One drumstick dropped to the dirt. "Shell?"

She waved her hand in front of her face. "Not Shell. Not him, of course. It's Vera."

He groped on the ground for his drumstick. "She's married?"

"No." She looked at him as if he were daft. "I caught her with Captain Maxwell."

"And he's married?"

"Yes." She resumed her pacing.

Roger let out a low whistle. "He's her commanding officer too."

"Sort of. Not really. He's the surgeon for our flight of six nurses, but Lieutenant Lambert's in charge of the nurses and Major Guilford over the whole squadron."

"Still, he's in a position of authority."

Her head sagged back. "I can't believe it. Vera and I have been friends for years. I never thought she was that kind of woman. Oh my goodness! I bet this has been going on since we trained at Bowman Field. That was two years ago. I feel sick."

"Yeah." He always felt sick when someone fell into temptation. It could easily be him.

Kay stood right in front of him. "What should I do?"

"Do?" He rolled the drumsticks in his moist hands. For once, no rhythm came to him.

"Should I report them to Lambert and Guilford when we get back to Rome?"

"I—"

She charged down to the water, back again, gaze fixed on the trees over Roger's head. "If I report them, will I look like a good leader, someone who can deal with tough issues and discipline those under my command? Will Lambert think I'm responsible? Or will she think I'm coldhearted? Vera will hate me, Alice too. Unity? There won't be any. How can I destroy what little unity we have? And what will I look like? Will I look like a good leader or just like a woman scheming to look like a good leader?"

Roger stared at her, clutched his drumsticks, and sorted through her mountain of words. "Well—"

Kay let out a cry and shook her fists in front of her chest. "What is wrong with me? Why am I even thinking about what I look like? Who cares! Only one thing matters—doing the right thing. Right?"

"Um, right."

She stomped up to him. "So what's the right thing to do?"

He stared up into her pleading face. How could he offer advice when he was about five minutes behind in her monologue?

She plopped down onto the rock beside him, her hip pressed to his. "If I report them, I'll have to report Mellie too, because she knew and didn't say a thing."

He edged away a bit. Any farther and he'd fall off. "Mellie knew?"

"Yes." She turned blazing eyes to him. "She's a Christian. She should know better."

Roger shrugged. "Christians still sin."

Kay collapsed forward, elbows on her knees, head in her hands. She looked so small, so defeated, so confused. Her red-blonde hair hung in damp strands around her neck.

More than anything, Roger wanted to pull her into his arms, or stroke her hair, or something. He had to comfort her. The turmoil made his legs jiggle.

For heaven's sake, what kind of friend was he? He jammed his drumsticks inside his jacket and rubbed her back, up and down, same as he'd do for one of his sisters. "You trust Mellie, right?"

"I used to."

"She must have had her reasons. Maybe she couldn't say anything—her word against theirs. Ask her."

Kay sat still, silent, and he stroked her back, her shoulders, warm and firm and soft all at the same time. Made him want her even more, but it seemed to soothe her.

"Can you ever be good enough?" Her voice came out small and weak.

"What?" This conversation gave him vertigo.

She sat up, dislodging his hand but engaging his eyes. "Mellie's a Christian and she ignored adultery. Georgie's a Christian and she breaks the fraternization rules. Can you ever be good enough?"

Part of him wanted to lie to make her feel better, but truth won out. "No, you can't."

Kay groaned and sank down over her knees again. "What hope do I have? How can I ever be good enough to get the job I want, or a—a house, or—or—" Her voice broke, and her shoulders shook.

Oh boy. This ran deeper than grief and betrayal and indecision. "You're listening to the wrong voice, kid. That's your earthly father talking, not your heavenly Father."

"What?" She sat up and shoved stringy hair off her reddened face.

How could she look so beautiful when she was a mess? He faced the lake, gripped both knees, and wrestled his thoughts into words. "Remember when I told you God's mercy was a gift? You don't earn forgiveness by being good. He gives it because he's good."

"Yes, but this is—"

"No, it's not different. Now we're talking about God's grace. He gives us good things not because we're good, but because he's good."

"That doesn't make sense." Her face glistened with tears and rain.

Roger yanked his handkerchief from his pocket and handed it to her. "What did you do to deserve this handkerchief? Nothing. I gave it to you because you're my friend."

Her smile wobbled, and she blotted her face. "Thanks."

"God isn't like a candy machine. We can't insert a good deed and receive a blessing. Then we'd be in charge, not him."

Her gaze darted around, nowhere near his face. "Okay. All right."

"If he gives you the chief nurse job, it's not because you did something good, but because he loves you and wants what's best for you. And if he doesn't give you the chief nurse job, it's not because you did something bad, but because he loves you—and something else would be better for you."

"Oh . . ." Her gaze returned to him, bright with comprehension.

In the mirror of her eyes, his words reflected back to him. God could choose to give him gifts too, no matter what Roger had done in the past. God could choose to give him Kay's love, even if he didn't deserve it.

That thought stuck like a rock in his throat. He swallowed it and lurched to his feet. "Say, we'd better get back before they drag the lake looking for us."

"Oh dear." She gathered her hair over one shoulder. "I look a mess."

The perfect opportunity to slice the romance out of the moment. He grinned. "No kidding. Drowned rats have nothing on you."

She gasped, stood, and gave him a playful punch in the arm. "Some friend you are."

He led the way up the embankment. "Hey, I gave you advice and a hankie. You expect a compliment on top of that?"

"Not from the likes of you."

"Don't you ever forget it." He glanced behind him to shining, kissable Kay. Fragile Kay. Some gifts were too precious to open.

# 27

**Istres**
**November 10, 1944**

Kay fluffed Mellie's bridal veil over her shiny black hair. "You look absolutely gorgeous."

"Thank you." Mellie had turned out to be as innocent as her pure white gown. Kay had confronted her, and Mellie told the whole story. Over a year before, she'd stumbled upon Vera and Maxwell kissing, but they'd threatened her into silence. When the threat resolved, Mellie demonstrated her forgiveness by extending mercy and not reporting them.

"Tom will do cartwheels down the aisle when he sees you." Georgie wove her needle through Mellie's hem in some unnecessary repair.

"I just wish . . . I wish . . ." Mellie's voice warbled.

Kay grabbed her friend's shoulder. "No blubbering. You'll ruin your makeup."

Regardless, tears glistened on Mellie's thick lashes. "I wish Papa could be here."

"Oh, honey!" Georgie enfolded her in a hug.

Kay whipped out her handkerchief and blotted her friend's tears before they could leave trails in her face powder. Mellie's father had been trapped in the Philippines when the Japanese invaded and was interned in a prison camp for civilians. Poor Mellie had only received three postcards in the past two and a half years. "No tears. Your father will be thrilled for you. Tom's a wonderful man."

"He—he is. But Tom's mother. She should be here too. He's her only child."

"It's wartime, honey." Georgie patted her back. "We have to make do. You don't want to wait any longer to marry Tom, do you?"

Mellie sniffled, blinked, and stood up straight. "No, I don't."

Georgie smoothed the sleeves of the wedding gown she'd labored over. "You just think about that man waiting for you by the altar and how much he adores you."

"She's right." Kay opened her compact and dabbed powder under Mellie's eyes. "Now let's get you down the aisle. You only have a few days to enjoy married life before we go back to Italy. Don't waste one more minute on the two of us."

"All right." Mellie lowered her eyes, pulled in a deep breath, and then raised her chin. "I'm ready."

Georgie arranged the lacy veil over her friend's face and then leaned through the doorway to the sanctuary and waved to the chaplain.

A few chords, and the organ changed to the wedding processional. Just over a week before, that same organ had offered solace in time of death and grief, but today it made the ancient stone walls vibrate with joy.

Kay would lead the way. She patted her pinned-up curls and straightened the russet-colored bolero jacket Georgie had made to cover Kay's sleeveless grass-green ball gown. Then she strolled down the aisle with her bouquet. Madame La Rue, who owned their house in Istres, had insisted on providing flowers from her garden, including fragrant sprigs of dried lavender.

Every man and woman in the church turned and smiled at Kay, but she wasn't the main attraction, nor did she want to be. So she fixed her attention on the men up front.

Tom MacGilliver stood by the chaplain in full dress uniform, his sandy blond hair neat, his bright eyes trained on the door, waiting for his bride. Only fidgeting fingers conveyed nervousness.

Two men from his battalion stood with him, Lt. Rudy Scaglione and Sgt. Larry Fong. The chaplain had expressed concerns about a Chinese man in the wedding party, but Tom had silenced him. Larry was an American citizen serving his country in combat. Any guests who had a problem with that were not welcome.

At the front of the church, Kay smiled at Tom and took her place. Who would have thought when she'd transferred anonymous letters between Mellie and Tom that they'd end up married?

Georgie came down the aisle in her long cobalt-blue gown and a jacket that matched Kay's. She beamed as if it were her own wedding, even though her boyfriend, Hutch, had been unable to get a two-day pass to attend.

The organ music swelled. When Mellie appeared in the doorway, everyone stood.

A slight pause, and Mellie glided down the aisle, her full smile evident despite the veil. How much she'd changed. Two years earlier, Kay had met a shy, unsmiling nurse with yard-long hair coiled around her head like a helmet. Now, thanks to friendship, love, and the Lord's work, Mellie was a new woman, serenely beautiful and a beloved member of the squadron.

When she reached the front of the church, Tom tenderly took her hand and led her to the altar.

The chaplain began speaking, and for the first time, Kay allowed herself to scan the congregation.

There he was. Roger sat a few rows back on the groom's side of the church, which was kind of him, since Tom had fewer guests.

Kay's heart went into that stupid spasm it always did when she saw Roger. Falling in love was ridiculous. She had no control. None. Her heart rate, breathing, and emotions—all disobeyed her. Yet it was the most glorious feeling ever.

Roger looked phenomenal in dress uniform. He looked great in khakis and in his leather flight jacket, but the olive drab service jacket made his auburn hair and dark eyes come alive.

He shifted in the pew, grinned at Kay, and winked.

Another stupid spasm, but she returned the wink. If only she had the same effect on him as he did on her. At times she sensed something more from him—a spark in his eyes, the way he saw into her soul, the way he lingered when stroking her back and comforting her.

Then he'd call her "kid," and the moment would shatter.

For years she'd collected hearts with minimal effort and all the wrong motives. Now she longed for only one heart, motivated by love, but that heart eluded her.

Kay turned her attention to the chaplain and tried to listen to the words.

Time was running out. They'd both complete their stint in France this week and return to Italy, to separate bases. Weather permitting, Roger would finish his tour in a week or two. If Kay didn't earn a spot in the chief nurse program, she'd remain in Italy and might never see him again. If she went stateside, they could be hundreds of miles apart, but since he'd fly all over the country, they might see each other occasionally.

Her grip tightened on her bouquet. Everything depended on how Lambert reacted when Kay reported Vera and Maxwell's affair, and on how Roger acted tonight.

The wedding reception was her last chance to turn the friendship to romance. If she succeeded, the separation from Roger would be unpleasant but bearable. If she failed . . .

Kay shivered. She couldn't fail.

Tonight she'd titrate up the dose.

# 28

Roger tapped his fork on his cake plate and laughed at something Shell said. How could he pay attention when the five-piece band played at the wrong speed? "I Don't Want to Set the World on Fire" was meant to be slow but lively, and this crew drained out all the life.

His fork didn't carry a drum's authority, and the band maintained its doleful pace.

The flight nurses had transformed the officers' mess into a reception hall with flowers and streamers and other girly stuff. They'd even made cake and coffee. But the base band . . . ?

The clarinet squeaked, and Roger cringed.

"Hi there, gentlemen." Kay approached the table with Georgie.

Roger's mind leaped back to the Orange Club, except now Kay didn't have a predatory look. But she was more gorgeous than ever, curls up on top of her head, green dress swooshing over her curves, and one bare arm perched on her hip.

"Hi." Unlike at the Orange Club, he remembered his manners. He bolted to his feet and held out a chair, while Mike, Shell, and Bert Marino did likewise. Four chairs for two ladies.

Kay didn't sit. "Swell reception, isn't it?"

"Yeah." Several couples had joined the bride and groom

on the dance floor, and everyone seemed to be enjoying themselves in spite of the music. "It'd be better if I could get behind the drums and pick up the beat."

Kay tilted her head, a glint in her eyes. "Since you can't play, you might as well dance."

"Uh-uh." He backed up and shook his head. "I don't dance."

A playful smile rolled up her lips, and she held out both hands to him. "What's the matter? No sense of rhythm?"

The men at the table broke up laughing. Bert slapped Roger on the back. "A drummer without rhythm? That's like a pilot scared of heights. Oh wait—that's Coop."

"Ah, shut up." Roger elbowed him.

"You'd better prove them wrong." Kay grasped both his hands.

Her touch—cool as water, and like water on a parched throat, it made him realize how thirsty he'd been.

Kay tipped her head toward the dance floor and gave him a teasing smile.

He couldn't do this. He leaned closer so he could speak low. "I haven't danced since high school."

"All the more reason—" Her eyes went round with understanding. "Oh."

Roger nodded. Thank goodness she saw.

How was it possible for her expression to grow softer and firmer at the same time? "All the more reason for you to dance now. Prove your past is past."

"I don't—"

"It won't kill you." A little tug on his hands, and she led him to the dance floor.

No, it wouldn't kill him. It'd quench his thirst and make him thirstier than ever.

Kay twirled to face him and set one hand on his shoulder. "What shall we dance? The Charleston?"

He chuckled and succumbed to putting his hand on her waist. "I'm not that old."

"Might as well be if you haven't danced in a decade."

Twelve years. He racked his memory and settled into a simple foxtrot. Least he remembered something.

Kay moved with practiced ease, smooth and supple. "Is this the first time the new Roger has danced?"

"Yeah, it is."

"First time for the new Kay too."

Somehow that relaxed him and warmed him. Another thing they had in common. He looked deep into her eyes and studied the shade of green, shot through with gold.

The band switched to "A Nightingale Sang in Berkeley Square" at the same droning pace, but Kay smiled. "That's our song, the flight nurses."

"Nightingales." He'd heard them throw that term around.

"Mercy on wing."

"Remember, those are my wings you're using." Roger did a little switch-up in the dance steps.

"Not half bad." Kay's eyebrows arched. "So, those wings are about to carry you home."

"Less than twenty hours to go." Oh great. That sounded rude, as if he couldn't wait to get away from her. While part of him wanted to, the other part never wanted to let her out of his sight for the rest of his life.

She gazed at his chest. "Do you think your CO will give you that recommendation?"

"Yeah. He hasn't said anything, but I think he will."

"You'll be wonderful. You're a natural . . . if the way you're drumming on my spine is any indication."

What? Swell, that's exactly what he was doing. He stilled his hand. "Sorry."

"Don't apologize. I was just trying to figure out what message you were sending."

Roger's face heated. Message? How much he loved her? How holding her in his arms about drove him crazy? "Drummer's habit."

"Could be useful." She studied him in that intelligent, coy way she had. "You said you used to drum out the Morse code. You could communicate silently with your dance partner."

A grin escaped. Thank goodness she hadn't read his real message. "Yeah. A tap of the thumb could be the dot, a pat of the fingers the dash." He demonstrated on her lower back.

"That works. I could tell you, 'Watch out! Drunk uncle careening toward us.'" She tapped and patted his shoulder.

He squinted at the ceiling. "You said, 'Q-Z-O-T-F.'"

"Smart aleck." She gave his shoulder a light slap.

He rocked her into a neat turn. Not half bad, indeed. "And I could signal you, 'Lecherous old goat wants to cut in. Mayday! SOS!'" He drummed out the SOS: dot-dot-dot, dash-dash-dash, dot-dot-dot.

She laughed and dipped her forehead to his shoulder in a way so natural and right that his dots and dashes slipped around to the far side of her waist.

He pressed her warm, slender body too close, but he couldn't let go, couldn't stop swallowing and quenching and thirsting, swallowing and quenching and thirsting.

The music shifted into "Let's Get Lost," even slower, more romantic.

Kay softened and snuggled closer, her cheek on his shoulder. She didn't have to tap out a message, and neither did he.

Dozens of people danced around them, but Roger didn't care, only saw them to avoid them. If any man tried to cut in, he'd kick him into the Étang. He never wanted to let go of this woman again.

Why should he have to? What if she was a gift from God? Wouldn't it be rude to turn down a gift from the Lord Almighty?

Kay sighed and raised her head. Only inches away, her facial features blurred, but her expression couldn't have been clearer. The softness of her eyes gleamed affection, slight hooding revealed desire, and a curving down at the corners showed vulnerability.

An urge flared in his chest to protect her, to love her, to have her. He could kiss her right now, on the dance floor, in full sight of everyone, and she wouldn't stop him.

No, she wouldn't. She'd give herself to him, her love, her kisses, and—if he didn't restrain himself—her body. He'd seen that blend of desire and vulnerability before, knew well how to take advantage of it. He could have his way with her, know her as no man had ever known her, fully and completely. What if she didn't stop him?

Somehow, for her sake, he had to stop himself. He wrestled the flame inside, but it scorched him, repelled him. He couldn't win this fight on his own, and his soul cried out. *God, help me.*

Kay's eyebrows drew together, and she pulled back an inch or two.

Just enough. Roger hauled in a breath and hefted up a lopsided smile. The other side of his mouth remained hung up on the imagined kiss.

She smiled too, and far more coordinated.

"So—" His voice croaked. He cleared his throat. "Looking forward to Italy?"

Dark eyelashes brushed over her cheeks. "I suppose. I love France, but . . . well, Lieutenant Lambert is in Rome."

Talking about their separate futures—that should break the spell. "I'm sure she'll send you to the chief nurse program."

"I hope so."

"Why do you want it so much? Want to boss people around?"

She laughed. "I have to admit that's part of it."

He spun her around. "What's the other part?"

She glanced away, across the room, where Tom and Mellie chatted with Georgie. "I've only told Mellie about this. It sounds strange."

"Strange? Why?"

"You grew up in a house, right?"

"Sure. Big old farmhouse packed to the rafters with red-headed Coopers."

"Well, I grew up in tents, never in the same location more than three months in a row. After I ran away, I shared apartments with as many girls as we could squeeze in. I've never had a house. That's what I want more than anything."

"A house." His voice sounded thin, about to crumble, like the connection between them.

Those gorgeous green eyes brimmed with emotion. "Last year Georgie invited me to her home in Virginia, and I had a room of my own for the first time in my life. I kind of—I fell apart. Mellie was there. She listened."

And the connection crumbled away to nothingness. He swallowed over his parched throat. "You want a place to call home. Someplace to set down roots."

"Yes."

The one thing he could never give her. As a drummer, he'd drag her from hotel to hotel. What if he tried to be a teacher? What if he failed? Then where would she be? She'd be longing for the security of her father's tent—that's where she'd be.

If he gave in to his love, to his desire, he'd destroy her dreams.

"Thank you for listening. You always understand." Kay slid her hand along his shoulder, and she played with the hair at the nape of his neck.

Felt so good. Too good. He loved her too much to let her stray down this dead-end road. He stiffened his shoulders and dislodged her hand from his hair. "Kay, don't."

She searched his face, her jaw slack. "D-don't what?"

Everything inside him screamed, but he grasped her hands and begged her with his eyes and voice. "Please don't flirt with me."

She blinked, and her face went pale. "But . . . but . . ."

But he'd been flirting too, and now he was rejecting her. Man alive! He was the biggest heel in the history of the world, but he had to do this. He gripped her hands hard, knowing this would be the last time he'd ever touch her. "I'm not the right man for you."

Her mouth tightened, and she flung down his hands. "Whatever makes you think—"

"May I cut in?" Grant Klein tapped Roger on the shoulder.

Roger chomped off a curse word. "Not now, Klein. Get lost."

He raised a smug smile and held out one hand to Kay. "I don't think the lady wants to dance with you."

Her mouth warped, and her eyes shot shards of flak at Roger. "I don't want to dance with either of you ever again." She flounced out of the mess hall, snatching her jacket from a chair on the way out. As she reached the door, she pressed one hand over her mouth, and her shoulders slumped forward.

*Dear Lord, I broke her heart.*

"What'd you do to her, Cooper?"

"None of your business." Roger headed back toward his table, where his friends stared at him.

"Where do you think you're going? I'm not through with you." Klein spoke too loud, his voice slurred. Must have brought his own booze.

All around, people hushed.

Roger's arms turned to iron, and his fists balled up. So Klein wanted a fight. Fine with him. "Let's take it outside."

He strode out of the hall, Klein on his heels. The door

banged shut behind him. In the rain, in the cold night air, Roger spun to face his foe. "What's your prob—"

Pain zinged through his jaw. He doubled over, clutching his chin. "What—"

Klein stood with his fist still high, his body open and undefended.

Roger ducked in, pummeled him in the gut with a series of rabbit punches.

A fist slammed down on Roger's back, ineffective, and Roger landed an uppercut square in that pretty-boy chin.

Klein reeled back, crumpled to the ground, and curled up in a ball.

What a coward. Roger stood over him, chest heaving, jaw throbbing. "You through with me now?"

The pilot eased himself up on one elbow and wiped his mouth with the back of his hand. "She doesn't want you, you know that? She spit you out, just like she did to me."

Roger's chest contracted. She only spat him out because he'd crushed her, but why humiliate her in front of Klein? "Girl's smart. What can I say?"

He moaned and wrapped his arm around his belly. The man was going to retch.

"Go sleep it off." Roger lumbered away toward quarters. He moved his aching jaw side to side. Nothing broken, but he'd have a honey of a bruise in the morning.

Served him right for hurting Kay.

He stumbled on the dark path, but truth eased his pain. Better she have a moment of heartbreak now than a lifetime of heartache as his wife.

# 29

**Istres/Le Tubé Airfield**
**November 15, 1944**

One more day and she'd never have to see Roger Cooper again.

One long day.

Kay carried her barracks bag across the runway toward the C-47. Why did they assign her to his flight for the return to Rome? Why couldn't they have put her on one of the other two planes?

Roger stood by the nose of the C-47 with Mike Elroy, both frowning and pointing east.

Her heart seized with a fresh burst of anger, grief, and humiliation. She positioned herself behind Louise and beside Georgie, so Roger couldn't see her. Not that he'd look her direction anyway.

A blast of chilly wind gave her an excuse to hunker down into her overcoat. Colder than the pilot's heart.

Sergeant Whitaker stood at the cargo door and took Kay's barracks bag to be stashed in the back, and Kay sat along the right side of the fuselage with the six nurses of her flight. Squadron equipment was lashed in place in the rear of the cabin.

"Are you okay, Mellie?" Sitting next to the bulkhead, Louise Cox leaned forward to talk around Kay.

"I am." Only a touch of melancholy dimmed her newly-wed glow. "But I wish they'd transferred our squadron from the MTO to the ETO like they did the hospitals and Tom's engineer battalion."

Georgie patted Mellie's arm. "First thing tomorrow morning, we'll ask Lambert for a transfer to one of the squadrons based in England."

Kay's two closest friends would leave Italy too. All the more reason to beg for an appointment to the chief nurse school.

Vera's and Alice's laughter floated down from the cargo door, and they took seats beside Georgie.

Kay's stomach turned at the sight of her former friend. Tomorrow she'd turn in Vera and Maxwell. This was more than a one-time indiscretion and couldn't be overlooked.

Lambert would have to credit her for doing the right and difficult thing. Kay would sacrifice a longtime friendship, all pretense of unity, and the hope that unity would earn her a recommendation. But perhaps the road to Kay's goal ran through disunity.

Masculine voices rose from the rear of the plane, and Kay's stomach turned in the other direction. She gazed down at her seat belt and fastened it, unfastened, fastened, unfastened until heavy footsteps passed her into the cockpit.

He didn't even say hello.

Her throat swelled shut. Would she ever get used to the loss of his friendship?

A light touch to her arm. Mellie gave her a compassionate smile, echoed by Georgie.

Kay sniffed and pulled the collar of her overcoat higher. How dare Roger make her the object of pity?

One engine sputtered and roared, and the plane vibrated. Kay hugged herself, glad the cold excused her behavior.

What was wrong with her? She could still feel that man's embrace. She was an expert at interpreting men's messages, and Roger had sent them loud and clear. He'd held her so close, so intimately, his hand stroking her back. And he'd worn the look of a man enraptured. The heat of it! For one moment, she thought—hoped—he'd throw propriety aside and kiss her right there on the dance floor.

Kay no longer doubted he found her attractive and desirable.

Hot moisture trickled down her cheek, and she swatted it away before her friends could notice. Roger desired her, but he didn't want her.

The second engine added to the din, and Kay gripped the gray-green wool of her coat. Why on earth had she flirted with him? Why had she played with his hair? She'd titrated the dose too high, too fast.

And now he thought she was still a floozy.

Her face convulsed, and she mashed her lips together to stifle a sob. He'd told her, "I'm not the right man for you."

Deep inside, he didn't believe she'd changed. And deep inside, Kay knew she'd never be good enough.

———

Winds buffeted the plane, and the instruments hopped all over the place.

Roger fought the control wheel. He never should have flown today.

Army Air Force Weather Wing assured the three pilots they'd have smooth flying from Istres to Ciampino, but he should have listened to Mike and to his own instincts. For weeks, the French mistral wind had blown steadily from the north, but today's weather didn't feel right.

Sure enough, they hadn't even reached Toulon when they'd encountered a thunderstorm. They'd cut northeast to avoid it and followed the curve of the Riviera until fog obscured all landmarks.

Roger missed his gum, but with the huge shiner on his jaw, chewing hurt too much. "Pettas, any closer to getting coordinates?"

Cuss words greeted him. "How can I? No radio nav aids, can't see the ground, and wind speed, airspeed, and direction keep changing. Can't keep track."

A pocket of turbulence bumped the plane, and Roger struggled with the controls. The planes had climbed to nine thousand feet, as high as they could go without needing oxygen. C-47s only carried a handful of walk-around oxygen bottles for emergency use.

Sandwiched between the murk below and the murk above, Roger searched for his companion planes. They'd put distance between them to avoid collision in the turbulence, but now they'd gotten separated. Since they were over enemy territory, he couldn't use the radio to locate them.

"What should we do, Coop?" A furrow creased Elroy's forehead, making him look his age for once.

"Head east as best we can, pray the weather's better on the far side of the Apennines. If we can find Italy's east coast, we can follow that down to friendly territory, find an RAF field to land on."

"Should we turn around?"

"If I knew where we were, sure. But if I turned around now, we could end up in Berlin. Besides, we're probably about halfway there."

Elroy sighed his understanding. "Least our fuel looks good."

For now. This northerly jaunt added at least two hundred miles to his route. Any engine trouble and he was sunk.

Only two weeks had passed since another plane from his squadron had crashed, killing all aboard. What had that pilot experienced before he crashed?

Roger drew in a deep breath. He couldn't afford to fail today, not with six nurses in the back of his plane, including the woman he loved.

The woman who hated him with a passion.

In his stomach, the turbulence duplicated the weather outside. No matter how many times he reminded himself he'd acted in her best interest, he couldn't shake the guilt. He'd hurt her horribly. And he hurt just as bad.

---

The plane jolted. Kay bumped Mellie's shoulder and apologized again.

Georgie and Alice looked pale, and Louise chewed on her lips, but Kay didn't worry. Roger Cooper might be a jerk, but he was an excellent pilot.

And she'd never have to fly with him again.

Tomorrow morning she'd talk to Lambert, and if Lambert wouldn't recommend her for the program, Kay would go straight to Major Guilford and beg him.

The war was bogged down on all fronts in Europe for the winter, and it plodded along in the Pacific. Kay still had time to train as a chief. After the war, many nurses would marry and start families, so Kay would be in a good position to gain a chief nurse job in a hospital.

She could buy a home.

The plane dropped. The seat belt cut into Kay's lap, and a couple of the girls gasped.

Thank goodness none of them had tendencies toward airsickness.

Kay closed her eyes to take her mind off the jostling plane and its pilot, and to focus on her only remaining dream.

Her own house. She didn't need much—a sweet one-bedroom bungalow with a kitchen and living room and indoor bathroom. After she'd come home from work, she'd cross a neat green lawn and climb three steps onto a porch, where she'd set up a wicker table and chair for summer evenings. She'd open her very own front door and walk across the wooden floor.

Her heels would tap out a beat, ka-thump, ka-thump, "I'm home, I'm home."

But no one would hear. No one would receive the message. A sob filled her throat, and she scrunched her eyes shut.

———

The lack of fog was a mixed blessing. Roger's crew could see the ground, but the Germans on the ground could see the plane.

Yellow tracer fire zipped up to his right, and he eased the plane to the left.

A pocket of turbulence knocked him into Elroy's shoulder. "Pettas, anything?"

"What do you expect? Mountains everywhere. Never flown up here before. Can't find any landmarks."

Roger grimaced. The Italian boot was about two hundred miles across, almost two hours at the slower speed he had to fly in turbulence. What if the Luftwaffe sent up fighters? What was his chance of downing a second enemy plane?

Cracks rang out, and the right wing jerked up. Smoke peeled from the engine.

"We're hit!" Elroy cried.

Orange flames licked out. "Have to put it out. Open cowl flaps."

Mike turned the dial to the right of his seat. "Cowl flaps open."

"Fuel and oil shut off." Roger flipped off the right fuel selector valve and shoved the mixture control valve and the throttle.

Elroy gazed out the window. Once the propeller stopped

turning, he pushed a button on the overhead electrical panel. "Prop feathered."

"Ignition off." Roger reached down to the floor and activated the engine fire extinguisher. Never had to use it before.

A sick feeling filled his belly. He'd never have to use it again either. He'd never make it to Allied territory. He'd never fly again.

While he trimmed the plane for single-engine flight, he weighed his options. The turbulence and the longer route had gobbled up fuel, and flying on only one engine would burn through what little remained. He had no idea where he was, but friendly territory lay at least 150 miles away.

"Coop?" Elroy's voice sounded small. "We have to land behind enemy lines, don't we?"

"Yeah." The finality of that word socked him harder than Klein had. Putting down in the northern Apennines? He'd need a miracle to find a field long enough and flat enough.

With a giant sigh, he pushed the control column forward to decrease altitude. "Look for a field. I'll head east and pray we hit the Po Valley, but right now I'll take anything."

"Coop?" Whitaker stood in the doorway to the cockpit, face drawn. "Did I hear right?"

"Yeah." His heart sank faster than the plane. "You'd better . . . prepare the ladies for an emergency landing."

"At least we know procedures."

"Yeah." Another sock to the jaw. They knew procedures from experience. Pettas and Whitaker had been with him in March when he ditched in the Mediterranean. Georgie had been there too.

Lt. Roger Cooper was about to lose his third plane. Number one when Grant Klein crashed into his parked plane and killed Clint Peters and Rose Danilovich. Number two when Vesuvius knocked out an engine. And now number three.

How many would survive today? Would any of them? At

best they'd be guests of the Germans for the duration of the war.

Not only had he failed Kay and broken her heart, but now he might kill her. *I'm so sorry, Kay.*

Pettas leaned in the door. "I sent a position report as best I could. Whit's got the doors open, everything lashed down. Any papers you need destroyed?"

"Yes." Elroy passed back flight plans.

Roger checked his instruments. Down to one thousand feet. Now to find a field.

He scanned the landscape. What was that? He squinted at a pale green patch ahead and to the right. "Elroy? See that? Let's check it out."

"Looks promising."

The plane wanted to turn right, so Roger let it. The closer he got, the better it looked. He could only afford to circle the field once. On the ground, the Germans would take them prisoner, but in the air, they were a big fat target.

He pulled alongside the field. Though open and smooth and long, it lay on a slope. He'd have to land heading uphill. "Oh boy."

"Don't think we can find better than this."

"I agree. Gear down."

Elroy turned the lever, and Roger set the latch. While flying the landing pattern, they increased rpm, made a power reduction, and lowered the flaps.

"Airspeed one hundred. It looks good, Coop. I think it'll work."

"It'd better." Ten lives depended on it. Roger turned into the approach, eyeing the field.

Sweat trickled down his temples. *Lord, help me. Don't let me kill these people.*

The field rushed up to him, trees along either side and at the far end. "Get ready to cut the engine. And . . . now!"

Roger pulled the control column toward his chest to get the nose up.

Elroy flipped levers and switches at lightning speed.

The wheels settled down. Roger pressed the brakes with his toes, maneuvered the rudder with his heels, jammed the column all the way to his chest.

The plane bumped and rolled and banged Roger around.

Elroy cried out and slumped to the right.

Roger's head cracked on the side panel, and pain shot through his skull.

How many people had survived?

# 30

Kay hunched over, her hands grasped under her thighs. Her chin banged her knees, she bounced between Mellie and Louise, and the floor of the plane blurred. When would it stop?

Vera screamed, then Alice.

*Stop, stop, stop. Make it stop.*

A final shiver, then stillness.

She was alive! Kay straightened up and pushed back her hair. "Everyone okay?"

"Yes," said Mellie, echoed by Georgie.

"Vera's hurt," Alice cried. "A crate got loose, slashed her leg."

"Help her out. Everyone out." Kay fumbled with her seat belt.

Footsteps thumped from the cockpit. Roger burst through the door and stopped, gripping the doorjamb. His gaze swept the nurses, then landed on Kay. A sigh collapsed his chest, as if he were actually glad to see her. "Thank God."

For one moment, Kay's heart cried out that he cared, that he loved her. But reason silenced that voice.

A trickle of blood ran down his temple, and a giant yellowish-green bruise covered one side of his jaw. How had he developed a bruise so quickly? And why was he still looking at her, mouth slack, forehead creased?

Vera screamed but clamped off her cry.

Roger blinked and snapped his gaze to Vera. "You hurt? We gotta get off now. We put out the engine fire, but I still don't trust it."

"Vera's hurt." Kay glanced to her right.

Louise slouched against the bulkhead, light brown hair sheeted over her face. The blanket she'd placed between her head and the wall had slipped down.

"Louise!" Kay shook her friend, pressed two fingers to the carotid.

Roger stepped closer. "Is she . . . ?"

"She's alive. Unconscious. Must have hit her head."

"Thank goodness. Everyone off the plane. We'll be POWs, so take your coat, hat, gloves, anything warm you can carry."

Prisoners of war. A cold shiver ran through her. She'd trained for this but never seriously considered it. Kay stood on wobbly legs. She looped her musette bag over her head, added Louise's bag, and unhooked Louise's seat belt. "I'll take her feet. You get her shoulders."

"No. I've got her. Get off the plane." Roger slung Louise over his shoulder and headed down the aisle.

Sergeant Whitaker beckoned at the cargo door. "Everyone out."

Alice helped Vera down the aisle, and Mellie and Georgie followed. What about Sergeant Pettas? Mike Elroy? Where were they?

Kay dashed into the radio room. Pettas sat at his desk, burning papers with a lighter. In the cockpit, Mike sat slumped against the window, eyes wide, one hand pressed to his chest.

"Mike! You all right?"

"Got the . . . wind knocked . . . out."

Kay grabbed his hands and raised them over his head as high as the ceiling allowed. "Take slow deep breaths. Be calm."

"Gotta . . . get off."

"I know. Can you walk?"

"Don't know." He got halfway out of his seat, moaned, and sank back down.

"I need help! Someone!" She couldn't carry him alone.

Roger stepped into the cockpit, chest heaving, face flushed. "What are you doing here? I told you to evacuate."

"Mike's hurt, dazed."

"I know. Had to get the ladies off first. That means you."

"Where's Louise?"

"Whit's carrying her." He shouldered past Kay and helped Mike to his feet. The copilot sagged to the side, and Roger struggled to hold on.

"Don't be stubborn. I'll get his feet." Kay did just that.

Roger grabbed Mike under the shoulders, and they maneuvered him out of the plane, Pettas following.

At the cargo door, Pettas took Kay's position, and the men carried Mike toward the trees. Kay stayed on the plane and rummaged through the cargo for a medical chest. Surely they had one on board. She shoved aside crates and barracks bags until she found one.

"What are you doing?" Roger leaned inside the cargo door. "The engine's smoking. The plane could blow any second."

She opened the chest and pulled out supplies. "We have wounded."

Roger groaned and hoisted himself inside. "Come on. We'll take the whole thing. We've gotta move."

They dragged the chest to the door and carried it across the field to the trees. Kay glanced behind. Smoke curled out of the right engine, puffing a message to the Nazis. How long until they were discovered? How would the Germans treat them?

Kay stumbled over a rock but kept moving, light-headed, her life turned upside down and inside out.

They plunged into the woods, where the rest of the party sat in a small clearing. Louise lay with her head on Mellie's lap. Her eyes were open, and she gave Kay a weak smile.

Kay set down her end of the medical chest and dashed to Louise's side. "You're all right. Thank goodness."

Mellie stroked Louise's hair. "We'll have to keep her awake in case she has a concussion."

Louise pointed to the medical chest. "Some aspirin would be nice. I'm sure to have a headache."

"I'll say." Kay glanced around. Mike sat up, leaning against a tree, pale but conscious. Georgie and Alice examined Vera's leg. "Georgie, how bad is it?"

"A long gash, not too deep. Oh, you brought supplies. Bless you." She scooted over to the chest and pulled out gauze and sulfanilamide powder.

Kay joined her, found an aspirin bottle, and shook out two tablets. Apparently the Lord didn't want her to report Vera's affair. He could have found a less dramatic way to stop her.

"*Hallo.*"

She spun around at the unfamiliar voice.

Two men stood there, Italians in civilian clothing, with rifles strapped across their chests.

Heart thumping, Kay eased her hands up in surrender, fingers coiled around the tablets.

The younger of the men grinned. *"Americani?"*

"*Si.*" Roger stepped forward, hands in front of his chest. "We surrender."

The younger man laughed, a boy really, a teenager. "No, we are friends. We are partisans."

"Partisans." Roger's hands drifted down. "You speak English."

The boy puffed out his thin chest. "*Si*. My uncle lives in New York. I visit him often before the war."

Kay relaxed her grip on the aspirin before her sweaty palms could dissolve the tablets. She slid to Louise's side, passed her the pills, and exchanged a wary look with Louise and Mellie. In the long run, would it help or hurt them to be found with partisans?

The older Italian man glanced around, one hand on his rifle.

"The Germans—the *Tedeschi*—they'll be here soon," Roger said.

"Tedeschi? No," the boy said. "Not here. The Tedeschi put the Italian Ligurian Army in charge here. Traitors. And the *Brigate Nere*."

"Brigate Nere." The older man spit to the side as if the words tasted foul.

Kay knew nothing about the Brigate Nere or the Italian Ligurian Army, but they seemed to be aligned with the Nazis.

"We see your plane." The boy pointed to the field. "They will too. We must hide you."

Hide? Hope flickered, but reality doused it out. How could they hide a party of ten?

Roger rubbed his hand over his chin—the side without the bruise. "We have wounded. We have women."

"*Si*. We want to help. Your planes bring us guns and bullets and medicine. Now we help you." The boy made a sweeping gesture. "We have friends. The SOE, the OSS. They will take you home."

"SOE?" Louise whispered. "OSS?"

"SOE—British secret agents," Kay said. "OSS are Americans." She'd heard of these agents, working behind enemy lines, coordinating partisan and Allied activities, rescuing downed airmen. Maybe they could rescue airwomen as well.

"I don't know." Roger scrunched up his face. "Sounds dangerous. The women . . ."

"Oh, please." Georgie's eyes widened. "I want to go home."

"I do too," Mellie said. "Tom will worry."

Alice wound gauze around Vera's leg. "Speak for yourselves. The Germans will treat us well. We're women. And the Luftwaffe makes sure aircrews are treated well. But if we sneak around, they'll think we're spies and kill us."

"She's got a point," Sergeant Pettas said. "Even more so for us fellas."

Kay clutched a button on her overcoat. This was why Lieutenant Lambert stressed unity. In times of danger and decision and stress, division could destroy.

She got to her feet. "Ladies, we all went through training at the School of Air Evacuation. What were we taught to do if shot down over enemy territory?"

Mellie jutted out her chin. "As an officer in the United States Army Air Forces, I have a duty to evade capture, and if captured, to attempt escape."

"Lt. Georgiana Taylor, serial number O-703631. And nothing more." Georgie clamped her lips shut.

"Well?" Kay tilted her head at Roger and crossed her arms. "I assume you were taught the same."

A sharp nod, and he glanced down to the leaf-covered ground, his eyebrows jammed together. "All right then."

Mike pushed himself to standing. "Coop, we should see what we can salvage from the plane. She seems stable."

"Come on, men." Roger plowed through the trees. "Rations, water, all we can carry."

Mike, Whitaker, Pettas, and the Italian boy followed.

Kay and Georgie jogged behind them. The men wouldn't think to get medical supplies, blankets, or extra clothing.

"Where are we going?" Roger asked the Italian boy as they ran.

"South. Closer to the *Americani*."

"Won't they expect that?"

"*Si*. When they ask which way you went, we point south. They won't believe us, will go north. So we go south."

In a strange way, it made sense. Kay climbed inside the plane and found her barracks bag. "Georgie, find yours, toss out anything you don't need. We can use the bags to carry rations and things."

"What about the other girls? We should bring them their bags, do the same."

"Good idea." Kay pulled out a stack of magazines, her skirts, her swimsuit, her . . . her ball gown. The same grassy green dress she'd worn to Mellie's wedding, dancing in Roger's arms, his face so close to hers.

"Have any room in . . ." Roger stood behind her, gaze fixed on the fabric in her hand.

Kay's cheeks flamed, and she shoved away the dress. "Plenty of room."

"Let me take that." Georgie relieved him of his armload of tins. "Oh good. Rations from the life rafts."

"Yeah." His voice rough, he turned away.

Kay's eyes burned, but she loaded her bag with tinned water that Mike handed her.

At the wedding she'd reverted to her old flirtatious ways and tried to manipulate Roger's heart and control him. This was her punishment.

———

Roger trudged through the woods, two of the nurses' barracks bags over his shoulders and his kit bag in hand. Since he'd transferred back to Italy on November 11, most of his belongings were at Ciampino Airfield, including the *dhol*. He only had his shaving kit, his Bible, a pair of drumsticks, and a change of shirt, socks, and undershorts.

The older Italian man led the way, Pettas and Whitaker assisted Vera, and Roger brought up the rear with the teenage boy, Enrico.

He never should have flown today. And he thought he'd become a top-notch pilot. Baloney. If they made it out of this alive, Veerman wouldn't give a recommendation to a man who lost yet another plane.

Nope, he'd blown his one good chance and thrown away a gift once again. And nine other people had to pay the price.

About fifty feet ahead of him, Kay struggled with a barracks bag far too heavy for her. She wouldn't be going to the chief nurse school. Not only had he broken her heart, but he'd dashed her dreams. Why did she have to suffer because he was a no-account?

The older man stopped and held up one hand. Roger stood still, held his breath, and strained his hearing.

Then the man flipped his hand forward. *"Presto."*

"Fast," Enrico said. "Go fast."

The woods opened up. A village lay cupped in a valley, open and exposed.

"Is that a good place to hide?"

*"Si."* Enrico jogged alongside him, out into the open. "Only today. Too close to the airplane. My friends will find better place. We move tonight in the dark."

Roger puffed from the exertion.

At the edge of the village, a middle-aged woman met them, ushered them through the back door of a house, and motioned them up a narrow staircase, speaking quietly in Italian.

They filed into a good-sized room, fitted with nothing but a table and chairs, and darkened by closed shutters.

"Quiet," Enrico said. "Do not open the window. Sleep. We go tonight."

Roger sloughed off the bags. "Let's lighten these, folks. Only essentials."

Enrico beckoned Roger to follow him downstairs. The other partisan waited down in the big kitchen, where the woman stirred something on the stove.

Enrico shifted his rifle strap on his shoulder. "You are the leader, no?"

Roger felt like saying no, but like it or not, he was in charge. "I am."

"We must tell the Americans."

"We brought our emergency radio from the plane." He pointed with his thumb up the stairs. "I could send a signal, but it wouldn't be coded."

"No, no, no." Alarm flashed in Enrico's large dark eyes. "The enemy will hear. We send messenger, a woman partisan they will not suspect. She will go to the OSS man in Genoa."

Genoa. At the top of the boot, on Italy's west coast. "Is it far?"

Enrico smiled and shook a finger. "No. We not tell you where you are. It is better you do not know."

That made sense. If the Americans were caught, they could endanger the partisans, who were risking their lives to help them.

Roger studied Enrico's face, the angles of manhood just starting to poke through the roundness of boyhood. "How old are you?"

"Fifteen." He pulled himself tall. "I fight for a year now. I will not work for Tedeschi."

Roger's throat tightened. These were the people the Twelfth Air Force helped with supply drops. Now he saw firsthand why they fought. Because the Germans took away every able-bodied man for forced labor and left women and children and the elderly to fend for themselves.

"Excuse me." Kay stood at the base of the stairs, one hand braced on the wall. She addressed Enrico, not Roger. "Could we please have some water? We're thirsty and we need to wash the wounds."

"*Sì.*" Enrico explained to their hostess in Italian, and the woman bustled around to meet the request.

Roger sank his hands into his trouser pockets, tapped out a rhythm on his thighs, and tried not to look at Kay, although she filled his peripheral vision. She'd been amazing today— calm, compassionate, authoritative, quick-thinking.

"You should have that looked at."

He faced her. "What?"

She pointed to her temple. "You're bleeding. Mellie or Georgie can take care of it."

He fingered the dried blood on his cheek. "Oh. Yeah." Mellie or Georgie, huh? She certainly knew how to put him in his well-deserved place.

The hostess handed Kay a bowl of water and some towels, and she chattered in Italian.

"For washing." Enrico handed Roger a ceramic pitcher of water. "For drinking. Do you have—how you say it?—for drinking?"

"Canteens. Yes, we have some." He had no choice but to follow Kay upstairs to deliver the water. At the top of the stairs, she paused, hands full.

Roger eased around her to open the door. He gripped the knob. They shouldn't be here. Women in enemy territory, hiding in plain daylight, wounded and scared. Brokenhearted.

In the dim cramped space, he faced Kay. "I'm sorry." The words came out throaty and grainy and insufficient.

She peered at him through dark eyes, the longest she'd looked at him all day. Her mouth softened a bit. "It's not your fault."

What wasn't his fault? The crash landing? The shattered friendship?

Kay nodded at the door.

Roger opened it. She was wrong. They were both his fault.

# 31

**November 20, 1944**

Not the most pleasant evening for a stroll.

Kay squinted ahead into the moonless night, careful to keep Georgie's black silhouette in sight before her. Roger and Enrico led the column, and Mike and Whitaker and Pettas brought up the rear, the routine they'd followed six nights in a row. Enrico served as their translator and guide as the partisans shuffled the Americans from shed to cellar to barn to bombed-out house. Traveling at night, Kay had no idea which direction they went, except that it always seemed to be up.

To her right, Mellie sucked in a loud breath.

"You okay?" Kay whispered and grabbed for her friend's arm.

"Yes, just lost my footing."

"Careful." Traipsing through a puddle had drenched Kay's feet, but her overcoat and hood kept the rest of her surprisingly dry and warm.

Mellie sighed. "Maybe they'll have food for us."

Kay's stomach rumbled. "Maybe." Since the Italians had so little food, the crew used their tinned Army rations, and sparingly.

"I hope I don't sound ungrateful. The partisans are wonderful to us, and I know Enrico and Roger do their best."

"I know." Kay adjusted her barracks bag over her shoulder. The group had sorted through the bags and discarded everything useless—high heels and cosmetics and hair curlers and skirts and swimsuits and even Mellie's wedding dress, at Mellie's insistence. Kay had kept only two sentimental items, her Bible and her doll Sissy, who now rode in her musette bag rather than in the less private domain of the barracks bag.

"Enrico's really taken to Roger, hasn't he?" From the tone of Mellie's voice, she had to be smiling. "I like how he calls him Ruggero."

"Yes." Kay's voice came out clipped.

"I'm sorry. I know you don't want to talk about him. This must be uncomfortable for you."

Kay made a face, invisible in the blackness. Any other woman Kay would have suspected of fishing for gossip, but not Mellie.

"Why?" Kay faked a sparkly spirit, although she kept her voice down. "What could be more fun than a vacation with a man who thinks you're a floozy?"

Mellie gasped. "He didn't say that, did he?"

Kay's foot skidded to the side, and she barely caught herself. "Not in so many words, but the message was clear."

"I can't believe that. You've been such good friends, and he's always respectful to you."

"Until I flirted with him."

"Oh." The word drifted away into the rain. "At the wedding. But I thought . . . well, it looked like you two were quite . . . close that evening. I thought something was happening."

So did Kay. Her throat swelled, but she shook her head to loosen her words. "He told me point-blank to stop flirting with him, that he wasn't the right man for me." Fresh pain lashed her heart.

"Oh dear."

A chilly raindrop hit her forehead, and Kay tugged her hood forward. The only sounds were the slap of shoe leather on wet pavement and the sniffles and grunts and shuffles of people on the move. Where were Mellie's sweet words of wisdom and insight?

The group halted. Enrico spoke softly in Italian to someone, a woman from the sound of it, and then Enrico led the group to the left, up a new road. Always up.

The group strung out again, close enough to see each other but far enough apart to avoid collisions in the dark. Enrico had partisan friends everywhere. They seemed to be spaced out every few miles to guide and to scout for enemy patrols.

"I wonder," Mellie said softly.

"Wonder what?"

"Roger. Well, I've known him for two years, and he never used to talk to women. Oh, he'd deal with us nurses, but only to get the job done. That was all. Until you and he became friends this spring. There must be a reason why he avoided women, something in his past."

Kay let out a noncommittal mumble. Even if he'd hurt her, she had no right to tell his secrets.

"Perhaps he didn't reject you because of you but because of him."

Because of him? A gust of wind blew drizzle into her face, and she angled her head away. Yes, Roger had been hurt by a woman, by a romance gone wrong. Was that why he'd rejected Kay? Did he have problems trusting women? Or did he have problems trusting himself with women?

*"I'm not the right man for you."* What exactly did he mean by that? She'd interpreted it as a brush-off, a way to avoid saying what he really meant—that she wasn't good enough for him. But what if he meant it another way—that he wasn't good enough for her?

That was plain silly.

Something bright shone up ahead, disappeared, reappeared. Kay's heart slammed into her throat.

A murmur worked its way down the line.

Georgie turned to Kay. "Take cover."

Somehow Kay passed the message to Louise behind her.

The road curved around a hill, and everyone scrambled for the downward slope to the right. Kay eased her way off the road, down through the brush, the mud.

"Get down. Lie flat. Stay together." That was Roger's voice, firm, low, calm, and coming nearer, working his way down the line. "Everyone here?"

Several feet below the level of the road, Kay flattened herself to the slope, damp grasses clammy on the side of her face.

"Vera, Alice, Georgie, Mellie, Kay." Roger crouched at her feet until she looked his way and nodded. "Louise, Mike, Pettas, Whit."

In the stillness of the night, a car engine rumbled. The light must have been a headlight. Who had cars in this area? Who would be out past midnight? Only the Germans or the Italian traitors, as Enrico called his countrymen who still chose to fight for fascism.

Kay hunched lower and pulled her hood over her face, longing to blend into the dirt, into the night.

Behind her, at the end of the line, Roger would be hunkered down too.

The new thought leached into her mind. Was it possible? Was he afraid of repeating history? Of getting Kay pregnant? Of hurting Kay? Of getting hurt himself?

She couldn't exactly ask him why he rejected her. What would be her motive? So she could counter his arguments. So she could convince him to take a chance on her. So she could manipulate him to do her will.

Kay shuddered.

"Lord, please," Georgie whispered. "Keep us safe. Hide us."

The engine rumbled closer. Light spilled down the slope, skimming over the nurses and airmen.

She should be praying for safety too. Why did her thoughts and prayers stray? *Lord, help me release Roger. You know I love him. You also know why he doesn't, can't, or won't love me.*

The sound of rubber on wet pavement, of water shooting behind tires.

Kay couldn't get any flatter, her cheek pressed into the mud. She'd tried to manipulate Roger to love her by flirting, but it didn't work. Just as she couldn't manipulate God to love her by being good. The Lord loved her simply because he chose to love her.

Roger had chosen not to.

Light flashed overhead, the engine and tire sounds peaked and then passed by.

Kay's back and arms and legs relaxed, and a strange, airy, sad peace filled her. She couldn't force Roger to love her. She couldn't control him, nor did she want to. Because she loved him. And that meant letting go.

*Lord, I release him.*

# 32

November 23, 1944

In the dim predawn light, Roger crouched behind a hedge and peered over the top. A vineyard lay before him, rows leading toward a two-storied home with a square tower and hills just beyond.

"This is the place," Enrico whispered.

"Good." After over a week of hiding by day and sneaking by night, they'd finally reached a more permanent refuge. If all went well.

"See?" Enrico pointed to the right of the house. "The cellar's in a cave in that hill. The Germans stole the *vino*, smashed everything to bits. They won't be back. Let's go."

Roger glanced behind him. The rest of the party huddled just behind the tree line, waiting. He motioned for them to stay put while he and Enrico checked things out.

"Let's go, Ruggero." Enrico vaulted over the hedge.

Roger patted his shoulder holster for security and followed, if less gracefully. Mike also had his pistol to protect the ladies if necessary.

The men scurried down a row between the grapevines, hunched over. At the end of the vineyard, they crossed an open yard, ducked between some outbuildings, through a gate in a stone wall, and approached the back door.

Enrico rapped out a knock. Knuckle, knuckle, fist, fist, knuckle. A secret code the partisans used, switching it up from time to time.

A wizened little old man dressed in black opened the door and ushered them in. His wife stood in an inside archway, wrapped in a black shawl.

*"Buongiorno, Signore e Signora,"* Roger said. *"Grazie."*

The signora raised one white eyebrow and sized up Roger, head to toe. She sniffed.

Not fond of guests, apparently. Or Americans. Or redheads. Or bad *Italiano*.

The gentleman talked with Enrico in hushed tones, pointing in the direction of the cellar. Roger could only make out *"Americani"* and *"amico."*

The signore lowered his head, grunted, and headed for the door, beckoning with short, sharp motions. Great. They were being kicked out. So much for a long-term hiding place.

At the door, the signore kept going, at a quick pace for a man his age, straight to the cellar.

"Is he letting us stay?" Roger asked Enrico.

*"Sì.* He is not happy though."

"I don't need a translator for that."

"The farmers bring some of their harvest here before the Tedeschi steal it. They feed many people. Signore is afraid you bring trouble, bring the Tedeschi. Then they starve."

An orange glow rose behind the hill. "I should get the group before the sun rises."

*"Sì.* I go with Signore."

Roger retraced his route, found the group, and led them to the cave. An arched doorway framed the entrance, but a huge wooden door lay hacked to splinters on the ground.

"We'll have to clean that up," Georgie said as she picked her way through.

"No." Roger gave her a hand to help her through the rubble. "If we clean up and the Brigate Nere or the Germans come by, they'll be suspicious."

"Oh," the ladies said, almost as one. Most of them—except Kay—took his hand to climb through the jumble of broken boards. Roger scanned the wood, looking for any piece close in size to a drumstick. When he'd thrown himself down on the hill the other night, he'd snapped one of his sticks in half.

"Oh my," Mellie said. "Isn't this charming?"

Roger headed down a long arched tunnel, faced with ancient golden bricks, lined with wine barrels on each side. A few oil lamps burned to guide the way.

"It smells funny." Alice pressed her hand over her mouth and nose.

It smelled like wine and oak and stone and earth. Most of the barrels had been smashed or hacked, and dark stains marred the brick floor.

Enrico and the signore stood talking at the end of the tunnel, where two vaulted alcoves sat side by side, each lined by empty wine racks.

"This is perfect." Kay pointed to the alcove on the right. "Ladies on the right, gentlemen on the left. We even have racks to hang our wet clothes and store our things."

Alice huffed. "Sleeping on brick. I wouldn't call that perfect."

"Yes, you will." Louise broke into a coughing fit. She'd been coughing a lot lately and running a fever. All the more reason to stay put for a while.

The women stashed bags on the wine racks, then shed coats, shoes, and socks.

Roger backed off to give them some privacy and to talk to the Italians.

Enrico and the signore were deep in conversation, and it

didn't look like a happy one, but the boy motioned Roger over. "We talk about food."

"Biggest topic of conversation in this group." Their tinned rations were running low. Roger glanced behind him to the raggedy party. To his surprise, Kay came over.

She held out her hand to the older gentleman. *"Grazie, Signore. Perfetto."*

The man's face softened, and he almost smiled. *"Prego."*

Roger didn't blame the man. Kay wore a warm smile. Her beauty shone even without makeup, even with dirt smudges on her face.

She grasped the signore's hand in both of hers. "Enrico, please tell him how grateful we are. It's so nice to be out of the wind and the rain. One of the girls is sick and needs to rest. And the cellar is lovely. We'll be very happy here."

As Enrico translated, the elderly man's face brightened, and he smiled and nodded.

*"Uno."* The signore lifted one finger and laid down a long string of Italian to Enrico.

"Signore says we can have one hot meal a day. Only one."

"One," Roger said. "That'd be great. That's one more than we're used to."

"That's a lot of work for the signora." Kay worried her bottom lip. "Can we help?"

"No, you need to hide." Enrico adjusted his rifle strap.

"Perhaps . . ." Kay narrowed her eyes. "What if we borrow an old dress, a shawl? One of us could go to the house early in the morning, help with cooking and chores during the day, then bring the food to the group in the evening. She shouldn't have to do all the work for us."

"That might work," Roger said. "I like the idea of paying our way. Ask him if there's anything else we can do, chores he could bring to the cellar. We'd be glad to help. We don't want to be a burden."

Enrico translated, and the signore's eyes moistened. *"Si. Si."* The older gentleman spoke some more to Enrico, then took Kay's hand, kissed it, and headed back for the house.

"Great job, Kay." Roger resisted the urge to nudge her in gratitude, because she'd clobber him.

Instead she gave him a smile, the first she'd given him since the wedding. "You did a great job too."

Roger's insides flipped around. Maybe she could forgive him, move on, and they could be friendly again. If they could work together, it would be best for the whole group.

"Just in time." Enrico laughed. "Signore first say no food. None. And you leave in two days. Now he say one meal a day, and you stay as long as you need."

Back in the alcove, Louise coughed and coughed.

Kay frowned. "I should give her some codeine so she can sleep."

"How are we doing on meds?"

"All right. Vera's leg looks good, but we used a lot of sulfanilamide on her wound. We have a bottle of a hundred codeine tablets. We'll be fine unless too many of us catch what Louise has."

"Let's hope we get out of here before long."

"Yes." A slight smile, and she returned to the ladies' alcove.

Roger felt lighter inside. A short conversation, not even a personal conversation, but a good one.

"Ruggero?"

"Hmm?" He turned back to Enrico.

The boy waggled his black eyebrows and grinned. *"Bella."*

He'd been caught watching Kay. Was his love that obvious? He couldn't let Enrico harbor that idea. He leveled a strong gaze at the kid and shook his head. "Just a friend."

Enrico gazed past Roger, down the tunnel, and he stiffened and gripped his rifle.

Roger slipped his hand inside his flight jacket to his shoulder holster and turned.

Three armed men marched toward them.

"Marco!" Enrico loped toward them. "Giovanni!"

Fellow partisans. Roger released his breath, eased his hand out of his jacket, and joined the four men.

"Ruggero, this is the man. The OSS man."

Roger scanned the threesome. They all looked like Italian partisans, wearing a motley collection of work clothes and jackets and hats.

The shortest of the three stepped forward to shake Roger's hand. "You must be the pilot, Lieutenant Cooper."

He laughed in relief at the Brooklyn accent. "Yeah, I'm Cooper."

"Capt. Tony Anselmo, Office of Strategic Services."

"I can't begin to tell you how happy I am to meet you."

Anselmo's smile tilted a scruffy dark mustache. "Want to go home, huh? Well, quite a few souls in Washington want to see that happen."

"Good."

"How are the ladies holding up?"

"Great. They're real troupers. One of the gals is sick, but she keeps up with the pack."

Anselmo peered past Roger. "Folks back home don't like to see women in danger, and the newspapers smell a story. The Army's managed to keep them quiet, saying it's in the girls' best interest. The more of a fuss we make, the more the Germans will be determined to find you. They know you're out here. They're looking. And they don't like to fail."

"No, sir. Any ideas on how to get us out?"

"We're putting together two plans, by sea or by air. Both are tricky this time of year, and it's shaping up to be a bad winter."

"Yeah." Thank goodness the women had heavy coats with

liners, and the men had their sheepskin-lined leather flight jackets.

"We'll leave Enrico here with you. I'll introduce myself to the crew, then return to my base, send a message. I'll use partisans for messengers and only come back when it's time to get you out."

"Any idea how long?"

Anselmo's dark eyes narrowed as if Roger had asked for a feather bed and a steak dinner. "These things take time."

"Yes, sir. I understand." Roger gave the man a hearty handshake. "I appreciate everything you're doing. We're all thankful."

"Celebrating?"

"Celebrating, sir?"

A smile twitched. "It's Thanksgiving, Cooper."

"It is?" Roger gazed down the tunnel toward his crew and the nurses, who would sit down to K-rations instead of turkey today. But they were alive and moderately healthy, with a plan in the works to go home. "It sure is."

# 33

December 6, 1944

"It's too much." Alice Olson piled the dirty dinner dishes into the basket. "The cold, the dirt, the hunger, the danger. And Signora yelled at me all day long. It's all too much."

Georgie tossed a cloth over the basket. "Just yesterday you were griping about never getting out of this cave, and now it's your turn to get out and you still whine."

"Leave her alone." Vera adjusted her kerchief over her hair. "You do your share of whining about how poor little Hutchie is doing."

"Be fair," Mellie said. "Hutch isn't next-of-kin like my Tom. The Army Air Force won't notify him. All he knows is Georgie isn't writing."

In the corner of the alcove, Louise broke into another coughing fit.

"Knock it off, Louise," Alice said. "For heaven's sake."

Kay held her breath and planned her words. Tension had escalated the past two weeks in the cellar. The boredom of inactivity brought out worse attitudes than the danger of the week on the run.

"Enough, ladies." Kay got to her feet, still weak and woozy from the respiratory ailment that had swept through the group. "Louise can't help coughing. It's not her fault she hasn't shaken the bug as quickly as the rest of us. We're out of codeine, and there's nothing we can do. As nurses, compassion is called for."

Alice lowered her head. "I know. Sorry, Louise."

"It's okay."

"Now, Alice." Kay nodded at the blonde. "Did Signora really yell at you?"

She gazed up with wide blue eyes. "She wouldn't stop."

"Does she yell at any of the rest of you?"

A chorus of "no" circled the group.

"I'll have Enrico ask her what the problem is. But we should remember she's putting her life at risk having us here, not to mention the frustration of communicating with people who don't speak her language."

Georgie leaned against the brick wall. "I'm trying to learn some Italian. I ask her the words for the tasks we're doing or the food we're cooking. She likes that."

"Great idea." Kay smiled at her friend. "As for loved ones, you all have folks who are worrying and don't have enough information. You can't do anything about it, and worrying only wastes energy."

Mellie scooted close to Georgie. "'Take therefore no thought for the morrow: for the morrow shall take thought for the things of itself.'"

"Exactly." Kay pulled a blanket off a wine rack and wrapped it around her shoulders. "We're all cold and dirty and hungry, we're all bored and uncomfortable and tired of being in danger. So have compassion on each other. Stop whining, stop snapping, and buck up."

"Yes, ma'am." Georgie gave her a salute and a wink.

"Let's get a game going." Kay leaned around the wall to the men's alcove. "Who wants to play bridge?"

"I do." Mike sprang to his feet and urged Pettas, Whitaker, and Enrico to join them.

Kay scanned the group. Four men and six ladies, but Louise

was too ill to play. "Have fun. I'll check on Roger, see if he needs anything."

"All right." Vera pulled two decks of cards from her musette bag.

Kay headed down the tunnel to the doorway, where Roger had guard duty. The men took turns. Over the past two weeks, Kay and Roger had inched their way to a wary friendship.

At the entrance, Roger sat by the pile of rubble, drumming on blanket-padded planks. He used his single drumstick and a scrap of wood.

"Hi." Kay leaned against the far doorjamb. "Are you warm enough?"

"Sure. I'm an Iowa farm boy. This is balmy and warm."

Snow fell in the darkness outside, adding to the several inches coating the ground. "Wish I could offer some coffee."

"Me too."

"Want some company?"

Roger laughed. "Why? Want to get away?"

Kay slid to the ground and arranged her blanket around her. "How'd you know?"

"I couldn't hear the words, but I got the gist. Alice whining, Vera snapping, Georgie and Mellie worrying about their men, Louise coughing, Kay soothing."

"Mostly right."

"Mike too eager to help, Pettas grumbling about not having any cigarettes, Whitaker threatening to raid the locals' food supply, and Coop goofing off."

Kay scratched her scalp under her kerchief. What she wouldn't give for a good shampoo. "Goofing off? Hardly. You're our trusty night watchman, our fearless leader."

"Fooled you, didn't I?" A slight smile, a strike on an imaginary cymbal in the air.

Why did he see himself that way? "Were you really that bad as a boy?"

"Oh yeah." Drumsticks flashed in the air. "Three boys in the Cooper family, then three girls, then me. I had three extra mothers doting on me, spoiling me. Then my little sis came when I was four, and the girls had a new pet. So I got more and more obnoxious to get attention. I was good at it. My pranks, my laziness, and my smart mouth got me in trouble at home and at school."

"You're not that boy anymore, you know."

He glanced her way, raised one eyebrow.

"You're not. You're smart and capable and an excellent leader. Your squadron, your crew, all the ladies here—everyone respects you and looks up to you."

"Until I got us all trapped behind enemy lines."

Kay pulled chapped lips between her teeth. "Could you have done anything to prevent it? Honestly?"

The drumsticks stilled. Roger peered into the distance, motioned Kay toward the wall, and eased back.

Kay sucked in a breath and pressed hard against the wall. What had he seen? So far only partisans had visited, but how long could that last?

He relaxed and smiled. "The goat got loose. Signore's chasing it."

The sound of angry Italian confirmed his words, and Kay straightened up. "No dodging the question. Could you have prevented this?"

Roger returned to his drumming in a low, steady beat. "No. I did everything I could."

"So don't blame yourself. You landed safely, and you've been our shepherd ever since. You got us through those first crazy days hiking at night in the mud, kept us moving when we wanted to stop, and now you're calm and firm. You make everyone feel safe."

He shrugged. "Couldn't do it without you." His voice came out low, and he coughed. "You're the only nurse who could lead this bunch, and you're doing it. They all listen to you."

"You're just saying that so I'll stop talking about you."

"Is it working?"

Kay laughed. "What would you like to talk about?"

"Anything at all." His sticks went tap-tap-tap, thump-thump-thump, tap-tap-tap, thump-thump-thump.

What letters were those? "How about the Morse code?" Memories of Mellie's wedding assaulted her, and she slammed her mouth shut.

He paused. "The . . . Morse code?"

Of all the idiotic things to say. She gestured with a blanketed hand. "I need to brush up. We're hiding in enemy territory. It could save lives."

"Yeah, like the partisans' knock." He knocked on the doorjamb. "They alternate knuckles and fists, like dots and dashes."

Kay remembered another way to send Morse code with thumbs and fingers, and from the way Roger wouldn't look at her, she had a hunch he remembered too.

Regardless, it could be useful, and brushing up on the code would be a pleasant diversion. She cleared the roughness from her throat. "First we need code for everyone. I'm Kay, and *K* is dash-dot-dash, right? What's *R* for Roger?"

"Dot-dash-dot."

She smiled. "They're opposites."

"They are." He grinned and tapped the two letters, with the drumstick for the dot and the wood scrap for the dash. He handed her a square board about the size of a book. "Rap on that."

"*K* . . . dash-dot-dash." Fist, knuckle, fist. "*R* . . . dot-dash-dot."

How appropriate that they were opposites. Opposites attracted. Opposites complemented. But ultimately, like oil and water, opposites didn't mix.

# 34

Roger and Mike walked the length of the clearing, just beside the trees, counting strides to estimate the field's length and its suitability for landing a plane. Roger struck the frosty night air with his new drumsticks to help keep count. Enrico had carved a pair from olive wood, not varnished, but nicely shaped and smoothed with Signore's sandpaper.

At the base of the field, Enrico and Captain Anselmo waited. "What do you think?" the OSS man asked.

"I counted 1142," Mike said.

"And I got 1137." Roger tucked his drumsticks inside his jacket. "Our strides are close to a yard, so it's about three thousand feet long and plenty wide. A short landing but not dangerous."

"Great. I'll radio the coordinates."

"First I need to check the center of the field for obstacles."

Anselmo squatted in front of the radio. "No. I can't have you out in the open."

"It's three o'clock in the morning. The partisans secured the area."

"As best they can. We need to get out of here well before daylight."

Roger's lower jaw hardened. "Sir, if one of our C-47 pilots flies in here—those are my buddies, mind you—and he hits a ditch and cartwheels, you know what'll happen. Those four crewmen are dead, the Nazis are alerted, the ten of us are captured or worse, and you and Enrico are captured—and much worse."

Anselmo slipped on his headphones. "The chance of the landing even occurring is close to nothing. First you have a two-day hike out here with most of your party weak and sick. Then the C-47 has to fly over enemy territory without being sighted and has to locate this spot. The landing is the least of our worries."

"You said only Mike and I could approve the field. I won't do it unless we can make sure it's clear."

Mike stepped forward. "I'll go with you. We can spread out, see more of the land."

Anselmo gazed up at them from under a ratty cap. "Half an hour. No more."

"Ruggero?" Enrico twisted his rifle strap. "Come back, okay? You need to finish teaching me algebra."

Roger clapped the kid on his scrawny back. "Wouldn't miss it." He felt bad for the boy, missing school because of the war. The least he could do was teach him some math and help him with his English using the few books the group had.

At the end of the field, Roger and Mike spread out about twenty feet apart, and they headed down the center in the feeble moonlight, feet crunching in the snow. Anselmo said it was supposed to snow later in the day, which would conceal their footprints.

Roger picked up a rock the size of his fist and hefted it into the trees. Mike poked at something with his foot, moved on.

It didn't look bad. Not too rough, fairly level.

Something cracked in the woods to the left.

The men dropped to the ground. Roger's breath raced,

curling over the surface of the snow. He wormed his hand down into his trouser pocket and found his clicker. He clicked twice.

Silence amplified every breath.

He clicked again.

Thump, tap, tap, thump.

Roger faced Mike and sighed in relief. The partisans' latest knock. He got to his feet and brushed snow from his face, jacket, and trousers. Mike mimed wiping sweat off his forehead, and Roger nodded.

They continued down the field and tossed aside some more rocks, but it was as good as they could hope for.

In the safety of the trees, they headed back to find Anselmo and Enrico.

"What do you think?" Roger asked in a low voice. "Looks good to me."

"Same here. I think it'll work."

"When I get back, first thing I'll do is eat a big steak dinner, then I'll take a long, hot shower. Then I'll sleep for a week until I get days and nights back in order. What about you?"

"I'll telegraph my parents, then eat fried chicken. Nothing else. Just chicken, dripping in grease."

Roger's mouth watered. "Sounds good."

"After you get cleaned up, are you finally going to ask Kay out? Take her someplace nice?"

Roger's stomach jolted, and not just because he hadn't had a good solid meal in almost a month. "Kay? Of course not. We're just friends."

"You're not interested in her? How's that possible? Not only is she beautiful and smart, but she's . . . well, she's just about perfect."

Ever since the crash, he'd suspected that Mike had a crush on Kay. Now confirmed. He burrowed his hands into his jacket pockets to conceal the fisting.

"So why not?" Mike asked.

Roger shrugged. He didn't care to discuss his past with Mike. Not that he didn't trust the man, but they didn't have that kind of friendship. "I don't date because I don't want to get married. The big band life is no kind of life for a dame. The wives get fed up and leave. I can't blame them. No roots, no home. I could never put someone through that." Especially not someone he loved.

"Oh." Mike pulled his coat collar up to his ears. He was a good man, a solid man, the kind of man who could provide a home and a future for a woman.

The inside of Roger's mouth felt sticky, tasted sour, but he had to say it. "You're crazy about her, aren't you?"

Mike let out a wry chuckle. "Doesn't matter. Not when she's crazy about you."

"Nonsense."

"Come on. I've seen how she watches you, seeks you out."

Worse than he thought. After his loutish behavior at the wedding, she had every reason to hate him. But the evasion had turned him into a hero in her eyes, a shepherd, she said.

They had to get out of here and soon.

Maybe Mike could help her forget Roger. Wouldn't that be great? He worked a smile into place to perk up his voice. "Say, when we get out of here, they'll send me stateside. She'll get over me, guaranteed. Then she'll see what a swell guy you are and fall for you."

"Yeah, right."

"I'm not kidding. You're the kind of man she ought to fall for. For now, get to know her more as a friend. When we get out of here, I'll back off and get out of your way. I promise."

Mike grunted, but he seemed to walk a bit taller, shoulders back, chin lifted.

Roger slipped out his drumsticks and rapped a beat on his thighs as he walked.

An image flooded his mind—Kay looking at Mike with the same admiration she lavished on Roger. Kay in Mike's arms, playing with his brown hair instead of Roger's red. Kay kissing Mike.

More than anything he wanted to strike a tree with his drumstick, but he'd break a stick—and reveal his true feelings.

Why should it bother him? Kay used to date dozens of men, and it never bothered him.

Truth silenced the rhythm. That was before he loved her.

# 35

December 23, 1944

Kay folded a blanket and stuffed it in a barracks bag.

"I'll leave this here. It's vile." Alice held up a khaki blouse and wrinkled her nose. "On Christmas Day we'll arrive in Naples and receive clean hospital pajamas. Just imagine."

Kay needed to correct her but carefully, because only hope would propel Alice through two nights of hiking in the snow. "Take it. Remember, we shouldn't leave anything behind that could incriminate Signore and Signora in case the Germans raid the place." Also, the rescue mission's success wasn't guaranteed, and they might still need their supplies, no matter how vile.

Georgie wrapped a scarf over her head and tucked it into her coat. "I still think Enrico should come with us. I'm worried about him."

Mellie looped her musette bag around her neck. "He doesn't want to leave. The partisans are his family."

Roger entered the ladies' alcove. "Ready to go?"

"Oh yes!" Georgie hooked arms with Mellie and Louise and strolled down the tunnel. "*Arrivederci*, old cellar."

While the rest of the group headed out, Kay peered into

the wine racks to make sure nothing was left behind. Her throat felt strange.

"You're not as enthusiastic as the others." Roger leaned back against the rack and crossed his arms.

Everyone else had left. Kay rubbed her hand over the smooth wood, inhaled the scent of old wine and earth, and savored the glow of oil lamps on golden bricks. "As hard as it's been, I'll have good memories of this place." Most would center on Roger—working with him, consulting together, chatting during guard duty, practicing Morse code.

"Mm." His face had become too gaunt, and he needed a close shave since the men's razors had reached their limits, but his gaze shone with compassion. "It's become home."

Her throat clogged. More than home, it had become family, and two days from now, they'd all be separated, never to be this close again. She'd probably never see Roger again.

He set his square hand on the rack about a foot from her hand. He patted with his fingers, tapped with his thumb, patted with his fingers. Dash-dot-dash . . . *K*.

A watery, wavering smile tugged at her lips. She signaled back . . . dot-dash-dot . . . *R*.

He stood too close, his odor filling her nose, as her stink certainly filled his nose. But she didn't mind because it was his scent.

Roger tapped and patted on the wood. *T-I-M-E-T-O-G-O.*

"I know." She grabbed her bags, snuffed out the oil lamp, and walked with Roger to the entrance.

Enrico and Giovanni, another partisan, helped Louise onto a mule.

"I'm sorry to be such a bother," Louise said. "I feel silly. I can walk."

"I'm sure you can." Mellie patted Louise's leg. "But why not enjoy the royal treatment, princess?"

Louise rolled her eyes. "You'll spoil me rotten."

Her pale cheeks, the dark circles under her eyes, and the thinness of her voice told a different story. The lingering pneumonia and the poor diet were taking a toll. For Louise's sake, the rescue needed to take place on schedule.

*"Andiamo."* Giovanni motioned the group toward a path up the hill.

Kay wound her scarf over her filthy, kerchief-wrapped hair, then pulled up her hood for good measure. The temperature was well below freezing, and a half-moon cast a silvery glow on the snow.

The group tramped up the hill in silence. Cold seeped through Kay's shoes, and the slick leather soles threatened to slip from under her as she climbed. Each step required concentration and care.

They proceeded down the hill, then up another, a winding path along the side of the slope.

A shriek. Ahead of Kay, a nurse slid off the path, tumbled down the slope.

"Alice!" Vera shouted.

"Oh my goodness." Kay worked her way down the hill, grasping bushes, careful so she wouldn't tumble too. "Alice! Alice, you all right?"

About twenty feet down, Alice lay curled in a ball. "Oh, my arm. Something's wrong. I think it's—broken."

Alice did have a dramatic flair. Kay sat in the snow beside her. "Let me take a look."

She sat up, cradling her arm to her chest.

Kay gently reached into her friend's coat sleeve and palpated the arm. Something was definitely wrong. It wasn't quite straight. "I think you made the right diagnosis, Dr. Olson."

"Oh . . ." Alice groaned. "What horrible timing."

Roger scrambled down the hill and crouched beside them. "Are you okay?"

"Broken arm, I think." Kay gave him a wan smile.

"Man alive. Does it hurt a lot?"

Alice nodded, and tears puddled in her eyes.

Roger tilted his head, beckoning Kay over to the side. He leaned in close. "I don't mean to sound callous, but we have to cover ten miles tonight. It's already nine, and the moon sets at one. The farther we can go while the moon's up, the better."

"I know," she said. "I'll put it in a sling and give her some morphine. She should be able to walk. We can splint it when we stop for the day."

"All right." He glanced up the hill where the rest of the group huddled, watching. "That'll have to do."

Kay and Roger helped Alice up the hill. Mellie and Georgie rummaged in the barracks bag with the medical supplies and found gauze and pins and morphine. The ladies helped Alice out of her coat and jacket, bound her arm to her chest with gauze, and pulled her jacket and coat around her shoulders.

Vera stashed the bottle of morphine back in the bag. "We can't go on. We need to go back and reschedule."

"Can't do that," Roger said. "The OSS, the Twelfth Air Force, the partisans—you know how hard they worked to set this up, how long it took. We might not get another chance."

Vera's eyes flashed. "She can't go on. It's heartless to make her."

Kay stood in front of Alice and grasped her good shoulder. If worse came to worse, she'd stay behind with her. "Be honest. Can you do this?"

A look of determination filled Alice's eyes, a look Kay had never seen before. "I can and I will. We're all in this together, and I refuse to hold anyone back."

Louise patted the mule's neck. "We can take turns riding the royal steed."

"And we'll all help you." Georgie slung Alice's musette bag over her shoulder. "We're the nightingale sisters, remember?"

Kay's eyes watered. The nickname had applied originally to Georgie and Rose and Mellie, and then to Kay and Louise, but never before to Vera or Alice.

"Come along." Mellie headed up the path. "We nightingales need to be in our nests before sunrise."

The group continued on their way, with Vera and Georgie flanking Alice.

Roger fell in beside Kay. "Good job, kid. Unity."

"Unity." Despite their differences, despite their history, despite the hardships of this ordeal, they were indeed unified. "I can't believe it."

"I can. You're an excellent leader. You work with each person's strengths and weaknesses, bring out the best in them."

Kay pulled her scarf over her mouth. That was what leadership was about, wasn't it? It wasn't about control but about helping people work together for a common good, and she liked it. Whether or not she ever became a chief nurse, she could use this skill.

She walked along the snowy path on the wooded hills by Roger's side, in companionable silence, occasionally bumping up against him.

Although cold nipped at her face and her feet, warmth snuggled inside her.

# 36

December 25, 1944

Behind Roger, the whole company hummed "O Come, All Ye Faithful" as they marched through the predawn gray. He didn't stop them. Their voices weren't any louder than the crunch of their shoes in the snow and brush, and the songs raised morale.

Directly behind him, Kay did not sing. He smiled at her. "Not singing?"

She laughed. "Of course not."

He knew why, thanks to one of their late-night talks. "I wouldn't mind."

"That's not the point. Pettas is off-key, and no one cares. I just don't want to. Every time I try, too many memories come back. I'd rather focus on who I am now, on my heavenly Father rather than my earthly one."

Nothing remained of the brassy glamour girl. Her nose was red, she wore no makeup, she'd lost too much weight, and a greasy strand of hair poked from under the kerchief and scarf and hood. She'd never looked more beautiful to him.

Roger returned his attention to the path so he wouldn't trip and make a fool of himself.

In front of him, Enrico pointed. "There it is. I see Marco and Captain Anselmo."

Excitement surged inside, and Roger charged forward, grasped Anselmo's hand, and pumped it. "You made it. Are we really pulling this off?"

"Looks good so far. The partisans have secured the area, and lookouts are stationed around the perimeter. Now we wait. The plane's supposed to arrive at 0805, right after sunrise."

Roger could barely see his watch in the dim light—0748. No time to spare.

"How's everyone?" Anselmo peered around to the group. "I heard one of the girls broke her arm."

"Yeah. Alice did, and they think she'll need surgery. It doesn't look right. And Louise gets weaker every day. We need to get them out of here."

Anselmo scratched his dark mustache. "Here's the plan. The field lies east to west. We have colored panels laid out on the snow in a straight line to signal the plane. The pilot will approach from the east along the north side of the field. If all is clear when he comes in sight, I'll lay out the final panels to complete the *T* pattern. When the pilot receives the signal, he'll circle the field and land from the east. You'll meet him at the southwest corner. Then he turns, takes off, and hightails it out of here."

"We should get in position."

"I agree. Speed is vital."

The group headed to the rendezvous point in high spirits. Roger had to shush them when "Joy to the World" got too joyful, but he couldn't stop grinning. He'd done it. He'd helped get them out of this mess.

The more he thought about it, the less he blamed himself for the crash landing. He would have flown that day, regardless. No one had ordered him. The other two pilots flew, and they'd arrived safely in Rome, according to Anselmo. Every decision he'd made had been the right decision based on the information he had. And he'd made a solid landing. Everyone survived.

Now he'd helped lead them out. He was sure to earn a recommendation for the Hank Veerman band.

They turned along the southern edge of the field, behind the trees. A glow rose from the east and spilled golden light on the snow. Anselmo motioned for them to stop, and the group clumped together, softly singing "I'll Be Home for Christmas."

Kay met his eyes and winked at him.

He winked back, but his heart seized. Soon he'd have to say good-bye to her forever. How could he do that? Over the past six weeks, Kay had become . . . well, almost as if she were the other side of his brain. They worked well together, perfect partners.

Like husband and wife.

Roger spun away and gripped a tree trunk for balance. He couldn't allow himself to think that way. Marriage required more than love, more than partnership. Kay needed a home and stability, and he couldn't give it to her. Besides, he'd promised Mike he'd back off and give him a chance with Kay. He'd keep his word.

"Listen," Mike said.

The group hushed, and Roger strained his ears. Sure enough, engines throbbed to the northeast. But was it the rescue party, enemy aircraft, or something else?

He listened harder, and the rhythm spoke to him, a rhythm he knew well. "That's a C-47."

"Something else too." Whitaker narrowed his eyes.

"They sent an escort," Anselmo said.

An escort? Fighter planes? Roger thumped Anselmo on the back and laughed. "Best Christmas present ever. Thanks, Santa."

The OSS man tipped half a smile. "It isn't over yet."

Roger wanted to grab the orange cloth under the man's arm and spread it out himself.

Something rustled in the brush to the east. A partisan jogged toward them, gesturing wildly. He and Anselmo conferred in Italian, in strident tones.

"What's going on?" Roger asked.

Anselmo's lips set in a hard line. "Two members of the Brigate Nere stopped one of the lookouts. They're not buying the partisan's story. They sent out a radio message. A German patrol's coming."

Roger's breath rushed out. "We have to move fast."

"No. We have to call it off."

"What? But—"

"No." Anselmo crossed his arms and fixed a firm gaze on Roger. "If you were flying a C-47, making a drop behind enemy lines, and you failed to get a signal, what would you do?"

"I wouldn't make the drop."

"Why not?"

He groaned and looked away to the fresh layer of snow that wouldn't be marred by airplane tires, to the orange *I* that wouldn't become a *T*. "Because if I did, I'd alert the Nazis to the partisans' position. A lot of people could die."

"People like Enrico."

Roger's eyelids flopped shut. He couldn't let anything happen to that kid.

"It's my decision anyway. I outrank you." Anselmo clapped his hand on Roger's shoulder, then addressed the rest of the group. "I'm sorry, but we have to call off the mission. The Brigate Nere called in a German patrol. We can't endanger the partisans."

Some of the ladies gasped. Pettas and Whitaker cussed.

Roger ached inside. If only he could do something, anything to restore the hope and joy they'd just lost.

The engine sounds grew louder, and the plane came in sight. The familiar lines of the C-47 screamed home and comfort and a good meal and a soft bed. He wanted to reach up and pluck the plane from the sky, force it to whisk these people to safety, all of them, the partisans too. He'd pile them all in.

"Look," Mellie said in a low, sad voice. "They sent P-47 Thunderbolts."

Georgie leaned her head on Mellie's shoulder. "They really wanted to help us."

And they couldn't. Roger punched a tree, grimaced, and shook out the pain in his hand. How much longer until they could arrange another rescue attempt? They'd have to start from scratch. And now they'd have to go on the run again with the sick and injured and weak.

The group stood in silence and watched the planes fly by, east to west, toward the Mediterranean, toward Naples. Without them.

Tears glistened on the ladies' cheeks. All but Kay. She put her arms around Alice and Vera and murmured soothing words.

Roger stepped forward. "I'm so sorry, ladies."

Vera gave him a calm gaze. "Don't be. These people have endangered themselves enough already."

They'd be endangering themselves again. The Americans needed to find someplace to hide for the day.

Roger stared at the sunlight, bright on the snow. He'd been looking forward to becoming a daylight creature again. "Where can we go?"

"We have a spot about a mile to the west." Anselmo motioned for Marco to run onto the field and gather the orange panels. "We need to move fast."

After Enrico helped Louise back on the mule, everyone shouldered their bags. A few sniffles, a gulped sob, and they followed Anselmo two by two, shoulder to shoulder.

It was Christmas Day.

Roger gazed up to the bright sky. Almost two thousand years earlier, a weary twosome had bedded down in a filthy stable, no room in the inn. "Guess you know how we feel, Lord."

# 37

December 31, 1944

In the corner of the dank cellar, Vera pulled her blanket around her shoulders. "This is the worst New Year's Eve ever."

Kay leaned against the cold brick wall. The last rays of sunlight slanted through narrow windows close to the ceiling. Roger sat cross-legged on a stack of crates by the far window, keeping watch on the village street outside, his back to the ladies, drumming on his knees.

To think, a year ago she and Grant Klein danced the night away at the Orange Club in Naples. She'd worn her long grassy green gown, her hair curled and rolled and pinned just right, her face powdered and rouged, her lips painted red.

Now she sat in a damp cellar, where little rat feet scurried among the boxes and crates. She wore a stinking uniform with ragged trouser hems and holes in the knees. Her stomach cramped with hunger and dysentery. Yet she was happier than she'd been on the dance floor.

Forgiveness from God, friendship with these ladies and with Roger, and even the growing experience of the evasion— all gave her a sense of peace and rightness.

Still, the glum mood in the cellar needed to be vanquished. Low spirits made for slow feet, and they had twelve miles to cover tonight. Once again they moved every night, not only to throw off the enemy but to reduce the burden on the villages where they stayed.

Kay sat up straighter and draped her blanket over her knees. "All right, 1945 will be here in a few hours. Let's fantasize. Where do you think you'll be a year from now? The war will be over, I'm sure of it, at least in Europe. Who wants to go first?"

"I'll play." Georgie tucked a well-worn novel into her musette bag. "I'll return to Virginia, where they'll throw a parade in my honor in Charlottesville. And Hutch will commit some stupendous act of heroism and be promoted to a general, and we'll get married. He'll open a pharmacy in Charlottesville, and we'll buy a house outside town with plenty of land for my horse Hammie, and we'll adopt Hutch's little friend Lucia from the orphanage in Naples."

Kay grinned. "That's quite a year."

"Best ever. How about you, Mellie?"

She leaned her head back against the wall and gazed at the ceiling. "The Americans will liberate my papa from Santo Tomas, and he'll come home. He'll love Tom, I know it. Tom will get an engineering job and build bridges all over the world. He'll have plenty of work in Europe with the war damage. And maybe . . . well, we'd like to start a family."

Mellie's embarrassed little smile made everyone laugh.

"Your turn, Louise." Mellie nudged her friend.

Louise lay on the floor, covered with several blankets. "I just want to—I want to get better."

"You will," Georgie said. "And then?"

"Then I want to go home to Colorado, to the ranch. Maybe I can talk Rudy into giving up the big city for the country. I sure hope so. I miss him."

"Well, I don't miss Gordon." Alice adjusted the gauze that bound the splint to her swollen, crooked arm. "I'm tired of how he plays around with anyone in a skirt. I'm breaking up with him first thing. Then I'm done with nursing. I'm going to study art. That's what I love."

Kay smiled. "Good for you."

"How about you, Vera?" Georgie leaned forward. "Are you going to marry this mysterious nameless boyfriend of yours?"

"I plan on it." Vera gave a smug smile.

Kay's stomach turned, and she exchanged a glance with Mellie. So Vera still had designs on Captain Maxwell. If they ever got out of here, Kay still had to deal with that situation.

"Your turn, Kay." Mellie looked too eager, probably to steer the conversation away from Vera's adulterous plans.

"Me?" She'd shared bits of her dream with some of the ladies, but only Roger knew all of them. Well, almost all. Not the dreams that involved him.

"Yes, you." Georgie laughed. "This was your idea after all."

"All right." Kay worked her fingers through holes in her blanket. "I hope Lieutenant Lambert will recommend me for the chief nurse program. After the war, I'd like a job in a hospital as a chief. If I can't, I'll work my way up."

"I can see that." Louise coughed. "You'd be a good chief."

"Then you'll buy a house," Mellie said gently. "Tell us what it's like."

Kay's eyes watered. "It's just a little house, one bedroom, painted yellow like the sun. I'll have my own kitchen, and a comfy wingback chair in the living room, and closets, and a front porch with a wicker chair and table."

"By yourself?" Alice frowned. "You'll live in a house alone?"

Kay's throat clamped shut.

"Hush now, Alice," Georgie said. "If the Lord wants her to get married, he'll bring a man into her life."

Silence fell among the ladies, a pitiful silence that made Kay's eyes water more. Over by the window, Roger's drumsticks lay still.

Had he heard her? Heard the longing in her words . . . in her silence?

She didn't want a home alone. She wanted a home with him.

———

## January 7, 1945

Roger helped Anselmo spread out the map on a dry spot on the floor, while Kay and Enrico looked on. Both daylight and rain streamed through holes in the roof of the stone shed, and the rest of the party huddled by the walls, trying to sleep.

Roger studied the map. "What's the plan, Captain?"

Anselmo traced the curve of the bay between Genoa and La Spezia. "This is the only spot in the Mediterranean where the German Navy is still active. They're weak but present. We have moonless nights between January 10 and January 18. However, we also need smooth seas. We're sending our Navy boys in on an Italian fishing boat. This is the area we're looking at. It's fairly isolated." He pointed to a spur of land about ten miles north of La Spezia.

"We're not far." Roger tapped a spot inland and to the north.

Enrico held his chin high. "Partisan territory."

"For the most part." Anselmo gazed from under heavy dark brows. "Tonight we'll head to this cluster of villages, all within ten miles of the pickup. We'll have you zigzag between the villages, with the exception of this one."

"Are the Germans there?" Kay asked.

"No." Anselmo pointed to a crossroads. "This is the best of all, only six miles away, and we're saving it for last. When we receive word that the boat is coming the following night, you'll move here. After dark, you'll head to the coast and wait. Can the ladies do it? You'll have steep hiking along the coast."

"Yes." Kay gazed around to her napping friends. "Our shoes are in bad shape, and everyone's weak. But more than anything, they want to go home."

Roger drank in the smooth curve of her neck, the strong set of her jaw, the compassion in her eyes.

"All right, Cooper." Anselmo folded up the map and handed it to him. "Tonight Giovanni and I will go to the coast, set up the radio and beacons. When we get the signal, I'll send a message with Giovanni. Enrico will stay with you. Both men know the terrain, the villages, the people. You just keep the party together and moving."

"I'll do that, sir." Roger tucked the map inside his flight jacket.

"I know you will. Say, what are your plans after the war?"

"I want to be a drummer in a big band."

Anselmo's face puckered up as if he'd bitten into a rotten apple.

"I know." Roger fingered the drumsticks inside his jacket. "No money, no stability."

"That's not what I meant. It's just a waste of your talents."

Roger squirmed. "Drumming is my talent."

"Not the only one. Don't you see how everyone in this group respects you? Because you respect them all, officer and enlisted, male and female. You treat them fairly and make sound decisions. You lead and they follow. Those are rare and fine qualities."

Roger shrugged and got to his feet. He needed to hit the sack. "They're my friends."

Kay smiled up at him. "It's more than that."

"I agree." Anselmo stood and straightened his coat. "You could do great things in this world if you put your mind to it."

"You could be a teacher." Enrico scrambled to his feet and grinned. "You teach me algebra and English."

Roger stared at the boy, at his latent dream spoken out loud yet again.

Anselmo pulled out his blanket and settled down in a corner of the shed. "I was thinking captain of industry, but if education is in your blood, aim for principal."

Roger barked a laugh, then clamped his mouth shut for the sake of the sleepers. "The only experience I have with principals is being paddled—a lot."

Anselmo tipped his service cap over his eyes. "Think about it."

"I'll forget about it. Best for everyone." Roger stomped to another corner and squatted by the bag of blankets.

"What's wrong?" Kay leaned against the wall beside him. "Why do you get touchy when anyone says you should teach?"

"Nothing's wrong." He wrestled out a blanket, didn't matter which one. They were all threadbare, dirty, and smelly. "Just tired of people nagging me."

"Nagging you? Sounded like they were encouraging you."

"Feels like nagging."

"Why? Because you don't want to teach? Or because you want to teach but don't think you deserve it?"

Roger sucked in a breath and jerked his head toward Kay, so hard he almost toppled over. He braced himself against the wall.

A slight lift of the eyebrows, of the corners of her mouth. She nudged his foot with her own. "Remember that day by the lake at Istres when you gave me advice?"

"Yeah." His voice rasped.

"A wise man told me God gives us good things not because we're good, but because he's good."

"Not the same."

Kay lifted one shoulder. "Maybe it is, maybe it isn't. That's between you and the Lord." She headed for the ladies' side of the shed.

Roger yanked the blanket around him, got as comfortable as he could on the dirt floor, and closed his eyes. Between him and the Lord. It wasn't anyone else's business. What did Anselmo and Enrico know? They didn't know what he was like.

A rock jabbed his ribs as truth jabbed his brain. They knew him as he was now, not a goof-up but a leader.

Roger opened his eyes. He'd changed. Could his dream change too?

# 38

**January 15, 1945**

The nurses sat in the cellar of a home in the crossroads village, silent but exultant. Kay studied the small window at shoulder height that opened to the alley behind the house. The orange glow of sunset filled the cellar. Only a few more hours and they'd head to the coast, where the boat was scheduled to arrive around two in the morning.

The inside door to the cellar banged open, and Giovanni scrambled down the narrow steps, wild-eyed, and he spoke to Enrico in quiet but frantic tones.

Kay's breath stilled. She stood and joined Roger, Mike, and the partisans.

"What's up?" Roger asked.

Enrico's dark eyebrows drew together. "A German patrol is in town, searching house to house. They come from the west. Two soldiers search, one driver in the car."

"Man alive." Roger ran his hand through his hair. "We're only about six houses in."

"We need to leave now," Mike said.

"No." Roger grasped his copilot's arm. "That's what they want. They want to flush us out. We need a plan. Kay, get the ladies ready. Keep it quiet."

Kay's hands felt numb, but she nodded. She returned to the nurses.

"What's going on?" Vera asked, a bit too loudly.

"Quiet." Kay squatted in front of them. "We have to leave very soon. A German patrol is in town. We'll have to move fast. Get ready."

"Oh no." Georgie clapped a hand over her mouth, and her eyelids fluttered. "We were so close."

"We still are. Get ready and stay calm."

Mellie squeezed Georgie's shoulders. "We will."

Georgie lifted her chin. "Yes, we will."

The ladies put on their outerwear, looped musette bags around their necks, and piled the few remaining barracks bags by the window.

Kay returned to the men. The map was spread on a table upside down, and Roger was drawing a map of the village on it. The town was shaped like a Y, with the long leg pointing to the sea. Blocks represented the houses, with a bunch of dots in one house on the long leg—where they were now.

Roger beckoned her close to the map. He traced an arrow running from the back of the house, down the alley, connecting outside the village with the main road to the sea.

"That's our route," Kay whispered. "Won't they . . . ?"

Roger pressed a finger to his lips, his brown eyes serious. He traced a second arrow running from the back of the house in the other direction and into the street in front of the German car. "Diversion," he wrote.

Kay's breath quickened. The partisans would do that for them? Just so they could escape?

Roger pointed to the house next door, drew two swastikas inside and one in the car, then he retraced the diversion arrow.

Kay nodded. They'd time the diversion when two of the Germans were inside.

Roger ended the diversion arrow close to the car, drew an

X, then mimed honking a horn. The driver would make a racket, but he'd wait for his colleagues before he chased the partisans.

He pointed to Kay then to the window. That was the signal to escape. Kay nodded and wiped her palms on her trousers.

Starting at the X of the diversion, Roger drew a line heading inland through town, branching at the fork in the road at the piazza.

All right. That might work. The Germans would chase the men—two of them—and they'd go in two directions. As Italians, they could blend in and evade capture. Meanwhile, the Americans could escape to the sea.

Someone stamped upstairs.

Kay startled.

Roger stared at the ceiling, then motioned to Enrico. Oh no, was Enrico part of the diversion? He was just a boy. They couldn't let him.

Then Roger turned to Kay and laid one hand on her shoulder. His eyes—she'd never seen that look in them—as if he were memorizing everything about her, and so firm, so fond, so sad. He pressed his lips into a straight line and headed to the window where Enrico waited.

Terror ripped through her heart. Good Lord, no! Not Roger! He couldn't be part of the diversion.

Kay dashed after him, grabbed his arm. "No," she whispered.

Roger faced her and nodded. He took her by the shoulders and leaned close to her ear. "Need two to divert."

She shook her head, over and over. No, not him.

He pointed at Giovanni, at the group, at the window. Giovanni would be their leader. They did need someone who spoke Italian. That left Enrico . . . and the Americans.

Tears filled Kay's eyes. Roger would never ask his men to sacrifice. He'd do it himself. "I'll go with you."

"No," he murmured. He gestured with his head to the ladies. They needed her.

Her love and her grief welled up and melded together. She placed her hands on his chest and tapped dot-dash-dot . . . *R*, her Roger, the man she loved, the man she'd always love.

His eyes scrunched up, and he mashed a kiss to her forehead, stayed there, his fingers tapping on her shoulder.

Kay struggled to concentrate on the message with his warm lips full on her forehead, with grief straining at her heart.

*K*, he tapped.

She nodded gently so as not to end the kiss.

He drummed out a message, his fingers insistent. *R-U-N*. She gulped back a sob and tapped, *Y-O-U-T-O-O*.

Roger broke away and climbed out the window. Gone, just like that.

Georgie slipped an arm around her shoulder. "He'll be fine, sweetie," she whispered.

Kay slapped her hand over her mouth. She'd never see him again, would she? He wouldn't live the day.

---

Roger crept down the alley with Enrico, heading inland, creamy plastered houses on one side, a rough stone wall on the other. Everything inside him ached from Kay's despair. But he had to do this so she could escape. If there were any other way . . .

He gritted his teeth. There wasn't. Enrico had offered to go alone, but if the Nazis caught him, they'd torture and execute him. With two of them, they stood a better chance, and Enrico had scouted out hiding places this morning. Always thinking ahead, that kid.

They turned down a narrow passageway to the main street, down broad stone stairs.

Enrico peeked into the street, popped back into the

passageway, and held up one hand. Roger pressed back against the cool wall. An eerie silence enveloped the village. No one would dare provoke the Germans.

His heart hammered out a rhythm he hated, the rhythm of fear. But he had to do this. *Lord, let this work. Let the women and my crew escape. Please.*

His stomach squirmed like a worm on a hook, which was what he was.

Enrico peered around the corner and raised one finger. The Nazis must have entered the house next door to the hiding place. Now to make sure they were well inside.

Roger set his hand on Enrico's shoulder. They might not see each other again. The boy faced him with dark eyes wide. He might be brave, he might be bold, but he was still a frightened little kid inside. Roger squeezed his shoulder. *"Grazie, il mio amico."*

One side of his mouth twitched up. *"Prego."*

"Let's go."

The men sauntered down the street toward the German car. With Roger's red hair and American pilot's crush cap and leather flight jacket, he had to be a mighty tempting worm, even in the falling twilight.

He strolled closer and closer to the jaws of the Nazi fish. The closer he got, the lower the chance of escape.

Roger poked a loose cobblestone from the road with his toe and kicked it down the street.

The fish snapped. The driver looked their way. Stared.

"Now!" Roger stopped in his tracks, turned, and sprinted down the road.

The car honked.

*Run, Kay! Run.* And Roger ran, harder than he'd ever run before, despite his weakened condition. They crossed the triangular piazza at the fork in the road. Enrico ran right, Roger went left. *Lord, keep the kid safe.*

But Enrico was young and fast, and he could blend in with the locals.

Roger dashed down the narrow curving street, counted off the buildings to his hiding place, then went down two more, where a cellar window sat at street level. He kicked in the window. A great crash, the tinkle of falling glass, a scream.

"Take that bait, you stupid stinking fish." He hurried back to the building Enrico told him about, an abandoned bakery. Roger tested the door. Unlocked, thank goodness. He stepped inside and shut the door.

Yeah, it was a bakery, all right, with a long counter, a big double brick oven, and crates and barrels. Enrico told him he could hide in a barrel.

Maybe a scrawny teenage boy could fit inside, but not Roger Cooper.

He glanced around frantically. The oven?

His stomach turned. He'd never been claustrophobic, but an oven?

Shouts rang out down the street.

No time to be picky. Roger opened the lower oven door. A giant brass pot sat inside, and he slid it out and poked his head in. Long and wide, but only about two feet high. Big enough.

He crawled inside. Wasn't this how Hansel and Gretel coaxed the witch to her doom? What if someone started a fire?

Roger groaned. What choice did he have? He tried to pull the door shut, but of course the handle was on the outside. He leaned out, hefted the pot back inside with him, closed the door as best he could, and slid the pot in front of the door.

Curled up with his knees to his chest, his head close to the door, he pressed hard against the wall and willed himself invisible.

What a strange place this would be to die. Even his parents, who believed he'd never amount to anything, couldn't have imagined an ending like this.

Dark, stuffy, no air. Ash tickled his nose, and he sneezed. He couldn't afford to do that again. He worked a handkerchief free from his shirt pocket and covered his nose.

Someone pounded on a door. Glass smashed, two men shouted in German.

Roger gritted his teeth and pulled his body as far from the oven door as possible. He eased his pistol from its holster. If discovered, he'd shoot and make a break for it.

One set of footsteps pounded up the stairs in the front of the building, and another clomped through the store up front. More glass smashed.

Prayers tumbled in Roger's head, unintelligible. His nose itched. A sneeze would kill him. He pressed one finger hard against his upper lip until the compulsion to sneeze passed.

The footsteps drew nearer. Pottery smashed, wood scraped on tile.

He held stone-still, one finger on the trigger, another jammed under his nose so hard his eyes watered. *Lord, please, make him blind.*

Closer and closer. The upper oven door squeaked open.

Roger trained his pistol on the oven door, praying he wouldn't have to shoot.

The door opened. Light slipped around the edges of the pot. The soldier shoved the pot back, right into Roger's knees.

He bit back a cry, kept the pistol level. One word and he'd fire.

*"Sind sie hier?"* a voice said from across the room.

*"Nein. Niemand."* The door slammed shut. *"Wohin gehen sie?"*

*"Ich weiss nicht, aber wir werden ihnen finden."* Footsteps thumped back to the street.

A long low sigh fluffed out the handkerchief. Silence, except his own galloping heart.

He was alive! He was actually alive.

A second thrill turned up a smile. They'd followed him and not Enrico. The kid would be fine. The Germans would break into some house and find a family with one extra child. Enrico would have taken off the hat and coat they'd be searching for. He'd live too. *Thank you, Lord.*

A third thrill, and he stretched out his cramped legs. By now, the girls would be well on their way to the coast, to freedom, to home.

The thrills fizzled out and fell as ash. He wouldn't be going with them.

# 39

A car honked.

"Roger," Kay whispered—a prayer, a plea, a dirge.

Giovanni opened the window, climbed into the alley, and beckoned everyone out. Mike, Pettas, and Whitaker helped the nurses, then shoved out the barracks bags, containing not much more than blankets at this point—and Roger's kit bag.

Kay gazed around the narrow, twilight-gray alley, her head light, her senses overwhelmed by the blaring horn. The women clutched one another's arms.

After the men climbed out, Giovanni motioned them down the alley toward the sea.

Away from Roger. The horn stopped honking, voices shouted in German, and an engine revved.

Kay braced her hand against the clammy plaster wall. *Run hard, Roger. Please, Lord, let him escape. Enrico too.*

But where would they hide? The Germans would turn the village inside out to find them.

Giovanni stopped and held up one hand. He crept down a passageway to the main street. A minute later he returned and continued on the way. The ladies followed the armed partisan, with Whitaker and Pettas behind them, and Mike with his pistol to the rear.

Dread swirled in an oily black pool in Kay's stomach. If the Nazis caught Roger or Enrico, they'd execute them on the spot.

At the last house in the village, Giovanni again scouted around to the main road. The land lay open for a good hundred yards where the road entered the village. They'd be clearly visible.

When Giovanni returned, he pointed up the wooded hill that flanked the village, then swept an arc with his arm back toward the road.

First they'd have to climb the six-foot-tall stone wall that kept the hillside from spilling into the alley. Pettas and Whitaker made stepping stools of their hands and hoisted the ladies up. Kay waited to go last. She gazed down the alley. Maybe Roger could circle back and join them. But no one entered the alley. Sounds of thumping doors and shattering glass assaulted her ears. *Please, Lord, don't let the Germans find them.*

Vera climbed onto the wall, stood, and swung back her barracks bag.

Too much momentum. Kay gasped. Vera tottered on the edge and plunged to the cobblestone road.

Vera crumpled to the ground, cried out, clamped it off.

Kay and the men dropped to their knees around her.

"Vera," Kay whispered. "Oh my goodness."

"My ankle." The brunette clutched her leg, her face writhing in pain.

Kay exchanged a glance with Mike. They had no time for first aid and no mule to transport her.

"Go on without me." Vera yanked off her shoe and probed her ankle, wincing. "It's bad. I can't walk."

"We won't leave you," Mike said.

"You have to." She gripped Kay's shoulder and pulled her close, face to face. "Tell Frank I love him."

"I'll do no such thing." Not just because she wouldn't pass a message from a mistress to her lover, but because she would not leave the nurse behind. "We'll work it out."

Mike took Vera's hand and helped her to standing. Whitaker scrambled up the wall and lifted Vera under the arms, while Pettas and Mike pushed her up.

Then Whitaker heaved Vera over his beefy shoulders and forged his way up the hill. He couldn't do that for long, but then they could take turns supporting her as she hobbled.

Kay climbed the wall next and scanned the village, desperate for a glimpse of Roger.

Mike hoisted himself up, glanced at Kay in alarm, and motioned her to the protection of the trees.

They threaded their way up through the woods. Leaves slipped under Kay's feet, and moisture seeped through the holes in her soles. Although they'd left the snow behind at higher elevations, the temperature hovered right above freezing.

Inside she shivered more than on the many treks through snow. Roger.

Over half an hour passed before they returned to the main road. Darkness had fallen, and they braved the main road, which wound through wooded hills. Whitaker and Pettas linked their arms like a chair and carried Vera, while Mike manned the pistol.

Kay walked at a sharp pace, lungs tight, ears pricked, eyes darting back and forth, searching for places to hide if necessary.

A bang sounded behind them, muffled by distance, retorting through the trees. And another.

Kay wheeled around and sucked in a breath. What was that?

Mike took her elbow, led her down the road. "We need to hurry," he said in a low voice.

"What was that?"

He didn't answer, he didn't look at her, he kept walking, his face unreadable in the darkness. But the tightness of his grip spoke volumes.

*Oh, Lord. Oh no.* Two gunshots.

Kay gasped and sank to her knees. *No, no, no.*

Mike pulled on her arm. "Come on. We have to go. We have to get to the boat on time. They won't wait."

She stared up at him, her mind dazed, muddy, reeling. How could she go on? How could she?

He squatted in front of her, set his hand on her cheek, and leaned close. "We don't know what happened. Could've been the Nazis firing wild shots at our men and missing. Could've been Roger shooting at the Nazis. Could've been some farmer putting his mule out of its misery. Might even have been that German car backfiring. We don't know."

If so, why did Kay feel as if the bullet had barreled through her heart?

Mike caressed her cheek with his thumb. "Right now, we need to move on. Your friends need you."

The ladies stood nearby, clumped together, holding each other, hands pressed over their mouths. Yes, they needed Kay to lead them, to escape. That was why Roger had caused the diversion in the first place.

Kay pushed herself to her feet and propelled herself forward. She tried to shove aside all thoughts but escape, but one image persisted, burning into her mind . . .

Roger and Enrico on their knees, hands tied behind their backs, pistols shoved to the base of their skulls.

*No, no, no. Lord, no.* Kay clutched her arm around her stomach and forced her feet to move, one step, then another.

---

Two shots rang out. Roger jerked, banged his head on the roof of the oven, and rubbed the sore spot.

Enrico! Did the Nazis catch him, kill him? What about the ladies?

He coerced his brain to think. No, the shots came from the inland side of town, not the direction the ladies were heading. But Enrico . . .

Why, those dirty rats. Roger shoved aside the pot so he could climb out. He'd hunt them down and shoot them like the rodents they were.

He paused at the oven door. Would he really? He'd get shot himself. And what if they were just shooting at Enrico while he ran . . . and they missed? What if those weren't even gunshots? Then Roger would endanger himself for nothing.

He sighed and rearranged the door and the pot. All he could do was follow the original plan. If Enrico lived, he would come for Roger when all was clear. If he didn't come, before daylight Roger would slip out of town and into the woods.

Then what?

Where could he go? Back to the last village where they'd stayed? Maybe the host family would let him in, hide him, and contact the partisans somehow. Maybe the partisans could contact Captain Anselmo.

A plan with more holes than his trousers, but the only one he had.

He huddled in the ashy cold and prayed for Enrico. The poor kid. Youthful enthusiasm and a clever mind had gotten him into this mess. Knowing Enrico, the boy would be proud to die for a good cause and for people he cared about, proud to die a hero.

Hero.

Nothing but a word for a good man who was dead. Too many heroes in this stinking war. Wouldn't be any good men left around afterward.

Roger's nose felt stuffy, and his eyes felt moist. Had to be from the ash. He wiped his face with his handkerchief.

A soft creak, a thud.

Roger tensed, slapped his damp hankie over his mouth and nose again, and readied his pistol. They came back. They'd be more thorough this time around.

Feet shuffled, wood scraped over tile.

He aimed his pistol at the entrance. He didn't intend to join Enrico among the ranks of dead heroes. If he did, he'd take a Nazi or two with him.

"Ruggero?" A quiet voice.

Enrico! He was alive! "Enrico? That you?" He kicked aside the pot, shoved open the door, and slithered to the door. In the darkness, he could just make out a skinny silhouette.

A flashlight shone in his eyes. "Ruggero!"

Roger tilted his head away from the beam and crawled out of the oven. "I heard gunshots, thought you were dead."

"*Si*. Thought the same about you at first."

"Any idea what it was?" He brushed ash from his jacket.

"A goat. The last goat in the village. The Tedeschi shot it out of spite."

"The ladies? Did they escape?"

"They must have. That's why the goat died. We must leave now."

He kicked his cramped legs. "Let me work out the kinks first."

"Don't know the word *kinks*, but we must leave now. The Tedeschi called in the Brigate Nere. They'll probably burn the village and shoot the civilians."

A hollow pit formed in Roger's chest. "No."

Enrico shrugged. "They do that."

He clamped his hands behind his head and slammed his eyes shut. The townspeople had done nothing wrong. Only a few of them had harbored the Americans—and they'd harbored innocent women, at that. Why should hundreds of people suffer?

"They're running away, the whole town. We join them and escape."

"You can. I'd stick out too much."

Enrico shone the flashlight at Roger, and he laughed. "You look like old man."

The ash. He whisked off his service cap, shoved it inside the pot in the oven, grabbed a handful of ash and smeared it into his hair.

"Here. Saw this when I looked for you." Enrico dashed for the doorway and returned with a tattered coat and cap.

"Great." Roger tugged on the coat over his leather flight jacket. Barely fit.

Enrico set the cap on his head. "Now you old Italian man."

"*Si.*" With his legs so stiff, he'd have no trouble doddering. "I'll need my grandson to lean on."

They picked their way through the broken pottery and glass to the front door. On the main road, mothers pushed carts loaded with small children and belongings. Older children carried little ones. Elderly couples lugged sacks over their shoulders.

Roger hesitated, his stomach twisting. For two months he'd been in hiding. He hadn't been out among people.

Enrico tucked Roger's hand around his arm. *"Andiamo, Nonno."*

He lowered his head and shuffled forward. *"Si, si."*

# 40

January 16, 1945

Kay didn't bother taking off her shoes but waded into the cold black water to the motorboat a few feet from shore. What did it matter? Her shoes were ruined, and she'd get new ones if the boat succeeded in taking them to the port of Leghorn.

What did anything matter?

A small wave chilled her to the knees. She stopped and peered behind her into the dark, willing Roger to come clambering down through the brush to the beach. But he wouldn't. If he'd survived, he was trapped in enemy territory with the Nazis on his trail.

Captain Anselmo took her elbow and guided her to the boat. "Don't worry. I'll search for him."

"Thank you." Her throat felt as briny as the ocean. With the captain's assistance, she climbed over the side of the boat and flopped inside.

"Stay low." A man whose voice she didn't recognize put a hand on her shoulder. "Any more, Captain?"

"No, she insisted on going last. Thanks for your help. Godspeed."

"Aye aye, sir." The motor revved, and the boat wheeled around and headed out to sea, bucking and rolling.

Kay huddled on the cold floor with Mike, Pettas, and Whitaker nearby. The rest of the nurses had gone out on the first trip.

"How far to the fishing boat?" Whitaker asked.

"Quiet," the sailor said. "And lie low."

"What if I get sick?"

"Then you get sick."

Kay curled up. Puddles of seawater soaked through her trousers. She'd never been airsick, but the small craft heaved more than any airplane.

She hugged her stomach. She didn't care if she threw up, didn't care if she died. The man she loved was dead, or at the very best in the greatest danger of his life.

*Why, Lord? Why? Take me too.*

And Roger had died for nothing.

The boat jolted over a wave, and the truth jolted her mind. No, he hadn't. He'd sacrificed himself for his friends, for the nine people now on their way to safety and freedom.

He'd died for her sake, so she would live.

She wiped her eyes and steeled her jaw. For his sake, in his memory, she would *live*.

———

**Leghorn, Italy**

Kay steadied herself on the narrow gangplank down to the dock. Army photographers swarmed the nurses and airmen.

Kay ducked her head. Not only was she filthy and sloppy, but she couldn't manage a smile.

"That's enough for now." Lt. Cora Lambert shooed the photographers aside. "You can take more photos after they've had meals, baths, and medical exams."

The familiar voice and face turned up the corners of Kay's mouth.

Alice squealed. "Lieutenant Lambert! I'd hug you, but . . . you don't want us to hug you."

The rest of the girls laughed—quick, joyous, relieved, nervous laughter.

"Let me take a look at you." Lambert set her hands on Mellie's and Louise's shoulders, closing the circle. "You're a sight for sore eyes."

"Well, we are a sight." Georgie adjusted the grungy kerchief over her hair.

A few feet away, the air crew had a more subdued talk with a fair-haired officer, most likely Major Veerman—he did bear a resemblance to the big band leader.

Fresh grief coiled around Kay's heart. Roger had earned a recommendation, and now he'd never play drums again.

"Come along, ladies." Lambert waved them onward. "What would you like first? A bath or breakfast?"

"Breakfast!" Five voices all at once, and they laughed.

Kay didn't, but she worked up a smile for her friends' sake. She doubted they could keep anything down. They were accustomed to so little food, and seasickness had taken its toll.

Army Air Force personnel ushered them into a dockside building. A long table heaped with breakfast food lay before them, and the ladies rushed in.

"Eat slowly," Kay said. "We haven't had a full meal in over a week."

"And we haven't had food this good in two months," Georgie said.

Vera hobbled to the table with a crutch the sailors had fashioned for her from a mop. "Is . . . Captain Maxwell didn't come?"

"Hmm?" Lambert assisted Louise onto a bench. "I asked if he wanted to, but he's been busy this week."

"Oh." Vera plopped down, and the crutch clattered to the floor.

Kay took a seat, and her stomach clenched. She had to report them, but perhaps she'd wait until Vera had healed some.

Lambert joined them at the table. "After you eat, we'll fly you down to Naples. You'll be admitted to the hospital for exams and treatment—as well as baths."

"When can we send telegrams to our families?" Georgie scooped a small serving of scrambled eggs onto her plate.

"In Naples. Meanwhile, this gentleman would like to hear your story." Lambert motioned over an officer. "May I introduce Captain Freeman with Army Air Force intelligence?"

Kay sighed and spread butter on a piece of toast, all she felt like eating. If only the interrogation could wait. Roger Cooper would infuse every tale, and she couldn't bear it.

The stories poured out, disjointed and out of order, but this wouldn't be their only interrogation.

Kay kept quiet. Her throat refused to swallow. The bread turned to paste in her mouth. She stood and pressed her hand to her stomach. "Excuse me. Where's the . . . I need to—"

"Oh! Come with me." Lieutenant Lambert took her arm and led her down a hallway. "I'm sorry, Kay. Too much food too fast."

She hadn't swallowed more than one bite, but she nodded. In the refuge of the bathroom, she sat on the toilet, waiting for the meal and the stories to finish, rocking back and forth to keep the tears at bay.

After half an hour, she went to the sink and saw herself in the mirror for the first time in weeks—the filthy thin face, the too-large eyes, the red nose. She turned on the water and scrubbed her face and hands and ragged fingernails, cool brownish water streaming down the drain. After she blotted her face dry, she only looked a bit better. The grief in her eyes couldn't be washed away.

Back out at the table, her friends looked at her with concern. She wrangled up a smile and held up her hands. "Clean."

"Oh!" Georgie stared at her palms. "Goodness' sake. I haven't washed my hands before a meal in so long, I plumb forgot. What would my mama say?"

"May we?" Mellie raised pleading eyes to Captain Freeman.

"Of course."

While the nurses headed for the washroom, Kay sat and nibbled her toast.

Lieutenant Lambert scooted next to her. "The ladies said wonderful things about you."

"That's nice." She swallowed, and the morsel went down.

"They say you unified them, held them together."

So much of that was Roger's doing—his calm, wise strength. *Oh God, please let him be alive.*

Lambert leaned one elbow on the table and studied Kay. "Awhile back, you asked me for a recommendation for the chief nurse school."

She gazed into Lambert's brown eyes. "I did."

"Not only have you put your personal life in order, but you've turned into a true leader. I would be proud to recommend you."

Kay's vision shimmered, and she mumbled her thanks. She'd embrace that dream and live it.

---

Northern Apennines
January 23, 1945

Even growing up in Iowa hadn't prepared Roger for this cold. At least in Iowa he had a toasty farmhouse. Here in the partisans' mountain hideout, he had no such luxury.

Roger tugged his coat tighter and pulled his knees to his chest. The partisans had built the hideout in a narrow gorge, with a ramshackle roof of boards and branches, more for concealment than shelter.

Four partisans sat in a clump deeper inside the gorge, discussing sabotage plans in Italian and shooting Roger nasty glares for the increased German attention he'd drawn to the area.

As if he wanted it himself. Running from the Nazis meant he could be shot, wearing civilian clothes guaranteed instant execution as a spy, but hiding out with partisans meant he could add the extra delight of torture.

Roger scratched his beard. He'd left behind his shaving kit, Bible, and his other belongings when he helped the ladies escape. If they'd survived, all this would be worth it. *Please, Lord. Let Kay be alive and safe. All of them.*

Enrico worked his way down the tunnel with a woman behind him, a nondescript-looking lady in her thirties with shoulder-length black hair. "Ruggero, this is Maria."

"*Buongiorno*, Maria."

"She's a courier." Enrico squatted beside Roger. "She knows where our friend is in Genoa."

"Will you go?" Roger asked her. "Tell him I'm here?"

Maria frowned and spoke in Italian to Enrico. A spirited discussion followed with lots of head shaking and hand waving.

"Translate," Roger said through gritted teeth.

Enrico sighed. "She doesn't want to go for one man. She went once for the group, for the women, but doesn't want to go now. Too dangerous. She says the work here is too important."

Roger rested his head against the rock wall. The partisans had been busy. They expected a big Allied push in March or April and were wreaking as much havoc as they could behind German lines and planning uprisings in the major cities.

Enrico tapped Roger's arm with the back of his hand. "I tell her you're a pilot. You drop supplies to the partisans."

"I won't fly again. They'll interrogate me and send me

home. Standard procedure when you spend time behind enemy lines."

"She doesn't have to know that."

He fixed a firm gaze on the kid. "Yes, she does. Tell her."

Enrico groaned and spoke to Maria, a lot more words than Roger told him to relate. As he spoke, Maria's eyes engaged Roger for the first time, and she leaned forward.

"What are you saying to her?"

Enrico waved him off and kept talking. Roger couldn't pick up more than a handful of words, but he could translate the hand motions. Enrico was telling how they'd created a diversion and helped the nurses escape, how Roger hid in an oven, how the Nazis shot the goat.

Maria tucked in her lips and blinked too much. "*Si*. I go."

"You'll go?" Roger clasped her hand. "*Grazie. Grazie.*"

Enrico gave Roger a smug smile. "She goes for the great war hero."

Oh brother. If his parents heard that, they'd die of laughter. Yet Roger smiled. No matter. Getting a message to Anselmo was his only chance.

# 41

**45th General Hospital, Mostra Fairgrounds, Bagnoli, Italy**
**February 2, 1945**

Flashbulbs burned Kay's eyes. She smiled, stiff and phony, as she'd been doing for the past two weeks. She and Georgie and Mellie sat on chairs between Louise's and Vera's hospital beds, and Alice sat up in bed beside Vera.

"Great. Swell. One more. And one more. Now with the two lovebirds."

The reporters and photographers had a reason to renew their frenzy today—Tom MacGilliver had a week's furlough to see his wife. If only the Army had sent them someplace romantic and private for the reunion, but no, the Public Relations fellows wanted a spectacle.

Tom led Mellie to the hospital aisle, and Kay took advantage of the break to rub the bright spots from her eyes.

Major Barkley, the PR officer, grasped Mellie's shoulders and angled her to face Tom. "Just like that. Put your arm around her, Captain."

"Captain." Mellie smiled up at her husband. "I'm not used to that."

"Neither am I." He put his arm around her waist.

"Now kiss her," Barkley said.

While bulbs flashed, Tom grinned and complied.

"I see my headline," a reporter said. "MacGilliver the Lady Killiver."

Kay winced. Poor Tom. No matter how good he was, he never seemed to be able to break free from the reputation of his father, a notorious executed murderer.

"All right, gentlemen." Tom held up one hand. "That's enough. The ladies are in the hospital for a reason. Some are sick, some recovering from surgery, and they all need rest."

"I quite agree." Lieutenant Lambert opened the door and swept her hand toward the opening.

Major Barkley, a dark-haired man in his forties, tugged down his jacket over his paunchy stomach, sniffed, and led the men out.

Lambert closed the door behind them and groaned. "So sorry. What good does it do to have a private ward for you ladies if the vultures have access?"

"We understand." Mellie snuggled close to her husband.

Kay put her chair back where it belonged, while a ward nurse assisted Alice to her bed. Louise's pneumonia was responding to penicillin, Alice had undergone surgery on her arm, Vera wore a cast on her broken ankle, and everyone had plumped up and regained color. Georgie had finally been able to write her beloved Hutch and was waiting to hear back from him.

Kay wanted to get out of the hospital, but the Army hemmed and hawed about the nurses' fate. A recommendation for the chief nurse program did no good here in Italy. And she wanted to leave the peninsula more than anything. Every day she asked if anyone had heard about Roger, and every day the Army brass said they hadn't.

Her friends told her to hold on to hope, but each day hope felt flimsier.

She marched to the door, to Lieutenant Lambert. "May I take a walk? Please? I'm desperate for fresh air."

Lambert exchanged a glance with the ward nurse, then nodded.

A sigh flooded out of Kay, and she strode down the hallway. Another sigh of relief that none of her friends joined her.

Right outside the hospital building, Kay stopped to drink in the unsterilized, unmedicated air. Where to? Mussolini's Mostra Fairgrounds outside Naples had been converted into a large American hospital complex, complete with a medical supply depot and a blood bank. Giant colorful murals trumpeted the joys of fascism, but were now defaced by GI graffiti.

"Kay?"

The masculine voice made her heart jump briefly, but it didn't belong to Roger.

No, it belonged to Capt. Frank Maxwell. A grin covered his handsome face, and he held out one hand for a handshake.

She didn't take it. "Good afternoon, Captain."

"I'll say. I can't tell you how glad I am to see you."

Kay crossed her arms over her bathrobe. Why would he be happy to see her? And why wasn't he dashing inside to see Vera? Two weeks had passed without a sign of him. Sure, the 802nd was based all the way up in Siena, but they flew to Naples almost daily.

"Is Vera . . . how is she?"

She was frantic with worry that her lover had forgotten her. "She'll be thrilled to see you." Venom leaked into her voice.

"I'm . . . I'm not going in. I just need to make sure she's all right, deliver a letter."

"A letter?"

He pulled an envelope from inside his service jacket, his cheeks twitching.

Kay narrowed her eyes at the man. "Let me guess. You're going back to your wife."

Maxwell's gaze jerked up to her, then darted around, making him look like the rat he was. "Well . . ."

"You found someone else." The venom tasted vile on her tongue.

He pressed his lips together and held out the letter. "Please, just give her the letter."

"I'll do no such thing." Kay marched away. "Tell her yourself. Tell her cheaters cheat. That's what they do. That's what they always do."

"Kay . . ." Defeat tinged his voice.

She marched around the corner under the gray overcast.

Why did a rat like Maxwell walk this earth in freedom when good men like Roger Cooper didn't?

---

**Northern Apennines**
**February 8, 1945**

Roger paced the snowy mountaintop in dwindling light, drumming the air.

Captain Anselmo sat before his SSTR-N1 radio set. He tuned dials and flipped switches and adjusted cables between the battery, power supply, transmitter, and receiver. The parts were designed to be carried inconspicuously by one man, some parts under his coat and one concealed in a fake loaf of bread.

Roger glanced at his watch—1802. Anselmo was supposed to contact Naples at 1800. "Got a signal yet?"

"No," he said in a crisp, annoyed tone. "Might have to move you to a new spot, try again tomorrow."

"Or stash me in Genoa until the US Fifth Army marches in."

"No. I run too many operations. I can't take the risk of having you there. You stand out."

Roger tapped a paradiddle on a tree. "Then let me help the partisans. I can't sit around and do nothing."

"No. You're under strict orders from your commanders not to get involved."

He huffed and whacked a branch, sending down a shower of snow. "So I'm supposed to sit around and wait for the Germans to find me and execute me, or for the Communists to get fed up and do it themselves, so they can throw the Nazis off their trail."

"Hush. I've got it." Anselmo pressed the headphone to his ear and wrote on a notepad.

Nervous energy propelled the drumsticks, slicing the air. It had taken two weeks for Maria to find Anselmo and for Anselmo to find Roger. The OSS man brought the great news that the rest of his party had escaped to Leghorn. Kay was safe.

This was Roger's first opportunity to get a message to the outside world. He had to keep his drumsticks quiet so signals could be heard.

As Anselmo tapped on the transmitter, a tiny lightbulb flashed on and off. Then he wrote on his notepad, decoding the message. He frowned and rubbed the back of his neck. "Verify Cooper sing sing sing?"

"Huh?"

"That's the final part of the message. They received the message that I found you, but they want to verify it's you. That's standard. Now we have to figure out the puzzle."

"Sing, sing, sing? Like the song?"

"The song?"

"Yeah. Big Benny Goodman hit—'Sing, Sing, Sing.' "

"Of course. That's it. They want to prove you're an American and know the song. The response they're look-ing for—it's 'Benny Goodman.' " Anselmo slipped on his headphones and flipped the switch to transmit.

Something squirmed inside. "Wait. It's too easy, too obvi-ous. It was a huge hit. Even the Germans might know it."

Wrinkles etched Anselmo's brow. "You're right. Why would they ask that?"

Roger paced to the tree and rapped out a drumroll. "They want to prove it's me, right? Not just any American, but me."

"Right."

He wheeled around. "Krupa. The answer's Krupa."

"What?"

Roger marched back. "Veerman's on the other end. He knows I'm a drummer. He wants the name of the drummer in 'Sing, Sing, Sing,' and it's Krupa. Gene Krupa."

"Yes." Anselmo's eyes lit up, and he scribbled on his pad.

Roger glanced over his shoulder to make sure he spelled the name right.

For the next few minutes, Anselmo tapped and scribbled and coded and decoded, and Roger couldn't stop grinning.

They'd gotten through. Maybe they'd try to get him out of here, get him back to his crew, to Kay.

If he could send her a message right now, what would he tell her? That he missed her more than a hot meal, clean water, flush toilets, and a mattress? That he loved her more than any human being he'd ever known? That life felt incomplete without her?

A joyful sense of purpose filled his lungs. Perhaps he'd tell her he wanted to take a risk.

# 42

**Northern Apennines**
**February 13, 1945**

Once again, Roger crouched by the edge of a makeshift landing field right before sunrise. Once again, Captain Anselmo held the last signal panels, waiting until all was clear. Once again, Roger prayed the plane would land.

Enrico squatted beside him. "I'll miss you, Ruggero."

"You can come with me. There's room."

The boy shook his head. "My work is here."

Roger handed him a scrap of paper. "My Army address and my parents' address. Write me when this whole thing's over."

"I will." Enrico stared at the paper, and his cheeks puckered.

Roger clapped him on the back before the kid could start crying.

Engine sounds arose to the east, beautiful American engine sounds. Anselmo held the orange cloth and didn't move, and Roger scanned in all directions. Any minute now the crash of partisan feet through the underbrush could kill this dream.

But no one came, and the planes grew nearer. Anselmo ran out onto the field, laid down the cloth, then ran back to Roger. "I don't need to tell you to make it fast."

"No, you don't." He held out his hand. "Thanks for everything. I'll never be able to thank you enough."

Anselmo shook his hand hard. "Aw, scram. I'm tired of being your nanny."

Roger smiled and glanced up. A C-47 passed by, plus half a dozen P-51 Mustang fighter planes. "They sent the cavalry."

"Sure did."

The C-47 turned for the approach. It was going to land. The ordeal was actually over. After almost three months, it was over.

The plane rushed down the field, and the wheels touched. Roger stood and saluted Enrico and Anselmo, his throat thick. As soon as the plane stopped, he sprinted onto the field, to the open cargo door. Propwash kicked up dirt and snow, and Roger gripped his hat, turned his face from the assault.

He hoisted himself up through the cargo door. Two pairs of hands dragged him inside, and he lay flat on his stomach, panting, his palms flat on the cool, American-made floor.

Someone shut the cargo door and shouted down the length of the plane. "Let's get out of here."

The plane pivoted, the engines roared, and they jostled down the field.

Roger grabbed the pole on the floor that the flight nurses used to secure the litters. Might as well lie still until after takeoff.

"Another prank from Lieutenant Cooper. Making us fly all the way up here to pluck you from trouble, huh?"

That was Major Veerman, mock outrage in his voice.

Roger laughed. He laughed so hard, the cold metal floor hurt his ribs. He switched hands, rolled onto his back, and grinned up at his CO. "You know I can't resist a prank, sir."

"I see you're out of uniform, yet again. Where's your cap, Lieutenant?"

"Stuffed in a bread oven in some little village."

"And that scruffy beard. Don't know why I bother." But the grin on Veerman's face said otherwise. He held out a hand and helped Roger up into a bucket seat. "Hungry?"

"You have . . . food?" Longing filled his voice.

"Sandwich and coffee sound good?" Veerman handed him a paper-wrapped bundle and a Thermos.

"Good?" Roger ripped off the paper. He smelled ham and cheese and butter and mustard and bread. "Sounds great."

"Go slowly. Your crew overdid it and made themselves sick, most of the nurses too."

The sandwich stopped three inches before his mouth. "They're really safe? All of them?"

"Yes, all safe, thanks to you."

Roger sagged back against the fuselage wall, and his eyes flopped shut. "No. Thanks to God. Thanks to the OSS and the partisans and the whole group working together."

"With the right man in charge."

He shrugged and took a bite of the sandwich. The swirl of familiar but strange flavors overwhelmed his taste buds. He swallowed, and the bite plunked into his empty stomach. "Where are they? My crew? The nurses?"

"They're all at the same hospital outside Naples, where we're taking you now."

In a couple of hours, Lord willing, he'd be in Naples. "Can I see them today?"

"Probably. The physicians and intelligence officers will want some time with you, of course." He sniffed. "But first you need a bath."

"No kidding." He laughed at Veerman's wrinkled-up nose, the same look his sisters used to give him when he came in the house covered in mud. He definitely wanted a bath and a shave and a clean set of clothes before he saw Kay.

Kay. His chest felt light and cool. Today. Today he'd see her.

"Let me fill you in on some of the plans."

"All right." Roger bit into his sandwich.

Veerman crossed his ankle over his knee. "You'll have a week or two in the hospital for interrogation and recuperation."

SARAH SUNDIN

A week or two with Kay. He drank coffee straight from the Thermos, had to stop himself from drinking too much, too fast.

"Then we'll fly you home. You'll have a two-week furlough at home, and then . . . well, I'll let the Public Relations officers brief you on the rest. You'll like a furlough at home, won't you?"

"Yeah. Swell." Two whole weeks at the Cooper farm? His family probably hadn't even noticed he'd gone missing.

He took another swig of coffee. That wasn't fair. Even if he'd disappointed his family, they did love him.

"Your family's in Iowa, right?"

"Right."

"Any chance you could get over to Chicago for a day or two?"

"Sure. Why?" Another bite of sandwich.

Veerman crossed his arms over his leather flight jacket. "My brother's there. He wants to audition you."

Roger almost choked. He chewed and swallowed. "Audition? Me? Now?"

"I knew you'd like that."

"Sir, I—I'm grateful, of course. But I haven't touched a drum in three months. I haven't sat behind a full drum set in almost a year."

"He'll take that into consideration. He loves the idea of having a war hero in the band, especially since I told him how dependable you are."

Roger turned the triangle of sandwich in his hands. "Thank you, sir."

He'd done it. He'd achieved his goal. He'd prayed, and God had given it to him. A gift.

Roger opened his sandwich, closed it, chomped off a bite. Why did his heart feel heavy? Wasn't this what he'd always wanted?

Yeah, but deep inside, he hoped God wanted him to be a

teacher. Maybe even to get married and have a family and a home.

But he didn't. He wanted Roger to be a drummer.

What was wrong with that? Roger sat taller and chugged some coffee. Nothing was wrong with that. Drumming was a fine dream. A fine dream.

---

## 45th General Hospital

Kay filed into an office in the hospital building with Lieutenant Lambert, Georgie, Mellie, and Mike Elroy. Major Barkley stood behind a desk with an officer Kay hadn't met before—handsome, in his thirties, smooth sandy hair, tan complexion, no wedding ring.

Just the kind of man Kay would have liked back when . . . back when she wasn't in love with Roger Cooper.

"Yes, yes." Barkley scanned the group with a smile. "Perfect."

"Have a seat, ladies . . . Lieutenant." The other officer gestured to five chairs.

"Yes, pardon my manners." Barkley came from behind the desk. "May I introduce Capt. Don Sellers, who will be assisting me."

"Good afternoon." He nodded, his gaze lingering on Kay.

She turned her gaze to Barkley instead, settled in her seat, and pulled the bathrobe over her pajama-clad knees. When on earth would they be allowed to wear real clothes again?

Major Barkley stopped in front of Mike. "The congenial, clean-cut pilot."

"Copilot, sir."

"Humble too. Excellent. Crowds will love you." He scooted in front of Mellie. "You're the one with the father in the Japanese prison camp, right?"

"Not anymore, sir." Mellie's wide smile broke free. "The

US Rangers liberated Santo Tomas. I received a telegram the other day. He's on his way to Pearl Harbor to recover."

"Still a great story—the plucky nurse serving her country while her beloved father was locked up by the Japs. The little old ladies will open up their wallets."

Their wallets? Kay and Georgie frowned at each other.

Barkley moved down. "And cute, perky Georgie Taylor with the cute, perky Southern accent. The ladies will consider you their new best friend. And then . . ." His eyes gleamed and locked on Kay. "Then we have our bombshell. The fellows will buy bonds by the fistful."

"I'm a nurse, not a . . . Did you say bonds?"

"Pardon my colleague, ladies." Captain Sellers leaned against the wall, his long legs crossed at the ankle. "He enjoys his job a bit too much. And yes, Lieutenant Jobson, he did say bonds. War bonds."

Kay sank back in her seat. They were going on a war bond tour. How long would that last? How long until she could go to the chief nurse school?

Sellers lit a cigarette and tucked the lighter back in his pocket. "You have to understand the situation at home. The Battle of the Bulge was bad for morale. The war is far from over, and the American people are tired. They're tired of war, tired of rationing, tired of giving. But you people will capture their attention. The Army is sending you on a bond tour after a two-week furlough. You'll have luxury accommodations all across the country."

Georgie chewed on her lower lip. "I'd rather stay here and serve as a nurse."

"I'm sorry." Lieutenant Lambert leaned forward in her chair to see Georgie. "That isn't an option. Army policy states that anyone who's been behind enemy lines cannot remain in the theater."

Mellie let out a deep sigh, and Kay gave her friends

sympathetic looks. Of course they'd prefer to stay on the same continent as their men.

Lambert straightened her skirt. "The other three girls need more time in the hospital, so they can't go."

"They'll miss out." Major Barkley gripped his hands over his protruding belly. "Just think. A whole month of fancy dinners in Washington DC, adoring crowds in Oklahoma, lounging on the California beach. You'll have the time of your life."

A whole month. Plus two weeks furlough. Plus travel time. Kay's plans turned to dust. "When do we leave?"

Captain Sellers angled a puff of cigarette smoke toward the ceiling. "Not for another two weeks at least. We need to wait until . . ." He turned to Barkley.

The major glanced at his watch. "I can tell you now. We need to wait for the fifth member of your party—your pilot, Lieutenant Cooper."

"Roger?" Kay's hand fluttered to her mouth. "He's alive?"

Lieutenant Lambert gave her a soft smile. "I was just notified today."

"The Twelfth Air Force flew in a rescue mission this morning," Barkley said. "They arrived at Capodichino Airfield about two hours ago."

He was alive? He was in Naples? Kay's breath puffed through her fingers in quick, incredulous bursts.

"I knew it." Mike laughed and slapped the armrest of his chair. "I knew he'd make it. Good old Coop."

"Thank you, Lord," Georgie said.

*Yes, thank you, Lord.* Kay stood on wobbly legs. "I have to see him. I have to see him now."

# 43

Roger brushed the nurse's hands away. "I can button my own pajamas."

"Sorry, sir. It's hospital policy."

"Not my policy." Sitting on the edge of the bed, he twisted his shoulders away from her and buttoned up the pajama top. Clean cloth against a clean body for the first time in three months. With a close shave and brushed teeth, he almost felt like himself again.

He gazed down the length of the deserted ward. "Where's my crew, the flight nurses?"

"The men are out for their daily constitutionals. They'll be back soon."

"And the nurses?"

"Another building."

"Which one? I need to find them now."

She offered a bathrobe and a condescending smile. "Lieutenant Cooper, you are a patient here. You can't simply come and go as you please. The doctor hasn't even examined you."

"Sure he has, right before my shower and shave." He stood and pulled on the bathrobe.

"That was the admitting physician. Now you need to see the ward physician."

He jammed his feet in the slippers. "No, now I need to find my friends. They might not even know I'm alive."

"You'll have plenty of time—"

Roger held up one hand to silence her. Voices came from the doorway, all the way down the ward. Feminine voices.

"I'm sorry, ma'am. As a nurse, you know hospital policy does not allow visitors without physician approval. He hasn't been examined yet."

"But I need to see him, need to know he's all right."

That was Kay! Her voice sounded better than the sound of the shower pelting his skin. "Kay!"

"Roger?" She peeked around the nurse at the door, her face lit up, and she reached an arm to him. "Roger!"

He shouldered his way past his nurse and ran down the ward.

"Sir! Lieutenant Cooper!" she called after him.

The nurse at the door blocked Kay's path. "Ma'am, you can't. Hospital policy."

He didn't care about hospital policy, only about Kay. When he came barging toward the door, the nurse startled and stepped away.

Kay stood there, wearing pajamas and a bathrobe, her red hair glossy and fresh, her hands over her mouth, her eyes glittering.

And his life was complete again. He threw his arms around her waist, lifted her right off her feet, carried her down the hallway, around the corner, and away from prying eyes. He set her on her feet, took her face in his hands, and studied every gorgeous inch of her. "You're all right. Thank God, you're all right."

"You—you're alive." Her mouth bunched up funny, like she was about to cry.

"Ssh." He pressed a kiss to her forehead, same as he'd done in that Italian cellar a month earlier.

She held him tight, her hands firm on his shoulder blades. "I thought—we heard gunshots. Enrico?"

"He's fine." His lips swept over her forehead, and he savored the silkiness of her hair, her clean, feminine scent—her living warmth. "A goat."

She pulled back to look him in the eye. "A goat?"

"The Nazis shot a goat out of spite."

Her face reddened. "I thought you were . . . you were . . ."

He couldn't let her finish that sentence, couldn't let her cry, so he silenced her with a kiss on the mouth.

On the mouth.

On the softest, sweetest lips he'd ever . . .

For heaven's sake, what was he doing?

He eased back. Kay looked at him, her lips parted and moist and inviting, her eyes wide and adoring and vulnerable. So vulnerable.

Her face rose to his. Her eyes fluttered shut.

He couldn't kiss her again. He couldn't. But how could he resist the woman he loved, the woman he longed for, the woman who filled him and refreshed him and satisfied him more than food and water?

His lips found her, tasted her, drank her in. He held her close, one hand buried in her hair, the other caressing her back. Never before had he kissed a woman like this. Never before had he loved a woman.

Her heartbeat thumped against his chest, spoke to his heart, and the beats synchronized in perfect, irresistible rhythm.

"Oh, Roger." She rested her cheek on his shoulder and sighed.

He stroked her hair, breathed in the smell of her. "My Kay."

She settled a kiss on his jawline. "I love you so much."

"I—I—" He loved her too. But where would love lead? Love would lead to marriage, to disaster. He shouldn't have—man alive! Why did he kiss her?

She rearranged her arms around his waist and gazed up at him with dreamy green eyes. "I've never been in love before. It's wonderful, isn't it?"

What had he done? What had he done to her? His heartbeat disconnected from hers and careened out of control.

Roger set his hands on her waist and pushed himself away. "Shouldn't have done that. I made a mistake. Shouldn't have."

Her gaze swam around as if she'd just woken up, a look he'd seen several times during the evasion. "Shouldn't have done—done what?"

He raked his hands back into his hair. He wanted to rip out his own heart and stomp on it, kick it, mangle it, anything so he could take the pain in her place. She hadn't done anything wrong. He was the one without self-control. "I shouldn't have kissed you."

"Shouldn't have . . ." Groggy confusion yielded to comprehension. "You're not saying . . ."

He gripped his hair until it hurt, gripped it even harder. "I'm sorry. I shouldn't have kissed you."

Her gaze hardened, and her jaw jutted out. "How dare you? Last time you pushed me away because I flirted with you, but this time—you kissed me! You did."

"I know. It's not your fault. It's mine." He implored her with his eyes. "Don't you see? No good can come of this."

She crossed her arms, her color high. "Why? Because I'm a two-bit floozy?"

"What?" He stepped closer, stopped himself. "That's not what I said—not what I think. You're wonderful, everything I could want in a woman."

"Except you don't want me."

Roger groaned and gazed at the ceiling. "I do. That's the problem. But I'm no good for you. Don't you see? I'll never amount to anything."

"Why would you say that?"

He returned his gaze to her, to her gut-wrenching hurt. "I got an audition with the Veerman band."

A spark of light entered her eyes. "See? You will amount to something. I knew you would."

"Yeah. I'll be a drummer, drifting from town to town, hotel to hotel. I can't give you what you want most of all."

"What makes you think you know what I want?"

Roger ruffled his hair, smoothed it, then gave her a firm gaze. "You told me what you want. A home. You want a yellow house with a wicker chair on the porch. I can't give you that."

She hugged herself, and her expression changed—to a lost little girl. "If I . . . if I had you, I wouldn't need a house."

His head sagged back. "You say that now. But how long would that last? One year? Maybe two? Then kids would come, and you'd want to settle down, plant some roots. Kids need a home, a school, a church—and I can't provide those things. You'd be miserable. I refuse to do that to you. I'd only disappoint you."

"What gives you the right to decide what makes me miserable, what disappoints me?"

"It's not a right. I'm not deciding. I just know."

Kay stood still and quiet so long, he ventured a glance. The lost look had vanished, and only strength remained. "So you refuse to love me because you'd disappoint me?"

"Yes." The word stung on the way out.

"Well, congratulations. You don't have to wait—you've disappointed me right now." Chin high, she marched away.

Roger leaned his forehead against the wall, rapped it on the wall, and pain zipped through his skull. What was new? He'd been disappointing people all his life.

# 44

From Algeria to Tunisia to Sicily to Italy to Southern France. Two years in the Mediterranean Theater of Operations, and now Kay was going back to the States.

She shielded her eyes and gazed around the airfield, the rugged mountains in the background, the bright blue sky. Many wonderful things had happened here.

So why did her anger at Roger Cooper overpower everything? She couldn't stand to open her Bible and see Roger's hypocritical notes. And prayer felt as effective as shouting into the wind. Her words flowed back into her own ears, unheard, unanswered.

She sighed and climbed the steps of the four-engine C-54 Skymaster transport plane, leaving Italian soil for good.

After she stashed her bag in the back with the rest of the luggage, she followed Georgie and Mellie down the aisle of the plane, set up with upholstered seats like a true passenger plane from her stewardess days.

About a dozen officers filled random seats. Georgie and Mellie found two seats together along the right side of the plane, and Kay slid into the row behind them.

She settled her musette bag on the floor by her feet. Only a few months earlier she'd flown immediately after Roger Cooper had spurned her and she'd ended up trapped behind enemy lines with him. History had better not repeat itself.

No, this time she'd be trapped for a month on a bond tour with him. But this time she wouldn't let him close, wouldn't let him anywhere near her heart.

She sensed him pass by on his way down the aisle, so she tipped her head away as if fascinated by the view out the window. The past two weeks in the hospital she'd managed to avoid him, except for one short meeting. He hadn't been able to look her in the eye.

Good. He ought to be ashamed of himself, kissing her like that.

Like that . . .

She tried to shake the memory, but how could she? That kiss—the yearning, the power, the connection of it. And it was a mistake, he'd said. A mistake.

Oh, he was perfectly fine kissing her. But not loving her. That's when he'd pulled back, when she said she loved him. She was good enough for clandestine kisses in the hallway but not for love and marriage.

All that talk about not being able to provide a home for her? Nonsense. Hadn't she told him it didn't matter to her? She'd gladly sacrifice that dream to be with him. If anything, she'd be the perfect band wife because she was used to living on the move.

What nonsense, a big fat lie. It was kinder than saying the truth—that she was desirable and kissable but not the sort of girl to bring home to mama. Because she wasn't. She'd never be. Why did she even try?

Her throat thickened, and she crossed her arms.

"May I join you?" Capt. Don Sellers, the public relations officer, indicated the seat next to Kay.

She shrugged. "If you want. But I plan to take a nap."

He sat and draped his overcoat across his knees. "An excellent idea. You ladies went through an ordeal."

The engines built to a roar, one at a time, and her annoyance built to a roar too. "The ordeal would be over and we could get on with our lives if it weren't for this tour."

His gaze bored into the side of her face. "Why don't you want to go, Lieutenant? The other ladies are sad to leave their men, but you seem downright angry. What would you be doing if it weren't for this tour?"

Kay faced him. "You really want to know?"

"I really want to know." His eyes were an unusual shade of light brown, an arresting shade.

She narrowed her own eyes at him. "I was admitted to the chief nurse program at Bowman Field. The next class starts on Monday. I could have made it, but thanks to this tour, I'll miss this class and the next, and who knows if there will be a class after that. But don't you worry—I'll smile and wave and bat my eyelashes and sell your war bonds."

Sellers's smile grew from studious to appreciative to an outright grin. "You slapped him so hard his head spun, didn't you?"

Kay stared at him. What on earth was he talking about? "Excuse me?"

He inclined his head toward the front. "The pilot—Cooper. He made a pass, and you slapped him."

"Where on earth did that come from?" Her cheeks heated. "I was talking about the chief nurse program."

"And in that speech I saw you're a spitfire." He chuckled. "Would've loved to see his face."

Kay clutched the armrests as the plane jostled down the runway. "I've never slapped him." Although she should have.

He pulled a silver cigarette case from the breast pocket of his service jacket. "Well, something happened. The evasion reports talk about you and Cooper working as one, close friends. And I saw your face when you found out he was alive, heard your voice when you said you had to see him. But since then, you two have avoided each other, and you're furious about the tour. Something happened." He plucked out a cigarette and offered one to her.

She shook her head. A perfect stranger. How dare he? Her chest heaved, desperate to spin a lie to save face, but she couldn't lie. "It's none of your business."

"I disagree." He slid the case back into his pocket. "My job is to keep the five of you happy and pampered. Barkley runs the show, but I manage you folks. If there's a problem between you and Cooper, I need to know."

Kay put on a stiff, sweet smile. "Lieutenant Cooper and I are both professionals and we're both adults. We will get along and not cause any problems. That's all you need to know."

Sellers leaned closer until his shoulder almost touched Kay, and a trace of masculine cologne reached her nose. "I need to know one more thing. Are you dating anyone?"

Only a year ago, she would have added him to her lineup. Now his smooth confidence, easy charm, and good looks did nothing for her. "No, I'm not, nor will I for the duration of this tour."

He settled back in his seat and lit his cigarette, a smug smile creasing his handsome face. "We'll see about that."

Kay groaned and pressed up against the fuselage. This tour got worse and worse.

---

Washington, DC
March 7, 1945

Maybe this bond tour wouldn't be so bad after all. Roger glanced behind him to the drum set on the makeshift stage in front of the Lincoln Memorial.

"So tell me, gentlemen." Major Barkley spoke into the microphone and grinned for the audience. "How did the ten of you get through this ordeal?"

"I tell you, sir, it wasn't easy, but we had a philosophy." Roger spoke from the script Captain Sellers had prepared from their evasion reports, polished to appeal to the public and censored to protect Captain Anselmo, Enrico, and the partisans.

"Yes, sir, we had a philosophy." Mike's earnest voice worked well with the script, and he could keep a straight face while mouthing the corniest lines. "We decided to accentuate the positive."

Barkley tapped his finger to his chin. "Say, that reminds me of a song."

Cheers erupted from the crowd gathered in front of the Memorial on their lunch break.

"How about it, folks? Lieutenant Cooper, they tell me you're a fine drummer."

"I get by."

"He gets by." Barkley gave a knowing glance to the audience. "Do the fine people of our nation's capital want to see if this young man gets by on the drums as well as he does in the cockpit?"

More cheers, and Roger headed to the drum set, slipping out his sticks from inside his lightweight leather flight jacket.

Three dames in short red, white, and blue star-spangled outfits pranced onto stage. One of them scanned Roger head to toe and winked at him.

He gave her the briefest smile, polite but uninterested. After all, the girls would join them on the bond tour. As if having Kay around weren't complicated enough.

The bandleader raised his baton, and Roger launched into a lively beat for "Ac-cen-tchu-ate the Positive." The trio sang in harmony with little dance steps and much mugging, and the audience loved them.

Just yesterday Barkley learned Roger could drum, listened to him play, and had Sellers rewrite the script. Now Roger could practice before his audition with Veerman. Drumming would also keep him occupied during the tour.

They arrived in New York on Saturday, took the train to DC, and spent Monday and Tuesday being interrogated by Army brass, one-on-one, thank goodness, so he didn't have to be in the same room as Kay for long. Today they were putting on two performances, more on Thursday and Friday, then away for two-week furloughs.

Offstage, the three nurses waited for Barkley to pretend to interview them for the crowd. Kay hadn't looked Roger in the eye since he'd kissed her, and words were chilly and few.

This time she wouldn't forgive him. He didn't blame her, since he couldn't forgive himself. If only he had one iota of self-control. Then her heart and their friendship would be intact.

Sure, he'd done the right thing letting her go. Maybe the realities of the bond tour—hopping from city to city and living on the rails—would make her realize it too.

That didn't ease his guilt. If he hadn't kissed her, he wouldn't have needed to push her away.

He thumped out the final beat, and the audience cheered. Roger stood, bowed his head, and headed down rickety stairs offstage.

"Let's hear it for our three little nightingales," Barkley called. "Come up and join us, ladies."

Roger stepped to the side as the women climbed the stairs. Kay walked past as if he didn't exist.

The crushing ache in his chest intensified.

"That was swell, Lieutenant." Charlie Poole, the stage-hand, ushered them toward the tent they used between shows. "You're a top-rate drummer."

"Thanks." He smiled at the kid.

Mike lagged behind to listen to the women speak.

Inside the tent, Roger sank onto a camp stool. "Say, Charlie, how old are you?"

He pulled himself taller and ran his hand through unruly straw-colored hair. "Eighteen, sir."

"Liar."

Charlie glanced around the tent, but they were alone. "All right, I'm sixteen, but that's old enough for a job, you know."

"I know. What about school?"

He flapped a hand at Roger. "Ah, I'm no good at school, sitting still and doing what Teacher says. Why should I when I can get a man's job and a man's wages?"

"Believe me, I understand." Roger rolled his drumsticks between his hands. "I only stayed in school because of band." And the girls.

"Well, I ain't got band, but I got strong arms and a strong back."

"That'll get you far." But he'd get further with some basic skills. "Say, you like math?"

He grimaced. "Hate it."

"Only 'cause no one ever made it interesting. You like music?"

"Who doesn't?"

"Did you know math's like music?" Roger pulled over a crate and tapped out some rhythms to show him the numbers in the beat.

Charlie drew up a camp stool beside him. He listened and asked questions, and something lit in his gray eyes.

The nurses breezed into the tent with Mike and the PR men. Kay walked beside Captain Sellers and said something to the man. He laughed and patted her shoulder.

Jealousy twisted everything up inside, but he had no right. She was free to date anyone she chose, including weasels like Don Sellers. But Roger also had no reason to be jealous. Although Sellers was handsome and attentive, Kay kept a professional distance.

Even after Roger had treated her so poorly, she hadn't reverted to her old ways. She could have, just to spite him. But she didn't.

The ache pressed so hard he could barely breathe. He loved her so much.

"Isn't that song fun?" Georgie threaded her arms around her friends' waists. " 'Ac-cen-tchu-ate the Positive,' " she sang out.

Mellie joined in with her pretty soprano, and Georgie slipped into the harmony.

Major Barkley rushed up to them. "You can sing?"

Georgie smiled. "Sure, we love to sing."

Barkley paced back and forth, waved Sellers over. "The Andrews Sisters have nothing on these three. Those dizzy dames on stage—fire them. We'll save money and a whole lot of headaches. You"—he turned to the nurses, his arms flung wide—"you're the Nightingale Sisters. You'll sing both songs."

"No." Kay's face blanched. "Not me. I don't sing."

Concern propelled Roger to his feet, but if Kay explained, Barkley would understand.

But Barkley laughed. "A looker like you? Sure you can sing, doll."

"No, I can't." Her voice warbled. "I really can't."

"No need to be modest. You can always sing soft, but with a face like yours, we need you onstage."

Kay turned paler than after the C-47 crash. "I assure you, sir. This isn't false modesty. I sing horribly. I'm tone deaf."

"You'll do fine." He walked away from her. "Sellers, start a new script."

"Sir." Roger stepped into his path. "The lady said she doesn't sing. You can't make her."

"Excuse me, Lieutenant." Kay's eyes flashed at him. "I can speak for myself."

Roger froze at the sensation of her gaze fixed on him, her words directed at him for the first time since the kiss. He swallowed hard. "I know you can."

She blinked and spun to the major. "Please, sir. I can't sing. You really don't want me to. Trust me."

"Nonsense." He waved her off and headed for the tent entrance. "You'll do fine. Excuse me, folks. I have three dames to fire."

Kay covered her face with both hands, her shoulders slumped.

"I'm so sorry, sweetie." Georgie hugged her. "We'll figure something out."

Roger gripped his drumsticks in one hand. Behind enemy lines, he could protect her. But now when she faced her old deep fear, he couldn't.

# 45

*Evil, evil, evil to the core.* The train chuffed it out, louder and louder.

Perhaps Kay should have taken Georgie up on her invitation to spend her furlough in Virginia at the Taylor home, a place Kay loved. But Kay sensed Georgie needed time alone with her family. Meanwhile, Mellie was meeting her new mother-in-law in Pennsylvania, Mike had gone home to Florida, and Roger to Iowa.

But Kay had no home to visit and no family to welcome her, so she was on her way to Tulsa with the PR men, band, and stagehands to prepare for the tour.

*Evil, evil, evil.*

Her father's voice grew louder and more insistent and more logical as the train crossed the prairie, land she knew well from her family's roving travels, as he preached that God required perfection in order to forgive.

Apparently her father hadn't skewed the message so badly after all. Because she sure didn't feel forgiven right now.

Captain Sellers shifted in the seat beside her. "You're quiet, Kay."

She kept her gaze on the flat grasslands rushing past her window. "I told you. I don't sing and I don't want to be here."

"You're very upset by this, aren't you?"

Her jaw edged forward. "Does it matter how I feel? Orders are orders."

"It matters to me."

"Because if I'm upset, it messes up your show." She glared at him.

Instead, compassion warmed his eyes. "No, because you matter."

She whipped her gaze back to the window. Baloney. She didn't matter to anyone. Not to her own family, not to Roger Cooper, and not to God.

For almost a year she'd fooled herself to believe the Lord cared about her, but recent events proved otherwise. If God cared, why did he let her throw herself at Roger to be rejected? Why did he thwart her only remaining goal? Why did he force her to get on stage and sing? Of all things, to sing? The one thing she absolutely couldn't do.

And the voices. Her father lambasting her for not repenting. Her sisters taunting her. Her mother's limp defenses of her middle daughter, dwindling away over time as she accepted the truth.

The truth that Kay was evil, evil, irredeemable.

"Tell you what." Sellers laid his hand on Kay's arm. "Why don't we have dinner tonight in Tulsa, and you can tell me more? Maybe there's something I can do."

Through the olive drab wool of her jacket sleeve, the warmth of Sellers's hand ignited a spark of hope. If he could do something, anything, to commute her sentence, she could handle one dinner out. "All right."

---

**Tulsa, Oklahoma**

In the Mayo Hotel's Crystal Ballroom, as silverware clinked on china and patrons conversed in subdued tones, Kay spilled her life story to Don Sellers, a man she hardly knew and barely liked.

Stories rushed out, stories she'd only told to Mellie and Georgie and . . . Roger. But she had a purpose, and Don listened and held her hand.

If she could make him see how singing would traumatize her—and the audience—and how she needed this chance at the chief nurse program, he might help.

Don stroked Kay's hand gently. "And here we are, trying to force you to sing in public."

"Do you see why I can't?"

"Of course, darling. It'd be cruel to make you. I'll see what I can do."

Kay offered a weak smile. "Thank you."

"Anything for you." His light brown eyes glowed.

Yes, he came on too strong, but at least he wasn't afraid to show his interest and wasn't ashamed to be seen with her. It felt good to be admired and pursued.

Roger certainly hadn't pursued her. He'd pushed her away. He never called her darling or took her to dinner or held her hand.

If he saw her right now, he'd think she'd fallen into her old ways. So what? Why shouldn't she? Why shouldn't she date a handsome man who cared about her? The old ways worked. The new ways only gave her grief.

The waiter cleared away the dessert plates, and Don reached for Kay's other hand.

She hesitated for only a second, then accepted, tilting a gaze up through her eyelashes.

Don inched closer. "About the second issue—the chief nurse program. That's the real reason you don't want to be here."

"Yes. I've worked hard for this goal for a year. With the war winding down, the program will close down and I'll lose my opportunity. After the war I'll have to start as a ward nurse, and it could take years to become a chief."

He caressed her hands with his thumbs, very pleasant. Nothing hesitant or confused about him. He knew what he wanted, and he aimed for it. How refreshing. "I might be able to do something about that."

"You could?" Kay's heart hopped.

"The more I think about it, the more certain I am. We don't need three nurses. Two will do. Sure, you're the best looking of the three, but Mellie and Georgie will suffice."

"Of course they would."

"I have quite a bit of influence with Barkley, and he calls the shots. He might let you go if we planned our strategy right."

"If you could, I'd be so grateful."

He slipped one hand free and set his finger under her chin. "I have an idea." Then he gave her a kiss, right on the lips, easy and assured.

Although stunned, Kay could mimic his poise. She arched an eyebrow at him. "That felt more like a kiss than an idea."

He chuckled. "I hope you like the idea as much as the kiss."

"Go on."

"We need to make plans to convince Barkley to release you. I have a few ideas and I'd like to hear yours. Perhaps we could discuss the situation this evening over drinks in my room."

So that's what this was about—getting her into bed. Kay stiffened and drew her hand away. "I'm not that kind of woman."

"I know you aren't. But you're my kind of woman. I knew it the moment I laid eyes on you." He pulled an envelope and pen from his jacket pocket and wrote something down. "You're gutsy, passionate, and brave. As I said, my kind of woman, a woman I'd like to help achieve her goals."

He slid the envelope to her.

She picked it up. It read, "Room 511, 9 p.m. Please join me."

The truth blared at her in dark, angular lines. Why did she keep denying it? Why not accept who she was and use it for a good purpose?

Kay tucked the envelope in her shoulder bag. "Nine o'clock."

---

## Outside DeWitt, Iowa

Mom passed Roger the jar of honey. "Who would've thought, of all our children, you'd be the one they call a hero? Never thought you'd amount to much."

"Thanks," Roger said, but only for the honey, which he slathered on a biscuit. He tried not to bump elbows with his sister-in-law Betty. The Cooper table had been built for a family with eight kids, not for thirteen full-size adults.

"That's what you told the reporter from *The Observer*, wasn't it, Mom?" his oldest brother, Joe, said from the far end of the table, his eyes glinting.

"That's what I told him." Mom folded the napkin over the remaining biscuits in the basket. "He asked how it felt that our youngest son was a hero. Surprised, I told him. Never had a lick of sense, that boy."

At the head of the table, Dad nodded. "Not a lick."

Roger swallowed. Honey had never tasted so bitter. "I did fine."

Joe nudged Dad with his elbow. "Remember, he's only called a hero because he crashed a plane."

"No kidding." Ted, the second oldest, laid down his piece of fried chicken. "How many planes have you lost, Dodger?"

That was what his brothers had always called him, a well-earned nickname for his work-dodging ways. "Three, but—"

"There you have it." Joe scooped up more green beans. "The real reason they're sending him on a bond tour—so he won't crash any more planes."

"Safer than putting him back in the air," Ted said.

"Come, now." Betty gave her husband a reproving glance. "Be nice. It sounds like Roger did his best not to crash, and he did lead all those nurses to safety."

"More likely they led *him* to safety."

Dad harrumphed. "In my day they didn't hand out medals for failure."

Despite the honey, the biscuit turned to dust in Roger's mouth. No matter what he did, he'd always be a failure in their eyes. Something reckless lurched in his chest. For the first time ever, he wanted to defend himself.

Roger wiped his fingers on the red gingham napkin in his lap. "You know what? I did good work over there. I worked hard and became one of the best pilots in the squadron, my commander said. And in the evasion, everyone relied on me, and I didn't let them down. I led, they followed, and we all got home safe. You know what else I did? I taught algebra to the Italian boy who helped us. And I was good at it. Really good."

His family stared at him, various shades of red hair glinting in the electric light.

Roger picked up his fork and knife, and he shrugged. "Maybe I should be a teacher."

Laughter galloped around the table, unbridled.

He tensed at the sight of his dream trampled and soiled. He should have kept it inside, pristine and untouched—and unrealized.

Six of his nieces and nephews ran in from the kitchen, where they'd sat at the smaller table. "What's so funny?"

Harv, the third-oldest brother, ruffled his son's hair. "Your Uncle Roger, always joking, that one. He said he should become a schoolteacher."

"Oh yeah!" Ten-year-old Frank grinned at Roger. "You could be my teacher. You'd be a lot more fun than mean old Mrs. Hoffman."

"Hush." The boy's mother swatted the back of his arm. "Don't talk about her that way."

"Fun." Dad shook his head, still covered with more copper than silver, even at the age of sixty-three. "Your uncle would be a fun teacher, all right. Nothing but play and nonsense all day long."

Roger clutched his silverware so hard, he was surprised it didn't snap. "I'm thirty years old, Dad. I think I can—"

"Yes, thirty years old. Thirty wasted years." Dad pointed his fork down the length of the table at Roger, his dark eyes hard. "I tell you what you're going to do. Tomorrow you audition for that silly band of yours. You play your drums for them if they'll have you. When you fail at that—or when you get bored—you come home and get to farming, as you should. We'll always find work for you here or on your brothers' farms, if you're willing to work for once. Lord knows I've tried to set you straight."

"Yes, you have, Copper," Mom said. "You certainly have. We all have."

Roger's bravado melted away.

"A teacher," someone said. More snickers raced around the table, and the family settled back to their meals, still smiling at the thought of Roger Cooper amounting to something.

They knew he couldn't. They knew he never would. And they'd known him all his life.

Thank goodness he hadn't dragged Kay down with him.

On his plate, golden fried chicken and crisp green beans and half of a flaky biscuit formed a triangle on the simple white plate.

Roger had lost his appetite.

# 46

**Tulsa, Oklahoma**

Kay crossed the black-and-white marble lobby of the Mayo Hotel. All around, officers in uniform and businessmen in tailored suits gave her appreciative glances, and she smiled back.

That was all she was, all she'd ever be—a beautiful woman who could attract men's attention and use it for her own good. She'd always done that, and tonight would be no different.

Over a decade before, she'd promised a lovesick farm boy a night in this very hotel if only he'd drive her to Tulsa. He'd complied. But then she'd waited outside the hotel while he registered and she'd ditched him for the YWCA. She'd used him to escape from her family, to achieve her goal.

Tonight she'd do something similar. Don Sellers thought he'd use Kay's desperation to get what he wanted, but Kay planned to use his desire to get what she wanted.

A sleek aluminum elevator door emblazoned with the Mayo's elegant logo slid open. Kay stepped inside and pushed the button for the fifth floor.

After the door shut, the elevator chugged up, the chains clanking, "Evil, evil, evil."

She belonged on the fifth floor. Didn't her own father say

she couldn't be redeemed? Roger knew it. That's why he'd kissed her and pushed her away. Don knew it. That's why he'd propositioned her.

If she was so bad, she might as well use it to get what she wanted, her best chance for success in this world, her best chance for a home.

The elevator dinged. The fifth floor.

Kay stepped out, and the doors shut, leaving her alone in the silent hallway.

Her chest tightened. What was she doing? What on earth was she doing?

She blew off a long breath. She was regaining control. That's what she was doing.

All along she'd had a policy never to let a man have his way with her. That would give him control. But this time, the situation was reversed. This time she'd regain control.

Kay squared her chin and walked down the hallway. Although she'd vowed never to sleep with a man, she'd also vowed never to sing in public.

Tonight she had to pick one or the other. Not a difficult choice.

One night with a handsome man, and she wouldn't have to endure the terror of singing in public. She wouldn't have to bear the pain of seeing Roger every day. She could get away from Oklahoma and its taunting voices. She could go to the chief nurse school, and her life would be as it should.

She strode down the hall, past rooms 501, 503, 505.

Her shoes tapped on the floor, muffled by maroon carpet with emerald green accents. Heel, toe. Heel, toe. Ba-bump, ba-bump.

Like her heartbeat.

"The heartbeat itself is a drum message from God," Roger had told her almost a year before, drumming on the table at the Orange Club. "With every beat, he sends his message. His life, his love. His life, his love."

Kay stopped and slammed back against the wall to silence her footsteps, the beat, the message. But her pulse thumped in her ears. Ba-bump, ba-bump. *His life, his love.*

She pressed her hands over her ears. "No, I don't believe it," she whispered.

His life?

What life? A life of humiliation and pain and solitude? A life with every goal thwarted?

And what love? She'd never be loved. She was only good for the tawdry imitation of love that men like Don Sellers offered.

For almost a year she'd believed a lie, that she could receive God's love.

But her mind swam with the year's memories. Hadn't she indeed felt his life inside? Hadn't she basked in his love—unearned, undeserved, cleansing, transforming? Hadn't he changed her?

Kay's hands squeezed her ears, her temples, as if she could squeeze out the truth. Yes, she'd been changed. Yes, she'd been loved.

"But why, Lord? If you love me, why?" Her voice trickled out.

It was too much—Roger's rejection, her family's voices, the singing, the humiliation, the frustration, the blocked goals. "It's all too much."

Her Army Nurse Corps pumps formed russet wedges on the maroon carpet, new shoes to replace the Oxfords that had fallen apart during the evasion and escape.

*It's too much. It's all too much.* Hadn't Alice Olson spoken those very words in the wine cellar? The dirt, the cold, the hunger, the illness, the danger, the constant worry—all too much. And Kay had comforted her and helped her through.

She wrapped her arms around her stomach. Was her current situation any worse? Did it really matter that Roger didn't love her, or even that her own family didn't love her? Couldn't God's love be enough now, just as it was back in the evasion?

Kay raised her head and smoothed her hair, her mind still churning. But the singing—she couldn't bear it. And the chief nurse program—she'd worked so hard for it.

She pushed away from the wall and wobbled for a moment. Then she set her feet back on their path, past rooms 507, 509.

Room 511, painted on the door in stark black on white. The brass door knocker glinted in the muted light. This door led to the future she longed for, the position, the chance to lead . . . to home.

Kay reached in her purse and pulled out the envelope with Don's invitation. It would be so easy. She could take everything she wanted.

Once Roger had told her that if God gave her the chief nurse job, it wasn't because she'd done something good, but because he loved her and wanted what was best for her. And if he didn't give her the job?

Kay slid the envelope under the door and walked back to the elevator, her heart straining. If God chose not to release her from this tour, not to let her become a chief nurse, then that was best for her.

She simply couldn't imagine why.

# 47

Chicago, Illinois
March 13, 1945

The Marine Dining Room of Chicago's Edgewater Beach Hotel. Roger stood inside the doorway and scanned the rows of tables on red-carpeted tiers surrounding the stage. How many evenings had he and Lou spent in this room, watching the bands and the dancers, dreaming of making the big time?

Now it was his turn.

A sense of awe at the enormity of God's gift stilled his feet. How could it be that an Iowa farm boy had an audition with Hank Veerman and his orchestra? Only by God's mighty hand.

"Thanks, Lord," he whispered and strode forward, determined to prove his heavenly Father right and his earthly father wrong. Even if he failed, he'd do his best.

Roger crossed the hardwood dance floor. On the stage, a dozen band members lounged and chatted, while the clarinet player laid down a swinging little riff.

"Well, lookie here. It's the big war hero." A portly man tooted "Reveille" on his trumpet.

Roger raised a hand in greeting. "Afternoon, fellas."

The clarinet player rested his licorice stick across his knees.

"Two months in hiding with six delicious dolls? If I'd known the Army offered gigs like that, I'd have enlisted."

The piano player kept tickling the ivories. "As if they'd take a bum like you."

The clarinetist adjusted thick glasses that must have landed him on the 4-F list—unfit for military service. "Ah, the Army—"

"Who's talking about the Army? The dames wouldn't take you."

Roger joined the laughter. Nothing like the camaraderie of a band.

"Lieutenant Cooper?" An almost-familiar voice sounded behind him.

He turned to an almost-familiar face. "Major—Mister Veerman. It's a pleasure to meet you, sir."

"Pleasure's mine. My brother raved about you in his letter." The bandleader shook Roger's hand. Shorter and younger than the major, but the family resemblance was strong.

"Thanks for the audition, sir." He swallowed a comment about being rusty. Veerman would find out soon enough, and the major said he'd warned his brother.

"Let's see if you drum as well as you fly." Veerman motioned to the drum set. "Drumsticks are in the trap set."

Roger reached into his waist-length "Ike" service jacket. "Brought my own."

"Lucky sticks?"

"No, just special." He stroked the olive wood, carved by Enrico and varnished by Roger yesterday in the Cooper barn. He'd considered bringing Kavi's *dhol* drum but decided it might be too exotic.

The bandleader clapped his hands. "All right, you lunkheads. Let's give flyboy here a chance to show what he's made of. Mary Jean? Where is that dame?"

"Right here, boss. Just enjoying the scenery." A blonde

sashayed from the corner of the room, her red-flowered dress swinging past shapely legs, skimming an even shapelier figure. She climbed the steps to the stage by Roger. "Well, hello there, Red," she purred. "I hope you stay on. I love a man in uniform."

"Yeah?" the trumpeter said. "If that's so, why do you work so hard to get 'em *out* of uniform?"

The boys in the band howled in laughter, and Roger pretended to rearrange the items on the trap set tray to his left.

"Ah, shut up, Pinky," Mary Jean said.

"All right, boys. Enough. First song is 'Let's Get Lost.' Lieutenant, all the music is on the stand before you."

"Thank you, sir." He didn't need it for this number. He knew the song well, romantic and painful. He'd danced with Kay to this song at Tom and Mellie's wedding, where he'd wanted to get lost with Kay.

He shoved away the memory to concentrate on his work.

Veerman raised his baton, and Roger opened with a soft, swishing beat. He was rusty, no doubt about it, but with leisurely songs like this, he'd do fine.

His technique might be rough, but he still knew when to switch it up, when to build, when to add a flourish, when to fade away. He kept his eye on the bandleader, the singer, the soloists, the music, learning the ways of this band.

Veerman led them through four more songs, only one with any swing to it. That was the way of things. When Roger left the States, the sound was big and boisterous. But in the summer of '42, the musicians' union called a strike, forbidding its members from making recordings. Desperate for business, the record companies had their singers perform a cappella.

The public's taste followed, and after the harshness of war, gentle songs suited them. They wanted crooners. They wanted Bing Crosby and Frank Sinatra. The band had become mere background music.

Not as much fun as a rousing swing song, but it would pay the bills.

"That'll do for now, boys. Take a break." Veerman set down his baton and waved Roger over. "Let's have a seat."

Roger followed the bandleader to a small round table with a compass rose pattern on top. He sat in a black curved-back chair, and his right leg jiggled.

Veerman offered Roger a cigarette, then lit one for himself. "My brother said you'd be rusty."

"Yes, sir." To his surprise, he didn't feel disappointed. The audition itself was a gift, and he'd done his best.

"If that's how you sound rusty, I'm looking forward to hearing you polished."

"Yes, sir. I'll be able to practice on the bond tour. Perhaps I could audition again—"

Veerman held up one hand. "I like what I heard. I want to sign you on as a backup drummer after the Army discharges you."

Roger's leg stopped jiggling. He couldn't breathe. He had a spot? In the Veerman band? A band that played all the great clubs and hotels across the nation?

"Don't look so surprised. As I said, I like what I heard. Too many fellows want to show off with flashy skills, but you know how to read a band, how to support the musicians and the singer and not overpower them. I like that."

"Thank—" He coughed to clear the croak from his voice. "Thank you, sir."

"More importantly, I trust my brother." He puffed out a curl of smoke. "He said you're reliable and hardworking, a man to count on. I could use that around here. You'd be a good influence on these clods."

Roger rolled his drumsticks back and forth on the table under his palm. Reliable? Hardworking? A man to count on? A good influence?

Major Veerman said that about him. A man who'd worked with him for a year and knew him well.

The sticks rolled smoothly on the table, polished with care by Enrico. He could still see the boy's eyes light up when he grasped the quadratic equation. He could see Enrico looking to him for guidance, see his crew and the nurses. They'd all relied on him, and he hadn't failed them.

He hadn't failed. In fact, he succeeded.

Back and forth the sticks rolled, back and forth his mind rolled, settling into peace. The audition was a gift, a great gift. But the Lord had offered an even greater gift and far more subtle.

He'd offered a choice between two good dreams. For some reason, the Lord believed in Roger even when Roger didn't believe in himself.

His jaw felt tight, and his eyes watered, from the cigarette smoke, he told himself.

"Well . . . ?" Veerman tapped his cigarette in the ashtray.

The drumsticks came to a rest. "Thank you, sir. I've dreamed of this opportunity since high school."

"You're welcome. Glad I could make your dreams come true."

With one finger, Roger stroked along the grain of the stick. "Sir, have you ever had a dream change on you? When you discovered something new about yourself, perhaps?"

Veerman settled back in his seat and puffed on his cigarette. "Come to think of it, I have. I wanted to be a trumpet player, then discovered I wanted to lead a band."

Roger tucked his drumsticks inside his jacket. "You know what I want, sir? I want to be a math teacher. I always did but never thought I was the kind of man who could be counted on, the kind of man people would trust with their kids. Now I know I am. And that's what I want."

Veerman's blue eyes didn't register shock or amusement, only understanding.

"You know what else I want? I want to get married, buy a little house, a yellow house, maybe have some kids." He'd never voiced all of this before, and it felt good. More than good, it felt real.

The bandleader sighed, stood, and shook Roger's hand. "Can't say I'm not disappointed you won't sign with me, but you'd better follow that dream."

"Yes, sir." A surge of joy and determination raised a grin. "I plan on it."

If only he could convince a certain redhead to join him.

# 48

**Tulsa, Oklahoma**

Keeping busy wasn't difficult. Kay found a bookstore, had lunch in a diner, saw a movie, and visited the hospital where she'd trained in nursing school. To her delight, her former chief nurse remembered her—and well.

But twilight cast shadows on Tulsa's streets, and Kay needed to return to the Mayo.

A long gown in the window of a dress shop caught her eyes, and she paused. A medium shade of green, but muted, like the leaf of a rose. Short sleeves, a sweetheart neckline, and the fabric gathered into a diamond-shaped panel at the waist. Kay could tell it would give her curves where she was lacking.

It looked to be her size, she had the money, and she wanted to replace the gown that had burned in the wreckage of Roger's C-47.

She closed her eyes against the assault of memories—Roger holding her in his arms as they danced, watching startled as she shoved away the dress in the crashed plane, lifting her off her feet in the hospital, carrying her around the corner, kissing her with abandon.

Kay clenched her jaw. The store was closed, but tomorrow she would buy the dress and form new memories.

Besides, she would need to get away from the hotel and Don Sellers. Now she had two men to avoid on the bond tour. Only Mellie and Georgie's friendship and the Lord's love would see her through.

Meanwhile, ten long days remained before her friends would return.

Kay strode down the street to the hotel. "Just you and me, Lord."

Two-story-tall classical columns flanked the hotel entrance, and the doorman held open the door for her.

"Thank you." Kay crossed the lobby at a swift pace, chin down, feet flashing on the black-and-white marble. She planned to order room service and avoid the PR officer.

A gentleman stepped in front of her, wearing olive drab trousers.

Don.

Kay sighed and looked up to him with a benign smile.

He studied her with those light brown eyes, his expression unreadable—amusement, annoyance, regret, concern? "There you are. I've been looking for you."

"I've been out."

He pulled the envelope from his trouser pocket. "I found this under my door this morning. Apparently I missed your knock last night. You must think me rude."

"I didn't knock. I decided not to join you."

His eye twitched. He gazed down, sighed, and took her hand. "I apologize, Kay. I came on too strong. Why don't I take you out to dinner tonight and we can get to know each other better?"

With a sweet smile, Kay freed her hand and rested it on her shoulder bag. "No, thank you. I already know you as well as I care to."

"Pardon?"

"You said I was your kind of woman, but you're mistaken, because you're not my kind of man."

Don's face reddened, and his mouth pressed into a knife edge, severing her last chance.

Kay tilted her head. "Let me guess. Suddenly you're no longer able to get me out of the bond tour and into the chief nurse program."

"Looks that way."

She patted her chest and heaved a dramatic sigh. "I'm so glad I found that out before I gave you my body."

His eyes flashed golden fire. "Enjoy singing on stage, Lieutenant. I'll make sure you get a solo."

As he marched away, Kay raised her face to the art deco chandelier and breathed a prayer. In an instant, the answer brought up a giggle. All she had to do was sing—one note— and Barkley would chase her right off the stage.

---

## March 19, 1945

A day in the spring sunshine at the Tulsa Zoo had perked up Kay's spirits after a week of solitude. Bears and monkeys and birds and alligators—finally she'd had someone to talk to, even if they bellowed, howled, squawked, or snapped back at her.

She crossed the lobby of the Mayo Hotel, anticipating an evening of listening to the radio and reading the new issue of *Vogue*. At the registration desk, an Army officer thanked an employee for his key, an officer so familiar Kay's heart leapt.

"Mike!"

He spun to face her and grinned. "Kay!"

She closed the gap and hugged him. What was she doing? She'd never hugged him before. She pulled back, straightened her garrison cap, and gave him an apologetic smile. "Sorry. I'm so happy to see a familiar face. How was Florida?"

"Warm." Like his smile against a new tan. "It was great seeing my family and friends. They spoiled me rotten."

"I'm glad." She looked him up and down. Like all of them, he'd put some healthy pounds back on. "You're early. It's Monday. You don't have to be here until Friday."

"I know." His gaze skittered away. "Um, how was your furlough?"

Kay groaned. "Let's put it this way—I longed for the wine cellar. At least there I had company."

"That's what I thought. That's why I . . . Say, have you had dinner?"

"I had a hot dog at the zoo."

"I already ate too. Just thought—well, after our evasion, I never turn down a chance to eat."

Kay smiled. "I do have overwhelming urges to sneak food into my purse."

Mike laughed, then he took off his service cap and ran his hand through his straight brown hair. "Say, you don't suppose . . . would you like to . . . if you'd like, we could sit down and talk."

His halting ways formed a delightful contrast to Don Sellers's suave self-assurance. "I'd like that. Today I was reduced to having a long conversation with an alligator."

Mike flashed a smile and gestured to tables and armchairs around the lobby. Kay picked a low round table in a quiet corner and settled into an upholstered chair.

Next to her, Mike leaned his elbows on his knees and fiddled with his hat, his lips tucked in. "I need to be truthful. I don't know how to say this, but you're the reason I came back early. I was worried about you all by yourself."

"That's sweet of you."

He wrinkled his nose. "That's not entirely truthful. I wanted to—well, I wanted some time with you before everyone else arrived."

"Oh." So he'd finally worked up the nerve.

Mike turned his hat in his hands. "It's no secret that I'm—well, I think you're swell."

A soft smile rose. No, it wasn't a secret, and he had a touchingly awkward way of confessing it.

"It's also no secret—it's none of my business, but I know something went wrong between you and Coop."

Kay winced.

"I'm sorry. I shouldn't have said that."

"Don't apologize. As you said, it's no secret."

"I know both of you are hurting, and I hate it. And I don't want to be a vulture swooping down."

"I know."

He sat up straight and looked her in the eye. "I just want to ask if I have a chance with you in the future. If I don't, fine. Tell me straight. I can take it. But if I have even the slightest chance—well, I'll wait."

Kay gazed into his earnest blue eyes. Why couldn't she have fallen for Mike instead of Roger? Mike knew what he wanted and aimed for it, but he was also willing to wait without pushing.

He was a kind man who adored her, a man who wouldn't change his mind, wouldn't kiss her and throw her away.

Mike set his cap on his head and scooted forward in his seat. "It's all right. I understand."

"Wait." She reached forward and grasped his forearm. "Wait. Let me think a minute."

"I can wait."

She nodded and closed her eyes. The Lord had redeemed her. He could choose to give her a good man and a home and a family. Even though Roger had rejected her, she didn't have to give up that dream.

"Mike?" she whispered.

"Yes."

"I'm not ready." She looked at him through moist eyes. "But I like you and respect you and trust you. Let's get to know each other as friends, then maybe when I am ready . . ."

He covered her hand with his own. "I'd like that."

---

**DeWitt, Iowa**
**March 21, 1945**

Roger swept his Bible from his dresser and tucked it in his barracks bag, thankful that his friends had rescued his kit bag from that Italian cellar.

Dad leaned in the doorway of the bedroom. "You ready to go? You'll miss your train."

He had plenty of time. The train didn't leave Cedar Rapids for another three hours. Today he'd follow the Mississippi River to St. Louis, then tomorrow he'd head to Tulsa and his future. "Just a few minutes."

"If you're late . . ." Dad flapped a hand at him. "Well, you're on your own. You're not my responsibility anymore."

"No, sir. I'm not." He looked under the bed, found an errant sock, and tucked it into his bag.

Dad leaned against the doorjamb. "Still can't believe you turned down a perfectly fine job."

Roger's mouth dropped open. "Perfectly fine? You've spent the last fifteen years telling me drumming is a waste of time."

"It is. But you had a job offer. What else are you going to do?"

Roger gritted his teeth, yanked on his "Ike" jacket, and buckled the waist strap. "I already told you. I'm going back to college on the GI Bill. I went to the admissions office at the University of Chicago while I was in town, and they'll take me back soon as the war's over. A year or two, and I'll be a teacher."

"A teacher." Dad crossed thick arms across a sturdy chest. "Might as well shoot for being president. You were better off with that band. At least you're good at drumming."

All he could do was stare at his father, his thoughts a murky mess. "I've been playing drums since I was fifteen. That's half my life. And this is the first time—the first time—you've said I was good at drumming."

Dad harrumphed. "'Cause it's a load of foolishness, that's why."

Foolishness. In his father's eyes, everything he did was foolish. Roger tugged shut the straps of his barracks bag, harder than he needed to, and his fingers could barely operate the buckles.

All his life he'd absorbed his family's words, believed them, and then made those words come true. How many dreams had he rejected because he believed he'd never amount to anything? From teaching to loving Kay Jobson, he'd turned down God's gifts because he believed he was unworthy.

No more. Never again.

Dad's feet shifted, and the floorboards creaked. "What do you think you're going to teach those children anyway? How to laze around all day, chew gum, play with sticks, and get out of real work?"

Roger's fists coiled around the strap of his barracks bag, and he prayed for strength and patience. "Math, Dad. I'll teach them math."

"Poppycock."

He straightened, slung the *dhol* across his chest, and swung the barracks bag off the bed. "Yes, Dad. Math. I'm good at it. And I'm good at teaching. And I'm dependable and hardworking."

"More poppycock."

"Guess what? People can change." In two giant steps, Roger stood inches before his father, man to man. "You know what else I plan to teach them? I'll teach them that they can amount to something, no matter who tells them they can't."

Dad edged away from Roger, eyebrows high.

One more step, and Roger thrust his finger in his father's face, careful to keep his voice low. "Because I have amounted to something. Because I will continue to amount to something. And if I can, anyone can."

He turned and jogged down the stairs and stepped outside into cool air crisp with the promise of good paths and great gifts. Yes, he had amounted to something.

# 49

A knock on the door, and Kay startled, sitting up in the armchair in her hotel room. Who could it be? Don Sellers wasn't stupid enough to bother her again, Mike Elroy wasn't bold enough, and the rest of the party wasn't due until tomorrow.

She set aside her Bible. She needed an evening in God's Word to fortify her for Roger Cooper's return, and the notes in Roger's handwriting helped her steel herself to the sound of his voice. Her gratitude for the role he'd played in her life would allow her to tamp down her hurt and anger so she could treat him with distant cordiality. Nothing more.

Kay crossed the room in stocking feet and opened the door. Georgie and Mellie burst in, laughing and smiling.

With a squeal, Kay yanked them both into a hug. "What are you doing here? I didn't expect you till tomorrow."

"We know. We decided to surprise you."

"You succeeded. Oh, I missed you so much."

Georgie pulled back and gave her as stern a look as her sweet face could muster. "I told you to come with me."

"You needed time alone with your family, and you know it."

"Still." Georgie glanced around. "Oh, look at this. Can you believe we each get our own room—and our own bathroom?"

Mellie sat on the twin bed. "I don't know how I'll sleep without the flap of canvas and the song of the cicadas."

"You'll just have to suffer through." Kay curled up in the armchair. "How was your visit to Pittsburgh? Do you like your mother-in-law?"

"I do." Mellie's face glowed. "She's wonderful. I can see why she and Tom have been so close. It was uncomfortable at first, but we got along well. After all, we both adore Tom."

Georgie flopped down on the bed on her stomach. "I hope Hutch's family likes me."

Kay laughed. "How could they not? How was Virginia? How's your family?"

"Nope. Before we get started with chitchat, I have news." Georgie kicked off her shoes and waved her feet in the air. "We have a solution to your dilemma."

"My dilemma? Which one?"

"The Nightingale Sisters." Mellie slipped off her service jacket. "Georgie and I talked about it in the taxicab from the train station. It's her idea and it's brilliant."

Georgie rested her chin in her hands. "You can sing—without singing."

Kay arched an eyebrow. "I already do that."

Mellie laughed. "No, no. Listen. Georgie and I will sing, and you echo in a spoken voice, like this: 'Ac-cen,'" she sang.

"'Ac-cen!'" Georgie almost shouted, tipping her head from side to side with each syllable, unbearably cute.

"'Tchu-ate the positive,'" Mellie sang.

"Just like that, all through the song," Georgie said. "I have the lyrics worked out for both songs. It'll be darling. You just have to speak in rhythm. Can you keep rhythm?"

Mellie nudged her. "Haven't you seen her dance?"

Kay swung out one foot and wiggled her toes. "I can feel the rhythm fine, but I can't make my voice hit the right notes."

"Wonderful." Georgie nodded. "You just stand on stage with us, right in the middle, speak in rhythm, and the audience will love it."

Kay's heart felt mushy, but she'd grown a taste for mushiness in the past year. "Not as much as I love it. I think I can do that. I'm sure I can."

"Thank goodness." Mellie's eyebrows tented. "My heart was breaking for you all during the furlough. I'm glad Georgie's so clever."

"I am." Georgie rolled onto her back and flung her arms over her head in triumph. "Put me in a room with Roosevelt and Hitler, and this war will be over in a jiffy."

Kay laughed. The tour would still be a trial, but her friends had lifted one load from her shoulders.

---

## March 23, 1945

Roger set the newspaper on the seat of the taxi and leaned forward, gazing through the windows at Tulsa's big buildings, glowing in the setting sun.

Great news from Europe. The day before, Patton had led the US Third Army across the Rhine River. The Allies were surging forward in Germany, and they were sure to launch an offensive in Italy soon. Unstoppable.

He draped his arm on the seatback in front of him and tapped out a rhythm. Although the odds were against him, he felt unstoppable too.

Why couldn't the cab drive faster? He had lots to do tonight. First he had to find Kay, second he had to convince her to talk to him, and third he had to declare his love and his intentions. Wouldn't be easy, any of it. Kay had loved him not long ago, but he'd hurt her badly. Even if she forgave him, she might not trust him.

Regardless, he had a whole month to convince her he loved her and wanted to spend the rest of his life with her.

"Would you stop that, mister?" The cab driver—a lady—flicked her head toward Roger's tapping hand.

"Oh, sorry." He leaned back in the seat and shifted the drumming to his thighs. He hadn't pursued a girl since high school. Even then he hadn't worked at it—a grin, a wink, an invitation.

Kay wouldn't succumb to mere charm. Over the past year, he'd gained her love without trying, but now it would be hard work. Maybe impossible.

The driver pulled to the curb. "Here you are, mister. The Mayo Hotel."

"Thank you." He paid her, grabbed his barracks bag and *dhol*, and strode into the hotel.

There she was, standing in the lobby, talking with Mike, Georgie, and Mellie, her back to him, her golden-red hair beckoning.

Roger swallowed hard. Part one—finding Kay—complete. Parts two and three loomed before him like the rugged Apennines.

He forged ahead, determined to scale those mountains.

Next to Kay, Mike caught his eye and smiled.

Roger waved back.

Mike circled his arm behind Kay's back in a proprietary way, pointed to her, grinned like a madman, and gave a thumbs-up.

Roger's feet and his smile froze, colder than the Apennines.

The promise.

Way back at Christmastime, scouting the landing field, he'd promised Mike that if they escaped, he'd back off and let Mike have a chance with Kay. Apparently Mike had taken that chance. Apparently it was going well.

He'd been in plenty of pickles the past year, ditching a loaded C-47 in the Mediterranean, dodging Japanese Zeros in narrow jungle canyons, hiding from Nazis in an Italian oven, but this pickle he'd created with his own words.

This time he couldn't—he wouldn't—get out. He'd given his word and he refused to break it, even though it shattered his own heart.

"Look!" Georgie called. "Roger's here."

Kay turned and looked at him in the cool, empty way you looked at a stranger, at someone you didn't know and didn't mean to know.

Roger's hope dissolved in that cool emptiness. He could work with anger, grief, embarrassment, any emotion at all, but not this—this apathy.

He'd lost her.

Despite the yawning void in his chest, he wrestled up a smile and approached the group. "Hi, everyone. Good to see you."

"Good to see you too." Mellie's smile was as warm as Kay's was cool. "Did you have a nice furlough?"

"Yeah. Swell." No need to mention the audition and the change in his plans. None of that mattered anymore. Thank goodness he hadn't told anyone about the audition . . . except Kay. "Listen, I'm beat. Long trip. I'm going to check in and hit the sack."

"I'll go with you," Mike said. "Good night, ladies."

"Good night, Mike. Night, Roger." One voice was conspicuously absent.

In a fog, Roger went to the registration desk and got his key for room 509.

"Right next door to me," Mike said. "I'm in 507. They sandwiched us between Barkley and Sellers, making sure we don't have any wild parties."

Roger had to chuckle. "Always a danger with us." He

headed for the elevator across squares as white as his job hopes and as black as his romantic hopes.

Inside the elevator he forced his muscles to smile in feigned interest. "So, things are going well with Kay?"

"Sure are." Mike leaned against the elevator wall, hands in his trouser pockets. "I came into town on Monday. We've been to the zoo, the movies, dinner."

"Great. That's great." His voice came out stiffer than he wanted, and his smile hurt as if nailed in position. He needed to be happy for Mike and Kay, two people he cared about, two people who deserved to find love—and why not with each other?

But tension coiled inside him, tighter and tighter. He opened his room door, said good night to Mike, and tossed his belongings on the twin bed.

Then he stared at himself in the mirror over the dresser. He threw a punch at his reflection, another, a third, stopping inches from the mirror, daring his reflection to strike back and make contact, hard contact.

Then he shook, shook, shook his fists at his image in the glass.

Kay had given him her love, and he'd let it sift through his fingers.

# 50

**Tulsa Bomber Plant**
**April 2, 1945**

For almost a mile, four-engine B-24 Liberators were parked nose-to-tail on the assembly line at the Tulsa Bomber Plant.

Kay tipped up her hardhat-covered head. Men and women of various ages and races scrambled over and inside the planes, riveting and welding and whatnot, while cranes and other heavy equipment rumbled pieces into position in the massive building.

"Can you imagine working here?" Mellie shouted over the noise.

Kay shook her head. "I thought working *inside* a plane was loud."

Georgie adjusted the strap for her hardhat. "And tomorrow we'll see where our C-47s are built."

The ladies followed Barkley and Sellers, Roger and Mike down the assembly line. At this factory, Douglas Aircraft built bombers, but the company's Midwest City plant in Oklahoma City produced over half of all C-47s. At the end of the tour, they'd visit the Douglas factories in Santa Monica and Long Beach, California. Along the way, they'd stop to put on their show and encourage folks to buy war bonds.

The sole purpose of today's show was to show gratitude for the people building planes for the war effort.

Far ahead of her, Roger stopped and chatted with a workman, Mike at his side.

For half a minute, she allowed herself to watch Roger, the way he moved and talked and held himself, allowed herself to taste the bittersweet flavor of loving a man who would never love her.

Mike waved.

She hitched up a smile for him. Mike was sweet and attentive, and in his shy way he hadn't even tried to hold her hand. Fine by her, since her heart stubbornly resisted switching allegiance from the pilot to the copilot.

Besides, she disdained juvenile games. She refused to incite Roger to jealousy, or punish him with anger, or manipulate him with tears. She'd maintain the charade that she'd lost all interest in Roger Cooper.

He'd made his decision, and she'd be mature about it.

On the outside, anyway.

Her gaze betrayed her and slid from Mike to Roger. He looked straight at her, and the zing of connection shot through her like an arrow.

Kay jerked her head toward Mellie. "Say, what do you think—our soldiers and Marines landing on Okinawa on Easter Sunday?"

Mellie blinked thick lashes over dark eyes. "Oh. Yes. A strange day for an invasion, I suppose. Maybe that was the point."

"Surprise. Yes, of course." Her cheeks warmed. How often did she blurt random war news to her girlfriends? But it served its purpose. Ahead of her, Roger and Mike ambled along.

"Nervous?" Mellie said.

About the tour? Absolutely. Today's shows officially started the tour, and a long month stretched before her.

"I hoped Georgie's idea would help."

"It did." Kay whisked up a smile. Georgie's idea had reduced terror to queasiness.

Major Barkley motioned the ladies onward and outside, where a makeshift stage awaited. They would put on two shows to cover both lunch breaks, and the first group of several hundred had already gathered on the tarmac.

In a tent beside the stage, the ladies removed hardhats, fluffed their hair, pinned on garrison caps, and fixed lipstick and powder.

Mellie adjusted her khaki necktie while studying herself in a handheld mirror. "Don't you think it's funny that we fought so hard to wear trousers on the job, we're performing for women in coveralls, and they want us to wear skirts?"

"Just be glad they don't make us wear those short sparkly skirts the showgirls wore in Washington DC." Georgie imitated one of their prancing little dance moves.

"That could be arranged." Don Sellers directed a cool gaze straight to Kay and puffed cigarette smoke down over his lower lip.

Why had Kay let those lips touch hers even for a second? A dozen nasty retorts pinged through her brain, but her tongue rejected each one.

Roger stepped forward. "If they get to wear sparkly skirts, Mike and I want to wear them too."

"Sounds fair," Mike said with a firm nod.

"Why shouldn't we show off some leg?" Roger lifted his trouser leg a couple of inches. "I've got killer gams."

Georgie and Mellie burst into laughter, and Kay couldn't restrain a smile, although she leveled it at Sellers.

The PR man let out a quick derisive snort and tilted his head to the tent entrance. "You're up, boys."

Applause penetrated the canvas walls, and Roger and Mike headed out with Sellers on their heels.

"That was sweet of Roger." Georgie managed to sound innocent and probing at the same time. "Protecting us like that."

"Wasn't it?" Kay made her voice sound grateful yet detached. No matter how kind he was or how much her friends nudged her, she would not let that man into her heart again.

In a few minutes, Charlie the stagehand leaned into the tent and motioned to the ladies. "Knock 'em dead."

Georgie wagged her finger at him. "That would violate our oaths as nurses."

The boy laughed and held open the tent flap.

Kay followed her friends and climbed rickety stairs to the stage. With each step, trepidation quivered in her fingers, and she stubbed her toe on the top step.

They passed behind the band, behind the drums.

"Kay!" Roger said in a loud whisper.

She faced him, stunned that he'd addressed her.

He held his drumsticks as one in his fists, at a diagonal, like a soldier with his sword at the ready, with the fierceness of a warrior. "You don't have to do this."

Kay stood trapped in his gaze. He'd heard the ladies practice. He knew she didn't have to actually sing. Why this concern for her?

Because he knew her too well.

Her pretense of distance couldn't disguise the intimacy of their friendship. He knew how traumatic this would be, knew the memories this would unearth.

"Mellie and Georgie can sing by themselves." He cocked his head to the front of the stage. "You don't have to do this."

She eased back to sever the connection. "Yes, I do."

With her chin high, she strode away. Hundreds of people sat on the tarmac, waiting for a song Kay couldn't sing, and she stepped between Mellie and Georgie at the microphone.

Two decades before, she'd stood on stage between her sisters, all dressed in white. Jemima sang clear as the Nebraska sky and just as crystal blue. Kezia and Keren had always sung in charmingly childish atonality. Although Father insisted Kay should be singing well by the age of six—hadn't Jemima?—Mother defended her. Kezia was young, so young. Give her time. She was a Jobson. She'd sing beautifully as all Jobsons did. Please give her time.

But that night at the tent meeting, four-year-old Keren joined Jemima, their voices navigating the musical scale with ease, gliding and diving and soaring. And they'd seared Kezia with brutal smug glints in their eyes.

That night Father prayed over Kezia, calling on demons to flee her and heaven to save her. For months and years he prayed and berated and ranted. But that night, the night Keren sang, was the night Mother surrendered, the night Mother stopped loving Kezia.

"Kay?" Mellie hugged Kay's arm.

She blinked away the past and blinked in the present.

Mellie's deep brown eyes shone with compassion, and Georgie's blue eyes with encouragement.

These women welcomed her into their triangle, each as different as could be, yet strong together. They knew each other, loved each other, pushed each other, and supported each other.

This was true sisterhood.

Kay winked at one nightingale, then the other. "Let's knock 'em dead—in a healing sort of way."

Her friends chuckled, Major Barkley introduced them, and then the music started, driven by Roger's drums, but she shoved him out of her mind.

Georgie and Mellie sang, their gorgeous voices in perfect harmony, and Kay joined the song in perfect rhythm. She echoed their lines, added some sass, and the energy of the trio built as one.

Something warm and light stirred in her soul. Her blood

sisters snubbed her, but her nightingale sisters loved her. Her earthly father scorned her, but her heavenly Father—oh, what he had done for her.

He loved her, forgave her sins, and gave her gifts too numerous to count. She had a career and friends and life and health and so much more. Someday he might give her love and a home and a family. Whether or not he did, he was still good and he'd always love her.

The song ended with a boom of the bass drum and a crash of the cymbals.

The audience erupted in applause, and the ladies dropped curtsies, stymied by straight skirts.

Major Barkley approached the microphone with his cheesy grin, ready for the interview part of their show.

But Kay stole a moment, veered from the script, and wrapped her arms around her friends' waists, closing the triangle. She had so much to say, but her words jumbled up inside.

"I know," Georgie said.

And Mellie squeezed Kay's shoulder. "Me too."

Only one word croaked out: "Thanks."

# 51

**En route to El Paso, Texas**
**April 21, 1945**

Roger hadn't pulled a prank for at least six months, but he couldn't resist this one. A hobby syringe from a store in San Antonio, some Texas chili powder, and Donald Pompous Sellers's cigarettes, nabbed from his breast pocket during a nap on the train.

Out of the corner of his eye, Roger watched the PR officer across the aisle of the Sunset Limited. A puff, a frown, another puff, a contorted face, a long stare at the cig, another puff, and a fit of hacking like a twelve-year-old taking his first smoke behind the barn.

Decades of experience faking innocence allowed Roger to keep a straight face. Sure, the prank was childish, but Sellers needed a little comeuppance for the high-handed way he treated them—especially Kay.

This would probably be his last prank ever. But boy, was it a good one.

Sellers smashed the cigarette in the ashtray and lit another. He sniffed it, took a puff, and broke down coughing.

Charlie Poole gave Roger a sidelong glance, his gray eyes dancing.

Roger merely glanced over Charlie's shoulder. "How're those problems coming?"

"Done." The boy handed Roger a sheet of paper.

He shook his head. "Start again. You've gotta write down the equation, show all your work."

Charlie groaned and slouched in his seat. "Waste of time."

Like looking back in time at himself. "Believe me, I understand. I can do this stuff in my head, but that's not the point. There are three reasons to show your work."

"Yeah?" Skepticism lowered his voice.

"Yeah. One—it shows the teacher that you understand the process. Two—if you make an error, it's easier to find where you went wrong. And three—in the real world, you don't work alone. As a pilot, I did load calculations, and other people relied on me. When I turned in sloppy paperwork, didn't fill everything out 'cause I did it in my head, they had to work twice as hard to figure it out. That's not fair."

"Still don't like it."

"Neither do I. But I understand why it's important, and I do it. You will too."

Charlie grumbled. "All right, but it's a waste of paper, and there's a paper shortage, don't you know?"

"Then write small." A wink, and Roger handed the paper back to the kid. "Work on those. I need a nap."

"Sure thing, Lieutenant."

Roger stretched his legs out as far as he could, crossed his ankles, and leaned against the window. The tour schedule wore him out. Tulsa to Oklahoma City to Dallas to Houston, a side trip to Austin, and several days in San Antonio. Trains and hotels and restaurants and canteens and shows and shows and more shows.

Thank goodness he'd turned down Hank Veerman's contract. This was a crazy way to live.

His eyelids felt like lead. If only he could shut his ears from the sound of Kay's lilting laughter two rows ahead.

The sound scraped his raw heart, and loneliness carved into him. Mike spent most of his time with the ladies now, a place Roger didn't belong. The boys in the band had shunned him when Major Barkley fired their beloved drummer and the three cute little singers. They played together fine, but without camaraderie.

That left Charlie. If it weren't for the stagehand, he'd be alone.

Kay's red head and Mike's brown one poked above the seatback, too close together for Roger's taste, but they were chatting with Mellie and Georgie across the aisle. Despite all their time together, Mike didn't seem to be making progress.

If Roger were a better man, he'd offer pointers.

He pulled his service cap over his eyes and settled lower in his seat, but Kay's voice penetrated his ears and heart and marrow. Her laughter sang even if her voice didn't. Yet her stage performance grabbed him more than that of any silky-voiced songstress, and not only because he knew what it cost her. She spoke her lines with spirit, her hips swaying gently, her words right in time to the beat of his drums. As if they still worked together as one.

A sigh seeped out. He longed for the partnership and friendship they'd shared.

In Italy, after the girls had escaped and Roger was hiding with the partisans, he'd felt imbalanced and incomplete without Kay.

How much worse now, when he was in her presence every waking moment and never savored her company.

———

Kay shifted in the train seat, her legs restless. Mike leaned too close, not to flirt but to converse with Georgie and Mellie across the aisle.

They had plenty to discuss—the heartbreaking death of President Roosevelt, the rapid Allied drive across Germany, and the offensive in Italy pushing toward Bologna and the territory they'd covered on foot.

Kay laughed at Georgie's joke. They'd spent the last few days at the various air bases in the San Antonio area, including Randolph Field, the new home of the School of Air Evacuation. The sounds of C-47s in flight and the sights of nurses in their olive drab trouser uniforms only reminded her of lost dreams.

A letter caught up to her yesterday from the Army Air Forces' chief nurse school, which remained at Bowman Field in Kentucky. The next class would start May 1. It would be the last class. Kay would not be there.

"Isn't that swell, Kay?" Mike's voice strained in cheer, as if he knew Kay wasn't present in the conversation.

"Yes, swell." She managed a breezy tone and adjusted her skirt over her knees.

Why did his attention bother her today? He was good-looking and so nice. But she'd never dated a shy man before. With plenty of lively men vying for her affection, she'd never had to take the effort to encourage the quiet ones.

And she refused to encourage Mike with false interest. She didn't want him to hold her hand or embrace her or kiss her. Because she still loved Roger Cooper.

Kay groaned and sprang to her feet.

Mike's eyebrows bunched together. "Are you all right?"

"Sure. Just need to stretch. I'll be back." She headed down the aisle to the powder room.

Two rows back, Roger reclined with his cap over his eyes and his mouth slack in sleep. Kay's heart jolted. Why could she still taste that mouth on hers?

Charlie Poole glanced up as if to ask her something. But she didn't want to talk. She wanted to walk and hard.

"Lieutenant Jobson?" Charlie followed her down the aisle.

Kay set a smile in place and turned to him, right where the aisle bent to the side to skirt the restrooms. "Yes?"

"Are you good at math? Lieutenant Cooper's taking a nap, and I can't solve this problem."

"I'll see." She took the paper and glanced at the rows of equations. "Algebra?"

"Yeah. He's trying to teach me what I missed in school. It makes sense this time. He explains real good."

"I'm sure he does." Kay studied the equation, but $x$'s and $y$'s mingled in her vision. How many times had she watched him tutoring Enrico in their wine cellar?

"I'm glad he's going to be a teacher. He'll be swell."

Kay snapped up her gaze to Charlie's sparkling eyes. "A teacher? No, he's a drummer. He had . . . he had an audition with the Veerman band." A jab of guilt. She'd never asked how the audition went. Apparently it had not gone well.

"Sure, he had the audition. Hank Veerman offered him a contract, but he turned it down. Guess he hasn't said anything. He kind of keeps to himself, don't you know?"

"I know." The words rasped over her throat as the words drilled into her brain.

"Can you believe it? Cooper told Hank Veerman himself he'd rather be a math teacher. How many teachers sit around wishing they could be musicians, and here's a fellow, makes it to the big time and turns it down to teach. Don't that beat all?"

"Yes. Yes, it does." The paper trembled in Kay's hand. "I'm sorry. I can't help you with this problem. And I need to . . ." She waved toward the ladies' room.

"Oh! I'm sorry, ma'am." Charlie turned red and backed away. "Thanks anyway."

Kay plowed through the bathroom door. A teacher? A teacher?

Roger had lied to her. He told her he couldn't love her

because he was going to be a drummer and live on the road and he couldn't give her the home and stability she wanted.

She braced shaking hands on the sink. He wasn't going to be a drummer. He was going to be a teacher. What profession could be more stable than teaching?

She gazed at her pale face in the mirror, at the haunting realization in her eyes. His rejection had nothing to do with houses or families or living on the road. It had everything to do with her.

No matter what he said, he didn't think she was good enough for him.

Kay yanked on the faucet and splashed cold truthful water on her face. He was wrong. She was too good for him, the lying, cowardly jerk.

# 52

**Douglas Aircraft, Santa Monica, California**
**May 8, 1945**

Roger pounded away at the drums while hundreds of couples danced to "The Victory Polka." This would be their last show. Their month was well up, and today they were celebrating victory in Europe—V-E Day.

No more boys would fall to German bullets. Italy was free, France was free, and Germany was conquered. With the war over in Europe, the full power of the Allied armed forces could be turned on Japan, already in its death throes.

Today the workers at the Santa Monica Douglas Aircraft plant polkaed in sheer joy under the California sunshine. With everyone in trousers, it was hard to tell the fellows from the dames.

At the front of the stage, Georgie and Mellie sang, while Kay played the tambourine. This would be the last time he saw her. Since she hadn't spoken to him once in the past two weeks, that would be best. The rawness would slowly scab over.

But man alive, he'd miss her. Even from a distance, he couldn't get enough.

The song came to an end, Roger finished with a flourish on the cymbals, and the audience applauded.

"No, no." Major Barkley patted imaginary heads in front of him. "No, the applause should be for you, the fine workers of Douglas Aircraft."

Roger winced at the cheesiness but shared the sentiment under the cheese. These people had cranked out thousands of the C-47s that had ferried supplies, dropped paratroopers, and evacuated the wounded—and helped win the war in Europe.

After the applause died down, Barkley raised two fingers. "Today we have two surprises and two special stories."

Roger frowned. This wasn't part of the script.

"These are surprises for two of our nightingales." He grinned at the ladies on stage, who gave each other perplexed looks. "First, it has come to our attention that Lt. Georgie Taylor is engaged to be married."

Georgie's face went bright pink.

"Today we have a surprise for you, Lieutenant Taylor. Drumroll, please."

Roger's jaw hardened. What on earth was Barkley doing? Georgie didn't hide the secret of her romance with an enlisted man terribly well, but the PR man should have known better than to broadcast it.

"Drumroll . . . please?" Barkley directed a stiff smile at Roger. Oh, that was him. He did a drumroll.

"Ladies and gentlemen, may I present Lt. John Hutchinson."

Roger whipped around. Sure enough, Hutch ambled onto the stage.

Georgie gasped, dashed a few steps toward him, and stopped short. She probably didn't want to get the man in even greater trouble.

But Hutch grinned at her. "Didn't you hear him? He said *Lieutenant* Hutchinson."

"Lieutenant?" Georgie's eyes widened.

Hutch nodded and drew her into an embrace. They didn't kiss. They just held each other as if hundreds of people weren't watching.

Roger's grip on his drumsticks intensified. Hutch and Georgie hadn't seen each other since November, before the plane went down. Their reunion should be private.

But Barkley loved a show. "Lieutenant Hutchinson has served as a pharmacist, as a technical sergeant, since he was drafted in 1940. He was in Honolulu when the Japanese attacked Pearl Harbor. He landed with our troops in Sicily and at Salerno and at Anzio. For months, he endured German bombing at Anzio, earning medals for bravery along the way. His hospital landed in Southern France the day of the invasion and had to retreat in the Battle of the Bulge. But now he's been rotated stateside—after his commanding officer bestowed a commission."

Georgie lifted a tear-streaked face and fingered the gold second lieutenant's bars on Hutch's epaulettes. "So now . . ."

He kissed her forehead and said something Roger couldn't hear.

Just as well. The words—the moment—should have been between the two of them alone.

"Come on over, you two lovebirds." Barkley motioned them to the microphone. "What do you think, ladies and gentlemen? Shouldn't these two young people tie the knot?"

The audience cheered and applauded.

"That's what we thought." Barkley tipped his head to partially face the couple. "The Army Air Force has planned a beautiful wedding for you this Saturday. We're flying out your parents and have every detail arranged. That is, if the bride is willing."

Roger's hands fisted over the sticks. Barkley deserved a sock in the jaw.

Hutch turned his back on the major and lowered his face to within an inch of Georgie's, and they spoke in hushed tones.

"What's that?" Barkley said. "We can't hear you."

Roger scooted to the edge of his stool and laid aside his drumsticks. He couldn't clobber a man who outranked him, but he could certainly give him a piece of his mind.

Georgie peeked around her fiancé, her face flushed. "The bride is willing."

"Did you hear that, folks? We're having a wedding this Saturday. Then two of our little nightingales will be taken. As for our married nightingale, Lt. Mellie MacGilliver—she's about to receive a surprise too."

Was Tom here? Roger craned around to look behind him but didn't see any sign of the engineer.

"For three long years, Professor Hiram Blake was imprisoned by the Japanese for no crime other than being an American. For three long years, he lived in barbaric conditions at Santo Tomas in the Philippines. But now he's free. Now he's here."

"Papa?" Mellie clapped her hands over her mouth and wobbled.

Kay steadied her friend.

Behind Roger, a gentleman in his fifties came onto the stage with faltering steps—emaciated.

"Papa!" Mellie ran to him and embraced him.

"Isn't this touching, folks? She hasn't seen him for over three years, didn't know if he lived or died for much of that time. So how about it, Lieutenant? Professor? Come to the microphone. These good folks need to hear from you."

No, they didn't. Mellie clung to her father, sobbing, and the poor man could hardly stand. How could they be expected to speak to a crowd?

"That's enough." Roger bolted from his seat and wrapped his arms around Mellie and her father. "Hutch! Georgie! Follow me."

He shepherded them to the stage stairs, where Mike stood, jaw dangling. "Mike! Get this gentleman into the tent, give him a chair, a crate, something to sit on."

"Will do." Mike guided them down the stairs.

As he passed, Hutch clapped his hand on Roger's shoulder. "Thanks, Coop. We needed some privacy."

"No kidding." Now to face Barkley. He headed back onto stage.

"Come on, everyone!" Barkley waved his arms around. "Let the nightingales know you want to hear from them again. Give them a big hand."

The people obliged, eager for drama.

Barkley spotted Roger. Although he kept his grin in place, his eyes shot poison arrows.

Roger marched to the microphone, aware of Kay a few feet to the side, all by herself now. "Ladies and gentlemen, while we'd all love to hear from them, some moments are too sacred for spectacle. These people have been through a great deal. They deserve time to catch up on the past and to plan for the future—in private. Don't you agree?"

More applause, but subdued.

Major Barkley gave a clipped laugh. "There you have it, folks. The protective leadership of Lt. Roger Cooper that saved this group from capture by the Nazis during two long months behind enemy lines. How about some more stories, Lieutenant Cooper? Or another song, Lieutenant Jobson?"

Roger's stomach contracted. He would not allow Barkley to use Kay this way. "Ah, who wants a bunch of boring old stories on a day like this? On a day of victory. You want to dance, don't you? Not some plodding little love song—how about 'In the Mood'? What do you say?"

Whistles, cheers, stomps, applause.

Roger returned to the drum set. "In the Mood" was an instrumental piece, so Kay was off the hook.

The bandleader raised his baton, the trumpet player tooted the intro, and Roger joined in with the rest of the band.

Kay headed toward the stairs, passing the drums, and she halted. For the first time since they'd left Texas, she looked Roger in the eyes.

The power of it almost made him lose rhythm.

Her gaze combined gratitude and guardedness. She hated what Barkley had done to Georgie and Mellie, and she appreciated what Roger had done. But she still didn't trust him.

He gave her a quick "it was nothing" smile and returned his attention to his drums.

After the song concluded, Barkley dismissed the workers back to their jobs. After all, he reminded them, the war wasn't over yet.

The band packed up their instruments, and Roger and Charlie dismantled the drum set.

Barkley strode over to Roger. "Listen, pal. I'm in charge. Not you."

"I know that, sir."

"I hope you enjoy the next seven weeks."

"Seven weeks?" Roger looked up from his work to the major's red face.

A slick smile with narrowed eyes. "The Seventh War Loan Drive. You're a hit. The Army issued orders for all of you to tour up and down the West Coast. Seven more weeks."

Seven more weeks with Kay. Joy and dread swirled in his gut.

Barkley stepped closer and shoved his finger in Roger's face. "Remember, I outrank you. I hold the power to discharge you from the Army once the Japanese surrender. No more stunts like you pulled today. Understood?"

He swallowed past the thick sludge in his throat. "Yes, sir. Understood."

# 53

Santa Monica, California
May 12, 1945

The strangest wedding Kay had ever attended.

Standing at the front of the church, she wore the green gown she'd purchased in Tulsa, Mellie wore a new gown in a rich gold that made her skin glow, Georgie wore a confection of white, and Hutch, Roger, and Mike wore their olive drab service uniforms.

The Army Air Force had flown both sets of parents to California, but no other friends or family were present. Hutch barely knew Roger and he'd just met Mike. The Army had filled the church pews with military and industry bigwigs, the lavish wedding and reception a gift of gratitude for their faithful service.

Mainly, they wanted a crowd for PR pictures.

Kay fixed her gaze on Georgie and Hutch, side by side, hands entwined. It might be the strangest wedding ever, but it also might be the happiest. Both of them beamed pure joy.

Georgie was so petite and sociable, and Hutch so tall and quiet. They complemented each other, brought out the best in each other.

Why wasn't it the same with Kay and Mike? With him,

there was . . . nothing. He was nice. So very nice. And good and kind. But she felt nothing for him other than general appreciation.

Hutch, for all his quiet ways, carried himself with confident strength. Mike, as if he were waiting for approval.

Kay sighed and glanced across at Mike. He grinned at her.

She glanced back to the bride and groom, but her gaze landed on Roger. Always on Roger.

He looked straight at her, and her breath snagged in her throat. He wore an expression she'd seen a lot recently, an expression she'd never seen before the tour, and she still couldn't make it out. She wanted to label it regret or longing or sadness, but it wasn't quite any of those.

Kay knew what she wanted her expression to communicate—that he didn't matter to her anymore. Not in a petulant way, just a way that said his rejection hadn't hurt her one bit.

A sigh rose inside her, but she stifled it. How on earth could she pretend for another seven weeks?

---

Kay leaned across the sink in the church bathroom and reapplied her lipstick. Finally, after three tries, she did a decent job of it. Her hands shook so.

The emotion of the wedding, rejoicing for Hutch and Georgie while aching from her own heartbreak, and the guilt she felt for thinking of herself on her friend's special day—it churned up everything inside her.

If only she could skip the reception, but she'd promised Mike. She leaned her forehead against the cool mirror and closed her eyes.

She'd been careful to be honest with him, to treat him as a friend, and not to flirt with him, even as she prayed she'd fall in love. But logic didn't budge her feelings.

A few hours. Only a few more hours. She could do this.

Kay smoothed her hair, adjusted a few bobby pins, and headed out.

Four Army cars sat by the curb in front of the church. Although the Miramar Hotel was less than a mile from the church, the PR officers insisted the wedding party travel in style.

Two cars pulled away from the curb. Mellie, her father, and the Taylors climbed into the third car.

Roger poked his head inside. "That's all right. I'll catch the next one." He shut the door, and the car pulled away.

Kay paused on the sidewalk, trapped.

Capt. Don Sellers motioned Roger to the last car, and the pilot slid into the backseat.

Roger peered out, caught sight of Kay, and blanched. "I—I thought you went with Mike, in the other . . ." He gestured with his thumb in the direction of the hotel.

No one else from the party remained. She couldn't possibly ride alone with Roger Cooper. "It's not far. I'd rather walk."

Sellers captured her arm and gave her a steely grin. "No, you don't, doll. I promised your commanding officer to take good care of you. I insist you ride." He guided her to the car.

She glared at him, plunked down in the seat, and snatched her skirt inside.

The door slammed.

Kay stared straight ahead, her cheeks heating. As long as they both remained silent, she would survive. Five minutes. It couldn't take longer than five minutes.

The car rumbled down the road. Kay wrapped her hands around her purse and stared out the window, but she remained insanely aware of Roger's solid presence less than two feet away.

"I'm sorry," he said. "If I'd known, I would've switched places with someone."

"That's all right." A perfectly chilled tone, marred only with a slight tremor.

Silence vibrated in the air, and Kay held her breath. Five minutes. If she counted to three hundred, it would be over.

"Mike's looking forward to this evening, to the reception."

What? Kay sneaked a glance at him.

Roger held his service cap in his lap and traced the brass eagle emblem. "You'll dance with him?"

Was that a question, a command, or a warning? Something snapped inside her. "Don't worry. Your friend's safe. I didn't line up another five dates for the evening."

"Huh?" He raised startled eyes. "I didn't—that's not what I meant."

"Wasn't it?" All the emotion churned right into a boil. "You don't believe I've changed."

His eyes widened into outright alarm. "That's not true—I do—I—"

Kay shook a finger in his face. "Guess what, Roger Cooper? I might not be good enough for you or even for my own parents, but I'm good enough for the Lord and for my friends, and that's what matters."

"Kay . . ." His voice turned low and gravelly. "Why would you say that? I don't think that way."

Now was the time to give him a piece of her mind. Why not? She had nothing to lose. "Why else would you lie to me?"

"Lie to you? I never lied to you."

The fire in her cheeks matched the fire in her chest. "Is that so? I seem to remember you pushing me away because you wanted to be a drummer and live on the road. Remember that? Yet now I find out that all along you really wanted to be a teacher. Last I heard, teachers don't live on the road."

"Man alive." Roger leaned his head on the seatback and raked his hand through his hair.

"Sounds like a lie to me. All because you were too cowardly

to tell me the real reason . . . the real reason . . ." Her voice choked up on her, and she shook her head to clear it.

"Kay." He rolled his head on the seatback to face her, his hair tousled, his eyes liquid brown. "That wasn't a lie. It was true when I spoke it."

"Was it now?" She relished the slice in her voice.

"Yes, it was. I've planned on being a drummer since high school, but I've always wanted to be a teacher. I never told anyone, because I thought I wasn't responsible enough. When I got the audition with the Veerman band, it seemed like a sign that God wanted me to be a drummer."

Kay didn't nod or murmur or give him any confirmation. She'd just watch and see how deep he could dig this hole.

"But at the audition—" He huffed out a breath. "Well, I saw the Lord was offering me two good paths. I've changed this past year, and I've learned about myself. Now I know I'm responsible enough to teach, and that's what I want, that's what I chose."

"You didn't tell me." She stitched the words together with an icicle.

Roger groaned and ran his hand through his hair again. "Believe me, I wanted to. That was the first thing I planned to do when I arrived in Tulsa. But it was too late. You were with Mike. I didn't want to interfere."

"Didn't want to . . ." Her thoughts ricocheted in her head, refusing to assemble in any order.

The car came to a stop, and the driver stepped out. The dusty pink Miramar Hotel rose before her, surrounded by lush palm trees and bright flowers.

Kay snapped her attention back to Roger, to that same expression she'd noted all month, but more pronounced and perfectly clear—regret *and* longing *and* sadness.

He was right about one thing—it was too late. She flung open the car door before the driver could get to it, then leaned back inside to glare at Roger. "You didn't want to interfere? How gentlemanly of you."

She marched down the walkway, skirt swishing around her ankles.

"Kay, wait!"

She had no intention of doing so. Mike waited for her at the hotel entrance, and she stretched a smile in place.

# 54

Roger trudged up the walkway past palm trees and flowery bushes that mocked him with their cheer.

Up ahead, Kay breezed over to her date. "Hi, Mike. I'm so glad to see you," she said, too loud, too merry.

Mike's gaze slipped over Kay's shoulder to Roger and hardened. Never before had they been angry with each other.

Roger held up one hand, closed his eyes, and shook his head. It was nothing.

Mike put his hand on the small of Kay's back, guided her into the hotel, and shot one last look at Roger. She certainly needed Mike's protection, because Roger couldn't seem to stop hurting her.

He waited on the sidewalk to provide time for them to go in and time for him to collect his thoughts. She thought he'd rejected her because she wasn't good enough? Why would she think that? He'd never said anything close. He'd told the truth that day, every word.

Would he have kissed her that way if she weren't good enough? Would he love her so much if she weren't good enough?

Didn't she know how much he loved her?

Realization slammed into him, and he sagged back against the pink stucco wall. How could she know? He'd never told her. In fact, he'd worked hard to conceal his feelings.

He forced his mind to return to that hospital in Naples, to that hallway, to the memory of Kay in his arms, kissing him, murmuring, "I love you so much." And what had he said in return? He'd told her he shouldn't have kissed her. He'd pushed her away.

That's what she heard. She didn't hear that he loved her so much he couldn't bear to ruin her life. She only heard that he didn't want her, and her history filled in the blanks—she wasn't good enough, he didn't think she'd changed.

Roger pressed his head hard against the wall until stucco prickled his scalp. Nothing could be further from the truth. But now it was too late.

Nothing he could do about it. He pushed away from the wall, brushed stucco from his hair and uniform, shoved his hat on, and headed inside.

The doorman informed him that the Hutchinson party was in the Garden Room, and he showed Roger the way.

In the Garden Room, a stage awaited the band from the bond tour, and groups stood around chatting. Roger stood in the reception line like a good guest, gave Hutch a hearty handshake, kissed Georgie on the cheek, and wished them a lifetime of blessings.

Then he stood alone in a sea of strangers. The band wouldn't start playing for a while. What could he do now other than keep a respectful distance from Kay?

"Coop?" Mike tapped him on the shoulder. "I need a word with you."

Roger sighed at his copilot's stern voice. Never had that phrase resulted in anything good in his life. "Let's go in the hallway." At the last wedding he'd attended, Grant Klein had given him a shiner. Today it was Mike's turn.

Down the hallway, out of sight of the wedding guests, Roger turned and braced himself for a fist to the jaw.

Instead, Mike crossed his arms. "What did you do to Kay?"

"Nothing." Roger raised both hands in surrender. "I didn't do anything. Just clarified something that happened months ago."

"She's upset."

"I know. I didn't mean to upset her, didn't mean to talk to her at all. I'd never come between you two."

"Not intentionally."

Down the hallway, sunlight slanted through the doors, fresh from the Pacific. A romantic setting. "I think you'll find her rather receptive this evening."

Mike's jaw jutted forward. "I don't want a gal to throw herself at me just because she's angry with you."

Roger squeezed his eyes shut and pinched the bridge of his nose. "She won't do that. Not Kay. But don't worry, she'll get over me real quick now that she's had it out with me. I had my chance with her, and I blew it. She doesn't want anything to do with me."

The silence between them magnified the sounds of laughter on the other side of the wall.

Mike cleared his throat. "If you had another chance, what would you do?"

"I don't have another chance, and I never will." He fixed his strongest gaze on his friend. "Besides, I'd never cut in on another man's girl, understand?"

Mike's eyebrows drew together. "I know."

He clapped his friend on the shoulder and worked up part of a smile. "Well, if you aren't going to beat me up, let's go inside and have some cake."

"Beat you up?" Mike cracked a grin. "I wish I'd known that was an option."

---

One of the many reasons Roger had always enjoyed drumming was so he could avoid dancing and its temptations. But today, as his drumsticks swished a soft rhythm to "Dearly Be-loved," he longed to be part of the humanity on the dance floor.

Couples swayed to the music, some stiff, some making goo-goo eyes at each other, some practiced and comfortable. Roger was tired of being alone and remote and removed.

He tried not to watch Kay and Mike and to keep his gaze on Georgie and Hutch. The first time the newlyweds had ever danced together, Georgie said, but they moved as one.

Roger's gaze drifted to Kay. She kept her back to him, but the slight slump of her shoulders said she was still upset. In a flash, she swiped at her cheek. Ah, swell. He'd made her cry? At her friend's wedding?

That great urge to comfort her expanded inside him, but he'd lost that privilege. Never again would he stroke her back as she cried. Never again would they sit together on a snowy night and tap Morse code to each other. He'd lost those rights and many more.

No, he hadn't lost the rights. He'd given them away to a good man, and it was time Roger accepted it.

Down on the dance floor, Mike met Roger's eye, and he shrugged, one corner of his mouth sunken in resignation. He inclined his head toward the lady in his arms and shook his head. He was giving up?

Somehow Roger kept drumming, but he shook his head too. *No, don't give up.*

Mike gave a firm nod, cocked his head to Roger, then back to Kay. He was backing off and giving Roger another chance. Something in the determined set of Mike's jaw and the soft acceptance in his eyes said that even if Roger didn't step in, Mike would still step back.

Roger's head kept shaking side to side, his heartbeat ac-celerated, and he had to use every ounce of training to keep his drumbeat steady.

Another chance? Now what?

Mike had asked what he'd do if he had another chance. What would he do? He'd never even considered the possibility.

Kay was furious with him, upset, humiliated, and she thought he'd lied. He couldn't do anything at all.

She furtively wiped her eyes again, and Roger's heart wrenched at her emotion. On the bond tour she'd shown no emotion at all in his presence, but now . . . ?

Now her mask had slipped. Now the truth was revealed. She cared. She might hate him, but she still loved him.

Roger's breath hopped around, and his palms moistened. Knowing she cared, he could work with her anger, with her grief, with her humiliation, but he had to move quickly before the wall of apathy rose again.

Now was the perfect moment. And yet the timing couldn't be worse.

Despite the song's sleepy rhythm, his clammy fingers slipped on the drumsticks. How could he tell her he loved her? She wouldn't give him five minutes alone and wouldn't listen to one word out of his mouth. And she certainly wouldn't want to hear what he had to say.

As he watched her dance with her head bowed, a sense of peace and rightness fell over him. Either God was offering him her love, or Roger was deluded.

If he was deluded, he'd go out in a foolish blaze of glory. At least Kay would know she was more than good enough for the likes of Roger Cooper.

And if he wasn't deluded, Roger would be an even greater fool to turn away from this chance.

This time he'd reach out for that gift, no matter what.

# 55

Another stupid tear dribbled out, and Kay rubbed it away discreetly. Why wouldn't her eyes stop leaking? Why couldn't she control herself?

Today, and for the next seven weeks, she had to live with the consequences of her outburst in the car. Her carefully built façade of not caring for Roger lay in ruins.

Mike rocked her back and forth to the music, never making her face the band, but every thud of Roger's drums shot painful vibrations through her heart.

She could still see his face in the car, the regret in his eyes. He hadn't lied to her back in Naples. He'd chosen teaching when he was on his furlough, after he'd pushed her away. He'd planned to tell her when he arrived in Tulsa. First thing, he said.

Why would he have been so eager? Only one reason came to mind, the girlish fantasy that he loved her and wanted to be with her, and he couldn't wait to tell her of his choice so they could be together forever and he could give her a home and a family.

An odd little whimper bubbled in her throat, but Mike didn't seem to notice over the music. Good heavens, she had to control herself.

In Tulsa, Roger saw her with Mike and didn't want to interfere. Was that it? Was that why he hadn't told her he'd switched career plans? Out of a gentlemanly sense of honor not to interfere with a friend's budding romance?

He hadn't lied. On the contrary, he was noble and loyal.

The music changed tempo, and the band launched into "It Had to Be You."

Stupid tears. She dipped her head to Mike's shoulder to conceal her face-wiping.

"Thank you, Kay," Mike said.

She blinked and looked up at him. "Thank you? For what?"

He raised half a smile and rubbed his thumb over her cheek. Kay winced at being caught blubbering.

"Thank you," he said, "for giving me a chance. But it's not working. It's not going anywhere."

She forced out a laugh. "I'm just having a bad day. I'll try to—"

"Try to what? Try to love me as you love Coop?"

"I don't love—"

"Yes, you do." Mike eased back and gripped her by the shoulders. "All the time I've known you, no one has made you happier, sadder, or angrier than Coop. I'm just in the background, a friend."

She raised a twitchy shrug. " I—I do like you. You're very nice."

"But you don't love me and you never will." His eyes were so earnest, always earnest. "And that's okay."

More protests formed on her tongue, but she couldn't lie to him. "I'm sorry."

"I said it's okay. I don't want this anymore. I thought I did, but I don't." He squeezed her shoulders, a new confidence in his expression. "I want a woman to choose me because I'm Mike Elroy. I don't want to be chosen because I'm *not* Roger Cooper."

Kay scrunched her eyes shut. "Oh dear. I wasn't using you, I promise."

"I know. You were straight with me from the start. I appreciate that. But I want something more. I want someone to talk late into the night with, like you and Coop used to do. I want someone to work with, finishing each other's sentences, feeding off each other's ideas, like you and Coop used to do."

"Used to do." Her voice came out small, as the lyrics for "It Had to Be You" loomed large in her head. Had Roger spoiled her for any other man?

Mike got a cryptic smile on his face and glanced around the dance floor. "Oh, I think you'll find things can change."

"No." She had to speak louder over a general murmur in the room. "He doesn't want anything to do with me, and I certainly don't want anything to do with him."

Mike released her shoulders, nodded toward the bandstand, and backed away. All around, couples paused in their dancing and stared at the musicians.

Kay's ears tuned in to the music. Something was wrong. The drumbeat didn't match the song. In fact, it clashed. Roger pounded, "Thump-tap-thump. Thump-tap-thump." The bass drum, the snare, the bass. Over and over.

What was he doing? She turned, and he riveted her with the most intense, determined look. Thump-tap-thump. Dash-dot-dash.

The letter *K*.

Her mouth flopped open. He was signaling her? Now? Here? Why?

Roger gave her a long, slow nod, but the intensity of his gaze never wavered. Memories flooded back to her, cherished and intimate memories—Roger kissing her forehead and tapping "*R-U-N*" on her shoulder, the silly messages they'd send when he sat on night guard, the way he ran down the hospital ward to her with the same expression in his eyes.

Kay stood alone, without a partner, on the crowded dance floor, and the murmuring couples shifted their attention from the errant drummer to Kay and back again.

He pointed one drumstick at her, like a teacher with a ruler, telling her to listen up or get her knuckles slapped. Then he changed his beat. Dot-dot. The letter *I*.

What was he doing? And why here? Why now?

Dot-dash-dot-dot—*L*.

The song toppled apart, and the musicians laid their instruments across their laps, giving each other quizzical looks.

Dash-dash-dash—*O*.

Kay held her breath. He wouldn't dare say that. He couldn't. He wouldn't.

Dot-dot-dot-dash—*V*.

Behind the intensity in his eyes lay tenderness she'd never seen before. He was. Oh goodness, he was indeed saying what she thought. How could he? After all this time?

Dot—*E*.

The bandleader marched toward the drum set, the room buzzed, and everyone stared at Roger, at Kay, at Roger, at Kay.

Dash-dot-dash-dash—*Y*.

All her emotions rolled together into an indecipherable muddle. Part of her wanted to yield to her love, throw herself onto his lap—right there at the drum set—and kiss him over and over.

Dash-dash-dash—*O*.

But every time she ran to him, opened her heart to him, he rejected her, shoved her away. Never again. Never again would she let this man hurt her.

Dot-dot-dash—*U*.

Fire rose inside her. The old proverb said, "Fool me once, shame on you; fool me twice, shame on me." There would not be a third time. Kay spun away and raced for the door.

"Kay! Kay, wait!"

Heavens, no. She stormed down the hallway and outside, where palm trees waved over flower-lined paths under warm spring sun.

She'd call a cab and get away, run away, anywhere, it didn't matter. No more bond tours for her. Let the Army catch her and lock her up for all she cared. At least she'd be away from Roger Cooper.

"Kay!" His voice thundered behind her.

"Don't you come near me." Her skirts tangled around her ankles as she strode away from the main hotel building toward little bungalows with sea-blue roofs, where Georgie and Hutch would spend their honeymoon.

"Stop and listen to me. Please, Kay."

"I can't think of one reason why I should." Green and blue swam together in her vision.

"I can think of one reason—so you don't fall in the pool."

Kay wiped her eyes. A pool, not three feet away. She sucked in a breath and stopped short.

"I take your reaction as confirmation that you received my message." Humor rang in his voice.

Humor? How dare he? She wheeled to face him. "I got your message, all right. I got the message that you—you're a snake. That's what you are. A copperhead snake."

A smile jumped onto his face. "Haven't heard that one for a while."

"That's surprising. It suits you."

"You suit me too. I'm in love with you."

A growl rose in her throat, and she marched away, paralleling the pool, past half a dozen sunbathers on lounge chairs gawking at her.

"Fine. Run and listen. I'm still having my say."

If only she could run in these heels. But even if she took them off and tossed them in the pool, he'd catch up with her. "Go away."

"After I'm done, but I've just started. I should have done this months ago, told you how I feel. I do love you, with everything in me."

"Nonsense." She turned onto a path that led between the bungalows, following the sea breeze toward the beach.

"I do. I love you so much. The past few months I've felt like someone chopped off my leg. I'm incomplete without you."

She passed a bungalow, and her mouth contorted. "How dare you? I won't let you draw me in again and then . . ."

"And push you away? Never again. I'm done resisting. From the day we met, I resisted my attraction to you. After I came back from India, I resisted falling in love with you. Then I resisted telling you how I feel. But no more. I'm done. I'm yours, Kay. I'm yours if you want me."

"I don't." Now it was her turn to resist, and it wouldn't be difficult.

"Kay, the road. Watch out."

She gasped and halted. Was the man trying to kill her?

Roger pulled up beside her and bowed his head. "May I escort you across the street, my lady?"

She shot him a glare, looked both ways, and strode across the street. "I hope you get hit by a car."

"Sounds like a plan. You're a nurse. You'll stop and take care of me."

Why did he keep following her? Why did he sound so annoyingly good-natured? "I told you to go away."

"Not until I've said my piece. I've known I was in love with you since we were in France. At Mellie's wedding, I wanted to kiss you. You have no idea how much I wanted to, but I was afraid I'd get carried away and ruin you like I ruined my girlfriend in high school."

She wouldn't let him sway her. She wouldn't. Up onto the curb and into a forest of short palm trees. She could smell the ocean, hear the waves.

"My love for you grew during the evasion. That kiss—I meant it, Kay. I meant it. But I couldn't see a future with you. I didn't want to drag you around on tours and make you miserable."

"Strange." She weaved around the palm trees. "You didn't ask me how I felt about it. You forgot I was raised on the road, in tents. I could've handled it, but you didn't even ask."

"I didn't." His voice lowered. "I'm sorry, darling."

Darling? He had no right. Brushing aside palm branches and arguments, she charged ahead.

"Now I can finish saying what I started in the car. I chose teaching for two reasons. First, because I like to teach and honestly think I'll be good at it, maybe even reach the kids who hate school."

Even though she agreed, she refused to nod and reduce the stiffness of her spine.

"But the second—Kay! Stop!"

Her foot slipped, and she scrambled backward. The land dropped off before her into a steep bluff.

From behind, Roger laid his hands on her shoulders. "If you keep running from me, you're going to get hurt."

Far below, a wide sandy beach sloped to the blue Pacific, flaming under the setting sun, but no path wound down the bluff to allow her access. She was stuck with Roger, the warmth of his hands relaxing her shoulders and eroding her resistance. But if she stopped running from him, she could get hurt even worse.

She tightened her muscles. "Let go of me."

"When I'm done." His breath ruffled her hair and melted her insides.

She could get away. His grip was gentle, and she knew him too well. If she darted to the side, he'd let her go.

Yet she felt bound. Bound by the weight of his hands, his solid presence only inches behind her, their long and deep friendship, the trials they'd faced . . . and curiosity. "Finish up then. Make it quick."

"All right." He brushed his cheek against her hair. "The second reason I chose teaching is because I love you. I want to marry you and have a family and a home, and I want to spend—"

"Don't you dare. Don't you dare offer—" Her voice broke, and she clapped her hand over her mouth, her eyes stinging.

Roger eased her back from the cliff, turned her to face him, and rested his hands on her waist. "Don't offer you what? Love, marriage, a home? I am. I'm offering you all of that."

She couldn't look at him, at his molten eyes, at his chest inching nearer, at his lips speaking impossible words. "Don't you dare," she said, her voice muffled by her fingers.

He eased her hand down from her mouth and smiled. "Don't dare what? Kiss you?"

"If you do, I swear I'll . . ." All the starch washed from her voice as he gathered her closer and closer.

With one hand he cupped her face. "Tell you what. The first time I kissed you, I pushed you away. This time you can push me away. Stomp on my foot, kick me in the kneecap, punch me in the gut, whatever you want."

"I don't want you to kiss me." She planted her hands on his chest, but her resolve drained away. He loved her. He'd pursued her.

"It'll only work if I kiss you. Then when you push me away, you'll break my heart to pieces. Isn't that what you want?"

An oddly compelling bit of logic, almost as compelling as his mouth drawing nearer, as the message in his brown eyes. He'd drummed his love for her, spoken it out loud, but his eyes—his eyes said even more. If she let him kiss her . . .

No, she couldn't.

"Please . . ." But her tongue couldn't form the word *don't*.

He descended, and his lips covered hers, not with the desperate passion of their kiss in Italy, but with the gentleness of respect, of regret, of a lifetime of promises he longed to fill.

The sweetness of the kiss paralyzed her. She couldn't respond, not as she should, not as she wanted to.

He sighed and pressed a kiss to her forehead. "All right. I'm ready. Give me your best shot."

Kay clutched the olive drab lapels of his jacket, her mind woozy. "That's what you want, isn't it?"

He shrugged. "It's what I expect."

Playfulness tugged at her lips. "Then I won't. If it's what you expect, I won't do it."

Roger pulled back and studied her face until the spark of playfulness ignited in his own eyes. "You won't? But how will you break my heart?"

"Maybe . . ." She wrapped her arms around his neck, every sense full of him. "Maybe I could kiss you back, really kiss you, and then I could push you away."

"You'd do that to me? To your old friend? I'd be devastated." Despite his teasing tone, his eyes said something more—that he really would be devastated. Because he loved her.

"Oh, Roger." Her voice choked, and she kissed the edge of his jaw, the manly roughness, and her fingers worked into his thick auburn hair. "I love you too. I do."

A moan rumbled in his throat, under her lips.

Kay's breath caught. Three times now, she'd played with his hair. Twice she'd confessed her love. Twice he'd pushed her away.

But this time he ran his fingers into her hair and sought her mouth, a lush kiss, equal parts love and desire.

Kay returned it fully, peeling away her last layer of guardedness and kissing him with all her love, all her joy, all her vulnerability, open and giving and receiving.

Roger let out a satisfied groan and burrowed a kiss into her neck. "Suddenly the next seven weeks are looking good."

She smiled, her lips tingling from his kisses. "They are."

"When do you want to get married?"

"What? Already?"

He straightened up and frowned. "You do want to get married, don't you?"

Kay stared up at him, her thoughts swirling. He'd mentioned marriage, not her, but it was so soon. Wasn't it? However, honesty worked its way to the top. "I do."

He grinned. "Those are the words I want to hear."

She pressed her hand to her forehead. "It's so soon, so sudden."

"Not really, considering what we've been through." He led her by the hand to one of the taller palm trees, leaned back against it, and gathered her in his arms.

She fiddled with the knot of his khaki tie. "I'm just—well, I can still barely comprehend the fact that you love me."

He kissed her again, short but fervent. "I'm enjoying convincing you."

"Me too." She caressed his shoulders, overwhelmed by the strength of him and by the freedom to show him her love at last.

"Here's the deal." He readjusted his arms around her waist. "We'll have seven weeks together for the bond tour, then they'll send us our separate ways until after the war's over."

"I know." A sad sigh leached out.

He kissed her nose. "Then I have a year or two of college before I can teach. We could marry then."

"That's such a long time."

Roger stroked her back, tender and . . . practiced. "I don't think we should wait that long."

Kay nodded. No, that didn't seem wise.

"We could get married after we're discharged."

"Whenever that is." With the Japanese fighting to the death for every square inch on Okinawa, Kay doubted that would be anytime soon.

"Or we could get married at the end of the bond tour."

"Seven weeks from now?"

"Mm-hmm." The glint in his eyes said he was serious.

Kay rested her head on his chest, her mind reeling. Seven weeks? That was so soon. And yet not soon enough. "I don't want a big spectacle like Georgie had. I don't want a bunch of strangers, or PR officers, or—"

"You and me. A little church. A few of our closest friends. What more could we want?"

The ocean breeze ruffled her skirt and her hair, and she raised a smile to the man she loved. "How about a bungalow by the sea?"

One side of his mouth twitched up. "I like that idea. I like it a lot."

He kissed her, and the rhythm of his lips on hers sent a message she received with joy. He loved her, he'd never leave her, and they'd make their home together forever.

# 56

No doubt about it. The dame was dangerous.

As Kay glided down the church aisle, Roger couldn't stop grinning. Most danger was meant to be avoided, but some danger was meant to be embraced, and he intended to embrace Kay Jobson for the rest of his life.

In a few minutes, she'd be Kay Cooper. His wife. Hands tightly clasped behind him, his thumbs beat out a rhythm. He wasn't nervous. Why would he be nervous?

A lacy veil muted Kay's face, but a flash of white told him she was smiling straight at him, trusting him with her heart and her body and her life.

*Lord, don't let me fail her.* A rush of peace stilled his thumbs. Life wouldn't always be easy, but he'd work hard for her and be true to her and love her to the death. And even if he did fail her, the Lord never would. She would always be provided for.

Kay lifted her long skirt a few inches and climbed the steps to Roger. No man gave her away, but Roger accepted her with all his heart. He held out his hand and drew her to his side before the pastor.

Her hand felt small and damp in his, her arm warm be-side his, and her breath puffed out the veil. Was she nervous too? He stroked her hand with his thumb, and she turned a grateful smile up to him.

The pastor talked and talked, and Roger strained to listen. Love as the Lord loves, sacrificially, unconditionally. Forgive each other's trespasses as the Lord forgives yours. Charity "beareth all things, believeth all things, hopeth all things, endureth all things."

Thank goodness it was all in his Bible because the words sifted through the holes in his brain. He and Kay would have plenty of verses to study, to make notes on, to live out together.

The pastor told them to face each other, and they repeated their vows, Roger with a throaty voice, Kay with a tremulous voice. He slid a simple gold band onto her lovely hand, and she eased one over his big sausage of a finger.

"You may now kiss the bride."

The moment he was waiting for. Roger lifted her veil. Kay's face glowed with love, but her eyes glistened too much.

His heart full, he cradled her beautiful face in his hands. "My wife. My love."

She raised her mouth, and he met her halfway—a sweet and gentle kiss. Then he pressed his lips to her forehead. "Know why I married you?" he murmured.

"I thought I did. Why?"

"So I could get my Bible back."

Her shoulders shook with repressed laughter, and he grinned at her, his gorgeous, clever, dangerous dame.

———

Knee deep in the Pacific, Kay swung her leg in the warm gray-blue water. "Almost three years together. I can't believe it's over."

"I know." Mellie leaned down and let an incoming wave soak her. "We've been through so much."

Georgie nudged Mellie. "You were so shy you could barely look anyone in the eye."

Mellie nudged back. "And you were a quivering mass of fear disguised behind a chipper smile."

"And you . . ." Georgie arched an eyebrow at Kay.

"I know what I was." Kay smiled and splashed both her friends. "More importantly, I know who I am now."

"Just think what we've been through." Mellie set her hands on her hips and gazed over the ocean as if the past three years' adventures lay before her. "Medical emergencies, and ditching at sea, and landing behind enemy lines. Not to mention dirt and bugs and washing our hair in our helmets."

Kay laughed, but Georgie fell silent.

Mellie turned to the brunette. "I know, sweetie. We all miss Rose. We always will."

Georgie nodded, her eyes moist. "But think how happy she is up in heaven with Jesus and Clint."

Sometimes silence was right. They'd seen a lot of death. They'd seen too many strong young men maimed and disabled by war. They'd seen enough illness and suffering for a lifetime. But they'd done their best to ease pain and misery, to heal the sick and wounded, and to ease the passage of the dying.

They'd overcome the objections of colonels and generals who didn't believe women were capable of handling depriva-tion and danger. They'd proven medical air evacuation was safe and effective, and now it was used in all theaters of the war. They were pioneers.

Georgie swished her hand through the water. "Three years ago, would you ever have imagined the three of us standing here, best friends, and all three of us married women?"

"No. Absolutely not." Kay shook her head so violently, she didn't see a wave, and it knocked her onto her backside.

Laughing hard, Georgie and Mellie helped her to her feet.

Kay wiped salt water from her face and smiled. "I never would have imagined it, but now I can't imagine it any other way."

"And look at the handsome husbands we snagged." Georgie grinned and faced the beach, where the three men lounged in the sun. "I'm thankful Hutch and Tom both finagled a furlough for your wedding."

Tom had returned from Europe only a few days after Hutch and Georgie's wedding, and he'd brought his dog, Sesame, to Mellie's relief.

Kay squeezed water from her ponytail. "I'm glad they stood up with Roger in the ceremony." Mike had been unbearably gracious about Roger and Kay's engagement and had accepted the wedding invitation, but his grandfather had passed away last week, and he'd gone home for the funeral.

"I think the boys are sleeping." Mellie's eyes twinkled. "Let's go dribble water on them."

"Mellie!" Georgie cried. "You surprise me."

"Come on." Mellie ran up the beach, sand kicking behind her feet.

Kay followed, laughing.

Roger wasn't asleep. He raised his head and rested it on his crossed forearms, and a smile edged up, higher and higher as she came nearer and nearer. His gaze slid down to her toes and back to her eyes. She could feel the heat gliding over her curves.

He'd never looked at her that way, and it scared and delighted her all at once. But now they were married. Tonight . . . well, tonight would be more than delightful, she just knew.

She gave him a flirtatious smile, and he sent it right back to her.

Mellie leaned over her dozing husband and squeezed out

her hair over his bare back. He jerked awake and cried out, and everyone laughed.

Hutch opened one eye and looked at Georgie. "If you do, I'll throw you in the ocean, and your curls will get frizzy." He finished in a falsetto.

She sank onto the towel beside him. "That's why I didn't get my hair wet in the first place."

Roger sat up, held out his hand, and drew Kay down to sit in front of him. He circled his arm around her waist, pulled her to his sun-warmed bare chest, and kissed her neck. "Mm. Salty."

Laughter broke the intensity of the moment, and she hugged his arm to her stomach.

Georgie shielded her eyes and glanced at the bluffs behind them. "To think this is the same place Hutch and I celebrated our marriage. We had a couple hundred complete strangers at a ritzy reception, and you're having a picnic for six on the beach."

"That's what we wanted," Kay said. "A celebration with friends, the three nightingales together."

"And their husbands." Roger rested his chin on her shoulder. "Husband. Husband. Great word, isn't it?"

"So is wife." Kay twisted to give him a quick kiss.

Hutch pulled one of Georgie's curls. "So, which nightingale will hatch the first egg?"

She gasped. "John Hutchinson! You ought to be ashamed."

He chuckled. "Why? It's a natural phenomenon. You're a nurse. You should know."

"I'm also a lady."

"And ladies become mamas. Even Southern ladies."

Kay soaked in the laughter, the friendship. What would she do without these women? "I can't believe this is our last time together."

"Last time?" Georgie's eyes rounded. "Heaven forbid. No, we won't let that happen."

"I have an idea," Mellie said. "Let's make a pact to meet once a year, right here."

Kay sat up straighter. "Or somewhere, anywhere. I like that idea."

"Then our children can grow up together." Georgie dug her feet into the sand. "The Red Cross said little Lucia will be sent over from Italy by the end of the year, and we can finally adopt her."

Hutch poked her with his toe. "Then we can add more hatchlings."

Tom patted his wife's flat belly. "Our hatchling will be the oldest."

Now it was Mellie's turn to gasp. "Tom! I didn't want to tell anyone yet. It's too early."

"You're . . . you're . . ." Kay leaned forward.

Mellie's eyelashes lowered, and a faint smile rose. "Pregnant Without Permission. Yes, I am."

Georgie and Kay shrieked as one.

"I'm sorry." Mellie's eyes pleaded. "I didn't mean to make the announcement on your wedding day. What horrible manners."

Kay reached over and grasped her friend's hand. "Don't you dare apologize. Now we have another reason to celebrate, and another wonderful memory for today."

Roger held up an empty Coke bottle. "Here's to Mellie's upcoming medical discharge."

Kay laughed. "Hear, hear!"

He drew her back to his solid chest and nibbled on her ear.

Her breath caught. Lunch had been eaten. Conversation had been shared. The ocean had been splashed in. Perhaps they should retreat to their . . .

"Bungalow," he whispered in her ear.

As much as she longed to be alone with him—with her husband—part of her ached at the thought of leaving her friends. Never again would they have such time together.

But Tom and Mellie sat forehead to forehead, probably selecting baby names, and Hutch and Georgie laughed together over something.

Their friendship had carried them through three difficult years together—three glorious years. But now the joys of sharing and support and encouragement were shifting from girlfriends to husbands.

Yet Kay knew they'd always be close. Through letters or phone calls or beachside reunions, they'd keep their friendship strong.

But things would never be the same.

"Kay." Roger set his hand on her cheek and turned her to face him. His eyes were smoky and his gaze firm. He'd never try to control her, but he'd lead with a sure and capable hand. "Darling, it's time."

She covered his hand with her own. What had she done to deserve him? Nothing. His love and this marriage were gifts from the Lord, gifts she'd cherish all her life.

"Yes." A smile rose, warmer than the sunbaked sand, and she pressed a kiss to his palm. "It's the perfect time."

Dear Reader,

Thank you for joining Roger and Kay on their journey. If you're on Pinterest, I have a board for *In Perfect Time*, with photos of events and locations (http://pinterest.com/sarahsundin).

The 802nd Medical Air Evacuation Transport Squadron was a real unit, the first to fly a true air evacuation mission. Although all characters in the 802nd in this story are fictional, with the exception of the commanding officer, Maj. Frederick Guilford, their movements, locations, joys, and challenges are real. The evasion incident is based on the true account of twenty-six flight nurses and medics of the 807th MAETS who crash-landed in Nazi-occupied Albania in late 1943. You can read more about this story on my website.

Likewise, the 64th Troop Carrier Group was real, as are its locations. On two occasions, unarmed C-47s of the 64th TCG downed Japanese Zero fighter planes over India and Burma, one while flying down a winding canyon. More about these stories on my website also.

In this series, I've sought to highlight some of the unsung heroes of World War II, who didn't receive accolades and honors, but who faced danger, experienced deprivation, and sacrificed for their country. I'm thankful and indebted for their service.

# Acknowledgments

Each novel I write presents unique challenges and unique joys. I'm thankful to the Lord for challenging me and giving me joy.

Supreme thanks to my husband, Dave, and my children, Stephen, Anna, and Matthew. They put up with weird moments like Mom buying drumsticks and a practice pad. Stephen, thanks for telling me about the Ring Nebula. It's perfect. And Matthew, thanks for demonstrating constant energy and activity, even if you Must. Touch. Everything. The drumsticks are now yours. Anna, I apologize for giving your brother drumsticks.

Thanks so much to Rachel Williams, director of the Mount Hermon Christian Writers Conference, who shared the memoir of her father-in-law, Lt. E. Eugene Williams, who piloted a C-47 with the 435th Troop Carrier Group based in England during World War II. An amazing story and so helpful.

I had the honor of talking to Dorothy White Errair, president of the World War II Flight Nurse Association and an actual World War II flight nurse (807th MAETS). Her daughter, Melinda Errair Bruckman, collects and preserves these amazing women's stories. Please visit their beautiful website at www.legendsofflightnurses.org. If you have information about any of the flight nurses, they'd love to hear from you.

Once again, Warren Hower of Hower Research Associates located rare documents for me—for this novel, several flight plans of the 64th Troop Carrier Group.

And special thanks to Sean Conner of the Mayo Hotel in Tulsa, Oklahoma (www.themayohotel.com). The website for this restored historic hotel contains fabulous photographs, but Mr. Conner provided even more detail, from the elevator to room furnishings to the hallway carpet. These details make the novelist's heart sing!

I couldn't have finished this novel without my sweet critique partners, Linda Clare, Judy Gann, Sherry Kyle, Bonnie Leon, Ann Shorey, and Marcy Weydemuller. Ladies, I appreciate your eye for detail and your support and encouragement.

Thanks always to my agent, Rachel Kent. Your calm and wise ways are invaluable to me. And thank you to my editor, Vicki Crumpton. Your keen insight always makes me see deeper into my story and challenges me to make it better. And to the entire team at Revell—from cover art to marketing to sales to contracts—you blow me away each and every time. I'm blessed to work with you.

And dear reader, I'm so thankful for you! Please visit my website at www.sarahsundin.com to leave a message, sign up for my quarterly newsletter, read about the history behind the story, and find tips on starting a book club. I look forward to hearing from you.

# Discussion Questions

1. At the beginning of the story, Kay has a "boyfriend in every airport." Why do you think she dates so many men? What need does this fill? What problems does it cause?
2. Roger Cooper goes out of his way to avoid women. Knowing his past, do you think his policy is wise or misguided? How do you handle known temptations in your life, or how have you seen others handle them well?
3. Both Kay and Roger grew up hearing lies about God or about themselves. How has that shaped their lives? How do they overcome this? Have you had to overcome lies in your life?
4. Kay's deepest longing is for a home. What do you think lies behind that? Do you think a house by itself would have satisfied her?
5. Sometimes it's easier for others to see our talents than to see them ourselves. This occurs with Roger and his gift of teaching. Has anyone pointed out a gift to you that surprised you—but turned out to be true?

6. Kay grows up believing she must be good in order to be forgiven. How has this affected her? Although most of us know this concept isn't true, how does it still seep into our thinking?

7. While Roger has easily accepted God's mercy, he resists God's good gifts in his life. Why do you think he does this? Have you ever resisted blessings in your life?

8. After Kay becomes a Christian, does her life get easier or harder? In what ways? How do you see this in your own life?

9. How does the ordeal in the second half of the book change Kay? Roger? Their relationship? How have ordeals shaped you?

10. Friendship is an important theme in the Wings of the Nightingale series. How are Kay, Mellie, and Georgie good for each other? How does their friendship evolve during this story? During the series? Do you have a set of good friends you can rely on?

11. Your turn to tell the story! What do you imagine for Roger and Kay in the future? How about Tom and Mellie? Hutch and Georgie?

12. If you read *With Every Letter* or *On Distant Shores*, did you enjoy following Tom and Mellie, and Hutch and Georgie?

**Sarah Sundin** is the author of *With Every Letter*, *On Distant Shores*, *A Distant Melody*, *A Memory Between Us*, and *Blue Skies Tomorrow*. In 2011, *A Memory Between Us* was a finalist in the Inspirational Reader's Choice Awards and Sarah received the Writer of the Year Award at the Mount Hermon Christian Writers Conference. A graduate of UC San Francisco School of Pharmacy, she works on-call as a hospital pharmacist. During WWII, her grandfather served as a pharmacist's mate (medic) in the Navy and her great-uncle flew with the US Eighth Air Force in England. Sarah lives in California with her husband and three children.

GET TO KNOW

# SARAH SUNDIN

★ ★ ★

To Learn More About Sarah,
Read Her Blog, or See
the Inspiration Behind the Stories
Visit
**SARAHSUNDIN.COM**